DALILA

By the same author

Choke Chain

DALILA

Jason Donald

JONATHAN CAPE
LONDON

1 3 5 7 9 10 8 6 4 2

Jonathan Cape, an imprint of Vintage Publishing,
20 Vauxhall Bridge Road,
London SW1V 2SA

Jonathan Cape is part of the Penguin Random House group of companies
whose addresses can be found at global.penguinrandomhouse.com

Penguin
Random House
UK

First published by Jonathan Cape in 2017

penguin.co.uk/vintage

A CIP catalogue record for this book is available from the British Library

ISBN 9781910702482

Typeset in India by Thomson Digital Pvt Ltd, Noida, Delhi

Printed and bound in Great Britain by Clays Ltd, St Ives plc

Penguin Random House is committed to a sustainable future for our business, our readers and
our planet. This book is made from Forest Stewardship Council® certified paper.

MIX
Paper from
responsible sources
FSC® C018179

Hundreds surge along the corridor. Parents lead their children by the hand. Couples walk side by side in silence. Some drag suitcases, others wear backpacks. She keeps pace with the rest, hugging her handbag to her chest. Her bare toes spread through the front of her shoes. As the corridor widens, the drone of suitcase wheels and the quickening clip of shoes hurry her along. She lifts her chin to peer between the bobbing heads of the crowd. Amber evening light reaches through the windows, cupping the back of each delicate skull. Collapsed human shadows scurry along the wall.

She cannot see where they are going, cannot see another way to go.

Ahead of her, a man carries a small child in the hook of his arm. He moves from the crowd and slips sideways through a door.

Two doors. Toilets. Male. Female.

She stops, looks back the way she has come, and enters the ladies' room. It's the cleanest room she has ever seen. Floor tiles as white as the sinks, made whiter still by overhead strip lights. There are no windows. The cubicle doors hang open. She lowers her handbag and stands still, thinking. She enters a cubicle, bolts it and presses her back against the door. For the first time in many days, she is alone. The stillness of it almost feels safe. She lays down her bag and as she bends over to remove her shoe, the toilet flushes. She jumps back, staring at the clear, swirling water. The bowl is bolted to the wall without a trunk to hold it up. It has no cistern, no chain to pull, only a single black eye on the wall behind. The water calms. But the black eye watches, unblinking. No longer is she by herself. It is here too.

Be strong, she whispers.

From under the inner sole of her shoe she removes a folded note. She unfolds it and gazes at the words. She has read and reread these instructions, considered each word and the implications. Closing her eyes, the memory of the words hovers in front of her, printed on her mind's notepad. When she opens her eyes, the mental copy overlays the notes in her hands, matching it exactly.

She tears through the note four times and lets the shredded pieces flutter into the toilet water. She waves her shoe in front of the black eye and watches it flush them away.

At the sink, she washes her unsteady hands, splaying her fingers under the warm water. She makes a fist and splays them again. Her stomach pulls and threatens to throw up its contents, but the feeling passes. She touches water to her face, bends forward and drinks from the tap. She presses two paper towels to her face and turns around so her eyes will not be tempted by the mirror.

Sawa, sawa, she says softly, and takes a deep breath. She tugs her cardigan and in English whispers, Okay. Okay.

She goes out. People continue to march across the tiles. She joins them, trusting the crowd's sense of direction, believing they must know where they are going. Soon the corridor veers left and descends underground. The flow of the bodies pitches and eddies, some opt for the staircase, most pour down the escalator. She takes the stairs, holding her handbag tight, glancing at the advertising colouring the walls. They spill into a wide hall filled with more people. The air is close, the sounds diffused, a slight tarpaulin smell rising from the carpet. It feels like the room is underground, but she can't be sure. There are no windows to confirm her position, only fluorescent lights fitted into the low ceiling, their light dispersing all shadows and any sense of time. The only exit lies beyond a row of booths manned by security officials. Two signs hang from the ceiling.

UK and EU Passport Only   **All Other Passports**

People appear to be congregating under one sign or the other. She approaches and notices blue, waist-high ribbons channelling the crowd into a long queue that snakes back on itself. Like livestock, travellers shuffle through the maze of ribbons. She joins the line for All Other Passports, and tilts her head to ease the knot from her neck. A hum of conversations hangs across the hall but no one dares raise their voice. Words are spoken in languages she doesn't recognise but now and then she picks out some English. Many people stand in silence. No one squats on their heels. No one sits on their bags. Children stay close to their mothers. After a few minutes, the woman in front of her shuffles two steps forward. She steps forward too. The people behind her follow suit.

A blue sign requests that she remove her passport from its wallet or holder to help speed up the examination of her documents. She buries her hand into her bag and finds her passport, opens it at the photograph. Her likeness stares out blankly. Her hair cropped as short as possible, only a shading across her scalp. Her full lips tucked down at the corners, the sinews flexing in her slim neck.

She closes the passport. The queue moves on and she takes three steps forward to close the gap.

People in the other line, the line for UK and EU Passport Only, move quickly. Each traveller holds open a maroon passport. The immigration officers glance at the identification, the person, and wave them on.

At the front of her queue, however, a security guard directs people to the next available booth. Four immigration officers are on duty. The first is a man with two chins. Next to him is a grey man with grey hair. Then, an old man with a neat moustache. Finally, a young Indian woman. These officers study every stamp on every page of the foreign passports, questioning the people attached to the documents, scrutinising their photographs.

The immigration officer with two chins withholds a man's passport and sends him to the row of chairs sectioned off at the front of the queue, beside the security guard. The man seems confused for a moment, but does as he is told. He sits, places his bag on the seat next to him. He crosses his legs, adjusts his bag, uncrosses his legs. No one in the queue looks directly at him. A few minutes later an immigration officer and a security guard approach the man. They speak quietly. The man stands up and follows them. As they walk the security guard casually clasps hold of the man's bicep and leads him through a grey unmarked door.

Three bodies now stand between her and the front of the queue. She folds her arms over her bag, rubbing her finger over the hardened scab on her wrist, picking at the edges of it.

At the front of the queue, she waits next to the guard and tries to calculate which officer she will get. Each one works at a different speed. The grey officer never smiles and directs his questions automatically. The one with two chins is friendly and chats to each passenger, but this one has a lizard smile. She trusts him the least. The Indian woman officer is young and smart, but probably ambitious. She hopes to get the old man with the neat moustache. Perhaps the world has been easy with his heart and there is still kindness left.

The Indian woman finishes first and the guard directs her to that booth. She walks up and stands behind the line marked on the ground.

The officer has glossy black hair, sky-blue eyeshadow and trim, plucked eyebrows. With two fingers, she signals for the next person to step forward.

Hi there, says the officer in a cheery English accent. Passport and landing card, please.

She steps forward and places both documents on the counter. She stands with her feet together.

The officer opens her passport. Just the one passport, yeah?

Yes.

Where are you travelling from?

Me, I come from Kenya.

The officer concentrates on a computer screen tucked into her booth. She looks at the landing card and types something into the computer. The officer has a metallic name badge pinned to her uniform with two words on it, Officer Nita. The pale blue of the uniform complements her eyeshadow. The neckline is open, almost casual without being feminine, while the rigid shoulder epaulettes carry authority. In the corner of this officer's left nostril a tiny hole suggests that the young woman sometimes wears a piercing.

How do you pronounce you surname?

My name is Dalila Mwathi.

It says here Irene is your first name?

That one is also my name. Dalila is my porridge name.

Your what?

My porridge name. The name my mother used for me, when I was very small, when I started to eat porridge. My English name is Irene. My name is Irene Dalila Mwathi.

Irene?

Yes.

Okay, Miss Mwathi, I'm going to ask you a few questions about your stay here, yeah? How long are you going to be here?

Dalila keeps her gaze steady. Three weeks, she says. I've come to visit my aunt . . . my cousin.

Which one? Your aunt or your cousin?

She's my cousin, I think. She is my mother's cousin but I always call her Aunty. She has a baby. I want to visit and see the baby.

Where does your aunt live?

In London. I have the address here.

Dalila digs into her bag and pulls out a handwritten letter with no envelope.

This is her letter, says Dalila. The address is there. She invited me to stay, to see London. Big Ben. To see her children.

Officer Nita reverse-folds the creases in the paper and reads the letter all the way through. She takes special note of the address and types it into the computer. She makes no eye contact with Dalila.

What is your aunt's name?

My aunt?

If you've known her all your life and you're staying with her, you should know her name, yeah?

Dalila dips her head. She thumbs the scab on her wrist. She is Nafula.

Nafula? Does she have an English name too?

Her name is Anne. She is my mother's cousin.

And you're here to look after Anne's children, yeah?

Dalila remembers her instructions, every word vivid in her mind. She's expecting this question and knows how to answer it. No, she says. I don't want to work. I only come to visit. I am a tourist.

The officer keeps her face unreadable as she flicks through every page in Dalila's passport. She re-examines the visitor's visa and letter of invitation. Dalila lowers her handbag, cradling it by her stomach.

Miss Mwathi, how do you plan to support yourself during your stay? Do you have any money?

I have money.

How much?

I have three hundred US dollars and, also, twenty thousand shillings.

Kenyan shillings, yeah?

Yes.

How much is that in pounds?

She hesitates. It is, maybe . . .

Do you have access to any other funds?

No. I will just stay with my aunt. I don't need so much money.

Officer Nita nibbles the inside of her lip as she studies the computer screen. Okay, Miss Mwathi, I have some inquiries to make. She points at the row of chairs. Just take a seat over there for me. You'll be here, with us, until I finish conducting those inquiries, yeah?

The officer's face closes over. Their discussion has ended.

Dalila looks over at the row of chairs. She turns back to collect her passport and documents but Officer Nita has taken them. For a moment, Dalila is trapped, unwilling to walk away from her passport yet uncertain about disobeying the authorities. She feels the people in the queue watching her and trying not to watch her. She lifts her chin, walks to the chairs and sits down, steadying her gaze straight ahead. The next passenger is directed to a booth, his papers are stamped and he is let through.

Dalila watches families pass easily through immigration. Single people are scrutinised more thoroughly, especially the men, their papers studied, questions asked, but they are all allowed to pass. So many different cultures step up to the booths, each person with a unique face. Each set of shoes different from the rest. An announcement is made, but the accent is so strange to her ears she struggles to rearrange the syllables into coherent sentences. The security guard's uniform is different from what she has seen in Kenya. The synthetic smell in this hall is different. The lighting is also somehow different. The stickers on suitcases are different. The flat-screen TVs hanging from the ceilings are different. Air vents are different. The number of white people is expected, yet unsettling and confusingly different from what she imagined. The hairstyles, different. The tattoos, different. Her eyes skip from one new image to another, trying to absorb all the differences of every new thing. She wants to look at everything, to turn around in her seat and examine every person, every surface, every item of clothing, but she doesn't want to be seen to be looking. Still, her eyes dart from one strange thing to the next. In this under-ground, windowless hall it is only her and a thousand different things and it is warm and getting warmer and she feels like she's been running, or should be.

Dalila glances down at the slimy texture on her fingers. It's blood and she realises she has been picking the scab on her wrist. She licks it off and watches a tiny bulb of red grow back. This she knows. Blood is not different. She sucks her thumb clean and presses down on the scab. Blood is always the same.

After ten minutes an immigration officer approaches her, a man she has never seen before. He says, Miss Irene Matty?

She nods.

If you'd like to grab your bits and pieces and follow me please, he says, indicating with his outstretched arm the general direction they will be going.

Dalila follows him behind the booths and through the same grey door the other man was taken. They enter what appears to be a stockroom. Metal shelves cover two walls. On them are boxes and small suitcases, items of clothing, toys, laptops and electronic components. There are two desks with computers and a two-way mirror that looks out across the passengers arriving at border control. The officer leads Dalila straight through into a waiting lounge with the same blue carpet as the hall and similar airport chairs to the one she has just been sitting on.

If you'd like to wait here we'll be with you in just a minute, he says, holding an open palm towards the room.

Four men are waiting in the room, all of them African. Two Somalis sit up straight discussing in whispers, the third hunches over his briefcase studying papers and the fourth reclines so far back in his chair he is almost lying down. Dalila sits near the coffee machine, as far from the men as possible. The machine stinks of burnt milk and a light blinks near the coin slot. From the corner of the ceiling, a camera films her and she guesses people are watching from behind the mirror on the wall. Dalila fiddles with the rough scab on her wrist, peeling back a corner till it bleeds and then rubbing saliva on her wrist to stem the bleeding. The scab is black and surrounded by frail pink skin showing the

8

original size of the wound. A wound from Kenya, now carried across the world. She runs her finger over the dried blood, trying to remember how it happened but she can't.

And then she can.

The memory of being thrown forwards across the room. The image of her arm stretched out in front of her, hitting the door frame a moment before her head did, her hand hooking on the door lock as she crumpled to the floor. The memory sits clear, but not the context. It simply happened and the flesh hardened trying to heal itself.

Officer Nita enters the room followed by a family and two security guards. Dalila recognises the family from the plane. The mother is crying and making a show of it. Her three children huddle close, the youngest clinging to her skirt. The father keeps shrugging off the security guards' hands.

Why you don't believe me? shouts the father.

Okay, Benton, says the Indian officer.

Why you don't believe me?

Okay, Benton, listen.

Don't put your hands on me! Why you don't believe me?

The father is a big man, his eyes wide with anger, but Officer Nita isn't intimidated.

Okay, Benton. Benton! I need you to look at me, she says. I am going to get my superior so we can sort this out, yeah? Now, take a seat.

The two security guards step closer and the family claim a row of seats. Except the father, who paces like a caged leopard in front of the mirror.

Very soon, Officer Nita returns with another immigration officer, an older, heavy set man with very short hair. He has a relaxed, unfussy mood about him but his eyes are hard. Officer Nita talks respectfully to him and Dalila assumes this man must be her superior. Dalila studies his face, trying to memorise his features, but all these people look the same, pale and plump, especially the men.

The father of the family also recognises the authority of this new immigration officer. He heads straight for him saying, Sir, sir, these people don't believe me. Every time they say all this bad things about my family.

But as soon as he approaches the guards hold him back. Shouting breaks out. Threats and orders fill the room.

Dalila turns her head so as not to attract attention. She breathes in and feels the wavering in her throat.

Under the threat of arrest the father sits down and stays quiet. The immigration officers leave and a short while later another immigration officer enters the room. He walks up to Dalila and says, Irene Delilah Mathi?

He looks a lot like the other white officers. Bald head, overfed. She thinks she has never seen this man before, but she can't be sure.

Are you Irene Delilah Mathi? he asks.

Yes.

Follow me please. We're going to go downstairs to search your bags, okay?

Dalila stands up and follows him.

Downstairs, her suitcase rests, unopened, on a long metallic table. A black man in uniform waits with his hand on her bag.

I am a customs officer, says the man, and I am going to search your bag at the request of the immigration officer.

Dalila nods. Only on TV has she heard a black man speak with an English accent. It confuses her and she is not sure if she trusts him more or less. He unzips her suitcase and opens it. It isn't full and the contents lie loose and dishevelled from the journey.

Where have you come from? he asks.

Me, I come from Kenya.

Did you pack this bag yourself?

Yes.

The customs officer takes out a pair of old running shoes and puts them to one side.

Are you carrying any drugs or guns or animals?

No.

He takes out her favourite pair of grey jeans, and feels through the pockets. He takes out the pair of shorts she bought a year ago at the Sunday market and the white blouse she wants to wear for job interviews. He piles them next to the running shoes. The immigration officer peers at the items but doesn't interfere.

Did you leave your bag unattended at any time?

No.

The customs officer unpacks the orange jersey her mother knitted for her two years ago and the blue long-sleeved T-shirt she wears to keep her warm in the winter. He takes out her Hello Kitty toiletry bag, which she has had since she was fourteen. He goes through her make-up, opens and sniffs her Nivea skin cream, examines her Close-Up red gel toothpaste. He sifts through her socks and underwear. He unfolds her cotton nightshirt with the dancing pandas, no longer white but dyed a very pale blue from being in the same wash as her uncle's jeans. He performs each task with a studied professionalism. When the bag is empty the customs officer sweeps his palm along the inside, feeling for items sewn into the lining. Satisfied with the suitcase, his eyes flicker over her face and rest on the handbag she is clutching to her chest.

Your handbag, please, he says, holding out his hand.

She gives him her bag and folds her arms across the empty space around her chest. Each hand clutches an elbow.

The customs officer unzips her bag and takes out a packet of tissues, a nail file, her glittery-blue plastic purse. He fingers through 500 Kenyan shillings and some change, pulls out her Kenyan ID card and studies her photo on the left and fingerprint on the right.

Irene Dalila Mwathi, he reads out loud.

Yes, says Dalila.

Her student ID card bears the same name. He finds a folded brown envelope, opens it. This unsettles Dalila, she doesn't allow anyone to touch this, and both officers notice her reaching for the envelope and then withdrawing her hand.

Cautiously, the customs officer pulls out a photograph. It's the one of her family standing in front of their old house in Nakuru. Her uncle, father and mother stand shoulder to shoulder at the front door. Dalila is standing next to her mother, holding her brother's hand. Her uncle's three boys sit on the front step. Everyone is dressed in Sunday clothes and all are serious except her uncle, who, as always, is smiling.

The next photo is of her father when he was young. He is holding up her brother, both are laughing. She always feels this photo makes the gap between her father's front teeth appear larger than she remembers.

The third one is her favourite. It was taken by her father. Her mother is standing by the cook fire behind the house, wearing her green-and-blue shawl. Dalila is only thirteen, squatting by the fire stirring sukuma wiki. A faint aroma of fried onions with steaming kale comes to her. It does every time she looks at this photo.

The customs officer lays the photographs aside and takes out an in-flight magazine from her bag. The title reads, *Think you know London? Think again!*

He looks at her.

Dalila lowers her head.

In her handbag he also finds a bread roll sealed in plastic and a tub of fruit salad from the in-flight meal.

Heat blooms into her face. Taking the magazine was bad, but stolen bread holds a deeper shame. She wants to explain, to invent an excuse, but the customs officer silently packs everything back into her handbag.

The immigration officer leads her back upstairs and along a narrow corridor with a series of yellow doors and glass-fronted interview rooms. The number for each cubicle is on the glass. Each room is identical. White walls, white desk and four grey chairs.

She is shown into a cubicle and told to wait. She sits and the officer leaves, locking her in the room. A little camera films her from above the door. On the glass is a small laminated poster stating, *Please do not lean on the red strip as it sets off an alarm.* It is only then that she notices the red rubber strip, like a bus bell, running the length of the wall. She rocks in her chair but catches herself doing this and forces herself to stop.

Stay calm, she thinks. Stay calm and remember your answers.

She closes her eyes and visualises her list of instructions but before she can really think about it Officer Nita enters the room. She starts her questions before she has even sat down.

Is this your first time abroad?

Yes.

I thought so because this passport is very new. When did you get it?

Dalila mentally checks her list of instructions but this question has no answer.

Me, I . . . I got it two weeks ago, she says. Before I came on the plane the passport was ready.

That was lucky, wasn't it?

What?

The officer sits down and opens the folder. You were very lucky your passport arrived just before your flight, she says, or you wouldn't have come on this holiday.

Dalila tries not to frown. Yes. I was lucky, she replies.

When is your date of birth?

On the twentieth of December nineteen ninety-four, says Dalila.

So you're twenty-one years old, yeah?

No, only twenty. I am twenty-one in December.

The immigration officer makes eye contact for the first time and Dalila looks down at her hands.

How long is your holiday?

Three weeks, says Dalila.

That's a long time for a holiday, isn't it?

Yes.

And you have a return ticket?

Yes, says Dalila, searching through her handbag and producing the ticket.

Officer Nita examines the ticket and checks it against her passport.

So, how many days are you staying for?

For twenty days.

Huh. Officer Nita raises her finger and touches the tiny hole in her nostril as she thinks. Twenty. Twenty. Twenty, she says.

Sorry?

It's just funny, yeah, she says. You're born on the twentieth, you're twenty years old and you're staying for twenty days. Don't you think that's funny?

I don't know.

What don't you know?

Dalila looks into her interrogator's eyes and says, I am twenty years old and I will visit the UK for twenty days.

Your English is very good.

In Kenya, we speak English.

How did you get the time off work?

I am a student. I want to study journalism.

So how did you afford to come here?

My uncle paid for me.

Your uncle?

Yes, my parents, they . . . they died. Last year. Now I live with my father's brother. He said before I start my studies I should visit England. So, now I come to see my aunt.

But she's not really your aunt, is she? You said she's more like your cousin, your mother's cousin?

Yes, replies Dalila. This is my only family. Only these ones are left.

Let's see the money you have.

Dalila produces a polythene sleeve with the US dollars and Kenyan shillings and lays it on the table.

Do you think that's enough money for a holiday in the UK?

Dalila glances at the pile of notes and then at the immigration officer.

I suppose you can earn some more while you're here, yeah?

This is a trap and Dalila's instructions have prepared her for it. No, she replies, I don't come here to work. Only to see my family.

Who are not really your family, says Officer Nita.

They are my family, my mother's family.

Do you have an address and contact details for the family you're staying with?

Yes, Dalila answers, and hands over a note with the address and mobile phone number.

Your aunt's coming to collect you at the airport, yeah?

Yes.

The officer pouts and taps her pen against her palm as she studies the paperwork.

Okay, Miss Mwathi, she says, I'm going to have to make some calls to follow up on our discussion here. In the meantime you'll have to—

The door swings open and an immigration officer leans in through the doorway. He has a mug of tea in one hand, a chocolate bar in the other, and a wide grin on his face.

Nita, he says, we got a shit storm in the holding pen. One of yours.

What?

That family you brought in about an hour ago? One of the little nippers pissed his pants and the father has started throwing stuff. It's all kicking off.

Shit, says Officer Nita. So you came to get me instead of helping out?

The man at the door dunks the chocolate bar into his tea. Sorry, love, he chuckles, I'm on my break.

Officer Nita grabs the paperwork on the desk and pushes past him.

The door slams shut.

Dalila sits in the silence.

Her fingers find the scab on her wrist. The interrogation that just took place plays over and over in her mind. She stuck to the story, answered the questions just as she had practised. Mostly. She had been told the story was good enough to get her through, but doubt picks at her.

The door opens again and another immigration officer stands in front of her. This one is young with a crooked mouth.

Miss, um . . . He looks up her name on the list he is carrying and reads it as if it is three separate names. Irene. Dalila. Mwathi.

Yes.

Right, well, I need you to come with me.

She is taken back to the holding pen, with her suitcase. The two Somalis are still there. Everyone else is gone. Dalila sits on the same seat as before. As soon as she sits an officer comes and takes the Somalis away.

Dalila waits alone. Another windowless room full of different things and she feels her eyes dart around as the anxiety starts to grow in her chest.

Blood is the same, she whispers to herself, glancing at her scab. But it's not enough to calm her this time.

Next to her, the drinks machine hums like a fridge. It is sponsored by Coke.

Coca-Cola, she whispers. Coke is the same.

Fanta – same.

Schweppes – same.

Sprite – same.

But the coin slot is different. To keep her mind occupied, she plays the game again.

Security camera – same.

Carpet pattern – different.

Fire sprinklers – different.

Recycling logo – different.

Dalila plays the game in her mind over and over, focusing on each item in the room. Every different thing is acknowledged, but each object that is the same holds a hint of home.

Her stomach growls but she dares not eat the bread in her bag. She is sure she is waiting for Officer Nita. When, after an hour and a half, Officer Nita does open the door, she is holding Dalila's passport and papers.

I've been in touch with your aunt, yeah, and she's waiting for you at arrivals.

Dalila doesn't know how to respond.

So, if you grab your bags, I'll take you to her.

Officer Nita leads, Dalila follows, cradling her handbag with one arm and hauling her suitcase in the other. They pass a shuttered coffee franchise. The departure lounges are empty, silent. Fluorescent light whitens the air yet along the windows night presses against the panes.

At a door, Officer Nita yawns as she swipes a card through a slot. They move through, into a larger, busier space, with travellers pushing trolleys full of luggage. Two people stare open-mouthed at the arrivals board. Over by the pillar, a teenage boy sits on the ground pulling clothes and books out of his rucksack. Dalila's eyes catch a sign for CHECK IN and a sign saying TAXIS and, further on, the word EXIT above automatic doors, and beyond that, movement, cars and the open night air.

Near the exit, Dalila spots a group of Africans. Three of them. A large woman in a green woollen hat, with a small child wriggling on her lap. A man, too young to be the woman's husband, but perhaps too old to be her son, sits hunched forward, staring into his phone. Dalila recognises none of them, but she wonders if these could be the people she is supposed to meet. The woman looks up and sees Dalila. She glances around the airport and nudges the man next to her. He looks up. The woman lifts the child off her knee and stands. She throws her arms wide and trots towards Dalila.

Irene, my beautiful girl, she calls out in English. Oh child, you have grown so much!

She wraps her arms around Dalila, pressing her cheek against Dalila's face. The woman holds tight, chuckling and swaying. Dalila's arm and handbag are wedged into the middle of this awkward embrace but she allows it to happen, knowing this is the final stage of her instructions, these must be the contacts she is supposed to meet. But underneath this knowledge, down at her core, panic flutters. She doesn't know these people, doesn't know what they expect from her, doesn't know how she should act.

We are so happy to see you, says the big woman, finally letting go of Dalila's neck. God bless you, madam, she says to Officer Nita, grabbing her hand and shaking it. Thank you. You are a very, very good and nice person.

That's alright, says Officer Nita, pulling back her hand. I just have a few questions.

But you are good. I can see your heart, persists the big woman. God bless you, madam. I have not seen my niece for many years. Thank you. You make everyone in my family so, so happy.

And your name is? Officer Nita asks.

Me? My name is Anne Nafula Abasi. She takes out a British driving licence and shows it to Officer Nita. Just now, you phoned me and we spoke together.

Anne is wheezy with excitement. She adjusts her green hat and takes the child's hand. This is my daughter, Helene, she explains to Dalila. To the child she says, This is your Aunty Irene. Say hello.

The child glances wide-eyed at Dalila before tucking her chin to her collarbone. Dalila braces her handbag, blinking at the child. To her mind Anne is too old to be this child's mother, but it's obvious Anne is in charge. She is big, confident, a true Mama.

Smiling, Anne switches to Kiswahili and says to Dalila, At least try to smile, girl. Do your part, so we can leave.

A knot of panic tightens in Dalila, she tries not to look at Officer Nita. The pressure to run or cry threatens to burst out if she doesn't make her body do something. She lets go of her suitcase, bends over and smiles at the child. But the little girl doesn't move.

Don't be so scared, laughs Anne, urging the child forward. This one, she is too shy, but soon you will be friends. Now, Irene, say hello to your cousin Markus.

The man steps forward. He is short, thick around the neck and waist. A round shaven head. Dalila judges him to be in his late twenties. He slips his phone into his back pocket and reaches both arms towards her.

Cousin, he says, you have grown beautiful.

She lets this man embrace her and kiss her cheek. Nice to see you, too, cousin, she says.

Officer Nita's phone chimes. She reads the message and rolls her eyes. Right, she says, handing the driving licence back to Anne. I have to get back to work.

God bless you, madam, says Anne. You are a good person. God bless you.

Officer Nita curls the corner of her mouth and waves once as she backs away. Goodnight, everyone, she says. And Irene, in three weeks' time, make sure you're on that flight, yeah?

Dalila nods and turns to face the people she has been left with. Anne is smiling and waving at Officer Nita as she walks away, but Markus is staring straight at Dalila.

Thank you, says Dalila in Kiswahili. I didn't know if anyone would be here to meet me. Thank you so much. I was told someone would be here but I was worried you wouldn't wait and I'd be—

Markus, take the girl's suitcase, interrupts Anne. You, girl, she says to Dalila, it will look better if you take the child's hand. Anne adjusts her green hat and says, Let's go.

Dalila shuts her open mouth. She takes the toddler's hand and the four of them walk to the exit. A first set of glass doors open automatically, ushering their group into a glass enclosure, a neutral space the size of the home Dalila grew up in. A second set of doors slide apart and the brisk, damp London air rushes at her, cool as petrol on her skin.

Anne leads them between parked taxis and across the road. They round the border of a floodlit car park till they come to a series of bus shelters. Markus places his hands on his knees and sits at the far end of the bench. He takes out his phone as if he is completely alone and begins thumbing the screen. Anne traces her finger along the posted timetable before sitting down on the bench. She lifts the child onto her knee and motions for Dalila to join them.

Are you really Mama Anne? Dalila asks in English.

We don't talk here, says the woman. Sit.

Markus glances sideways at Dalila and says, You have the money?

He unconsciously tilts his phone towards her. Something in that gesture makes her wonder if the question about money is coming from him, or if he is relaying a question that has just been sent to him.

But Mama Anne flaps her hand at him. Later, Markus, she says.

He turns his face away and thumbs a message into his mobile. Mama Anne looks down the road at where she expects the bus to appear.

Will I stay with you? asks Dalila in Kiswahili, thinking they can speak more privately in their native language.

Mama Anne looks up, surprised that she is being spoken to. We don't talk here, she replies in English.

But where are we going? Dalila persists. I was told you would help me. That once I got here you would help me to stay in the UK.

The Mama looks away and says, Sit.

Dalila doesn't sit. She moves her weight from one foot to the next. The air pushes down the back of her neck, it bites at her bare toes and edges up over her ankles.

It is very cold here, she says.

Yes, it is very cold. This is Britain. Get used to it.

The bus arrives. The hydraulics hiss as it stops.

Mama Anne has tickets for everyone and waddles down the centre aisle carrying the child. Markus puts his hand on Dalila's suitcase and motions for her to get on the bus. She climbs the steps and takes a window seat across the aisle from Mama Anne and the child. Markus shoves Dalila's suitcase onto a luggage rack and sits beside her, his bulk pressing against her. Dalila shifts over a little but she has nowhere to go. She turns her head and watches this new world out the window.

The bus swings left at a roundabout, past an area fenced off for airport utility vehicles, up a slip road and onto a dual carriageway. With every turn of the bus she feels herself becoming more and more lost in this vast city. Within a few minutes she is unable to remember the way back to the airport, but uncertain why she would ever want to return. A parade of foreign images swoop past the window. With a deep breath she tries to ignore her anxiety and focuses on one thing at a time.

Dust-free brake lights on the cars – different.

Lush grass on the side of the dual carriageway – different.

Hundreds of orange street lights – different.

Billboard advertising – different.

Old buildings, which must be houses – different.

Traffic lights – same.

Motorists obeying the traffic lights – different.

She stops watching the road and slowly exhales. All she has now are these three strangers. Her fate lies with them. Closing her eyes, she reads the list of instructions imprinted in her mind. Each step had gone to plan. Her 'Aunt' had turned up at the airport and played the part with a flourish. The child was a good sign. It proved these people had thought things through. They are professionals. Only two more things need to happen. First, she will give them the money. Second, they will arrange her asylum process, and then the plan will be complete. After that, she will finish her studies and restart her life.

Dalila opens her eyes. Mama Anne pouts a little, leaning her head gently to counterbalance the sway of the bus. Markus glances up to see what Dalila is looking at before attending to his phone again. The heat of his thigh presses against her leg, his elbow nudges her as he texts. He smells of Nivea and raw chicken meat and Dalila wonders if, in fact, it is he who is in charge.

They change buses in a brightly lit depot in the city. This time they sit upstairs. After a few minutes the child falls asleep and no one breaks the silence.

London is a swirl of lights and shopfronts, cars and narrow streets.

People use umbrellas – different.

Many stroll with their hands in their pockets and hoods pulled over their heads – same.

All the buildings are made of brick and stone. Dalila doesn't see a single sheet of corrugated iron. She spots rubbish bags and litter but no rubble. Neon advertising shines above every shop, the reflected light shimmers across the wet concrete pavement.

Mama Anne rings the bell and they get off. The child whimpers, so Mama Anne raises the little one onto her hip and carries her towards a maze of low concrete buildings. Markus carries the suitcase. Dalila follows, lowering her head against the gusts that twist between the buildings. Their group climbs stairs to the third floor and along an open balcony. Mama Anne unlocks a front door and goes into the flat. Markus stands aside, allowing Dalila to enter before he shuts the door behind him.

Dalila finds herself standing in a corridor. A three-seat sofa is pressed against the wall, leaving only just enough room for one person to shuffle past.

You wait, Mama Anne tells Dalila, before disappearing with the sleepy child into one room.

Behind her, Markus clears his throat. Dalila stands absolutely still trying to sense his movements.

Mama Anne returns, pushes right up to Dalila and says in English, The money, give me.

Dalila glances back as Markus steps up directly behind her.

Mama Anne takes off her green hat and with it all the charm she employed at the airport is gone. She switches to Kiswahili and says, Give me the money, now. All of it.

Dalila sinks her hand into her handbag and pulls out the plastic zip-lock pocket. Mama Anne snatches it and immediately starts counting the notes. It is three hundred US dollars and twenty thousand Kenyan shillings. She slips the dollars back into the plastic pocket and holds it up to Dalila's face.

Where did you get this?

Charles gave it to me, says Dalila.

Charles? Who is this Charles? I don't know Charles.

Charles Okema. He works for my uncle. He's a matatu driver, explains Dalila. He helped me. Charles paid Eddie to get documents to come here.

So this is Eddie's money?

Yes.

You met with Eddie?

No. I gave money to Charles and he paid Eddie for his help, his services. Then, after two weeks, Eddie gave us a plane ticket and some letters and three hundred dollars. He gave me a list of instructions and said I must memorise it. Then, I came here.

Mama Anne holds up the wad of Kenyan shillings. And whose money is this?

That is mine, Dalila answers. My uncle gave it to me.

Your uncle?

Yes.

Mama Anne watches Dalila's face, waiting for something else. She glances at Markus and back to Dalila. What did you say at the airport? she asks.

Dalila swallows. I said it was my money for a holiday.

What else did you say?

About what?

About me. What did you tell them about me?

I said only . . . what was in the instructions. I told them you are my aunt and I am coming to visit only for three weeks.

What did you say my name was?

I said you are called Anne Nafula.

Did you tell them my real name?

Your real name? I . . . I don't know your real name.

Mama Anne pouts and thinks. Where did you say we live?

I gave them the address that Eddie sent to me. I did everything exactly as the instructions said. Believe me.

But they kept you back, says Markus. They must have asked you a lot of questions.

Before God I swear, says Dalila, turning to look at Markus, I didn't say anything. I only told them what I was instructed to say. For two hours I said the same things again and again.

Mama Anne lifts her chin and whispers, If you are lying, Markus will—

I am not lying. I promise. I promise! I only said what I was told to say. I don't know anything else.

And the instructions, where are they?

I flushed them down the toilet before I got to Passport Control.

Mama Anne exchanges a look with Markus. She turns and walks back down the passageway.

What happens now? Dalila says. The instructions said I would meet someone here in London who would help me. Do you work for Eddie?

Mama Anne stops and turns. We don't work for anyone. I am my own boss. I do what I want. Do you understand? Sometimes Eddie asks for a gesture of kindness, that is all.

So, you will help me?

Mama Anne walks back towards Dalila and says, We only help Eddie. We need money to help you.

But I just gave you the money.

The big woman laughs, slapping the US dollars against her palm. This? she says. This is Eddie's money. It must go back to Eddie. If you want a place to sleep and food to eat, you need to pay rent. How much do you have?

Dalila lowers her head. Only what I gave you.

Mama Anne holds up the wad of Kenyan shillings still in the polythene bag. How much is this?

Twenty thousand, says Dalila.

It's not enough, says Mama Anne, rolling her eyes. Not even enough for food.

It is all I have.

Mama Anne's eyelids lower. Take off your shoes, she tells Dalila.

Why?

To see what money you have.

Dalila slips off her shoes and pulls out each inner sole. You see, she says, I have nothing else.

Markus pushes up behind Dalila. She feels his breath at her ear. He wrenches her handbag away and empties out the contents on the sofa. Mama Anne picks out the glittery blue purse, unzips it, and pulls out five hundred shillings.

Please, I only ask for a place to sleep, says Dalila. Eddie said you would help me. Please, Mama.

Calling her Mama has an effect. The woman sighs and points her chin at the sofa in the hallway. Tonight, she says, you sleep there.

Thank you, Mama, says Dalila.

Markus's hands rest on Dalila's waist as he shuffles between her and the sofa. He wanders down the hall and enters a room where Dalila glimpses a TV and at least three other men before he closes the door behind him.

Mama Anne pulls a duvet from the hall cupboard and dumps it on the sofa. If you make trouble, she says to Dalila, you are out.

I won't make trouble.

Mama Anne clicks her tongue and enters the room where she had put the child and closes the door.

Dalila sits down on the sofa. She replaces the purse, bread roll, fruit salad, passport and the photographs of her family into her handbag. Through the walls come voices. Sounds of movement from deeper inside, from the other people living in this flat. The deeper tones of male voices and then, light female giggles sprinkle across the room. It's difficult to determine how many are in the flat, impossible to know where they are from, what their intentions towards her might be.

She stands up. The front door is right there and beyond it, London. Great Britain. The great land her father had often talked about. But beyond the door is also darkness, and cold, a place with no instructions to follow. It is better to stick to the plan. Only one more step remains in the plan. She has given them the money, now they must help her.

She places her shoes neatly next to her suitcase at the end of the sofa and considers digging out her nightdress but the thought of changing clothes here in the hallway stops her. Better to just sleep in her dress. Tomorrow, when they trust her more, she will wash and eat, but now she must sleep. She lies on the sofa and tucks the duvet around her neck. A deep tiredness moves up through her body and into her head. The last time she slept was on the floor in her uncle's house.

The voices mumble in the background. Images of the day roll, unsummoned, across her mind. The food tray on the aeroplane. Her instruction list flushing away. The sky-blue eyeshadow of the immigration officer opening her passport. The pink razor burn on the man who escorted her to the holding room. She adjusts herself on the sofa till her neck is straight and her feet poke out from under the duvet.

You are here, she whispers to herself. You have made it. You are in England.

Unbelievable, improbable words. That she, Dalila Mwathi, could be on the other side of the world. Her father had always said England was the Father of the World. Now, here she is. With her heart, she reaches out, trying to feel the Englishness around her, but there is only the warm duvet and the hum of voices in the other room. For now, it is enough. She breathes out and allows herself to sink deeper into the cushions beneath her.

A door clicks open. Dalila wakes, listening without moving. Very light footsteps. A shape in the dark approaches the sofa. Dalila blinks as her eyes adjust. Markus is looking down at her, his hands hanging limp, his shirt hanging open.

What do you want, Markus? she whispers.

I want to help you.

Okay, says Dalila. Thank you.

Markus sits down next to her. The flat is silent. The chatter she fell asleep to has been swallowed. Dalila tugs the covers up around her neck.

Do you want me to help you? asks Markus.

Yes, says Dalila.

Markus shifts his weight and places his arm across the top of the covers.

Dalila flinches. I've paid my . . . my rent, she whispers. You saw me pay.

I saw you give rent to Mama Anne, says Markus, but this isn't rent . . . this is tax. He leans onto her, his mouth at her ear.

From under the duvet Dalila shoves upwards, forcing him back. No! Get off, she shouts. She wriggles under the duvet trying to sit up, to break free. Markus pulls his head back and shunts his forehead down against her chin. Her head snaps back, stunned. Before she can call out again his hand covers her mouth. He is quickly on top of her. Her arms pinned across her chest under the duvet, her two free fingers claw at the hand across her mouth. She twists, pushes with all her strength but can hardly move. Markus's free hand reaches down and starts to pull up the covers around her legs. The cooler air touches her exposed thighs. She kicks and thrashes but his weight is too much for her. He hooks his arm around her left thigh and wrenches it to the side, brings his face right up to hers. Stop kicking, he grunts, or this will get worse for you.

Dalila fights to free her face from under his hand. His fingers are pressed right up against her nostrils. Her lungs pull frantically, trying to inflate. Blood from her burst lip is filling her mouth.

Markus shifts himself between her thighs. His hand gropes at her underwear.

Not this, cries Dalila, but the words can't come out. Please God, not this. She wrestles under the duvet but can't free her arms, can't breathe, can't move. With enormous effort she pushes against his weight, trying to sit up, and feels herself rising, floating up out of herself, hovering over the sofa. She sees herself from above. Apart.

He pulls her underpants, trying to slip them off but her legs are too splayed. He tugs hard sideways, trying to rip them.

Uncle Markus, I'm hungry, says a little voice.

Markus looks up. The child is at the armrest of the sofa, rubbing the corner of her eye with her wrist.

Get out of here, hisses Markus. Go to bed. Go.

Markus shoves the child away with one arm while keeping Dalila trapped with his other arm. There is silence, and then, the child erupts into howling.

A light flicks on and Mama Anne comes into the hallway. She squints in the brightness and sees Markus on the sofa with his trousers down, his hand over Dalila's mouth.

You stupid boy, she says, pushing the child into the bedroom with one hand and in one fluid movement stepping close and slapping Markus across the ear.

You stupid boy, shouts Mama Anne, slapping him again and again. The child stands in the doorway screaming.

Markus jumps up, pulling at his trousers. Stop, he yells, shielding himself with his forearm. Stop. He lunges at Mama Anne, pulling her flailing arms down.

Dalila gasps for breath. The air rushes into her as she flops off the sofa and scrambles across the ground, away from Markus, till her back is pressed against the front door. A light switches on deeper inside the flat. People appear in the hallway shouting in English and Kiswahili.

Are you crazy? shouts Markus. What is your problem, huh?

You, says Mama Anne, wide-eyed and unafraid. You are a problem, for all of us. For our business. You don't think.

Markus looks at the hallway full of faces. He pushes past Mama Anne and sneers, What do you know, old woman?

She pursues him down the hall, shouting, I know you are a selfish boy! What if this girl talks? Huh? What then, stupid boy? We are all finished. Believe me. The Home Office will take everyone in this flat. And if she talks to Eddie? Then *you* are finished!

The argument moves into the kitchen. Two men and a woman blink and stare at Dalila before following the action into the kitchen. Dalila sniffles and touches her mouth. Her lip is swollen. There is blood on her fingers.

The shouting continues. The toddler's wailing gets louder, closer. A girl Dalila has never seen before appears in the hallway carrying the child.

You are hurt? the girl asks in English.

Dalila holds up her bloody fingers. I'm okay, she says.

You are okay?

Yes.

The girl bounces the child, trying to calm her down. She looks towards the kitchen and back at Dalila. You must go. Now, she says. Quickly.

Dalila doesn't move.

Markus won't leave you alone. Get your shoes. Now.

The girl disappears with the child into the bedroom. Dalila jumps up, slips on her shoes and loops her handbag across her shoulder. The girl returns without the child. She grabs an anorak from the cupboard, forces it on Dalila.

Take this, she says. Don't come back.

Dalila goes for her suitcase but the girl pushes her towards the front door. She unlocks it, opens it. Go, she says, run.

The door closes behind her.

Dalila runs. Arms reaching into the night, tears on her face, she runs.

The open anorak flaps behind her as Dalila sprints, instinctively, back the way she came, to the bus stop. Her breath steams out under the street lights. From behind her comes a noise. Wood scraping over concrete. Markus? The other men?

Glancing behind her, she stumbles, almost falling, yet spots no shapes within the black.

She races across a junction and along a wider road, her legs working hard. She passes houses on either side, a shop, another junction, she runs across a wet street, under the red glow of a traffic light, looking back, expecting to see her pursuers, she slams right into someone and screams, scrambling back to her feet, pressing her back against a hedge. The person she slammed into is a man, a white man, in uniform.

Hey, he shouts. What the hell you doing?

Stunned, her lungs burn, she can't answer, doesn't have time to answer. She looks back up the street and then again at the man's uniform. He's a postman. Only a postman. As he steps towards her she darts off, running for three blocks, head back, arms swinging.

Her ears ache in the icy air. Abruptly switching direction, she runs down a tree-lined street for four blocks, for five, moving fast enough for neither Markus nor her panicked thoughts to catch up with her. In her peripheral vision, over the roofs of parked cars, a figure in the road chases her. She speeds up, gasping for air, trying to keep going, scanning desperately for a place to hide, a weapon, a sign. The figure appears alongside her. It's a man on a bicycle wearing a helmet. His eyes flit up at her, delivering a concerned, questioning look. His expression is touched with alarm. He speeds up and pedals on down the road. It's enough to make her slow down, to stop.

She places her hand on a wheelie bin and tries to slow her breathing. Daybreak is approaching, the sky changing from black to indigo, it will be light soon and she'll be easier to spot when they come looking for her. A car rolls by. She turns from it, zips up the red anorak and strides along the pavement.

The girl. That girl in the flat told her to run. So she got up and ran. She just left. So, so stupid. How could she do that? What is she going to do now? She knows no one and her money is gone, all given to Mama Anne as payment. Dalila stops walking and places her palms against her face. She should go back. She could apologise for her behaviour and beg Mama Anne to take her in. She has to go back. She turns and walks back the way she came. The cold air seeps through the fragile layers of her clothing. She has to go back, if only for her grey jeans and her mother's knitted orange jersey.

Dalila places a finger against her swollen top lip. There is no blood but an image of Markus's face rushes up at her. She stops. The smell of his beery breath is distinct in the morning air. She can still feel the pressure of his hand across her mouth. She can't go back. Not to stay. Perhaps she could wait till Markus leaves and persuade that young girl in the flat to return her suitcase and then she'll leave.

As the sun rises, the terraced houses and shuttered shops all seem very similar and above them are concrete tower blocks of various heights. One street looks like the next. She tries to recall the specific architecture of the building she fled. An image of the child sleeping on Mama Anne's shoulder comes to her. She remembers Markus clutching her suitcase, walking through gusting wind in the middle of the night, but she can't picture the building. She has the address memorised, but the way Mama Anne questioned her last night makes her suspect that the address she gave to the immigration officers was not where she ended up. Dalila stands at a crossroads. She studies one road and peers along another.

More people emerge onto the streets. Traffic starts to queue at the junctions, people in cars wait patiently for the lights to change. Half a block away, three heavyset men in dirty jeans and fluorescent waistcoats walk up the pavement. A fourth comes out of a newsagent's and joins his friends. He unwraps a packet of cigarettes and lights up, exhaling smoke into the brittle dawn. They move as a pack, each man with a shoulder-swaying gait. To avoid them, Dalila crosses the street. She catches up with a couple of women in saris and overcoats, trailing close enough behind them for a casual observer to mistake them for a group of three. She follows them for a while till one woman calmly looks back at Dalila and whispers something to her friend. Before the other woman turns around, Dalila steps off the pavement, weaves between standing traffic and heads off down a different street. Three African women get off a bus, all talking at the same time. One of them opens a pushchair and places her child in the seat. Dalila hurries behind them, trying to disguise herself as one of their group. Using women as cover, she weaves her way deeper into the maze of London, her arms crossed over her handbag, fingers tucked under her armpits, her feet bloodless and numb in her open-toe shoes.

The sun rises without warmth. Its mute grey light illuminates objects, while also drawing colours from them. In the distance, taller towers and a crane mark the horizon. Assuming the biggest towers mark London's heart, she heads towards them, moving only to keep warm, knowing there is no way back.

People walk by with a hungry focus, their eyes set on the middle distance. Lots of them wear headphones. Many queue at bus stops, staring into their phones. Hundreds flow into and out of Underground stations. All nationalities mix together but it's the white people who fascinate her. She tries not to stare but she has never seen so many whites before. Thousands of them. The streets of London aren't as crowded as the avenues of Nairobi, but, for Dalila, these white people embody more space. Their bodies press out against the seams of their clothes, many of them stout as African businessmen. Even the thin ones seem big, as if the space around them is packed with prominence.

With so many similar white faces, only the extremes stand out to Dalila. A man with plump pink cheeks. The charcoal tattoos crawling up a teenager's neck. The ash-grey of a man's unshaven chin. A woman's bronze face and her shocking-pink lips. Here and there, she sees some of the whitest faces she has ever seen. Pale fragile complexions with fine blue veins visible through their opaque skin.

But no face is actually white and Dalila becomes fascinated with each person's subtle shading. She is surrounded by people the colour of eggshell and bread, of yams and potatoes, of cashews and oats. Hair the colour of melon flesh and peeled pears, of aubergines and roasted coffee beans. Most beautiful are the eyes. Sparkling irises of topaz and opal, tiger's eye and lapis lazuli.

All these colours and black clothes. Almost everyone wears dark overcoats, black jackets, deep blue jeans and charcoal suits. Only Dalila weaves through the crowds in her sunflower dress and red, oversized anorak.

London itself feels like it leans towards her. Glorious buildings of cold stone. Gift shops covered in Union Jacks. Portraits of the Queen and mugs shaped to look like Prince William. Black taxis look exactly like the ones she's seen in the movies. *Mr Bean. Four Weddings and a Funeral.* An ambulance rushes by with an unfamiliar sing-song to its siren. She sees performing statues, long buses that bend in the middle, three-year-olds in pushchairs and grown men wearing backpacks like schoolchildren. She remembers walking to school and a feeling descends on her, a loneliness, a memory of when the world was vast and she felt tiny and fragile before it.

She enters a large clothing store and walks the aisles, stopping under a ceiling vent blowing warm air. She fingers through blouses to disguise herself among the purposeful. An African woman stands behind a small desk at the dressing rooms, counting a customer's items and handing them a numbered tag. Dalila watches from behind a rack of pyjamas. Perhaps she could talk to her. She's a sister. She could ask if she knows of a place to stay, or where to get help. But how do you phrase that? Hello, I want to start a new life in the UK. Can you help me? She has to be more delicate, maybe pretending to only need one night's accommodation till her family . . . her people arrive the next day. She watches the sales assistant helping two customers. Dalila unhooks a set of yellow flannel pyjamas and commits to going over there. She'll smile and ask to try these on and hopefully push the conversation round to Africa or some other common ground and then, once they are talking like sisters, she will ask. There will be less shame in it this way. She carries the pyjamas over, but as she approaches another sales assistant comes across and talks to the African girl.

Dalila stands still, holding the pyjamas, waiting to be served.

But the African girl gathers up an armful of clothes on coat hangers and disappears through a set of grey doors.

Would you like to try those on? asks the new sales assistant.

No, thank you, says Dalila. She hangs up the pyjamas and slips out of the shop.

The afternoon draws on and hunger pulls at her core. She notices people eating, chewing chocolate bars as they walk, fingers dipping into crisp packets. People sitting on benches with paper cups of coffee and sandwiches, others stand outside takeaways eating chips from paper wrappings. She takes out the bread roll from her handbag. In the cold air her lip doesn't throb as much as she chews and after a while the gnawing in her stomach releases.

The city opens to a great brown river. A large white Ferris wheel sits on the bank further upstream. In front of her, a single barge chugs under the bridge. She crosses with hundreds of other pedestrians. Most hold their collars closed against the bitter wind while Dalila cups her hands over her ears.

She walks till her heels ache and her bare toes go numb again. Up one street, along another, looking for something, a sign, a plan.

The afternoon passes into a foggy evening. She stands at busy junctions without crossing, simply watching the green man flash, watching a street-cleaning truck with rotary brushes sweep rubbish from the gutters. She avoids eye contact and keeps to well-lit areas. Instead of hunger, a deep weariness takes hold of her legs. This worries her. She keeps going, feeling the weariness move up through her body and settle into her shoulders. Her world begins to shrink into a succession of lights and faces and noises as she shuffles along in a limbo of indecision, her limbs too numb to feel the cold. In the brightly lit entrance of an office building she sits down and unzips the red anorak, pulls her knees right up close to her chest and zips up the anorak over her shins up to her neck. She perches on the steps like a stuffed sack of yams and rests her head against the marble wall. It feels good to sit. Her breathing deepens. She thinks she can smell fire, woodsmoke, like the cooking fire her mother used to squat in front of to prepare ugali. As a tiny girl it had always been her job to collect sticks for the fire and then water for boiling. She would squat next to her mother and stoke the flames, the two of them speaking softly while they shifted pots from the centre of the flames to a cooler section on the grill. Her mother comes to her, standing with her hands by her sides. A deep sadness opens up, but her mother smiles at her, and sits down on the step while her father stands further off and looks out. They don't say anything. Dalila feels too ashamed to look up. They deserve a better daughter than her. Her mother places a hand on Dalila's shoulder.

Hello. Hello, miss? You need to wake up, miss.

Dalila stares at the woman touching her shoulder.

Do you speak English? Can you understand me?

Yes, says Dalila, still heavy with sleepiness.

Have you got anywhere to sleep tonight?

I'm sorry, I was resting.

Have you eaten anything today?

No. I am okay, I must go.

It's alright. I'm here to help, okay? My name is Melissa and I'm here with Shelter For All. Would you like a sandwich?

No.

It's alright, look, those are my co-workers over there and we help people who are homeless. We can give you a safe place to stay for the night. Get you out of this cold. Would you like that?

No. I will go.

What is your name, miss? No white woman had ever called Dalila *miss*.

Irene, my name is Irene.

Irene. You are safe with us. We won't hurt you. Why don't you come with me and you can have some soup? You like soup, don't you?

Yes.

Melissa smiles. Me too, she says, I just love soup. Come, it's alright. She slips off her woollen glove and reaches out. Dalila looks at the soft pale hand and when she takes it, it's warm.

Shivering, her teeth rattling, Dalila stares at the spire. Right up at the top, at the narrowest point, against the peach mist of London's night sky, stands a cockerel on one leg. The iron bird tilts into the wind. Melissa is talking and most of it swims by Dalila, but her tone is soothing.

The shelter is a church, with enormous wooden doors. Cut into one of the doors is a regular-sized entryway, through which they step.

Inside, an older man behind a desk greets them good evening. His whiskers and eyebrows curl about his wide face, his moustache twirls into tusks. He slides an open ledger towards them and Dalila pulls back, wary of this warthog man. Melissa takes her hand.

You're alright, she says. You'll be safe here. Everyone needs to put their name on the list.

Dalila struggles to write in the ledger, battling against the cold quivering through her bones.

Here, let me help you, says Melissa.

She signs Dalila into the ledger and writes the word *Irene* on a sticker, which she attaches to Dalila's chest.

You just keep that on, she says, with an easy smile. Come on, let's get you warmed up.

In the basement canteen at a table by herself, with a blanket wrapped around her, she listens to the wooden floor creak as Melissa moves and prepares the soup.

In the corner sit two men, both unshaven. One has matted, shoulder-length hair, the other has no teeth, his lips shrinking around his gums. They hunker over bowls of soup, dipping their bread, chewing slowly. Their trousers are soiled and worn through at the knees. A whiff of urine comes from their end of the hall. She has never seen white men like this. Never thought it possible. The toothless one catches her staring, but he turns back to his meal.

The soup is hot and salty but the tea is dreadful, needing more milk and more sugar. Dalila sips it anyway, warming her fingers on the mug. Melissa takes the seat opposite her and chats as if they are friends. Her face is open and earnest and Dalila hears none of what's being said, but she appreciates having this woman nearby.

It's late when Dalila is shown to the women's dormitory, which, Melissa explains, doubles as a Sunday school. Two women are already asleep, so she doesn't turn on the light. Each bed is a mattress on the floor with a sleeping bag. Dalila claims the nearest one. She takes off her anorak and lies down. The sleeping bag smells of detergent whereas the mattress holds a deeper scent of sweat from other bodies. When her vision adjusts to the dark she becomes aware of children's drawings on the walls. A box of limp, unblinking soft toys unnerves her. She rolls away from it, onto her side, and tucks her handbag into the bottom of the sleeping bag. She slips her wrists between her knees, and focuses on a hand-sewn banner of a satin dove soaring above a cross. For a long time, she lies there staring at the dove. Thoughts chop through her mind, fragmenting her. She was in college not so long ago and now she's sleeping on the floor on the other side of the world. How quickly it all changed. How deeply it all became ruined. Is she being punished? She wonders where she will sleep tomorrow and if Markus might be out looking for her. Where will she get more clothes? The breathing of the other women asleep in the room is deep and slow and Dalila wonders who they are and where they come from. Her thoughts evade conclusions and her stomach has that empty feeling she used to get before exams.

In her dream she's riding in a matatu. It's full of people and she is sitting at the back. It's hot. Traffic is heavy and the windows are darkened by amber dust. There's a jolt and a scraping along the side of the van and suddenly everyone is trying to get out. She, too, is climbing, over seats, over people. Someone is kicking a window, cracking it, breaking it. And then, somehow, she is out, running. The streets are empty but she isn't safe. She ducks into a mobile phone shop and goes to a rack of glittering phone covers. A man approaches and asks if she needs assistance. As she turns she recognises his face. It is her uncle. He and she are the only ones in the shop.

Dalila opens her eyes and sits upright, sweating, her sleeping bag kicked down around her ankles. She has no idea where she is. Her nose is blocked, her tongue dry. She listens for men's voices. A weak dawn has come. The patter of light rain thrums the window. She remembers being brought to this room, remembers the soup she had. Next to her is a sleeping woman with her arm across her face. The other woman has already left. Her rolled sleeping bag marks where she had been. Dalila gets up, puts on her anorak, rolls her sleeping bag, and leaves.

In the hallway, a heavy-hipped woman smiles and says, Good morning. The woman hobbles towards her, using a crutch to keep balance. Everything alright? she asks.

Dalila is unsure of exactly what kind of place she is in or how to act in this place.

The woman staggers closer and glances at the sticker on Dalila's anorak. Irene, is it? she asks.

Dalila nods.

Well, I'm Judith, says the woman, pointing at her own name badge. You're up bright and early, she says. Would you like a cuppa?

No, says Dalila, not quite understanding the woman's accent. Me, I'm looking for the toilet.

Right, well, it's just down there and on your left. And when you're done, why don't you join me in the canteen?

Downstairs, Dalila sits in the same seat she used last night. The clarity of this room in the morning light doesn't match her memories from the night before. A hint of damp hangs in the air and it's a little too cool to be comfortable. Dalila does, however, remember last night's tea, and when Judith offers her some she declines. Instead, she accepts toast, breaking bits off and trying not to eat it too quickly.

Melissa is here? Dalila asks.

No, her shift only starts at four.

Judith waddles over, crutch in one hand, tea in the other, and lowers herself into a seat next to Dalila. You're not long here, are you, love?

Dalila stops chewing, trying to decipher Judith's question.

Judith tries again. How long have you lived here, Irene?

Dalila puts down the toast and says, I came to this place, to this country, two days ago.

And do you have family here?

She glances at Judith and looks away.

What about friends? Perhaps some people you'd like us to call?

Dalila wants to look at Judith but she can't. I have no people, she whispers.

Saying these words releases something. It pushes its way up and tears flood her vision. She wipes her palm stiffly across each eye as if to push this thing back inside.

It's alright, says Judith. It's alright. So, you only just got here, then?

Dalila nods.

And did you travel all that way on your own?

Yes, says Dalila. She sniffs and says, I came alone on the plane. An agent arranged for me to meet his people at the airport. I didn't know them. They got money to help me stay in this country. But when I went with them, they . . . this man . . .

The raw thing inside her pushes up again, stronger than before. The tears flow and she finds herself unable to speak.

It's alright, love, says Judith. And this happened yesterday, did it?

He was going to hurt me, whispers Dalila. I ran away. She digs into her handbag and finds the packet of tissues. She blows her nose and apologises to Judith.

Not at all, says Judith. You've had a rough time of it. You sure you don't want some tea?

Dalila shakes her head.

A silence opens up between them. Judith lifts her mug of tea and sips from it. Then she says, I have always found that it's good to have a plan and get on with it, especially when times are tough. So, what do you want to do, Irene?

Me, I want to be a journalist, replies Dalila. A news reporter, like the women on NTV Kenya. That is my dream.

Judith puts down her mug and grins. Well, yes, why not? she says. You're well spoken. You'd make a fine reporter, you would.

I studied in college for only one year, says Dalila, but I didn't finish. One day I will complete my studies.

Good for you, Irene. You've got ambition, I can see that. But the point I was trying to make is, what are your plans *right now*?

Oh, says Dalila, as a surge of embarrassment hits her.

You see, our congregation only runs a night shelter during the week, Judith continues, so you can't stay here indefinitely. But we try to help people as best we can. Now, you said some people were supposed to help you claim asylum, is that right?

Yes, says Dalila.

Do you want to claim asylum?

Yes, I need this, says Dalila. If I go back to Kenya, my uncle, he will find me.

Well, if you're going to claim, you'll need to go to Croydon. That's the first step. Everyone has to go to Croydon, says Judith. It's in south London, not far from here. I'll make some calls once breakfast has been served. We'll make an appointment and get everything in order.

Thank you, says Dalila.

The warthog man enters the canteen and nods hello. He switches on the urn and starts preparing for breakfast.

Judith struggles to her feet and says to Dalila, Come on, I'll show you where the showers are.

*

Mid-morning, Judith takes Dalila into the cramped church office. She fingers through a pile of leaflets for asylum seekers and calls the Asylum Screening Unit in Croydon. It's a complicated process. After three attempts, Judith gets through and says she has a young lady wanting to claim asylum and recites some of Dalila's basic information. She gives them the office phone number and within half an hour the unit calls back asking more questions. Does Miss Mwathi need an interpreter? Judith says she does not, but she insists that a female case worker interviews Dalila. This is noted and the questions continue. How did she enter the country? What was her point of entry? Does she have tuberculosis? Does she have any children or dependants? Does she have scabies? Later, they call back again, repeating similar questions before confirming the time and date for the interview the following day. They inform her that Miss Mwathi will need four passport photos, uncut, with her full name and date of birth written on the back of each one and she will be expected to bring her passport and all other forms of identification including any documents and supporting evidence to back up her story.

When you get there, Judith tells Dalila, you just tell them your story. Tell it like a journalist, she says, smiling at Dalila, make sure you get all the details in.

The details. Dalila lowers her head and thumbs the scab on her wrist.

I know it might be hard but they can only help you if you trust them.

In her stomach, Dalila feels the story she needs to tell. It's a story she has only lived, she has never told it and she worries if she will be able to find the words.

Judith reaches over and takes Dalila's hand. Would you like me to pray with you? she asks.

Um, yes.

Judith takes hold of Dalila's other hand and bows her head. Dear Lord Jesus, I bring to You this beautiful young woman and I pray You'll guide her through these difficult days. In Your infinite wisdom You have brought her to this place. Let her feel Your love and guidance, Lord. May she know, that no matter how hard life gets, You hold her in the palm of Your hand as one of Your dearest children. May she understand that all things happen according to Your divine plan. May she embrace the hope You promised in Your Word, that all things work together for the good for those that love Him. I pray this in Jesus' name. Amen.

Amen, echoes Dalila.

When Melissa arrives, she gives her an easy smile and Dalila can't help but smile too. The two of them go to a photo booth at the Post Office where Melissa pays for passport photos. Dalila sits upright on the stool and pulls across the little blue curtain. On the digital screen in front of her is an image of her face. Her lip is still swollen from Markus's headbutt. The image is her, but reversed, not the person she is used to seeing in the mirror. The woman on the screen looks startled and thin.

By the time the photographs have developed, Dalila is shivering again.

Oh, you're frozen, aren't you? says Melissa.

Back at the shelter, Melissa rakes through the clothing cupboards as Dalila stands back and watches.

This one's nice, says Melissa, holding up a coat. Try it on and see what you think.

As Dalila puts it on, Melissa holds open the cupboard door so Dalila can see herself in the mirror. Dalila loves the colour, a vibrant banana-leaf green, but it smells of old perfume. It sits far too wide around the waist. She looks lost in it.

Here, try this, says Melissa, holding up a black puffer jacket. These are really cosy. It's not really a raincoat but it'll keep you pretty dry.

Dalila slips her arms into puffy sleeves. The coat fits neatly down to her waist and from there widens and hangs like a large bell around her knees.

That's good on you. It's a good fit, says Melissa. Here, zip it right up. See? That'll keep your neck warm against the wind.

Dalila looks at herself in the mirror. It's too puffy. The ribbed quilting makes her look like a grub. And black is a colour of sadness.

How does that feel? asks Melissa.

She focuses on the feeling. The fabric feels like a sleeping bag tucked around her neck and her hands, deep inside the pockets, are already tingling as they thaw. Is this the kind of clothing she will need in this place? If this English woman likes it, maybe this is what people wear here.

It feels good, says Dalila.

Melissa digs through a cardboard box and pulls out a pair of black woollen gloves and a black beanie with a small Thinsulate label on the front. You'll need these too, says Melissa.

Dalila slides her fingers into the gloves and puts on the hat, pulling it down to her eyebrows. It's snug and warm against her ears. She looks like a boy, one of those young men who grill corn cobs on the street. But she's warm. It's the most comfortable she has felt since arriving.

Both of them stand back and regard her image in the mirror.

We don't have any women's shoes at the moment, says Melissa, but we have some thick hiking socks that will be better than nothing.

Unzipping the jacket, Dalila says, I have no money for these things.

Oh no, not at all, Melissa says, you keep it. All these items are donated to the church. It's the goodwill of others that keeps us going.

Dalila nods and looks at herself in the mirror again. She turns and picks up the red anorak she had been wearing and gives it to Melissa.

I want to give this to the shelter, says Dalila, for helping me.

Thank you, says Melissa.

The next morning, Melissa and Dalila step off the bus in Croydon. A cardboard coffee cup tumbles in the wind. Dalila tugs her woollen hat down over her ears and squints up at the surrounding architecture. Melissa unfolds an information leaflet and holds it open towards Dalila.

The Asylum Screening Unit looks like this, says Melissa, pointing to a photograph. It should be around here somewhere. It's called Lunar House.

Dalila scans the horizon. The tallest nearby structure is a monument to concrete and blue-mirrored glass. The dust-free newness of it is almost beautiful. It is what she imagines a government building in the UK would look like, the neat lines, the air of importance.

Maybe it could be that one, she says.

Melissa peers at the building and glances down at the photograph. That looks about right, she says. Are you ready to go?

Me, I am ready.

As they walk towards it, the building appears to grow taller and more imposing. Dalila clenches her fists inside her pockets. As she breathes out slowly, Melissa looks at her and links Dalila's arm around her own. Nothing is said, but in Dalila's heart a hope begins to grow. If she gives herself openly and truthfully to this place, if they mark down her name and take her fingerprints and listen to her story, if they record it all into their computers then, in a way, she will be woven into its importance. And if her new papers come from here, with official approval, who can argue with that? What is safer than that?

Outside the entrance to Lunar House stands a queue of at least twenty people. Dalila and Melissa wait with them. At the door, a security guard in an armoured vest ushers people in one at a time. His eyes examine every face in the queue and when they land on Dalila she lowers her head. She can't help herself. Her little cloud of hope evaporates. What if she can't tell her story? What if she opens her mouth but the words don't come? And if the words do come, will they be big enough to hold all that has happened to her?

Hey, says Melissa, squeezing her arm. It's okay. There's nothing to be worried about. You just talk to them and they will help. Okay?

Dalila nods.

You know I'm not allowed in there, but trust me, you'll be safe. It's going to be okay.

Dalila nods again, trying to believe what Melissa believes.

When they reach the front of the queue, Melissa hugs Dalila. You have my number, right? Yes. So, just call me after your interview and we'll chat. Okay? You're going to be fine. Everything is going to be fine.

The guard steps aside and lets Dalila through. Inside, security is like an airport. She places her puffer coat, hat, handbag and shoes into a tray on a conveyor belt which rolls through an X-ray scanner, while she steps through a metal detector. Security guards go through everyone's possessions, picking out manicure sets, knitting needles, aerosol cans, perfume bottles and liquids. The liquids are treated with particular suspicion. Those individuals who have items confiscated are moved to one side and given a ticket so they can collect their belongings when they leave, the rest scramble to rethread their belts and help their children put on their shoes. Dalila pushes through the crowd and grabs her handbag and coat.

There are window booths, like at a bank. She steps up to the first available one and says, Good morning, madam. My name is Irene Dalila Mwathi. Me, I have come to claim asylum.

Do you have your appointment letter? asks the officer.

Yes.

Well, I don't see your name.

Dalila presents the appointment letter that was emailed to the shelter. She also gives the officer the self-completion form which she had filled out in her neatest handwriting. She hands over her Kenyan ID card, her passport photographs, her passport.

The officer types some details into the computer on her desk and asks, Where are you staying?

I don't have nowhere.

So, you need accommodation?

Yes.

The officer does more typing.

Is my appointment okay? asks Dalila. My name is in the computer?

The officer issues Dalila with a ticket, saying, Take a seat and wait for your number to be called.

Although the waiting area is large, it's full of people, the air as close as breath on her face. Three different babies are wailing. One mother paces the aisle bouncing her inconsolable child on her hip. Another mother tries to bottle-feed her crying infant with one hand and keep her toddler close with the other. Her husband pays no attention.

Dalila sits down on the end of a row of metal seats.

Many people disappear into their phones, playing, texting, talking, with no regard for the signs on the wall instructing them to *Turn Your Mobile Phones Off!* Toes twitch. People sigh. Children refuse to sit still.

She stands up, takes off her coat and sits back down, folding it over her lap. Her hiking socks have begun to slip off and are flopping through the toe-gap of her shoes. Checking to see if anyone is watching, she leans forward and places her handbag at her feet then quickly tugs her socks tight. She sits up straight and adjusts her sunflower dress across her knees.

For over an hour, she waits, watching the second hand of the clock sweep around. She wonders where she will sleep tonight. Melissa assured her that the Home Office would provide a place, but where? The leaflets mentioned she may be detained but Judith and Melissa both said that women seeking asylum are mostly placed in a hostel in the city.

Mostly.

The man sitting in front of her wears a brown suit jacket, similar to the one her father used to wear. She remembers him wearing it the day she started her degree. He put on his Sunday suit and drove her to college, stopped right in front of the gates. She was so excited to get started she immediately got out and shut the door. As she waved, her father beckoned her back. He rolled down the window, then went silent and seemed to have nothing to say.

What is it, Father?

Your mother told me to say she is very proud of you. I mean, your mother and I, we both want to say this. You are a good daughter.

She remembers the look that passed between them and she wonders if he can see her now, in this building, with her ridiculous socks.

A baby's crying becomes open-throat howling. The mother stands up holding the child to her shoulder, trying to gently bounce it into silence, but the crying continues, on and on across the waiting room.

At 11:21 a.m., her number is called.

She is escorted to a room where she is asked to confirm her name and date of birth and nationality. She is told to place the fingers of her right hand on a scanner and then her thumb. She obediently repeats the process with her left hand. She is told to look directly into the camera. There is an urge to smile but the atmosphere is too official so she mirrors the mood of the officers. Her escort takes her to an enclosed interview room and Dalila is left by herself to wait. She tucks her handbag and coat under her chair, sits with her knees together, straightens the neckline of her dress. She is expecting a female officer, because Judith specifically asked for one to be present at the interview.

Two white men in uniform enter the room. The younger one asks, Are you Irene Matty?

Dalila stands up and says, Yes, sir, I am Irene Mwathi.

She shakes their hands. The officers sit down. Both of them are plump and short-haired. The younger one has the tail of a tattoo curling out from under his shirtsleeve. The older one yawns and glances at his watch. They have a file with her ID, passport photos and letter. The younger one starts the procedure by confirming her age, date of birth, nationality and marital status.

He then starts explaining how the interview will proceed. There is something about his face, an expression he maintains in the cross section between his nose and eyebrows, which feels unfamiliar to her. As he talks, he straightens the papers into a neat pile, lightly touching the corners to ensure the papers are precisely aligned.

Do you understand everything I have explained to you, Miss Matty?

Yes, sir, I understand. Are you going to interview me?

The interview has already started.

Oh, yes, she says. But I . . . On the telephone I was informed there would be a woman.

The older officer leans back in his chair, arms folded across his chest. Our female officers are busy at the moment, he says. If you want, you can come back another day. It's no skin off our nose.

Dalila looks at his nose. No, she says. We can talk now.

The older one leans forward. Right, so let's get on with it. What are you doing in England?

Dalila fully understands the older one's expression and struggles to make eye contact with him.

I came to be safe, she says.

To be safe, right. From what?

It is not safe for me in my country. I cannot go back.

He points down at the tabletop and touches the tip of his index finger to the wood. We'll decide if you can go back.

Yes, sir, she says, startled by his manner.

The younger officer glances sideways at his colleague. He turns back to his papers and asks, Why aren't you safe?

My uncle is very dangerous. If he finds me, he will kill me.

Your uncle?

Yes, sir.

And what is his name?

He is called Kennedy Kimotho Mwathi.

As the younger officer writes this down, the older one leans back and says, Look, why don't you just tell us the whole story, from the beginning?

Dalila closes her eyes. She tries to see what happened to her as one thing, tries to feel where the beginning might be. Faces appear to her and then disappear. She feels herself sinking and in that sensation exists the urge to exhale and allow herself to be pulled under.

Sometime before lunch would be good, says the older officer.

The younger one clears his throat and says, Just take your time, Miss Matty.

Dalila digs out a packet of tissues in her handbag and blows her nose. She tries to see her story as a journalist would see it, with details, and as she does this the shape of it comes to her.

My family, they come from Nakuru, she starts. My mother, father and brother, we are Kikuyu. All the Kikuyu people are businessmen. Even my father, he had a small matatu business together with his brother Kennedy, my uncle.

A what business? interrupts the younger officer.

Matatus. They are like taxi vans, explains Dalila. My father was clever and the business grew very strong. Later they began driving tourists all over the country, to Nairobi, Mombasa, Thika, Malindi. Even, they would take people across the border to Uganda. When the business became too big, it was decided my father would stay in Nakuru and my uncle would move to Nairobi and manage all the vans from there. When my brother was eighteen he went to study business management at college in Nairobi. Two years later, I also went to Nairobi to study journalism. I want to be a news reporter on the TV or the radio. If I can stay in this country I will go to college and study very hard. I am a good student. I will even work to pay for my education.

The older officer raises his eyebrows. You won't study here and you won't work here. Is that understood?

Dalila doesn't understand. She looks at the young officer for confirmation.

While your asylum case is being considered it is a criminal offence for you to work or go into higher education, he confirms. If you do, you'll be arrested, detained and deported.

The younger officer lifts his pen as if to write and then asks, Is that why you came here? To get a job?

No, sir, I came for my safety.

Why are you not safe in Kenya?

Because of my uncle.

Tell us about him.

Her mind is still trying to process why she isn't allowed to study but she pushes these thoughts aside and tries to focus on her story.

After the elections, there were too many protests in Kenya, she says.

Was your family political? asks the younger officer, but the older one silences him with a hand on the shoulder.

Dalila continues. My family was not political, but protesters were blaming the Kikuyu people. Many Kikuyu were being killed. My brother went to Nakuru to make sure our parents were safe. When he was there robbers came to the house at night, they told my family to leave. My brother refused and they started fighting and the gang killed my whole family. My brother. My father. My mother. They murdered everyone in my house.

Dalila goes silent. She feels her father standing in the room behind her, senses his reassurance. She takes a deep breath and continues.

After the funeral, my uncle took over my father's side of the business. He took me to his house in Nairobi. He said I couldn't go to college because it wasn't safe. I was not allowed to leave the house. Every day I had to clean the house, cook food. I slept on the floor. He kept me as a slave. I stayed in the same house for ten months. It was like a prison. One day I refused to work. He became very angry, saying very bad things to me and then . . . he beat me with a belt. He whipped me.

Dalila stops again. Listening to her own voice, it was developing a tone she was hoping to avoid. The younger officer looks up from his note-taking and asks, Do you have any evidence of this abuse?

She tugs the neckline of her dress down across her shoulder. The scar on her collarbone is raised, still pink in parts.

What else did he do to you?

Her story only leads to dark places. Places she has never talked about. Places she doesn't want to describe. The inner part of her forces at the seams of her outer part. The thought of him coming towards her, placing his hand on her, causes her mind to drift, hovering again, watching the scene from the ceiling. Dalila blinks hard. She rubs a hand across her face trying to pull herself back, to be here, now, in this interview, to face these questions.

How did you get here? asks the older officer.

A friend . . . helped me, she says. He arranged for my documents and the flight.

Tell us about this friend.

Charles Okema. That one is a matatu driver for my uncle.

And how did you meet him?

Always, people were coming in and out of my uncle's house. You must know, in Nairobi the matatu businesses are like gangsters, believe me. They fight for territory, they pay the police, there is too much corruption. My uncle's business is now very big, his matatus go to everywhere. He has lots of . . . advisors. Lots of security. Charles was an advisor to my uncle and he came to the house every day. He saw me there. One day, my Uncle Kennedy took a boy, only fourteen years old, into the house. He said this boy had betrayed him. My uncle was so very angry. He beat the boy with his fists and when the child fell down my uncle kicked him. The boy cried for mercy, he called out the name of his mother, but my uncle only kicked and kicked until the boy died. Charles was there. Even me, I saw this.

The next day Charles spoke quietly to me. He said he knew about my family. He said the gang who killed my family, they were not political, they worked for my uncle. He said if I have money he will help me escape. I wanted to go, so I took money from my uncle's room and gave it to Charles. I was very scared, but after fifteen days Charles told me everything was in order. The next morning, very early, he took me from the house and brought me to the airport. He gave me all the papers and explained exactly what I must do. And so I came here.

The older officer runs his hand across his cheek. His eyes stay fixed on Dalila and in the silence she hears the prickle of his stubble against his dry fingers. He leans across and whispers something to his colleague. Then he says to Dalila, We've checked your data, and we see you came here on a tourist visa.

Yes, sir.

Where did this . . . Charles Okema get the visa and the plane ticket?

From Eddie.

Eddie who?

I don't know, sir. Me, I only know the name Eddie.

It's an offence to lie to us, Miss Matty, you know that, don't you? It won't help your case either if you are seen to be lying. Is that clear?

Now both men look at her, waiting.

Dalila lowers her head. I only know the name Eddie, she answers. I never met with him. I never spoke to him. Charles only—

Speak up please, says the older officer. I can't hear you.

Dalila swallows, sits up straighter. Charles only said the name Eddie. That is the truth.

Why didn't you claim asylum at the airport?

I was following my instructions.

What do you mean?

In the airport Charles gave me my passport with a tourist visa, a plane ticket, a letter and US dollars. Also, he gave me instructions. He said I must memorise them, do exactly what they say. After, I will meet people at the airport, friends of Eddie, these people will help me. They will show me where to get asylum.

Did you meet with these people?

Yes, they took my money and the man, he tried to hurt me, so I ran away. I couldn't be safe there.

She pauses, feeling her composure about to break. As she raises a trembling hand to her eyes, a powerful sadness descends. She tries to feel if her father is here with her, but he is not.

Please, she says, please help me. I have no people. I have no place to sleep. I have no money. I only want to be safe.

She reaches into her handbag for a tissue. The two officers watch her blow her nose and they wait till she has composed herself.

Where do these people live? The people you met at the airport, asks the older officer.

She recites the address she has memorised and the younger officer writes it down.

What are their names?

Anne Nafula Abasi and Markus, says Dalila, sniffing and wiping a finger across her eye.

The older officer leans in and whispers to the younger one. He glances at the notes and then checks his watch. Okay, I think we have enough here, he says, standing up and stretching. I reckon it's lunchtime.

The younger officer nods and stands up. As he gathers the papers he says to Dalila, You'll be provided with temporary accommodation for the next few days and meet with your case worker who will manage your case. The Home Office may need to disperse you to a more suitable city elsewhere in the UK. If this happens you'll probably be assigned a different case worker. You understand?

Dalila blows her nose and nods.

Thank you, Miss Matty.

A week later, Dalila is sitting on the front step of the hostel, where the Home Office has housed her. Tucked against the wrought-iron railings, she wraps her arms around her knees. Five pigeons peck at sodden crumbs on the concrete. There is one with a diseased foot. It's the most aggressive, hobbling on a red stump, chasing after specks, sometimes mistaking chewing gum for food. They remind her of the pigeons in Nairobi.

Pigeons – same.

Her nose is wet and has been running for days. Her lips, dry. As she inhales through her mouth, the morning air tastes clean as toothpaste.

Down on the pavement, two Syrian teenagers share a smoke. While one boy narrows his eyes and touches the filter to his lips, the other poses, like a TV policeman, smoothing back the hair above his ears. They glance up the street, and back over their shoulders. They tap their toes against the red postbox, too aware of themselves to ever stop moving.

Boys acting brave – same.

Red postboxes – different.

The boys are brothers. They arrived the day before yesterday. She has never heard them speak English and never seen them apart. Last night, she eased out of her bunk and tiptoed to the bathroom. At the far end of the hall something moved and she froze. The youngest brother was slumped against the wall, sobbing. The older one was trying to pull the limp boy to his feet. The sobbing was so deep, so forsaken, she felt her own tears threatening to surface. She slinked back to bed and stared at the dark ceiling, listening to the other women turn in their dreams.

The oldest Syrian boy drops the cigarette and twists it underfoot as the brothers go inside. Dalila curls and splays her cold toes inside her shoes, watching one pigeon toddle over and taste the cigarette butt.

She gets up and goes inside. A young man with a flipchart is leading a drop-in English class in the common room, so she wanders through to the canteen. Children's toys are scattered across the floor. Little boys and girls dash open-armed around the room. The dining tables have been arranged into a U-shape and volunteers are ripping open black plastic bags of donated clothes and dumping the contents on the tables. A few hostel residents are helping sort the items, but many are snatching the expensive-looking clothes. Coats and jackets are the most popular items. Baby clothes are in high demand, too. As Dalila picks through the clothes the faint smell of pencil-sharpenings comes off the fabrics. She finds a pair of jeans and some underwear still in their plastic packaging. She holds up a T-shirt with a swirling blue pattern.

Hiya, says a young volunteer. A loose woollen beanie rests on the back of her head as strands of black hair shape her plump face.

Hello, Dalila says to the young woman.

Just a second, says the girl, turning her back on Dalila. She steps behind a large gas heater and slowly wheels it closer. The heater has a glowing orange filament, but the moment the girl turns a dial on the top, blue flames ignite the second filament.

That's a bit better, don't you think? says the girl. She turns to Dalila and asks, Sorry, love, what's your name again?

Dalila, says Dalila.

Dalia?

Dalila.

Da-li-la?

Irene is my English name.

Irene. That's a lovely name. I'm Lyndsay. Are you looking for anything particular?

Maybe shoes, Dalila says, if you have.

Aye, we've got a few boxes over here. Lyndsay leans across the table and looks at Dalila's socks protruding through the open front of her plastic sandal. What size are you? says Lyndsay.

Six?

Right, well, you can look though those boxes over there. C'mon, I'll show you.

Some ladies' boots are stacked two by two, next to the boxes, the boot uppers flopping to the side like ox ears. Lyndsay bends over a box, peering into each shoe searching for the right size. Dalila squats and looks at the pile of straps and buckles and laces. She runs her hands across running shoes, pumps, slippers and sandals.

A boy riding a plastic tractor bumps into the box of shoes. She recognises the boy. It is Farnaz's son. She has been sitting with them at suppertime for the past few nights.

Salaam, little man, says Dalila, smiling at the child. She touches him on the cheek and he smiles back.

Farnaz comes over and says hello. She scoots her son off to play with the others and picks up a pair of black boots. Oh, these are very nice, she says. Irene, you need shoes?

Dalila nods.

Okay, I help you, says Farnaz, starting to rake through a box.

After a moment, Farnaz says, Today, I signed for Birmingham. Lots of Iranian people live there. Many people say Birmingham is the more beautiful city in whole of UK.

You will be happy there. I am sure, says Dalila.

Insha'Allah, says Farnaz.

Over the past week, Dalila has pieced together the system for managing the flow of people through this hostel. The Home Office are moving asylum seekers out of London, to Manchester, to Birmingham, to Newcastle, to Glasgow or Liverpool. The name of each city is on the cork noticeboard. If your name is listed under a city, that's where you are going. If not, you have to wait in the hostel till they find a place for you. Tomorrow is posting day and the tension in the hostel has been building.

Residents can request to be sent somewhere, but Dalila hasn't even heard of some of the cities on the list. She suspects most people in the hostel know very little about these cities. No one really knows how big they are, or how far they are from London. In the absence of facts, gossip serves as information. Most claim that Manchester is the best place to go, since everyone has heard of Manchester United, so it follows that the city must be as exciting and prosperous as its famous football team. To a lesser extent, the same logic applies to Liverpool. Birmingham is also popular because many have relatives there.

Dalila's hand finds a gold basketball shoe. The laces are knotted to its partner. She untangles them from other shoes in the box and holds them up. Her brother would have loved these. He was obsessed with Nike. She remembers him drawing the swoosh on a pair of white canvas shoes when he was still a small boy. When he was thirteen years old he saved up enough to buy a second-hand pair from the market. He scrubbed them with a toothbrush and kept them in a plastic shopping bag next to his bed. There was such pride in his stride when he wore them. That's what she remembers most, his smile as he laced them up, how he was when he wore them.

Dalila places the sole of her foot against the sole of the basketball shoe.

I think this one is good for you, says Farnaz, holding up a pair of black high-heeled boots. What size you want?

Six.

Ah, this is too small. I will find another. Farnaz turns to Lyndsay. Six, she says, do you have size six?

Lyndsay drags over another box and starts pulling out shoes.

Farnaz turns back to Dalila. Did you decide where you go, Irene?

No.

Why? You must sign your name for a city.

I don't mind where I go, says Dalila. God will decide.

If you don't choose, they put your name for Glasgow, pleads Farnaz. Glasgow is very bad, very dirty.

Dalila has overheard the rumours about Glasgow, and they weren't good. People said it is far, far to the north, in another country. It is always cold, covered in snow, very windy. Some people believe they don't even speak English in Glasgow and the locals are nasty, racist. They stab asylum seekers. Once you go there you are forgotten about. No one in the hostel wants Glasgow. Last week a woman's name was posted under Glasgow, and she burst into tears. People on that list try to swap. They plead to be sent to another city. Some refuse to get on the bus. Others hide and sleep in the park overnight hoping that next week they might be assigned to a different city.

Och, Glasgow's not so bad, says Lyndsay. I was born there.

Farnaz looks sideways at Lyndsay.

You don't believe me? says Lyndsay. I'll show you.

As Lyndsay walks off towards the canteen kitchen, Farnaz says to Dalila, Please, you sign for Birmingham. You come with me.

Lyndsay returns with a calendar. She flips through to February and shows them the picture. See? she says. That's Glasgow.

Under a blue sky, by a blue river, rest metallic, futuristic-looking buildings.

So, that's the IMAX Cinema and the Science Centre, says Lyndsay, pointing at the picture. And that one's the BBC headquarters.

BBC TV? asks Dalila.

Aye, it's BBC Scotland and next to it's the STV headquarters. It's a whole media hub right by the river.

With journalists? says Dalila.

Of course, they broadcast the news from that very building.

Farnaz studies the picture and shakes her head. I think it's so cold there, she says. She turns, picks up a pair of black boots and gives them to Dalila. These ones are better for you. Take them. Try them. They are better.

Dalila looks at the gold Nikes in her hands. Me, I like these ones, she says.

But it's not for women, says Farnaz.

Dalila slips her feet into the basketball shoes. The shape of someone else's feet rest under her own, and the gold shines clean. Dalila looks up at the two women and grins.

*

59

The next morning, the lists are posted. Everyone crams around the noticeboard. Farnaz gets Birmingham with two other women from Dalila's dorm. A Congolese woman picks up her little boy and begins crying. It is Glasgow for her. The Syrian brothers are going to Manchester. They hug each other and shake hands with a few men. She overhears them mention Beckham and Rooney.

The gathering begins to break up. A few men go outside to smoke. Some hold conversations in the common room. Most of the women head back to their rooms to pack.

Dalila steps closer to the board and scans the lists for her name. She sees what she expects to see. Her name is top of the list, under Glasgow.

Three of them take the minibus north at 11:30 a.m., the Congolese woman with her infant son and Dalila. Two other people on the list didn't show up. They were not to be found in the hostel, their bags were not on their bunks.

The driver is young, with a ponytail. He drives with a hand slung through the bottom of the steering wheel. He doesn't talk and doesn't glance at them in the rear-view mirror.

The motorway is perfect. No potholes. No stretches of dirt track where the tar is still to be laid. Nobody walking along the side of the motorway. No vendors selling food. No boys herding cattle. No children waving at the passing cars.

Roads – different.

After an hour the Congolese woman is still wiping away tears with the back of her hand. Her baby whimpers in its sleep.

Fields pass by, very green fields. Square patches of earth ploughed into neat rows. Every corner of the countryside is used and cultivated, even the trees are planted in straight lines, mist shifting through their upper branches. They pass green motorway signs, a grey river and a primary-coloured petrol station. They pass a scrapyard, a town built of concrete and a crumbling stone castle. Black-and-white cows stand on cold hillsides, their udders splattered with mud.

Cows – different.

She watches her reflection in the window gliding across this wet and confusing land.

After many miles, the rain comes. Droplets streak across the windscreen. She places her head against the cool glass. Vibrations rumble through her skull and grant her a dreamless sleep.

The van arrives in Glasgow after sunset. When the engine shuts off, the only sound is rain drumming on the roof. The Congolese woman's baby starts whining. The driver jumps out, slides open the side door and takes the woman's suitcase while she carries her baby. Dalila grabs her handbag and the bundle of second-hand clothes she had gathered at the hostel. Hunched over against the wind-blown rain, the group hurries across the car park towards an old stone building. Inside, Dalila wipes water from her forehead.

The baby starts openly wailing. The mother bounces her child, whispering to it, but the crying only gets more hysterical. The room is a cross between an open-plan office and a carpeted lobby with a reception desk. An older woman and a thin man sit at one desk, two mugs and an open packet of biscuits rest on the table between them. The woman stands up and goes to help the Congolese woman. She coos and fusses over the baby, but none of this stops the screaming.

The thin man approaches Dalila and the driver. He is taller than she suspected.

What time do you call this? says the thin man to the driver.

Don't start, alright? says the driver.

It's after nine.

Dalila stands back, unsure if this conversation involves her or not. Her eyes are still adjusting to the light and she needs to use the toilet. The baby's howling cuts right into her head, overwhelming any thoughts as soon as they form.

The driver hands a folder to the thin man and says, Just sign these, so I can clock off and get a pint.

A pint?

Aye, a pint, says the driver, maybe even two.

The thin man sighs. He scans the documents and says, Right, so we got two new arrivals?

Well, three, counting the baby.

Miss. Miss, says the thin man. What's your name?

My name is Irene, says Dalila.

Can I see your ARC card?

She shows it to him and he says, Could you sign here and here, please?

The baby lets out a piercing scream, causing everyone in the room to pause. The Congolese woman is now in tears herself as she tries to shove a soother into the infant's mouth.

Dalila looks at the papers, at the words, yet can't focus enough to understand their meaning. She signs the papers.

The thin man calls to his colleague. Maggie, I'm going to take this one over to Govan.

Right you are, says Maggie. I'll see you the morra.

Right, Irene, come with me, says the thin man. I'll take you to your accommodation.

He holds the door open and Dalila walks out into the quiet night. The rain is pouring less heavily. Across the dark car park she makes out three vans. Her body tightens and she can feel her heartbeat speed up. A powerful urge to just start running battles an even stronger urge to simply sit down and refuse to move. She quickly turns to go back inside and walks straight into the thin man, who drops the van keys.

Sorry, says the thin man.

He bends down, fishes the keys from a puddle and wipes them on his jeans. Sorry about all that in there, he says. I'm Paul, by the way.

Dalila looks at his offered hand. Without removing her gloves, she shakes his hand.

We're just five minutes away, says Paul. Then we'll have you out of this rain and in your warm flat. Come on.

She follows him, at a safe distance, across the dark car park to one of the vans. He gets in behind the wheel. The van is just like the matatus her father used to drive. She slides open the side door and takes a seat in the back.

Vans – same.

You can sit up front if you like?

It's okay, she replies.

His long fingers wrap around the steering wheel and they move off, driving along wet streets, between heavy stone buildings. Paul smokes as he drives. He winds the window open an inch and taps off the cigarette ash through the gap. A phone-in debate is taking place on the radio. The opinions are passionate, aggressive even, but the accents are too dense for Dalila to follow. She thinks it's about football.

The van pulls into a car park. Shattered glass sprinkled across the tarmac twinkles under the headlights. Paul turns off the engine. The wipers pause halfway across the windscreen.

Right, here we are, he says.

Dalila climbs out, cradling her handbag under her arm and the roll of second-hand clothes. Not a single person is out on the street. At intervals, lights illuminate a long empty road. As droplets pass under the orange bulbs it looks like a row of shower heads soaking the neighbourhood. Even through her puffer coat the cold closes in. She lifts her face to the rain. Three pale tower blocks, concrete and angular, disappear above the street lights, up into the dark. In a few windows, light presses against the curtains.

Dead streets – different.

Icy cold rain – different.

Paul tugs his hood over his head, grabs a folder from the passenger seat and trots towards the closest building, remotely locking the van.

Come on, he calls, let's get you inside before we get drenched.

She glances up at the closest tower. In Nairobi, her college was in the first four floors of a building like this.

Tower blocks – same.

The lobby stinks of bleach and urine. Graffiti is scrawled across the lift's metallic doors. The most legible words being IBROX YF.

Right, says Paul, I should explain how the lifts work. See the numbers above the door? This lift only goes to even-numbered floors and that lift only goes to the odd floors. You're on the seventeenth floor, so we'll take this one.

The doors open and they step inside the metallic-panelled lift. From the corner of the ceiling, a security camera records them. Paul presses number 17. Dalila's bladder sinks then rebounds as she is hauled up through the centre of the tower.

At the seventeenth floor the lift opens. Directly opposite them is a heavy door with the words EMERGENCY EXIT written in red. On the wall above it, the light fitting is caged in protective wire casing. They step out on to the small landing. Four green doors suggest four separate flats. Bleach still dominates the air and also, a stale suggestion of cigarette smoke. The space feels tight and Dalila can't shake the sense that she is, somehow, trespassing.

Paul fiddles with his bunch of keys, and opens a door. It only opens a few inches before the security chain pulls tight and prevents them from entering.

Yes? calls a voice from behind the door.

Hello. It's Paul, from the Housing Association. Remember I said we were coming?

The eye of an African woman peers at them from behind the chain.

You don't knock? You just come in? What is your problem? says the woman.

Who put this chain on the door? asks Paul.

Me. I put it.

Well, I'm not sure you're allowed to deface private property in this way.

You don't knock. Every time, you people just come in.

Paul sighs. Dalila can tell he's wrestling with how to handle this but all he says is, I'm sorry we're late.

The door closes, the chain is unhooked. As the door opens the African woman turns her back and walks deeper into the flat. Dalila follows Paul inside, noticing how he rolls his shoulders forwards as he walks, as if his stoop will hide his height, or apologise for his presence.

Three sets of women's shoes have been kicked off and abandoned just inside the front door. A coat hangs on the wall with an umbrella looped over the same hook.

Dalila slips off her gold basketball boots and places them neatly against the wall.

Paul opens his folder and says, Right, Maza, this is the girl I was telling you about.

She turns to face him. My name is Ma'aza. Ma'aza!

Right, Maza, that's what I said. He checks his folder, running his finger down a list. And this is, uh, Irene, he says. She's actually from Kenya, which is next to Ethiopia, right? So you're neighbours. You'll have a lot to talk about, I'm sure.

Ma'aza folds her arms and stands loose-hipped and tight-lipped. Her neck is long and lithe as a gecko's torso. Her eyes reach out and jab at what they see.

Maza has kindly agreed to share this unit with you, explains Paul, just on a short-term basis, you understand, till a more suitable place becomes available. I thought you'd be a lot more comfortable here than in a hostel.

Dalila offers her hand. Ma'aza glances at the socks on Dalila's feet. She turns her head away and concedes to a limp handshake.

We don't always get people to share but it's just for a short while, says Paul. Besides, I'm sure Maza won't mind showing you around the neighbourhood.

Ma'aza clicks her tongue and points at a door behind Dalila and says, She sleeps there.

The three of them turn to face the door then Paul pushes it open. Oh, I see you've moved all your things out. Are you sure about this?

I sleep in the living room, says Ma'aza.

Well, okay. Irene, it looks like you have the whole room to yourself. That's very thoughtful of you, Maza. Thank you.

A bare light bulb dangles from the centre of the ceiling. There is a single bed. Floral curtains. The carpet is green, the wardrobe is white. In the corner, a loose flap of wallpaper droops down like a banana leaf. Dalila lowers her handbag. She isn't sure what she expected but knows this place will never feel like home. Yet the blankness of this room is oddly encouraging. It reminds her that this arrangement is only temporary, till she gets her papers sorted. For now, it's all she needs.

Why don't I show you the rest of the flat? says Paul.

There is no window in the compact bathroom and the shower curtain above the bath holds a medical smell of plastic. The walls are cream-coloured, the same as her new bedroom, with identical textured wallpaper. The toilet seat is wooden. Tiles are missing from the bath surround. Black mildew is growing from the corner, spreading up the sealant between the tiles.

Now, this is the shower, says Paul. It works by pushing this button for 'on' and this one for 'off', and you can adjust the temperature with this dial here. Do you understand?

Dalila nods.

Have you seen a shower like this before?

She hasn't, but she nods again.

Always pull the curtain closed so the water doesn't splash on the floor and remember to pull this cord. Paul tugs the cord and a fan starts whirring. This is the extractor fan, he says. It'll suck all the steam out of the room when you're having a shower. And this is the heater.

He pulls the cord of the appliance bolted above the towel rack, but nothing happens. He yanks the cord a couple of times to no effect.

That one is broke, says Ma'aza. I told them before, but they do nothing.

Oh, says Paul, and did you fill out one of these? He holds open the folder and Ma'aza examines the form.

Yes, she says. I fill this out two times. And also for this.

Ma'aza holds back the shower curtain and points at the mildew and missing tiles. The water goes in there, she says. It's not healthy. They have to fix this.

Right, well, says Paul, we could fill out another maintenance request form if you like?

No more letters, says Ma'aza. They must fix everything.

Paul slips the form out of its polythene pocket and begins filling it out as Ma'aza steps closer to see what, precisely, he is writing down.

Dalila sneaks a look at Ma'aza, whose hair is combed back and plaited into a spike that juts out from the base of her skull. Standing directly under the bathroom light, Ma'aza's scars are more obvious. She has three neat little nicks through each eyebrow and a very tiny cross cut into the centre of her forehead. Beauty scars. While at college, Dalila noticed that some of the foreign girls, the Ethiopian ones, had similar markings but she never became friends with any of them. Her brother didn't like all these migrants and refugees from the north. The Sudanese, the Somalis, the Ethiopians. He said they only came to Kenya to make trouble. During her first week at college, he introduced her to all his friends, all Kenyans and mostly Kikuyu, and they became her friends and that's how it stayed.

Paul closes the folder. Ma'aza and Dalila follow him down the hall. He opens the door to the living room, into which Ma'aza has moved all her things.

Against one wall slumps a grey sofa with a green tartan blanket hanging off the armrest. Opposite is a pine chest of drawers and a glass coffee table pushed against the wall. A TV stands on the coffee table with a DVD player balanced on top of it. Discs are scattered across the table, also a mug, empty crisp packets, chocolate-bar wrappers, a hairbrush and magazines. At the far wall, tucked under the window, is a bed with a pile of unfolded clothes on it. Above the bedside table are photographs taped to the wall, which Dalila assumes are pictures of Ma'aza's family.

This is Ma'aza's space, and to enter the adjoining kitchen Dalila has to intrude across her territory. Paul walks straight across into the kitchen. Ma'aza moves about her room, hiding the clothes under the duvet, straightening the DVDs into a pile. When Ma'aza's back is turned, Dalila skips into the kitchen.

With an almost natural cheeriness Paul explains how the toaster works, how to fill the kettle, which one is the hot tap. Everything is machines. She watches as he switches appliances on and off, opens every cupboard and peeks through the oven door. This room feels even more uncomfortable than her bedroom. It reminds her of the kitchen in her uncle's house where she was forced to cook and often sleep. When Dalila senses a question is being directed at her from Paul, she nods. Otherwise she can't keep her eyes from flitting across to Ma'aza, who is now sitting on the sofa, flicking through TV channels.

Paul takes a wooden spoon from the drawer and jabs at the smoke detector on the ceiling. Satisfied, he turns to Dalila and says, Right, that's about everything. Do you have any questions?

Dalila shakes her head.

There's lots more information in this pack, says Paul, handing Dalila a poly-pocket full of leaflets and booklets. If you read through that, he says, it'll tell you where to get the bus and what services are available and, you know, stuff like that.

Thank you, says Dalila.

Before I go, is there anything else I can get for you?

Dalila lowers her head.

Well then, I need you to sign here and here.

As Dalila writes her name, Paul says to Ma'aza, Thanks for agreeing to this. Let's just try this arrangement for a few weeks. I think it could work out well for everyone.

Ma'aza's eyes prod Dalila.

Now, if you need anything, says Paul, just ask Maza, I'm sure she'll be glad to help. I'll be back in a couple of days and you can always call the Housing Association at the number on your copy of the form. Oh, and here is your key. Make sure you lock the door as soon as I leave.

Thank you, sir.

They shake hands as if a grand agreement has been settled. Paul leaves and Dalila locks the door. She looks at the key and closes her fingers around it.

The door to the living room slams shut.

Dalila goes to her bedroom and closes her own door, but the key in her palm, polished and shiny as a new coin, doesn't lock her bedroom door. She places it in her purse and then sits on the bed.

Near the carpet, under the window, freckles of mould are growing through the wallpaper. If her father were here, he'd know what to do about that mould.

Standing up, she pulls back the curtain. Her blurry reflection stares back from the double glazing. Behind the glass is a deep, ongoing gloom. She switches off the light and returns to the window. Heavy fog blocks out the view. She presses her forehead against the cold pane and tries to look straight down but all she sees is an orange haze from the street lights.

Laughter comes through the wall from the neighbouring flat, faint girls' laughter. To Dalila's ears it sounds like little girls giggling together. As she listens she hears the other voices of a whole family who are living right next door. There must be people directly underneath her too. Sixteen floors down, in bedrooms much like hers. Above her, too. People. In fact, all around her, people are watching TV, talking to their families.

Or sitting alone, like she is.

She lies down on the bed, stroking the duvet cover, twisting the linen into tight knots around each index finger. She takes a deep breath and lies absolutely still.

You are here, she whispers in the dark. You are here.

Dalila wakes. She sits up and rubs a knuckle against her eye.

The flat is silent.

She showers, wipes the bath, brushes her teeth and rinses the sink clean. Wrapped in a towel, she tiptoes back to her bedroom. The air is cooler here, her breath faintly visible. She pulls her clothes on and hangs the damp towel over the wardrobe door.

She sits on the bed and listens. Wind against the window. No movement inside the flat.

She picks up the information booklet given to her last night. The title reads, *Welcome to Glasgow: An Information Guide for New Arrivals and Refugees.* The cover photograph shows a statue of a man on a horse. On the man's head is a bright orange traffic cone. Inside are photographs of people sitting in classrooms, of children staring into computer screens and of a smiling policewoman in a fluorescent yellow jacket. There are maps and bus routes, addresses of shops selling halal food and African hairdressers. Helplines for legal support, domestic abuse, emergency medical treatment and the National Asylum Support Service.

A door opens and she hears Ma'aza shuffle to the bathroom. Dalila tries to read on but her attention is honed towards Ma'aza's movements. The toilet flushes, a door opens and closes.

She forces herself to study the booklet. A basic map of Glasgow shows a pale blue river, named Clyde, bisecting the city. A motorway, in darker blue, cuts across the city from north to south. The rest is a daunting tangle of streets and green patches for parks. Each neighbourhood has a peculiar-sounding name, Possilpark and Pollokshields, Dennistoun and Dowanhill, and she wonders which part of the city she woke up in this morning.

She stands up and pulls back the curtain. Greyness extends upwards, without change in tint or hue. It's the same colour directly above her as near the horizon. It isn't clouds. It isn't smog. No sign of the sun. The light of day comes from nowhere. A seagull swoops past and she steps back from the glass. She has never been this high up before. Far below are the silver roofs of warehouses, slate tiles, chimneys and empty streets. Not a single person is to be seen. In the distance, at the edge of the city, an aeroplane comes in to land.

Glasgow.

She feels the word in her mouth as she says it. Glasgow.

When she hears running water and the clinking of cutlery coming from the kitchen, Dalila moves down the hall and taps lightly on Ma'aza's door.

Ma'aza opens it halfway. Her eyes are still puffy and she's only wearing a long T-shirt.

Dalila glances at the kitchenette in Ma'aza's room and then lowers her head. Sorry, she says, I didn't mean to . . . I thought, if you want . . .

Ma'aza sighs, long and slow. You want tea? she says.

Dalila makes eye contact for a second and says, Yes. Thank you.

Ma'aza swings the door open and points at the stove. Make tea. I get dressed.

Ma'aza's room smells of buttermilk and perhaps singed hair. It has that close feeling of someone's personal space and Dalila slips across the carpet and stands safely on the kitchenette's linoleum floor while Ma'aza grabs some clothes from a chest of drawers, scoops a pair of jeans off the floor and disappears down the hall to the bathroom.

The stove is all dials and numbers and lights. Dalila opens and closes her fingers, wishing for a normal cook fire. Even after her father's business started to make money and they moved into a more modern house, there was always a cook fire out the back door. Cooking by the fire felt easier, comforting. But blackened pots and fanning coals are in her past. Anyway, it's not as if she has never switched on an electric stove. She can do this. She opens the fridge and finds a plastic jug of milk in the door. Sniffs it. Opens every cupboard and, eventually, she finds a pan, a box of tea bags, two mugs and a wooden spoon. Everything gets lined up on the counter. Now it's just the stove to figure out. She turns a dial to 6, but nothing lights up. She hovers her palm over the hotplate but it doesn't heat. She tries a different dial but still no heat.

Ma'aza appears behind her and says, You must switch on. She leans over and flicks a red lever on the wall. The lights beside the dials come on and the plates begin to warm.

Thank you, Dalila says. I have to learn everything.

They send you back before you learn anything, says Ma'aza.

I will learn very fast, says Dalila.

She places the pan on the glowing orange plate, pours in the milk and drops in two tea bags. With the wooden spoon she paddles the milk, watching the tea bags rotate on the surface.

Ma'aza unscrews a blackened Italian coffee pot and fills it with water and ground coffee. In Ethiopia, she says, we drink coffee. Tea is for children.

Ma'aza goes over and switches on the TV. Two presenters sit on a massive sofa and discuss newspaper headlines. Ma'aza examines herself in the wardrobe mirror. She rubs cream into her face and along her forearms then teases her hair with a comb. Side-on, Dalila watches her. She has always thought Ethiopians are blessed with their hair, loose silky curls that are half Arabian, half African. Dalila touches the velvet stubble on her own close-shaven head. Maybe now, here in this new place, she could let it grow again.

Steam rises off the milk. Brown bleeds from the tea bags. Dalila turns off the heat and squeezes each tea bag against the side of the pan till the milk turns a caramel brown. She lifts the pan and pours straight into a mug. When the coffee has boiled, she pours out a mug for Ma'aza.

Do you like sugar? she asks Ma'aza, who is pinning up her hair.

Give me three spoons.

Dalila smiles to herself as she takes the coffee to Ma'aza. Even me, I like three sugars, she says. We are like sugar sisters.

With a hairpin in her mouth, Ma'aza arches one scarred eyebrow.

73

Retreating to the neutral zone of the kitchen, Dalila rinses the pan and wooden spoon.

Ma'aza pushes past her, opens the circular door of the washing machine and scoops out an armful of damp clothes. At the window, she twists open a latch and, with a jolt of astonishment, Dalila realises that this window is, in fact, a glass-paned door. Ma'aza opens it and steps out into a rush of fresh air.

Placing her mug to one side, Dalila grips the door frame and tests the strength of the balcony with her toe. She edges forward and peeks over the railing. Far below, the ground appears to tilt, her stomach pulls up inside her and she jumps back into the kitchen. Ma'aza shakes her head and pegs socks and jeans to a small clothes horse. The garments shift in the wind.

The view from this side of the flat has tall modern buildings standing on what, Dalila assumes, must be the heart of the city. A motorway overpass crosses high above the grey-brown river. Closer, she recognises something. A tower. Silver and aeronautic, with what appears to be the front of a jumbo jet balanced on top. It is just like the calendar photograph she was shown back in London.

What is that place? she asks Ma'aza, pointing at the tower.

Ma'aza turns her head as she pegs a blouse to the clothes horse. That one is the Science Centre, she says. Also, the BBC.

The BBC. It is the same place. And that it should be so close, that she should be housed in a flat that overlooks it, feels, somehow, meaningful. This feeling quickly spreads. Perhaps God has led her here? Perhaps there is a deeper reason to the things that have happened to her?

She traps these thoughts and stops them spreading. Working is impossible while her claim is being processed, and besides, she hasn't even finished her studies yet.

But she could take a look.

Dalila picks up her mug of tea and presses the warm ceramic against her cheek. The terrain between her building and the satellite dishes on the BBC's roof seems simple enough to navigate. Perhaps a ten-minute walk, no more. She gulps down the rest of her tea and rinses the mug.

Armed with her welcome booklet, her key and her handbag looped across her shoulder, Dalila leaves the flat. She presses the button for the lift as a neighbour's door opens and an old woman with her little dog exit their flat.

Morning, says the woman as she lifts the dog into her arms and waits for the lift.

If there is a respectful way to address the elderly in English, Dalila can't find it, so she simply says, Good morning.

The lift arrives. As they descend the dog tries to sniff Dalila, but she edges away from it.

Outside, it's shadowless. A cool vapour hangs in the air, clinging to Dalila's puffer coat as she moves through it. She pulls on her woollen hat.

The old woman puts on a plastic hood and fastens it under her chin while her dog squats and, quivering with effort, poos on the deep green grass.

Dalila looks up at her building. The sky is corrugated cloud. Her new home is one of three identical towers of white concrete. Above the entrance is a security camera pointed at the door that doesn't close properly. On the wall a large sign reads, NO BALL GAMES.

From where she is standing she can't see the BBC centre. In fact, at ground level everything looks different. She isn't exactly sure which direction she is facing, or where she should be going.

She asks the old woman for directions.

The BBC, you say? replies the woman, as she pulls a plastic bag from her pocket. Well, that's down by the water. Toby and I are on our way there. You could come along with us if you like?

You are very kind, says Dalila.

The old woman puts her hand in the plastic bag, stoops over and scrapes up her dog's fresh excrement.

Never in her life has Dalila seen anyone do this. She closes her gaping mouth and looks around to see if anyone else witnessed this. As the old woman double-wraps the bag and knots it, Dalila considers simply walking away.

I'm Mrs Gilroy, the old lady introduces herself. She offers the same hand she just used to wrap the dog poo.

Dalila hesitates, trapped between disgust and politeness. She forces herself to take the woman's little hand.

I am Irene.

Right you are then. Shall we be off?

Mrs Gilroy clips the lead to her dog and they walk across the car park, picking their way through smashed glass. Though short and stout, the old lady sets a steady pace, dragging her tiny dog, whose scurrying legs stab at the ground.

It's a fair day, isn't it? says Mrs Gilroy. Toby here hates the wind. If it wasnae for me he'd just lie in his bed all day, but he needs his walk, don't you, boy?

The dog abruptly veers towards a lamp-post. Dalila skip-jumps to avoid it and crosses in front of Mrs Gilroy.

Aye, we all need to get out, says Mrs Gilroy.

Dalila pushes her hands deep into her pockets and walks on, ensuring this old woman stays between her and the dog.

The pavement is smooth tar while the roads are rougher, but still all tarred. There are no sections of unfinished road which descend into dirt tracks. Even the smaller side streets are fully tarred.

Pavements – different.

They pass an open derelict section of land. Rubbish clings to the weeds. A sodden mattress lies in the mud. Further on, they pass a burnt-out sofa, the exposed seat springs all tangled and rusted. Mrs Gilroy stops, takes the parcel of dog poo from her pocket and places it in a red bin attached to a lamp-post.

They move on.

At first, the neighbourhood appears only to be brick warehouses but after a few blocks the architecture changes. Four-storey buildings, topped with chimneys, rise up on either side of the street. Squat ochre structures, red as African dirt, with large windows and crumbling masonry. Through the windows Dalila sees curtains and the blue glow of TV screens so she assumes these buildings must be homes. Low walls decorate the entrances of these houses and on them grows a spongy emerald-green moss more vibrant than she has ever seen.

Moss – different.

As they approach the river, the tower comes into view.

Is that one the BBC? asks Dalila.

No, no. That's just an eyesore, says Mrs Gilroy. That tower's just a daft money-making scheme. It's for tourists. See, the whole thing's built like an aeroplane wing and it's supposed to turn into the wind. Only it doesnae. It's all for breaking down. Then the fire brigade comes out to rescue everybody. It's the Tower of Terror, so it is. They charge you a bloody fortune just to go up and take a look at Govan. You'll no get me up there. I've lived in Govan forty-three year and I'll tell you this, it's no any prettier from up there.

Mrs Gilroy points and says, That building further away is the Scottish TV studios, but that big square thing closer by, that's your BBC.

It's exactly what Dalila had imagined. Modern, clinical, with a lot of glass. A professional place. Two women in suits pass through the wide revolving doors. On the front steps five people stand and smoke. They chuckle and tap their ash on the ground.

Are those journalists? asks Dalila.

Could be, aye. There's a lot of folk coming and going from there.

I want to be a journalist, says Dalila. This is my dream. For me this is the most important job, to take the stories and tell them on TV so everyone will know what is happening. I always believed one day I will work for NTV Kenya.

So you're from Kenya?

Yes, I lived in Nairobi before, says Dalila. She squints up at the BBC building. The group of journalists shuffle towards the rotating door and go inside. I don't know what will happen now, says Dalila. Maybe I must leave this dream in my country.

You could read the news, says Mrs Gilroy. You've got a lovely face for it. How's your teeth? They're all for showing their teeth on the telly. Go on, show us.

Dalila can't help but smile.

Aye, you've got a good straight set, chuckles Mrs Gilroy. You're halfway to getting the job already.

Dalila raises her hand to her mouth, suddenly shy. Trying to change the subject, she points and says, What is that place?

Well, let's see now, says Mrs Gilroy. That'll be your Science Centre. Now, to my mind it looks like a great big slice of lemon. And that silver grape thingy next to it? That's your IMAX Picture House. I've no been inside. I'm no really bothered with the pictures. And that one? That's the Armadillo.

Across the river, a vast building, segmented like some silver sea creature, seems to have crawled out of the water and settled itself on the bank.

Now, you wouldn't think it, but there's a concert hall inside. And right next to it? That's a hotel. A posh one.

The curves of the Armadillo are mirrored in the hotel's glass facade, like two animals facing off.

What is Armadillo? says Dalila.

It's a . . . It's a beastie with a wee face. They come from your part of the world. It's got all these scales on its back like armour. You know? Armadillo! Mrs Gilroy makes a gesture with her hands indicating the size and bulk of the animal she is failing to describe.

Dalila nods. Yes, maybe I know this one.

She takes another look at the building. The similarity to the armoured scales of an armadillo is uncanny, but not exact.

For me, says Dalila, it is like a croissant, from your part of the world.

The words slip out too fast. Dalila's jaw tightens, hoping she hasn't been too direct with an elder.

Aye, right enough, says Mrs Gilroy. I can see that. You know, I think these buildings are all designed to look like something else. This place always makes me feel really wee, like Thumbelina. Do you know Thumbelina?

Dalila shakes her head.

No? Well, never mind.

Mrs Gilroy picks up Toby and cradles him in the bend of her arm. A seagull plummets and holds the air inches above the river. They watch it glide for a moment and then Mrs Gilroy stares up at an enormous crane standing dormant on the other side of the river, now a relic, a skeleton.

Aye, when I was young this place used to be heaving wi' ships and workers and the rest. My Sam worked here for thirty-one year. Now it's just a spot for tourists. Sad really, when you think about it.

The wind off the water carries the hush of motorway traffic from the city centre.

I also get sad when I think about this place, says Dalila.

Really?

When I was a small girl, my father said to me Great Britain was the Father of the World.

The old woman raises her eyebrows. Ho! That'll be right.

Dalila smiles. Believe me, it is true. My father said Britain was so, so rich. It could care for many different countries. I tried to imagine what such a rich country would look like. Sometimes I saw a *Mr Bean* on TV. Sometimes there was a picture in a magazine. I was hungry to know. In the UK, I believed, everything was new, everything clean. No rubbish. No shanty town. All people wearing nice clothes. All the old buildings would be broken down and they would build new clean places, like this place.

Mrs Gilroy starts to chuckle. You thought the whole city'd look like the Science Centre?

Dalila shrugs.

Aye well, it doesnae, does it?

No.

A jogger plods by and Toby starts barking.

Och, shoosh! says Mrs Gilroy, stroking the dog's head. Right, time to take this wee fella home, I think.

She puts Toby on the ground and untangles the lead from around his front leg.

Right then, she says, that's me.

Confused by this expression, Dalila replies, And this . . . is me.

Unlocking the front door, Dalila calls out, Ma'aza? Hello?

No answer. The lights are off.

She places her basketball boots at the front door and tiptoes to the kitchen. The clothes are still drying out on the balcony. The kitchen is clean. Maybe she should buy food, cook something? But with what money? And where is the market? She opens the cupboard and finds enough to eat for two or three days. But it's Ma'aza's food. Perhaps Paul will come back this afternoon? He might tell her where to visit the Home Office and then, somehow, she will get money.

There is nothing to do but wait. What else can she do? Someone will come.

She switches on the TV, flicks through the channels till she finds the news and sits down cross-legged on the sofa.

It is 5 News, a station she has never seen before. The anchor sits in a red studio and summarises the headlines. It's the same story that ran every night on the TV in the hostel. Boats, overloaded with people, trying to cross into Greece and Italy. Last night twelve people drowned, including two children. The news report shows two men, arm in arm, struggling ashore. It cuts to a pile of life jackets abandonded on the rocky beach. The report then switches to a scene of African men and women being rescued from inside the tiny dark hull of a fishing boat. She suddenly can't breathe properly. The air is too close. The next channel is better. A woman is digging in a garden and saying something about asparagus. She flicks through some more channels looking for dancing. Some singing and dancing would be nice.

At ITV News, she hesitates. This station can afford a male and female anchor and the frosted-glass desk they sit behind is quite sophisticated. The words MIGRANT CRISIS scroll across the bottom of the screen. A waxy-skinned politician is being interviewed in the studio. The government won't support planned search and rescue operations in the Mediterranean, says the politician, because it will only create an unintended 'pull factor'. It'll simply encourage more migrants to attempt the dangerous sea crossing and thereby lead to yet more tragic and unnecessary deaths. We have to focus our efforts on rooting out the people-smugglers who wilfully put lives at risk by packing migrants into unseaworthy boats.

The male anchor addresses the other guest in the studio by asking, Do you agree with this strategy?

No. Absolutely not, replies the guest. The British government seems oblivious to the fact that the world is in the grip of the greatest refugee crisis since the Second World War. People fleeing atrocities will not stop coming if we stop throwing them life rings. You know, boarding a rickety boat in Libya is still a seemingly rational decision if you're running for your life and your country is in flames. The only outcome of withdrawing help will be to witness more—

Dalila taps the mute button on the remote and the room is instantly calmer. She rubs her toes and tucks them in tighter under her thighs. The images continue to flip and flicker on the screen in front of her. Compared to Kenyan news studios, the ITV studio seems overly bright and vibrant, as if it doubles for a children's show in the mornings. Behind the anchors is a glass wall, separating them from the actual newsroom, a room full of desks and computer screens belonging to the actual reporters who are gathering the news. One of these reporters stands and moves across the office to a colleague's desk. Dalila leans forward, but then catches herself trying to look past the anchor to get a better view of the reporter in the background. The reporter wears a shirt, hair primly tucked behind her ears, and is obviously comfortable in this high-tech environment. What must that be like? To be immersed in information? To be connected to all the great cities of the world, and their neat newsrooms? To live every day in a dust-free world of sheen and lustre, where you can get up from your desk whenever you want, without getting into trouble, and casually walk over to a male co-worker and simply ask him a question?

The news show ends and she switches over to the BBC. Here the news anchor is an older black woman who is reporting on cricket. Dalila taps the mute button and the woman's crisp British accent fills the room. There are few things stranger, yet oddly charming, than when she hears a black person speak in this accent. It's so old-fashioned. Not xaxa. She wonders where this anchor is from. She has a Kenyan look about her, but she could be from Ghana or somewhere. The anchor has excellent hair. Probably a weave of fine-quality Indian hair, but as the camera sweeps closer for a segment change, it appears to be the anchor's own hair. The roots are too thin near the hairline at her forehead. This is, in fact, perfect hair. Glossy, obsidian folds resting lightly on her shoulders. Relaxed and straightened over many years. And that accent. It's flawless, like an actual English person.

They switch to a different studio and announce the news headlines for BBC Scotland. The backdrop to this studio is a still of the bridge and Science Centre she has just visited. As if they are reporting from the rooftop of the actual building she was standing in front of less than an hour ago.

Dalila jumps up and goes to the balcony window. A light fog has settled on the river. The outlines of the tower and the BBC building have dissolved and lost their definition. Still, it's thrilling to think that what's happening on the TV right now is happening in a studio right over there, just a few minutes down the road from where she now lives. She bounces back to the living room and perches on the sofa. Many of the reporters are women, even the ones covering politics and sports, and, as she watches, it is as if something starts to make sense, as if deeper, hidden reasons are allowing themselves to be partially exposed. Perhaps it isn't a complete accident that she finds herself here, in this particular place. If she thinks about all the hard work she has done and then considers that she is now living down the road from the BBC studios, the *actual* British Broadcasting Corporation, well, it's more than a coincidence. She could finish her studies here while she gets her papers in order and then she'll start applying for jobs. She'd apply to the BBC and the Scottish one. The STV? She might not even have to complete her studies. If she got some nice, professional clothes, she could even go to the reception and enquire about jobs. She could go in every week or every single morning, it wouldn't be a problem since both newsrooms are just down the road. It would show her persistence, her ambition, her dedication to pursuing her profession. If she goes in enough times they might take notice and give her a job, even a low-level job so she could work her way up. In her spare time, right now, while she waits on the Home Office arranging her papers, she could brush up on her skills. Maybe write some articles or even interview people about something.

And then, after working at the BBC for a year or two, things will have probably calmed down back home. It'll be safe to go back. As soon as she lands in Nairobi she could go straight to NTV and apply for a post there. She could even apply by email *before* she goes. With her experience of working in the UK, at the BBC, they'd be certain to accept her application.

She gets up, runs to her bedroom, opens the wardrobe door and lifts her chin at the reflection in the mirror.

This is Dalila Mwathi reporting to you live from the studios at NTV Kenya.

It doesn't sound quite right. She shouldn't use her porridge name. She starts over, trying to mimic a British accent.

Irene Mwathi reporting live from . . .

Her British accent is terrible. She tries again, in her own voice. I am Irene Mwathi and you have been watching NTV.

Unhooking a clothes hanger, she holds it in front of her chin like a microphone, straightens her shoulders and continues.

Yes, I am out here in the small hamlet town of Njoro, where disturbing reports are coming in of continued violence . . .

Do they still use microphones? Wouldn't it be a lapel mic? And her hair is so short. She can't be a reporter looking like this. She takes her black jersey and slips the neckline over her forehead, allowing the material to hang down over her shoulders like hair. Turning her face this way and that, she studies her profile in the mirror, and tucks a sleeve behind her neck. She stares straight ahead, imagining the local people standing back, giving her room. All eyes on her. The cameraman holding up three fingers, now two, now one.

I can report that the situation here is becoming increasingly volatile, she starts. There is a growing concern from the locals who feel trapped by the sporadic violence, which, over the past months, has haunted their village. But the government appears to be unable to . . .

The jersey isn't right. It looks more like a hijab than a wig. As she adjusts it, her scar becomes visible, that ugly grey welt from her collarbone to her jugular. She tugs up the neckline of her blouse, but it's still visible, and it's all she can look at. It's all anyone would ever look at. How can she read the news like this? How can she even speak to people?

It's all ridiculous. She's ridiculous. Talking to herself in the mirror with a stupid jersey on her head. She peels it off and sits down on her bed.

She should do something. Just sitting around this empty flat is pointless. She should at least look busy because Ma'aza might be back at any time. She gathers her few items of clothes and, unsure how to use the washing machine, she kneels at the bath and hand-washes them, wrings them out and goes to the kitchen. She opens the door to the balcony. Holding on to the door frame, she steps only one foot out and drags the clothes horse closer, all the while keeping her other foot safely inside the kitchen. Pegging her clothes up, she focuses purely on the task in front of her, refusing, even for a second, to glance through the railings at the abyss below.

Back inside the kitchen, she shuts the door and stares out. Fog hangs heavier across the city as the afternoon darkens into evening.

It is a struggle to remember what, exactly, she was expecting on her walk this morning. The architecture was beautiful, maybe inspiring. The people outside, the journalists, if they were journalists, were smartly dressed but it is hard to picture them now. She mostly remembers them smoking. Facing each other as they joked and giggled. Every now and then one of them would stretch an arm out behind them and tap their cigarettes. As the ash released, before it even hit the ground, the wind would carry it off.

Early the next morning, Ma'aza knocks on Dalila's door and opens it without waiting for an answer. Dalila pulls back the duvet and blinks at her.

Come, says Ma'aza, we must go.

Where?

To Festival Court. Come. Wake up.

Dalila lies back down, covers her eyes with her elbow. Today I can't. Me, I feel sick.

This is for you, says Ma'aza, laying a letter on Dalila's bed.

As Dalila props herself up with her elbow, the pressure in her sinuses shifts and the room itself seems to lean and then rights itself. The envelope is addressed to her but it has already been opened.

Ma'aza shrugs. I look inside for you, she says.

Dalila removes the single sheet of paper. The Home Office stamp decorates the top-left corner and there's a scanned photo of her face on the right. The letter is titled, **Immigration Act 1971 – Notification of Temporary Admission to a Person who is liable to be Detained.**

Paragraph A is titled, **Liability to Detention.**

Paragraph A reads, You are a person who is liable to be detained. That is all it says. That is the entire paragraph.

Dalila sniffs hard and looks up at Ma'aza. They will put me in jail?

No. This is not the letter for detention. It is the letter for reporting, says Ma'aza. She points to paragraph B. Look there. It says you take this letter to Festival Court and report to the Home Office. Your appointment is today. Nine o'clock.

Today? says Dalila, sitting up in bed.

You want safety or you want to sleep? asks Ma'aza.

Dalila rubs a finger along her eyelid and digs out a fleck of sleep gunk from the corner of her eye.

If you don't go, shrugs Ma'aza, you get in trouble. They reject your case.

She yanks the duvet off the bed. Come. Get ready. Wash your face, and bring your ARC card. I will show you where to go. Ma'aza marches off, leaving the bedroom door open.

Twenty minutes later, Dalila is dressed and ready. She swallows the two cold and flu tablets Ma'aza hands her and washes them down with her last sip of tea. Stuffing a wad of toilet roll into her pocket, she follows Ma'aza out of their building and across the sodden lawn.

The day is wet, yet rainless.

They pass an empty bus shelter and Ma'aza says, When you take the bus, you wait here. Okay?

Dalila nods. She glances back up the road from where buses might approach. Not a car passes. Not a cyclist. Not a single human being walks the street. No people anywhere. The silence is almost total. No children walk to school. No hawkers sell their wares. No matatu drivers call out. No donkeys drag carts. No one sells roasted corn. No dogs skulk by. No marabous watch from the trees.

Street life – different.

Where are the people? she asks, zipping up her puffer. Even yesterday, I didn't see many people in the streets.

Eh? They are in there, Ma'aza points. They stay in the houses.

Do they come out?

They like to stay inside.

Dalila quickens her pace to keep up. It gives me fear, this place, she says. It is like the film where there is a great virus. Everyone is dead and there are no more people, the streets are empty, the cars they have stopped, and everywhere is silent. Everyone is dead. Do you know this film?

Ma'aza rolls her eyes. I only like comedy.

It is very frightening, continues Dalila. The infected ones have become monsters and they eat the healthy ones.

Where do you see these films?

It was a DVD. I watched it with my brother in . . . I saw it a long time ago.

Ma'aza glances at Dalila, but doesn't slow her pace. She walks on, every step with purpose. After a minute Ma'aza says, Look there.

An old woman hobbles towards them. Wearing a blue plastic hood tied tightly under her chin, she cradles a toaster in one arm. The toaster cable slips loose and the plug rattles along the ground. The lady stoops down, wraps the cable around her arm and carries on. As she approaches, Dalila tries to acknowledge her, since she is an elder, but the old woman never lifts her eyes. They move past each other in silence. Ma'aza lifts her chin as if she sees something interesting in the distance. Dalila peeks back, watching the old woman shuffle onwards.

You see, says Ma'aza, there are people.

They walk for two more blocks, taking almost the same route as Dalila walked yesterday with Mrs Gilroy.

Ma'aza points down a road to a set of three identical buildings. You must go there.

You are not coming with me? asks Dalila.

No. I report tomorrow. Now I must go to see . . . some people. You take this, says Ma'aza, handing Dalila an umbrella.

Will I see you later? says Dalila.

Ma'aza pouts and shrugs and strides off back the way they came.

As Dalila arrives for her appointment the downpour starts. She pops open the umbrella, taking refuge beneath it. Water pours off the polyester canopy while she stands on the pavement and studies the buildings across the street.

An eight-foot-high iron fence surrounds the complex. Next to the main gate is a small Portakabin. At the gate, a sign.

Five young trees, brittle and leafless, endure behind the fence. Security cameras, disguised as lamps, scrutinise every corner of the empty forecourt. Three buildings share an identical utilitarian design, grey bricks then tan bricks with grey windows on the second floor under aluminium roofing. Each building has a specific name. FESTIVAL COURT 1. FESTIVAL COURT 2. FESTIVAL COURT 3.

She considers these words, lets their meanings take shape in her mind.

Festival. Court.

An Asian couple enter the gates. They approach the middle building, moving cautiously, their eyes lowered, their posture stooped.

What might happen when she enters? Will they detain her? Will they give her money? Will they send her away if she doesn't have the right paperwork?

On the ground, around her wet basketball shoes, are hundreds of discarded cigarette butts scattered across the pavement, sodden and swollen, like fat maggots. The understanding comes that she is not the only person to have stood on this corner, facing these buildings, searching for courage.

Clinging to the stem of her umbrella with both hands, she crosses the street. The guard in the Portakabin opens the door and calls to her.

You here to report?

Dalila doesn't approach him. She answers, Yes.

Got ID?

She holds up the letter close to her chest, keeping it safe from water damage.

Where's your ARC card?

Fumbling through her purse, she takes out the card and holds it up.

The guard stuffs his hands into the pockets of his neon yellow jacket. Building two, he says.

As she approaches the middle building a different security guard holds the door open and asks to see her papers. She shows him the letter and her ARC card. He reads them and examines the photograph, making sure it matches her face. Satisfied, he steps aside and lets her in. She shakes out her umbrella and enters.

Two people sit behind a reception desk, one male, one female, both in uniform. They stare at her but make no welcome. Hoping to figure out what she is expected to do next, Dalila walks up to them and says, Good morning.

Identification, says the female guard.

Dalila hands her the letter and her ARC card.

Name?

Dalila . . . Irene Dalila Mwathi.

Is this the first time you've reported?

Yes.

The man behind the counter leans back and yawns deeply. As he closes his mouth, his eyes settle on Dalila's face. An urgent need to swallow pushes under her tongue but she holds it.

I need your handbag, keys, mobile, belt and shoelaces, says the woman.

The expression on both faces behind the counter is exactly the same, and Dalila can't tell if it's disdain or simply boredom.

Dalila clears the phlegm from her throat. You want my bag?

You can't take that stuff inside with you, says the female guard. That's the rule. You have to hand in your handbag, your keys, your phone and any other photographic devices or metal objects. You're also required to hand over your belt and shoelaces . . . for your own protection. These items will be returned to you when you leave.

Dalila places her key into her handbag, zips it closed and hands it over. Straight away, the female guard unzips the bag and fingers through the contents. She removes certain items and places them in a clear plastic bag.

Dalila crouches and begins unfastening her shoelaces. She can't imagine why she's expected to do this. Her headache slides to the front of her face. She reaches into her pocket for the wad of toilet paper and then blows her nose. A guard's feet approach from behind. She looks up at him. The guard's loose pink face is impassive as he gazes down at her. She undoes both sets of laces and hands them to the people behind the desk.

I'll need your belt and the umbrella too.

Dalila unbuckles the belt and pulls it through. She picks up the umbrella and places it on the counter. The female guard puts the umbrella behind the desk and the rest of Dalila's belongings into the plastic bag.

Any other sharp objects? Pens?

No.

Are you carrying any pills or other medication?

I have paracetamol in my bag.

Any other pills on your person?

No.

Okay. Place this sticker on your chest, it's the number for your belongings. You can go through now.

The female guard points towards a metal detector at the entrance to another room. Dalila walks up to the metal detector and waits for yet another guard to wave her through.

He motions with his hand.

She steps through the false doorway, aware of it invisibly searching every inch of her body for a hint of non-compliance. The machine lets out a long high-pitched alarm. The guard approaches and points for her to go back through the detector. Once on the other side he tells her to take off her boots.

She does.

Any rings, jewellery or watches? he asks.

Dalila holds up her hands to show she has none.

He waves her through and this time the machine stays silent.

The guard with the loose face approaches and reaches for her neck. Dalila steps back, breath trapped in her throat.

It's alright, love, says the guard, I'm just going to check your coat.

He fingers the collar and feels for items in her pockets. He stands close enough for her to smell the coffee on his breath. Memories of hands, male hands, reaching for her neck flash across her mind and she turns her head and swallows hard, forcing the memories back down. When the guard moves across and examines her shoes she exhales slowly, opening and closing her fists. He peels back the tongue of each boot and peeks inside. He lifts the inner sole and checks for hidden objects then hands them back to her. Dalila notices her hands are shaking and she loses balance slightly trying to slip on her shoes.

She is led to another desk. There, her name, number and arrival time are marked down and she is given a ticket with a number on it. She is told to wait till they call this number.

The waiting room is full of people. Nearly every seat is taken. Many languages fill the air and the windows are steamed up from the inside. Children sit on their mothers' laps or on the floor and some busy themselves by folding paper toys. Men stand here and there, allowing the rest of their family to sit together.

To her left are two doors. The first is marked TOILET, the second PRAYER ROOM. A glowing drinks and snacks machine stands in the corner.

A number is digitally lit up and announced with a bleep. Everyone falls silent and dips their heads, checking their tickets. A woman stands up, raises her baby onto her hip, and shuffles down a short corridor off the main waiting room. People continue speaking as before, in small huddles, nodding and biting their lips. Some sit hunched forward, squeezing their knuckles, others appear drowsy and half asleep. A mother clutches her child, moving the little one from one knee to the other to gain a firmer grip as the child wriggles. Dalila stands, unsure of her next move.

My sister, please, says an old man. He motions for her to take the empty seat next to him.

Thank you. I am okay, says Dalila.

Standing is good, says the old man. Because, me, I don't believe you can walk in those shoes.

Dalila looks at her feet. Without laces, the tongue on each basketball boot flops forward.

Grey hairs pepper the old man's goatee beard. Something about his blue tie and stained shirt collar reminds Dalila of her maths teacher in high school.

If you choose to stand, says the man, looking up at Dalila, maybe you will stand a very long time. You could grow very tired, become weak and fall down. Because I am the only one to be seen talking to you, the others will assume you are my responsibility and I am too old to carry you out of here. So, out of concern for my weak limbs, please take a seat.

The old man fails to suppress his playful grin. He nods at the chair next to him.

Dalila sits with her knees pressed together, her hands on her lap.

I am Daniel, he says.

My name is Dalila, she says.

Nice to meet you, he says as he shakes her hand. Where are you from, sister?

Kenya.

Ah, Kenya is a marvellous country, says Daniel, switching into Kiswahili. He leans a bit closer. I lived in Nairobi for many years, I had a business there. Every time I go back I am always surprised by its microclimate. While the rest of Africa swelters, Nairobi nestles in a basin of cool. I'm sure you've noticed this. But for my old bones, it's almost too cold.

Dalila can tell by his accent he wasn't born in Kenya, but hearing the homeliness of her mother tongue feels like stepping into sunshine. She watches his mouth as he strums through the language. The African musicality of his vowels, the pop and roll of his syllables.

I much prefer Lamu, continues Daniel. What a gorgeous little town. An African jewel. Have you been to Lamu?

Dalila replies in her first language. I once went to Mombasa. I saw the ocean, but, unfortunately, I've never been to Lamu.

That's good, says Daniel. The less people go there, the longer it will retain its charm.

Dalila nods politely, not sure if he is joking or not. She looks at the ticket in her hand then at the clock. What happens next? she asks.

Daniel leans back and crosses one knee over the other. Well, I suppose, you and I will talk about our lives and get to know each other and then, if we have common interests, we might become friends.

Dalila looks at him. This time she smiles. I mean, what happens when they call my name? What should I do?

Ah. You should do as they say. He uncrosses his legs and leans forward. Luckily, the Home Office has made this easier for us by removing any recourse to free will. Daniel pauses for a response, his eyes glinting.

She smiles again, bigger this time.

Your number will be announced and you'll be told which booth to report to, he says. Then simply do as you're told.

Dalila nods, interlacing her fingers and squeezing them.

There is no need to worry, sister. You will get used to all of this.

Another number beeps onto the screen and everyone in the room dips their heads and checks their tickets.

Bingo, says Daniel, waving his ticket at Dalila. He stands up, buttons his jacket, walks over and sits in the first booth.

The minutes pass. Dalila notices that all the chairs have been welded together. She reads a Home Office poster showing a handsome, smiling couple from the Middle East who claim to be delighted at accepting an offer by the UK to return them to their community.

She reaches into her pocket and retrieves a wad of toilet paper, blows her nose and returns the wad to her pocket. Someone else in the room is sniffing. It is a pregnant woman in a grey hijab who is rocking back and forth. Tears wet her cheeks. She sniffs and touches the back of her wrist to her nose. No one goes to her.

The guard at the door looks at the pregnant woman and looks away. The woman continues to cry. It's not physical pain but a deeper brokenness. When those tears come they cannot be denied. Men lower their heads. Some strengthen themselves by staring out of the window. An older lady in a black hijab comes over and sits next to the pregnant woman. Without saying a word, she places her hand on the young woman's arm. They sit together as the woman softly sobs.

Two more numbers bleep across the screen. Dalila stiffens as she realises her number has been called. She stands up and shuffles in her flapping shoes to booth number four.

Behind the glass sits a big bald man with an enormous head.

When she sits down his mouth pulls at the corners as if to smile.

ARC please, he says.

Excuse me? says Dalila.

Give me your ARC.

My ARC card?

The man nudges up the bridge of his glasses. It's called an Application Registration Card, he says. If you call it an ARC *card*, you are in fact repeating the word *card* unnecessarily, aren't you?

Dalila keeps silent and hands over the card. She gives him the letter too. He slots the card into the machine and stares at the screen in front of him. His eyes flit from her face to the screen, verifying her photograph. He has almost no eyebrows and, in the light of the computer screen, his skin has a tinge of green, like a casaba melon.

Name? he says.

Irene Dalila Mwathi.

Address?

Flat seventeen two Iona Court, Glasgow.

Is this the first time you've reported?

Yes.

He types something on the keypad.

Place your right index finger on the scanner.

Dalila hesitates, confused.

The official sighs. He holds up his right index finger. Put finger . . . on red light, he says, pointing at the scanner in front of her.

Dalila places her finger on the warm glass surface.

He types more information into the computer, takes out her card and holds it up. You . . . take card to Post Office . . . Post Office give you money. Understand?

Dalila frowns.

The card is pushed back under the glass to her.

Now you . . . wait there, he says, pointing to a single chair in the corridor behind her.

He sits back, folds his arms and retracts his chin. After a few seconds of staring at each other, Dalila concludes their exchange must be over. She stands up, goes to the chair and sits.

Twenty minutes later, a woman in a white blouse walks up to her. Are you Mercy Kiguru?

Dalila glances both ways to see who this woman is talking to, but since no one else is nearby she decides to answer. No, she says.

No?

It is not I.

The woman fingers through the files cradled in her arm. How about . . . let's see here . . . Irene Dalila Matty? Is that you?

Me, I am Irene, nods Dalila.

Right then, come with me.

She follows the woman into a small office. There is a desk with a computer on it, filing cabinets and boxes on the floor. The bin next to the desk is overflowing with scrunched papers and cardboard coffee cups. Even though the room is stuffy the window is firmly shut. The woman sits behind the desk and Dalila takes the single plastic chair facing the desk.

Right, says the woman as she places the files to one side and opens the one with Dalila's name on it.

It says here that you speak English, is that correct?

Yes.

Good, then we can get through this quickly. I'm Ms Colgan and I've been assigned to be your case owner. This means I am responsible for controlling the progression of your case.

It is nice to meet you, Mrs Coligan, says Dalila.

It's *Ms* Colgan.

Dalila fights a flush of embarrassment as she tries to re-pronounce the name. Miz Col-gin, it is a pleasure to meet you.

They shake hands and the sensation of this woman's cold dry skin lingers on Dalila's fingers.

I understand that you went through Screening in Croydon almost two weeks ago and you've been transferred to Glasgow.

Yes.

Ms Colgan smiles, places her elbows on the desk and leans into them. First things first, she says. In the letter we sent you are the dates and times when you're required to report. Do you have the letter with you?

Me, I have it here.

Good, so you'll know you have to report here twice a week on Tuesday and Friday afternoons. If you fail to meet these reporting restrictions, even one time, then your case may be jeopardised. Do you understand?

Dalila nods.

And while your case is being considered it is illegal for you to work in this country. I want you to know that we take this very seriously. It's a crime to work in the UK without your Leave to Remain. If you're caught you'll be arrested and detained. Is that clear?

Dalila lowers her head. Yes, Miz Col-gin.

Soon you'll receive a Statement of Evidence Form through the post, says Ms Colgan. It's like an application form. You've to put in all the details of your case. Don't leave anything out. Explain exactly what happened to you and why you need to be in the UK to stay safe. Write every single detail down. Just tell the truth and you should be alright.

Dalila's stomach knots as she considers the truth, the details. These are not things she has been able to talk about and certainly not anything she ever imagined writing down. But in Ms Colgan's smile, in her eyes, are hints of kindness or, more accurately, there is an openness to her, a calmness. Perhaps, as they get to know each other, Dalila wonders if she might be able to talk to this woman.

You don't need to be concerned, continues Ms Colgan, I'll be conducting your asylum interview and working with your legal representation. Do you have a lawyer?

No, says Dalila, reaching up and holding the back of her neck. I don't have money for a lawyer.

You shouldn't need one. You and I will be in close contact throughout the process, but you are entitled to hire legal help if you wish.

Once you've had time to fill in your Statement of Evidence Form, I'll set a date for your asylum interview. You will bring this form and all the supporting evidence and documents to the interview. I'll conduct the interview myself and I'll be joined by two of my colleagues as witnesses. We'll discuss your situation in detail and then I'll decide how to proceed from there. Does that all make sense? Do you have any questions?

Dalila looks at Ms Colgan's blouse. It is white satin with a shallow V-neck and no shoulder pads. Do you work for the Home Office? asks Dalila.

Ha! Ms Colgan leans back in her chair, chuckling. Yes, I do. I actually do, someone has to, right? Now, you'll need one of these, she says, sliding a booklet across the table to Dalila. It's got all the information we've just discussed and here is my card with my number should you need to call me. Okay?

Thank you, says Dalila.

Don't worry about anything, says Ms Colgan. Just report on time, fill in the application papers and I'll see you at the interview.

Dalila exits the gates of Festival Court and crouches down to thread the laces through her golden basketball boots.

Jambo? Dalila hears someone say as they approach. Habari gani?

She looks up and sees the old man she met earlier in the waiting room. Mzuri, sana, says Dalila.

We meet again. It is me, Daniel, he says in Kiswahili.

Yes, I remember, says Dalila, standing up to shake his hand.

I am going to the library, says Daniel. Do you know where it is?

No, I'm not sure of anything.

It's just along the road, not far. I go there most days. I read the internet. If you don't mind walking slowly with a tiresome old man like me, then I will show you the way.

In one corner of the library two children sit on a beanbag and point at pictures in a book. On the other side of the hall, five old men sit in armchairs reading newspapers. There are shelves of CDs and DVDs. In the centre of the hall is a display of books with bright blue covers. The sign invites people to *Beat the Winter Blues with a Book!*

Daniel introduces Dalila to the librarian behind the counter and mentions that Dalila would like to join the library. After filling in some paperwork, they reserve an hour to browse the internet.

Upstairs, on the mezzanine level, is a suite of computer terminals with a few people sitting in front of the screens. One of them is a man Daniel recognises. The men shake hands and whisper their hellos. Dalila sits at the computer allocated to her.

She logs on with the pass code she was given and as soon as she is online the timer at the bottom of the screen starts to count down. She has fifty-nine minutes left.

Her fingers hover over the keys. The address bar on the search engine is as blank as her mind.

When was the last time she sat in front of a computer like this? Where was she? It must have been in the computer lab on campus, more than a year ago. No, it was actually in the internet cafe in the mall. Just after her brother went up north to check on their parents, she remembers going in there quickly to check if he had sent any news.

Her fingers type one word. *Facebook.*

She enters her email address and password. Her fingers recall the rhythm of typing these words faster than her mind can remember them. She has 478 notifications and 119 personal messages. She clicks on her home page. It is still that profile picture of her posing in the wig and red shirt that she thought made her look so professional. She can hardly see herself under all that eye make-up. That person doesn't feel like her any more, or rather she doesn't feel like that. A silly college girl trying to look grown up. It's an embarrassing photograph, but she is compelled to look, to see who she was.

Her timeline is full of new posts. She quickly scrolls down and then back up, reading random messages from her friends and classmates.

Sarah Wa Mum ur bro was the best. RIP.
Anthony Gamboa xaxa D. I heard about your fam. So sorry. May God be with you this trying times.
G. Talai So sorry 4 ur loss dada.
Beautiful Muragu People saying these crazy things about U Irene. Whats up?
R U OK?
Judy Mwenda pole for your loss. Call me
Eunice Ndirangu I'm really worried. Is how? Not seen u for months! Where ru???? Some people saying ur with yur uncle or something. Plz Plz Plz ☎ me. email. Anything.
Caleb Wairimu RIP Dalila Mwathi, you were always so sweet.

Judy Mwenda She not dead!!

Caleb Wairimu What? Sorry. I heard about the riots, about her family.

Muthoni Muragu Has anyone heard from Dalila **#whereisdalila**

JC Kinuthia No

Njeeh Kimenju She's not @ colle, not in class. Not seen her for ages.

Moses Kaire She's with her uncle.

Faith Ndungu I heard she moved to Thika.

N. Mutiso Missing you everyday girlfriend. Hope you're ok wherever you are.

Sam Mbuvi Condolences. May you RIP. You were a beautiful girl, a delight.

Kenny Kibue We mourn our friend.

Muthoni Muragu Dalila, If U read this call me!!! I know UR there. **#whereisdalila**

Esther Njanja You and your brother touched many lives in this college. May you both rest with God.

Muthoni Muragu Siz, just p.m. me or something. Friends milele!! **#whereisdalila**

The posts roll on and on. Dalila sets the cursor on her status update and, not quite sure what to say, she excitedly starts typing.

Saseni! Contrary to the many RIPs, sijadie, I'm alive! Safely in the UK. Glasgow is the address! Been a tough year with many shidaz, but niko poa! Nawamiss!

She doesn't know what else to write but this should put a stop to the rumours going around college. The word will get out that she is alive and well and then she can start to reconnect with friends one by one.

She hits ENTER.

Her parents never used Facebook, they weren't part of the xaxa generation. Her mother only got her own phone three years ago.

But everyone else uses Facebook, her friends, her teachers, her brother.

Samuel, her brother. The sense of him is clearer than her memories.

In her darkest moments her thoughts always reach towards her mother, her father. They were her earth, slipped out from under her. But Samuel exists to the side, his face opaque, like a silhouette in the moonlight. His outline is more defined when she doesn't look directly at it. It troubles her that she isn't more troubled by his death. His tragedy has somehow been lost in her own. His passing wasn't an event itself, it merely became part of the earthquake splitting through the centre of her life.

She types his name and clicks on it.

There is his face. Real. True. Like he stepped from the shadow towards her. She can feel his mood in the proud, self-conscious profile picture. Her big brother, athletic and gentle.

His page has become a memorial site with hundreds of good wishes and RIP postings. She scrolls through the litany of tributes. Many of her friends have posted condolences and photographs that she has never seen. She clicks on the album and flicks through the photographs. One shows a crowd of well-dressed people standing in a field. The next one is of people posing in a car park. No one is smiling and her brother is tagged in every shot. She looks for his face but he isn't there. In the next photo people in nice dresses wait outside a church. Recognition whispers something to her. The next picture is much the same as the last but the image hums with an unnerving chill. She recognises family friends, people who used to drive for her father, cousins and a few faces from college.

And then she knows.

This is the funeral.

This photograph was taken at her brother's funeral. Her family's funeral. These are her friends and family saying goodbye. It's everyone saying goodbye, everyone except her. This is the funeral her uncle forbade her to attend. She breathes in so sharply it makes a noise.

Flicking through more photographs she finds him, her uncle, standing by a car with some of his men. They are wearing suits, smoking. In the foreground, some of Samuel's friends are standing arm in arm, holding up her brother's basketball vest.

This picture has a ferocious silence.

Her heart starts beating so hard she's afraid she might scream. She pushes back from the desk and struggles to find a tissue in her pocket. Daniel turns in his seat and lowers his glasses to look at her. She blows her nose and raises her hand in a gesture to assure Daniel she is okay. She blows her nose again and when she looks at the screen a private message has popped up. She scoots forward to read it.

Muthoni Muragu Who is this? You are trespassing on my friend's page and I will report you to campus security.

Dalila stares at the little green cursor showing that Muthoni, her best friend, is online right now. She's not sure how to respond. Muthoni must be able to see that she is online and available for messaging.

Muthoni Muragu How did you get my friend's password? Hacking someone's private account is a serious offence!!
    Dalila Mwathi It is me.
Muthoni Muragu Who are you?
    Dalila Mwathi ni mimi Dalila.
Muthoni Muragu ur NOT Dalila. I know this!!
    Dalila Mwathi Believe me. It's me. We studied media and comm together.
Muthoni Muragu U can know all this from her page. U think I'm sooooo stupid. U R in big trouble. U can be expelled for this. If u r she, then where did we meet?
Muthoni Muragu not answering? U make me sick.
    Dalila Mwathi Noni, don't be like that! We met in the tiny mobile phone shop at Moi Avenue, near the place that sells nice fries. U were buying a Nicki Minaj phone cover. U helped me get the battery out

of my phone because yr nails were longer. It is me, Noni. It's Dali.

Muthoni Muragu OMG OMG OMG!!!!! Gff!

Muthoni Muragu Dali, is it really you??

Dalila Mwathi Yes! ☺☺

Muthoni Muragu They said u r dead. Killed!! But I knew, I KNEW. I knew I knew I knew!!!! ☺☺☺ R U ok? Are you sick? What? Sending you a big hug!

Dalila Mwathi I'm ok.

Muthoni Muragu R U in UK?

Dalila Mwathi Yes. Glasgow.

Muthoni Muragu Where is this place? never heard of it. Pictures? Where R they? Want to see u with yr nice clothes!!☺☺☺

Dalila Mwathi It's not like that. Glasgow is too cold. Things have not been easy.

Muthoni Muragu Don't worry girl. I'm glad u r safe. Everyone said you died. They say you ran away, people were looking for u. Some said u live with your uncle. It was crazy here! After a year the colle want to take u off the register, can u believe that? But I deferred u for 1 year so they are holding yr place. ;-)

Dalila Mwathi wow!! U did this? U R the best!!

Muthoni Muragu When you'll come back?

Dalila Mwathi I want to come back now, believe me. But I'm scared of my uncle.

Muthoni Muragu did u stay with him?

Dalila Mwathi at first I stayed but after he wouldn't let me leave. It was bad for me, Noni. Bad things happened, but I escaped, ran away.

Muthoni Muragu that Mungiki bastard! I'm so sorry Dali.

Muthoni Muragu How did you get to UK?

Dalila Mwathi 1 of my uncle's drivers helped me.

Muthoni Muragu he thinks he's a big man now.

Dalila Mwathi who? My uncle?

Muthoni Muragu yes

Muthoni Muragu I saw his photo on the back of the matatus. He is campaigning 2 b on the city council.

    Dalila Mwathi really?

Muthoni Muragu All these Mungiki are changing now. No more tobacco chewing, no more dreadlocks. These days they wear suits. True! No more gangstas, now they try 2 b businessmen. Even here at colle there are too many Mungikis. There R so many everywhere. If you speak against them it can be trouble.

    Dalila Mwathi This is bad for me. Maybe I can never go home.

Muthoni Muragu Don't think like that Dali. You come home soon, don't worry. Its better U B safe now. But don't tell people where U R. People talk.

She imagines people talking. Friends from college talking to other students who take the matatus home. The news of her whereabouts getting passed from one to the other. The loyal Mungiki students talk to the ticket boys or matatu drivers who are also Mungiki. The matatu drivers remember her name. They talk to her uncle. Her uncle must be furious that she has escaped, but when he knows where she has gone he will have a place to direct his rage.

    Dalila Mwathi I just put Glasgow in my status!!! Stupid stupid!!

Muthoni Muragu Maybe better you delete it quick.

Dalila clicks back to her home page to find her recent status update already has twenty-nine likes and eight comments. Friends from college wishing her well and asking about her life in the UK. She deletes the post as quick as she can and refreshes the page to make sure it's gone.

A warning box flashes up on her screen showing she only has two minutes of internet time left.

She sends Muthoni another message.

Dalila Mwathi I deleted my post but now I'm worried

Muthoni Muragu U B Ok. Don't worry. No one can find you in UK. But better to use private message or email.

Dalila Mwathi I feel sick, Noni. Pls don't tell people about me.

Muthoni Muragu You safe, girl. Believe that! Mungiki don't fly to UK.

Dalila Mwathi I have 45 sec left on this computer.☹ love you Noni. We chat soon.

Muthoni Muragu I love you Dali!!!

When Dalila gets back to the flat she locks and bolts the door behind her. Her head is tight as a watermelon and her body is full of thoughts, getting tangled in her chest, diving down to her stomach. Each one wriggling and slipping, too fast to properly grasp. That strange old man, what was his name again? Daniel. And Ms Colgan. Miz Col-gin. And why did they make her take out her shoelaces? Do they expect her to unlace her shoes at every visit? She should use Facebook again. Muthoni. Sweet, precious Noni. She is such a good friend, a true sister.

Ma'aza enters the hall, fidding with the zip on her hoodie. Did you sign at Festival Court? she asks. They swipe your card?

Yes, says Dalila, taking off her coat.

Ma'aza zips up and lifts her face. Okay, we go.

Again? I am not so strong today. I want to rest.

Ma'aza lifts her chest and puts her hands to her hips.

Dalila can't meet her eyes.

I am not your mother, says Ma'aza, shooting her arm out towards Dalila and snapping it back to its place on her hip. I don't take care of you. I don't ask for you to be here. If you don't have money, if you don't eat, I don't care.

Dalila turns her head away, wondering if it's perhaps safer to just leave.

You want your money? asks Ma'aza.

Yes.

So, we go to the Post Office, she says, her arm punctuating the air again. Don't take off your shoes. We go now.

*

Ma'aza strides down the street, chin up, never looking left or right, while Dalila looks at everything through the haze of a head cold. Seagulls swoop and peck at litter. Seagulls, the same as in Mombasa, and Dalila wonders if Glasgow is a seaside town. Old trees splay their branches and their roots buckle the concrete slabs around their trunks.

They approach what appears to be a bus depot. Dalila watches a mother pushing her child in a pram. The child is at least four years old, maybe older. A black taxi, like the ones she saw in London, U-turns and stops by the roadside. A white man sweeps rubbish from the pavement.

White cleaners – different.

Taxis – different.

Is this the city centre? asks Dalila.

No. This is Govan. City centre is other side.

They cross the road, towards a small shopping mall. At the entrance sits a man in wheelchair wearing an Iron Maiden T-shirt. His wheelchair is very modern. He doesn't beg or speak to passers-by, he just sits, with his tattooed forearms resting on his lap, waiting for someone, or something.

Beggars – different.

Inside, it's stuffier and smells of overcooked food. Many of the shops are vacant, their windows whitewashed from the inside. Ahead, she sees a shop called Farmfoods. It is filled with freezers and seems unlike any place the farmers she knows might visit. The malls in Nairobi are better than this.

Ma'aza pulls Dalila by the elbow into a brightly lit shop selling sweets, newspapers, stationery, drinks, magazines and cigarettes. The Post Office is at the back, behind the stationery and birthday cards. The staff work behind security windows and speak to customers through the glass with the aid of microphones. Though there are four windows, only two are manned.

Ma'aza and Dalila join the queue behind a man in a blue turban. Ma'aza, like everyone else, gazes straight ahead and makes no effort at conversation. Dalila holds her face in a neutral mask, trying to blend in, but her eyes scan the room, fascinated. What is most astonishing is what isn't happening. No one tries to push to the front of the queue. People don't swarm at the counter. No one sits on the floor. There are no children. No security guards, no guns. People merely wait, like tired school pupils, like inmates. The next person is called to the window and the entire queue shuffles one step forward.

Hundreds of glossy magazines line the far wall. Almost every cover shows a woman with glorious skin. On the top shelf are pornographic magazines with naked white women pouting and exposing themselves. Dalila lowers her eyes but can't help taking another quick look. Those pictures are right there, shameless in this public place, but no one seems to notice.

Pornography – different.

They move forward, following the queue as it doubles back on itself, now facing the people in the line behind them. A tall old lady at the back of the queue briefly makes eye contact with Dalila and then turns to whisper something to her podgy companion. When the podgy one glances up, Dalila feels heat rising in her face.

Another person is called to the counter and Dalila is forced to step closer to these old women. She glances at Ma'aza, who is texting on her phone. Dalila looks down at her feet, then lifts her chin and pretends to read a poster about banking with the Post Office. All the time, she can feel the old women's eyes on her, on her lips, her hair. Again the queue moves. Now she is standing right next to these women. The tall one fumbles with letters, the plump one makes a show of helping her friend. Dalila takes this moment to study them, their slack dry skin the colour of weak tea, their spider-web hair.

Ma'aza gets called to a window. She slides her ARC card through to the woman behind the glass. You have your card? asks Ma'aza.

Yes, says Dalila, holding it up.

After you report, you come to this place for money, okay? You must remember the way. I cannot show you every time.

Dalila nods and watches the clerk behind the counter swipe the card through a machine. The clerk studies the computer screen for a moment, counts out some notes and coins, prints out a receipt and slides it through to Ma'aza, who scrunches the notes and quickly shoves them in the front pocket of her jeans.

Then Dalila slides across her ARC card and, within a few minutes, she too receives her money. £37.41, which she mentally converts to Kenyan shillings and it seems to be a lot.

The two old women stand ready, each with a letter in hand, and don't look at Dalila. They don't look at her in that peculiar way women can curse you by refusing to look at you.

Leaving the mall through a different exit, Dalila braces herself against the wind. She follows Ma'aza past some warehouses, past a car repair shop, past an open plot of land strewn with papers rolling in the wind, till they come to a row of old houses, the ochre kind.

Wait here, says Ma'aza.

Dalila nods.

Ma'aza disappears into the building.

The wind pulls brown leaves from the trees. Dalila blows her nose and tucks her hands deeper into her coat pockets. She's alone on the street. And yet it's hard to believe she is here, alone, on this strange, cold street. Who would believe it? She had never even heard of Glasgow before coming to Great Britain. Still, it was dumb to mention Glasgow at all on stupid Facebook. What if the news gets back to Uncle Kennedy? His fury would be uncontained, but he won't come here. Certainly not. This city is a nowhere place. No one could find her here.

Her stomach pulls and curls in on itself. You're a stupid girl, Dali, she says out loud. A stupid, silly girl.

A dog comes towards her and she backs against the wall, moving away from it and up the three steps into the building's entrance. The dog sniffs the lamp-post, lifts its leg and carries on down the street.

Ma'aza comes out and says, Take this. You must have one.

She holds out an old Nokia mobile phone, the kind Dalila owned when she was seventeen.

Thank you, says Dalila, taking the phone. She looks up at the building and wonders what this place is. It looks like people's homes. Did Ma'aza just buy this phone from a friend? Maybe there is a shop inside. When she turns to ask Ma'aza, she sees her walking off down the road and Dalila hurries to catch up.

They march to a main road heavy with traffic. Across the road, cars queue up at a gleaming McDonald's drive-through and wait to place their order at the speaker, but the restaurant itself is empty.

Further on, three tower blocks come into view, identical to the cluster of towers they live in. Two of the towers stand hollow and windowless, the balconies marked with graffiti. The front of the third tower has gone, crumbled away as though made of sand, as if bomb-blasted. It's like a war-zone news report, thinks Dalila. One entire side of the building is completely gone. Tangled metal supports hang from the shredded concrete. Painted walls and coloured wallpaper hint at what used to be a living room, a child's bedroom, the tiles of a long-gone kitchen.

As they get closer, something near the top, about fifteen floors up, shifts. A slab of concrete the size of her bedroom wall loosens and falls to the rubble below. A second later, the shockwave shudders through their chests.

I used to live in there, says Ma'aza.

In there?

Yes, up there, she points, where they are breaking it.

Dalila looks, and only now sees the articulated digger partially obscured behind the tower. It's fitted with a long insect-like arm that scratches and pokes at the remains of a yellow-wallpapered room, pushing it, till the wall crumbles and smashes to the ground. The digger adjusts its position and starts prodding the next patch of colour.

How long did you live there? asks Dalila.

Fifteen months. Then they move everyone out. Put us anywhere in the city. But they put me in Iona Court. Our building is like this one. Next year they will move us again and destroy our building also, just the same like here.

When did you come here? Dalila asks.

I am in the UK for four years and seven months.

That long? And you don't have papers?

Ma'aza sighs and shakes her head. Listen to me, they never tell you anything. You only wait. Maybe they move you to a different place and then you wait there. Waiting is your biggest problem. This is not Africa. They don't use guns against you. In this place, they use papers and lies.

Ma'aza pauses, as if waiting for a response. To avoid her eyes, Dalila stares up at the crane.

They say they give you everything, Ma'aza continues, but they only take from you. They try to turn you against yourself. They want you to stay inside, to be alone, to do nothing. This is a broken place, you understand? Heavy hearts are a sickness here. That's why I go out every day. To forget about the waiting.

Ma'aza looks directly at Dalila. Moving is living, she says, believe me.

A block slams to the ground in a plume of dust. The two of them stand for a moment watching the metal arm claw at what used to be a bathroom.

Why do they do this? says Dalila.

She watches Ma'aza gaze up at the building and then along the road.

I believe it is like this, says Ma'aza, they don't hate us, but they don't want to see us. Like those two old donkeys in the Post Office.

Dalila lets out a snigger. I didn't think you noticed them.

Ma'aza shakes her head, smiling. I meet their kind so many times. They pretend we are not here. I believe this. We are like rubbish to them, something they don't want to see. So they hide us away in these dirty towers or detention centres. Maybe they threaten us or ignore us, hoping we will go away. But we stay. We are the rubbish that walks. We stand in their queues, sit on their buses and live on their streets. They cannot hide us.

They come to an enormous warehouse. The letters ASDA are lit up in green across the entrance and Dalila squints up, wondering what the word means. Inside, it's a wonderland of colour and movement. Fresh flowers decorate the entrance. The kinds of flowers her mother used to pick in those toxic polytunnels.

Flowers – same.

Beyond the flowers is a display of the most beautiful fruits and vegetables. Apples with skins as glossy as magazine pages. Straight carrots with the leaves trimmed off, each one as perfect as a drawing in a children's book. Potatoes without any grit, washed and ready for the pot. The smallest watermelons she has ever seen. Very long bananas, yellow, and cut from the stalk. Gorgeous polished violet aubergines.

Fruit and vegetables – different.

She picks up an avocado, but it's hard and not yet ripe. She brings a small apricot to her nose but the smell is faint and it's tight and unripe. The green grapes look full of juice. Seedless grapes they are called. But she's sure it can't be true. How can a fruit be seedless? Where would it come from if it were seedless? How could you plant more? The seeds must be soft. It must feel as though there are no seeds in your mouth.

Radio music plays gently across the heads of the shoppers and echoes up against the high metal roof. Above her, there is no ceiling. Broad ventilation pipes and thin wires weave between the rafters. Dust lies undisturbed along the cables. Extractor fans turn slowly behind their grills.

Ma'aza rakes her fingers across corn cobs. She palms one and puts it into a clear plastic bag. She adds four more. The bag goes into her basket and she moves on up the aisle.

You have the money from the Post Office? asks Ma'aza.

Me, I have it, Dalila answers.

They give you this once a week, says Ma'aza. You think it's a lot, I know, but everything in the UK is too expensive. You must be careful. Every week I pay maybe twenty pounds for food, five or ten pounds for phone cards, five pounds for toothpaste or shampoo. The rest I use for the bus, sometimes clothes. But if we live together we must put fifteen each for food and share everything. Also, soap and toilet paper, we can share these things. It's better like this.

Dalila nods. She agrees with herself to try this arrangement for a week. It could tighten things between them. They could live like a family, sharing. And if it doesn't work out, she'll shop by herself next week. She digs into her pocket and hands over fifteen pounds to Ma'aza.

They walk past fridges with pink meat, sliced and wrapped. Fat bloated chickens, plucked with the heads and feet already removed. Pizzas, covered in plastic, stacked like records in a music shop. Tubs of ready-made salad. Pasta and tuna swimming in mayonnaise. Couscous and diced red peppers. Then a fish stall with white and pink flesh resting on a bed of crushed ice. Prawns and crabs. Dalila looks for tilapia but they don't seem to stock it. They wander down an aisle entirely devoted to brightly packaged breakfast cereals, the kind only found in high-end hotels. Red signs highlight the items on sale and Dalila converts the price into Kenyan shillings and it all seems very expensive. They follow the smell of bread and find boxed cakes wishing anonymous children a Happy Birthday. Loaves of freshly baked bread are set out by a baker in a white hat.

They buy none of this food.

Instead, Ma'aza buys the cheapest sliced white bread. Tea bags. Coffee beans. UHT milk. A bag of polenta. Popcorn kernels. Six eggs. A bag of frozen white fish cutlets. And three dented, and therefore discounted, tins of soup.

We need sugar, says Ma'aza. Go to find sugar, but look for this style, she says, holding up the box of Asda's own-brand tea bags. Look for these markings, these are the cheaper ones.

Dalila sets out to explore the supermarket. A family walks by, the father with a trimmed black beard, the mother in a hijab. She sees an African woman too and her heart leaps as she wants to go to her and ask her many questions, but the woman is reading the label on a jar and so Dalila doesn't interrupt.

Towards the back of the shop she finds DVDs and CDs and flat-screen TVs and cameras. The very latest technology, but, curiously, no one around to guard it. It's just out. People can touch it. A child sits cross-legged on the floor watching a nature programme about a kingfisher. Dalila stands behind the child and watches the wall of screens. Many of them are even bigger than the TV in her uncle's house. Some are as big as the TV she glimpsed in Mama Anne's flat.

On the screens, the kingfisher hovers above the water, its wings a blur.

Mama Anne. Anne Nafula Abasi. That was the name she memorised. It was in her instructions, the ones provided by Charles Okema, who got them from Eddie. She wonders about Eddie. She never met him, but Charles knew him and said he was a good contact. That's the word he used. Contact. If her uncle finds out that she is in Glasgow, he might talk to Eddie, he might make Eddie talk. She thinks harder about Eddie and about the kind of man he might be. Eddie would probably give her uncle the same details that were in her instructions. And if her uncle threatened Eddie and charged him with finding his niece, Eddie would call Mama Anne and tell her to go to Glasgow. How long was the drive up from London? Seven hours? Mama Anne is tough, but old. Would she really come all that way by bus, just to convince me to come back to London? It doesn't seem likely. Anne is a Mama, she would send someone. Someone tough, loyal. Someone remorseless, who could drag me, thrashing and biting, back to London.

All breath leaves her body as she makes these calculations. She can't seem to keep her balance and Dalila slowly kneels down next to the little boy, hoping she doesn't throw up.

As early as tomorrow morning Markus could be here, in Glasgow, looking for her.

In super slow motion the bird dives straight down, plummeting underwater, the same bird on every screen. Silver bubbles glide across its feathers as the beak opens, silent and gasping.

She turns over in bed and pulls the pillow close to her chest. The dream she left was angry and argumentative, about something that mattered, and the mood from that dream lingers with more clarity than the content. Her sinuses are blocked and aching, the insides of her eyelids are itchy and soon she is in another dream where she is standing alone on a cold street wearing a very smart suit. She has an early appointment with her case owner, but she feels guilty for being in such an angry argument earlier. In the meeting she talks with her case owner very politely, very formally. They sit on two chairs not quite facing each other like visiting dignitaries on the news. There are many photographers and journalists present to record the event. During the meeting, Ms Colgan accidentally drops a pen. Still seated, Dalila stoops to pick it up and while bent down she reaches out and touches Ms Colgan's black lacquered shoe. She cups the shoe and foot in both hands. One journalist whispers to another and there is a frenzied flash of cameras.

The post arrives mid-morning. Dalila sifts through the letters and finds one addressed to her. She takes it to her bedroom and sits cross-legged on the bed as she opens it.

It's a Statement of Evidence Form. In the Explanatory Notes it states that this form is the basis of her application for asylum in the UK, and it notes, cordially enough, that the form has been provided to her free of charge.

She turns over one leaf after another. The form is over twenty pages long, with large empty panels for her to write down her story and explain why she is here and why she can't be at home.

Starting on the first page, she begins filling in her family name, her first names, her date of birth, nationality, current address in the UK and how she entered the country. She writes neatly, printing everything in block capital letters as instructed.

Part B is Family Details. She skips over Spouse and Children and under Parents fills in her father's Name, Date of Birth, Nationality but her pen halts over Present Address.

Present Address?

The box can only be left blank, profoundly blank. Why did she fill in her father's other details? She stares at the word for his name. The room begins to feel bigger, as if the bed and wardrobe are moving away and she is alone, kneeling on a vast carpet and that old realisation comes slamming back to her, freshly felt.

She no longer has a family.

All these boxes have to remain blank, because the details of her kin, which she protects and carries inside her, are inconsequential.

She hurriedly flips through the pages to Part C. The Basis of Your Claim. And quickly reads what she has to do next. It is mandatory to complete Part C1. She has to use this part of the form to tell the Secretary of State why she qualifies for asylum in the UK. Then she should complete one or more of the following sections according to the basis of her claim.

Dalila taps the pen against her bottom lip and bites down on it. She studies which sections she should complete as the basis of her claim.

Part C2 Your Race, Ethnic Origin or Nationality
Part C3 Your Religion
Part C4 Your Political Opinions
Part C5 Any other reason including possible membership of a
        particular social group

She reads the list again, hoping her eye has missed something. That which threatened her life, which tormented her, which she was forced to flee, fits none of these categories. Her uncle wasn't motivated by any of this. He did what he did because he could. He simply used her because she is a girl.

She turns to Part C1. Persecution, Harassment and Harm. The first question asks her to please explain why she is applying for asylum in the UK, describing any specific events that happened to her, and, where possible, giving dates on which each event occurred.

The memories of what happened crouch raw and angry inside her. Everything is there. All of it. Especially the floor tiles in her uncle's house. The pattern, she can see it. Squares next to squares, in rows upon rows. She feels the coolness of them under her bare feet and the coldness of those tiles at night when she slept on that floor, with only her bicep as a pillow. The face of her uncle comes to her, his smiling mouth up against her neck, her cheek, his tongue forced into her mouth.

Dalila puts the pen down and stares up at the light bulb as if it might burn the images from her head.

She goes to the bathroom and brushes her teeth.

In the mirror she notes that she is, in fact, quite calm. The memories aren't the problem, not today. She feels them flash up and settle down. Her frustration comes from trying to see all these images as one story, to step back and give it coherence.

She rinses her mouth and thinks about college. When piecing a story together, you jot down notes. That is what they taught her, that is what journalists do. She goes to the kitchen, gets a pencil and returns to the form. Her pencil hovers above the page as she tries to think how it all started. She writes notes, at first just single words and then a few phrases. The more the words appear on the paper, the more defined her story becomes.

She writes of her family home in Nakuru where she lived with her father, mother and brother. She writes their names for they share her story. Even though she briefly told her story in Croydon, she wants their names noted on this official record. She explains, once again, that her family are from the Kikuyu tribe, and the Kikuyu people are business people. Her father's business was matatus. It was a strong business and her father owned many vans and employed many drivers and they transported customers to Nairobi and Thika. Her father shared the business with his brother, her uncle, Kennedy Kimotho Mwathi. As the business grew her father ran things from Nakuru while her uncle was based in Nairobi. Together they had plans to expand their business to new routes, including Mombasa, Lamu and even into Uganda.

After the elections, there were many protests throughout Kenya. Protestors were targeting the Kikuyus, sometimes killing them. She makes it clear that her father was not political. He talked about cars and Chelsea Football Club, but never about politics. He didn't care about that.

One night a gang came to her parents' home. She doesn't know the details of that encounter but the results were deadly. They killed everyone in the house, her father, her mother and her brother. As God would have it, she was in Nairobi, at college, studying for her exams. Had she been home that night, there is no doubt they would have killed her too.

The police said that her family's murder was collateral damage from the political violence that was engulfing the nation. They never found the perpetrators.

She writes more, explaining how she believes the gang who murdered her family were not politically motivated but actually worked for her uncle. She was told this by a man named Charles Okema who works very closely with her uncle. He said her uncle killed her father, masking it as part of the political riots, in order to take over his brother's side of the business.

After the funeral, her uncle was in charge of everything. A vast matatu business that reached across the country and employed many, many people. He became a very powerful man.

Her uncle also took her.

She tells how he came to fetch her from her college dorm and brought her to his house. She didn't know her uncle very well. He didn't visit much when she was young. She was so upset after her family's murder she went with her uncle. He was the only family she had left. He told her to stay in his house for her protection. He even forbade her to attend her family's funeral. Later, she was forbidden to leave. She stayed in that house for ten months, forced to cook and clean and made to sleep on the kitchen floor. It was like a prison.

Dalila stares at her handwriting, at the pencil hovering centimetres above the page. There is more to tell. More, that she has never told anyone. Things that she struggles to write or to say. She dares not go into those memories lest they overwhelm her, and yet, without venturing into those painful places she cannot frame the story that will protect her.

Just write it, she whispers to herself. Just put what he did in one sentence.

After a few months in that house, she writes, my uncle pushed me to the floor and raped me.

She dares not lift the pencil and quickly writes the next sentence.

He raped me many times. One day I fought against him. I threw things at him and bit him on the hand. When he saw the blood he grew very angry. He took off his belt and beat me. The buckle caught my shoulder and cut across my collarbone. The bleeding didn't stop the whole night but he never called a doctor. I still have the scar from that night.

Dalila lifts the pencil and chews the end. Without pausing to read or correct the previous paragraph, she continues. My uncle has many advisors. I saw many people come into the house, businessmen, matatu drivers, even policemen. They all came to meet with my uncle. He is a big man with a big business and big men always have competitors. One day they brought in a boy, only about fourteen years old. They said this boy had betrayed my uncle. My uncle was so, so angry he beat the boy, he hit him with his fists and when the boy fell to the ground he kicked him. This boy cried for his mother but my uncle only kicked and kicked until the boy was dead. Many people saw this. I watched from behind the door and with my own eyes I saw him kill this boy. I knew then that my life was in danger. My uncle would kill me too, because of what I saw that day.

The next question on the form asks, If you claim to have suffered ill-treatment, who was responsible for the treatment? Give the name of any group or organisation involved.

She writes only the name of her uncle. Kennedy Kimotho Mwathi.

Question 3. Why do you believe that this treatment occurred? Why.

Why did this happen? This question has sat in her heart for months, wet and heavy as river mud threatening to pull her down if she ever steps into it. On distant days, when she feels disconnected enough from life that she can pretend to be objective, she can almost understand why her uncle had her family killed. Greed. Power. These things are real. They are in everyone. They make weak people do tragic things. But why would he keep her? Why torture her instead of simply ending her life? Why would an uncle rape his own niece? What reason can ever be applied to such actions? Those urges churn up from the swamp in men's minds. And on those horrible nights when he came to her, she never ventured into the dark deltas of male desire looking for nuggets of reason.

She touches pencil to paper and writes, I don't know why this happened.

Question 4 asks, Did you report any of the incidents which you have just described to the police or other authorities? If not, why not?

Dalila explains again that she was kept prisoner in the house, unable to leave, seldom speaking to anyone. But even if she could have gone to the police, she would not have. She saw policemen come to the house and discuss things with her uncle. She believes he is paying them. Also, she knows from her journalistic studies that the police are compromised. When women go to the station to report a sexual crime the police don't give them a proper Occurrence Book Number and log the complaint correctly. Instead, they just call a family member and tell them they have their daughter or niece at the station.

The next relevant question asks her to give full details of the specific events which made her finally decide to leave her country.

After my uncle killed that boy, writes Dalila, I knew I must get away. One of my uncle's advisors, a man by the name of

Charles Okema, also watched that boy die. The next morning before sunrise, Charles came to me. He said he knew about my family and what my uncle was doing to me. He said he could help me to escape.

I knew everything in my uncle's house. Even where he kept my passport and ID card and where he kept some money. One day when my uncle was away I took my documents and I stole money from my uncle's bedroom. I gave it all to Charles. If my uncle found out he would hurt me very badly but I didn't care any more. I had to leave or die. After two weeks Charles said everything was arranged. That night, Charles went out with my uncle as he did many nights. Charles made sure there was lots of beer and spirits for my uncle. The next morning very early, when everyone in the house was drunk and sleeping, Charles took me directly to the airport. He gave me all my documents and explained exactly what I must do. I went on the plane and came to the UK.

Dalila flicks through the next ten pages of the Statement of Evidence Form. There are questions about military service, religious practice, political memberships, none of which apply to her.

She rereads what she has written. It is as if the disparate, various things that had happened to her are now, for the first time, framed as one thing. Her experience has a single shape which she can study and, perhaps, come to understand. Yet, while all of it is true, it feels, somehow, insubstantial. It's a sad and unfortunate story, but only a story. She has no documents to prove what happened, no one to contact who would corroborate her version of events. All she has are words. If they are not enough, she has nothing else.

Dalila knocks on Ma'aza's door, hoping she might have returned quietly in the early hours.

No answer.

She opens the door and peeks in. The room looks the same as it did last night. She wonders where Ma'aza might be. In the few days they have lived together, no routine has been established. Ma'aza comes and goes at any time, without ever saying where she is going.

Dalila rubs the corner of her eye and shuffles into the kitchen. Through the window, clouds hover across the city. Fresh snow dusts the low hills on the horizon.

Another day is here and she is already in it.

She pours milk into a pan and places it on the stove. The teapot from the night before waits by the sink. She lowers two fingers into the pot and retrieves the wet tea bags. When the milk is warm she pours it into the teapot, adds three teaspoons of sugar and a tea bag. She stirs it around, sets it aside to steep.

Sitting cross-legged on the sofa she watches TV. The news is a horror show of bombings and beheadings in Syria. The story cuts to a huge crowd of Syrians marching across the border into Slovenia, hoping to get to Germany. Some carry small bags, others carry children. One person has opened an umbrella. When the news item switches to a segment on the Italian coastguard pulling the drowned bodies of children from the Mediterranean, it's too much for Dalila and she changes the channel.

Now she is watching a man talking to another man. Behind them stands an almost completed house. They talk about wine, about growing vegetables, about glass and the feeling of space, but the show also seems to be concerned with housebuilding. A fat woman appears carrying lots of papers. Though the house is extremely beautiful, the fat woman doesn't like it. There are problems. Then there is lots of driving while talking to the camera. Dalila doesn't understand this TV programme.

She goes back to the kitchen, stirs her tea till the warm milk turns brown. She takes the pot and a cup to her place in front of the TV and changes the channel. Now it is a show about shopping. An old man with sideburns and glasses takes two couples to a market. The old man gives each couple two hundred pounds, for free. Each couple must walk around the market and wisely spend the old man's money. The couples are very serious but the things they like are worthless. A cat statue. An old plate. Ornate candlesticks. Curiously, the couples have no idea how to barter. They pay over one hundred pounds for the cat statue and seem very pleased with themselves.

Dalila thinks about the money. She sips her tea.

Later the old man takes both couples to an auction where they try to sell the things they bought in the market. Dalila is certain no one will buy their stuff, especially the cat statue. But people bid more money for the porcelain cat than the Home Office will give her each month. In the end both couples make a loss. They shrug and smile. They hug each other, laughing. The old man doesn't get his money back. He looks at the couples over the top of his glasses and gives them a very strange smile. Dalila doesn't understand this programme either.

She turns off the TV and puts her empty mug in the sink. She goes to the window. Clouds are moving steadily across the city. A seagull rides the air currents and dips out of sight. On the street, seventeen floors below, an old woman waits at the bus stop. A heavy feeling begins to grow inside her. It's been two days since she left the house because she can't stop thinking about Markus. She pictures him sitting on the bench outside her building, hunched over his phone, waiting. Or she imagines him leaning on the gate post at Festival Court, looking for her.

She sits down and stares at her gloomy reflection on the TV screen. She stands up again and goes back to the window. The old woman is still standing at the bus stop. A blue car waits for the lights to turn and then slowly moves off. The feeling inside her grows heavier and she knows she must get out. It is Friday and this afternoon she has to report.

She walks to Festival Court with her woollen hat pulled down low across her eyebrows. But no one is waiting for her, no one even speaks to her. She goes through security, waits for over an hour, reports and leaves, walking straight back to the triple towers of her estate. Hers is the middle tower and she short-cuts across the car park of the south tower to get to her building. A movement catches her attention. It is a man lying on his back on the rough tarmac under a car. He taps at something behind the front wheel and then, with some difficulty, he stands and adjusts his glasses.

She recognises him as the old man from the reporting centre, the one who showed her the library. Relieved it's only him, she is about to turn and leave when he notices her and raises his hand.

Habari? he calls.

Mzuri sana. Dalila waves, struggling to remember this man's name.

It is me, Daniel, says the man in Kiswahili. He offers the back of his wrist in greeting to prevent touching her with his filthy hands.

I remember, she says. I am Dalila. Do you live here?

He glances up at the tower to his left. Yes. My flat is there.

Is this your car? Dalila asks.

Daniel places his fists on his hips and frowns at the car, appraising it. Yes, he says, at the moment, this is one of my cars. I bought it yesterday.

Daniel wipes his fingers on his trousers. He opens the door and gets in. The car starts first time and Daniel's grin is wide and proud. What do you think of this beauty?

For all the time she has spent around cars, and the men who love them, she still does not know enough about these machines to pick one out from the other.

It's good, she says. How many do you have?

Only two, for now.

The smell of grease and oil reminds Dalila, only and always, of her father. She wants to ask another question but decides to stay quiet.

Daniel switches off the engine and explains, These cars are my work.

Really? she asks in a lowered voice. But we are not allowed to work. What if they find out?

Ah well, technically, you and I are prevented from having jobs, Daniel says, but everyone has their work to do. Fixing these cars, taking care of them, this is my work.

He bends down and slips his tools into the pockets of a canvas bag and then rolls it up. Dalila shoves her hands deeper into the pockets of her puffer and raises her shoulders against the breeze.

When I first came here, says Daniel, I arrived only with the money I had saved. I knew I had to make this money work for me, because, as you say, I am forbidden from gaining employment. After making some enquiries I learned the police auction off the cars they have impounded. The first time I went there, I saw cars going very cheap and I said to myself, Daniel, you have found your work.

First, I bought a Toyota Corolla, a white one. Oh, these cars are very reliable. If you take care, they can run for a lifetime. It took me one month to fix the panelling and find the parts. I rode the bus here and there across the city looking for parts. This is how I came to know Glasgow, by riding the buses every day, talking to men in repair shops, visiting scrapyards, discovering the cheap places to buy spare parts, attending auctions. When my car was ready I sold it for four hundred pounds profit.

Dalila mentally converts the sum into Kenyan shillings. So much, she says.

It was a good sale. Soon, I bought another car and started repairing it. He closes the bonnet and says, This lady before you is number nine. She's old but still has many miles ahead of her. I think I might already have a buyer.

Where is your other car? asks Dalila.

It is here in the garage, he says, pointing at the door behind them. Another Toyota Corolla. They are the most dependable cars. I once had a car just like this in Kenya. The same colour too, says Daniel.

Cars are same, says Dalila. Roads, different.

Daniel adjusts his bifocals and peers at Dalila through the dirty lenses. I don't understand, he says.

Dalila shakes her head, feeling childish. Oh, it's nothing. It's just a silly game I play in my head. Ever since I arrived I, um . . . I compare things that are the same back home with things that are different. It's stupid, I guess.

Yes, yes, I understand. I do this too, says Daniel. So, let me see, it's the same that both countries drink tea, but the taste? Very different.

Dalila snickers. Yes, it is true. Why is that?

Daniel shrugs. I thought in the UK they like good tea, but they have no idea.

Her turn. Dogs are the same, she says, but the British pick up the, you know, the excrement, with their hands. This is very different.

Ghai fafa! Daniel shakes his head, giggling. I, too, have seen this. A strange mzungu business, picking up after dogs.

The giggles come for Dalila, and she flaps her hand as if to wave them off.

So, how long have you been in Glasgow, my sister? asks Daniel.

This is my first week.

Are you enjoying it here?

Dalila shrugs. It's okay.

You answer without saying anything, that *is* a polite reply, says Daniel.

I am grateful to be here.

Yes, I understand, says Daniel. When I first arrived, everything felt different. I didn't sleep well and I had all this paperwork from the Home Office. It was too much. I didn't understand it.

Dalila looks up at her building. She wants to go home, to be out of this cold, but she finds herself suddenly saying, My form came yesterday, the Statement of Evidence Form.

Yes, this is a big one, says Daniel.

But when I tried to write my story I . . . I don't know. Most of my form is empty, I have no evidence. It is only my word. My case owner said I don't need a lawyer but on the form it talks about having one and I don't know where to get one. Do you have one? Are lawyers expensive? They must be, in this country everything is expensive. So I don't know what to do.

Daniel doesn't answer straight away. He adjusts his glasses and nods as he looks out across the car park. Dalila realises he is giving her a minute to calm down.

Have you been to the Solidarity Centre? he asks.

No, what is this?

They are a charity for asylum seekers. I know them. They helped me. Maybe they can help you. It is too late to see them this afternoon. Can you come for me on Monday morning? I will take you there.

Waiting outside Daniel's building, Dalila tucks her chin under the collar of her coat and watches her breath appear and disappear about her face.

Damp cold – different.

Winter sunlight – different.

Breath – same.

Daniel arrives and the two of them set off. The morning is lit by a sharp, horizontal light reflecting whitely off shop windows. Steam dances above the tarmac and miniature clouds chase after every car's exhaust pipe. Daniel is animated, talking about cars and pointing out funny street names and explaining something about the trees in this country which she finds hard to follow.

They walk shoulder to shoulder and she's aware of his bad breath. Daniel doesn't limp but he favours his left leg. There is a stiffness to his foot and he prefers the security of the grassy verge over the frosted pavements.

They cross the road. Their shadows, narrow as twigs, stalk the length of the street.

I've noticed your English is already very beautiful, says Daniel. What work do you do?

I was a student, she replies, but I didn't complete my studies.

What did you plan to do after your studies?

In her mind it's the same scene she has had since she was twelve. She imagines standing on location dressed in a business outfit and wearing an expensive weave of glossy shoulder-length hair. As she says her lines into the camera the crowd keeps respectfully out of the shot. That's it. That's her dream.

It sounds stupid now, she says, but I dreamed of being a news reporter on NTV Kenya, a journalist, but I don't know any more. It is the dream of a little girl.

Ah, of course, says Daniel. I can see this now. You listen very well. You observe. Everyone needs to know someone with your skills. Your purpose is a listener. You are a story collector.

Dalila has never seen herself that way.

Yes, to listen is very important work, says Daniel. People like you will always have employment in this world.

The Solidarity Centre is only one block away from Festival Court. It looks like a corner newsagent. There is no sign. One shutter is pulled down over the window and the shutter over the door is only rolled up three-quarters of the way.

Three men stand at the entrance, smoking and stamping their feet against the cold. As they are about to enter the centre, Daniel recognises one of these men.

They clasp hands and nudge shoulders. Abbi, it is a long time, my friend, smiles Daniel. How are you?

Abbi shrugs and turns up his palms. You know how it is, he says, every day is every day.

And this? asks Daniel, pointing at the man's beard. This is new.

Yes, laughs Abbi, smoothing down the hair on his chin. You know, everybody, they want to be Bob Marley and the Wailers.

They smile and nod and Abbi fist-bumps one of the men.

Gentlemen, says Daniel, she is my good friend Dalila. She is new here.

Dalila lowers her head, feeling self-conscious. She shakes hands with each man but only Abbi speaks, saying, Welcome, sister.

Daniel raises his hand slightly, not to wave goodbye but rather to put this conversation on hold. He turns, ducks under the shutter and into the centre as Dalila follows.

Inside, the centre is really just one room. One room containing three rooms' worth of stuff. It's a nest of filing cabinets, posters, leaflets, a photocopier, a scanner and printer, boxes piled on boxes, used coffee mugs, pens and pencils, a tissue box and children's toys. The room is so small that Dalila finds herself standing behind Daniel, unable to enter any further.

By the door is a waist-high pile of plastic bags stuffed full of second-hand clothes. Against one wall, three people sit on a sofa. One woman perches forward, rubbing her fingers in front of the glowing bars of a portable gas fire. At the far end of the room, a thin man with a wilting ponytail stands behind a desk. He talks into the phone wedged into the crook of his neck. He hasn't shaved for a few days and he scratches the whiskers under his chin as he reads something on the screen. His desk is stacked with folders, loose papers, a stapler, printer ink cartridges and more coffee mugs.

In Kiswahili, Daniel tells Dalila, The purpose of this place is to help people like us. Phil is a good man, he knows many people. There are no guarantees, but he will try to help. He can advise you about your application. He is the man to know. I will introduce you, but first I must show you this.

Daniel lifts a large black ledger from the desk. The sticker on the cover is the face of an American Indian chief wearing an elaborate feather headdress. Around the edge of the sticker are the words, My Heroes Have Always Killed Cowboys.

He opens the book and explains, First you must register with the Solidarity Centre. It's a simple form. You tell them the basic story of your case and give them your contact details and the details of your friends. Then, most importantly, before you go to report with the Home Office down the road, you come here first and write your name and the time in this book. After you have swiped your card you come back to this place and sign out. Do this every time you have to visit the Home Office. It is safer.

Why? asks Dalila.

Because, my sister, they are taking people. More and more people go to report and discover they have been refused. They are immediately put into a van and taken to a detention centre. But not always. The Home Office is a place of secrets. No one knows for sure what they will do. So, if you sign this book, but you don't sign out at the end of the day, Phil and the other volunteers will start making phone calls. They can trace where you have been sent and try to help you. And, you know, sometimes their efforts actually work. It's always good to have someone on your side.

A woman in a headscarf hurries into the centre. Please, I am late, she says to Daniel.

Of course, says Daniel. He hands the ledger to the woman. She quickly signs it and dashes out the door.

Do you see that board? says Daniel, pointing to the whiteboard behind the desk covered in handwritten notes. Those are the people who have been taken recently, he says. Those are the ones in most need.

Dalila is a bit startled by the expression on Daniel's face. She takes another look at the whiteboard and reads the notes more closely. The top line reads,

MARY NARTEY / GHANA / YARL'S WOOD / REMOVED 8/11

Three lines down, she reads more.

YOUSIF MOHAMMED / ALGERIA / DUNGAVEL / RELEASED!
KARIM BEGUM / PAKISTAN / YARL'S WOOD
DENNIS KITUNGUKA / DRC / COLNBROOK / REMOVED 11/11
J. K. MAZOMBA / ZIMBABWE / DUNGAVEL

The list goes on for over thirty names. She is seeing something she doesn't understand. Who is Dungavel and Yarl's Wood? she asks Daniel.

Those are places, he says. Those are the names of detention centres all across the UK. Dungavel is the closest one. It is here in Scotland. If they take you, there is a strong chance they will take you there.

You think they'll put me in a prison and send me to Kenya?

Who can say what will happen?

I can't go back, Daniel. I won't even get out of the airport. Do you understand? I have to stay here.

Phil glances up from his phone conversation and Dalila realises she has been raising her voice. Daniel nods at Phil, letting him know there is no problem.

Can I call you back? says Phil into the receiver. He puts down the phone and smiles at Daniel. They shake hands like brothers.

Let me introduce my very good friend, Daniel says in English. This is Dalila Mwathi and she wants to register with the Solidarity Centre.

Pleasure to meet you, I'm Phil.

Nice to meet you, says Dalila.

Phil's shirt is crumpled, his jeans worn through at the knees. He doesn't look like a man people would go to for help. Well, he says, placing both hands on his head and looking down at his desk. Um, first things first, you have to fill in a registration form . . . which we have somewhere here, let me just see if . . . ah, here you are. Do you speak English?

Oh, this one is very educated, answers Daniel. Her English is perfect.

Really? Well, if you fill that out, please, says Phil, then, um, then we'll put you into the system. Maybe you can find a seat . . .

Dalila sits down on the arm of the sofa.

I am going to stand outside with the men, says Daniel.

Okay, Dalila nods.

As he leaves Abbi comes inside and starts collecting the empty mugs from all over the room. He steps over some boxes and pulls back a stained curtain to reveal a tiny sink, a kettle, boxes of tea and biscuits. He puts on a CD and starts hunching and dropping his shoulders to the rhythm of the reggae music, pointing at each person in the room.

People smile, glancing at each other.

But Phil flaps his hand and points at the receiver by his ear. Abbi turns the music down and says, Who wants some tea? He counts the raised hands, switches on the kettle and starts rinsing mugs.

Taking a pen from the desk, Dalila begins filling in the form. Most of it is the same list of questions she is sick of answering. Name, age, date of birth, date of entry to the UK, nationality, country of origin, phone number, address, next of kin and number of dependants. The next section is a large blank page asking her to detail the reasons she fled her country and the basic points of her case. As she writes her story, it comes easier, as though the shape of it is more apparent.

When the form is complete, Dalila sips her mug of weak British tea and glances around the room. A large map of the world is taped to the wall by Phil's desk. Her eyes automatically drift south, across the coloured patches of African countries, until she finds Kenya. The heavy equator line splits her homeland, cutting right through the centre of it. Her eyes move north, tracing the path she flew to get here, across the blue Mediterranean and the compact countries of the European mainland, until she finds the little island of the UK and the tiny dot of London. Even further north is Scotland. Someone has pasted a big red arrow to the map. The sharp end of this arrow points to Glasgow. YOU ARE HERE, declares the paper arrow. Dalila looks at the space between her feet, trying to imagine the ground as the spot on the map. Glasgow. An old, cloudy town north of Moscow, north of Newfoundland, a place closer to the North Pole than it is to Kenya. She looks around at the people in this tiny room and wonders if, like her, any of them could have guessed they would end up here.

Daniel stoops as he enters the Solidarity Centre, his smile a row of yellow teeth. Have you had time to talk to Phil?

Not yet, says Dalila. I have filled out my form but that is all.

Daniel leans over to glance at the form but Dalila lifts it to her chest, not yet ready to reveal her story to anyone.

Daniel straightens up. I understand, he says. Come. Let's see if we can talk to Phil.

Phil, my friend, says Daniel in English, we need your advising.

Ah yes, says Phil, looking up at both of them. There is a rare kindness to his eyes that Dalila has seldom seen in this country. Perhaps this is why people come to this man with their problems.

How can I help?

Not quite sure where to start, Dalila digs out the letter from her bag.

This morning, I got this letter from the Home Office, she begins. She flattens it out on the table and reads the first line aloud: I have arranged an interview for you to discuss your claim for asylum in the United Kingdom. She runs her finger down the page and reads out again, You should bring this letter to the interview. You should also bring any documents which you would like to submit in support of your claim.

Yes, says Phil, leaning over the desk, so this is the summons for your Substantive Interview. Who is your case owner?

She is Miz Col-gin, says Dalila.

Hmm, I don't know her, says Phil, but during your interview she'll listen to your case and decide if you're eligible for Leave to Remain.

It says here, Dalila continues, reading out a line from the letter, Your legal representative may only attend your interview if they are suitably qualified under the terms of Part V of the Immigration and Asylum Act 1999. Must I have a lawyer? I think lawyers are too expensive for me.

Phil turns to the desk and lifts a folder from which he pulls a sheet of paper.

These are the details of most of the solicitors who are likely to take on asylum cases, he says.

He grabs a pen off the desk and starts scoring through most of the names. We know for sure these offices aren't taking on any more cases, explains Phil. But you could try Mr Rafa. He takes on a lot of asylum cases. Now, I won't lie, he's a bit . . .

Phil makes a hand gesture Dalila has never seen before. She takes it to mean that Mr Rafa is unreliable or questionable in his methods, or perhaps his motives.

Daniel pushes his glasses to the bridge of his nose and peers at the list. This one, he is okay? he asks, pointing with his middle finger to the name at the bottom of the list.

From what I hear, they're okay, says Phil. But they're based in Dundee and they tend to give their asylum cases to their younger employees in order to get them a bit of courtroom experience.

Dundee? asks Daniel. Where is this?

It's the other side of the country. Not actually that far, really. About two hours away, but they probably won't make the drive. They do most consultations by phone and make the journey for court days. But they're good.

These are the only ones to help us?

To be honest, they might not even be of any help. I mean, look around you. Everyone's worried. Migration is suddenly a hot topic. The newspapers, well, they're going nuts. Downing Street is posturing but no one really knows what to do. So people are looking for assurances, they're all turning to solicitors.

Daniel nods and takes the paper. Dalila watches the resignation grow on his face.

Miss Dalila, says Phil. I see you filled out our registration form?

Dalila nods.

Would you mind if I look at it?

She takes a deep breath and hands the form to Phil.

He scans the details and says, So you're from Kenya?

Yes. Me, I lived in Nairobi before.

Phil reads over the private details of her story. His eyes express a quick intelligence, absorbing the implications and nuances of her story, without ever flinching at the horror of it. When he has read it all, he gives her a brief look. A look which seems to say, Thank you for trusting me with this. You are safe. I won't expose you.

When is your interview? he asks.

My interview is in four days.

He puffs out his cheeks and appears to be weighing up options. Okay, here's my advice, he says, leaning closer. Daniel steps closer, too, and now the three of them are having a private, more softly spoken discussion, in this room full of people.

The first thing you need to understand is that Kenya is on the White List, says Phil.

Dalila tilts her head to show she is listening, waiting.

Okay, so the White List is an unofficial list of countries that the Home Office deems safe enough to send people back to.

But, for me, Kenya is not safe, says Dalila.

I get that. I really do. You've got the Foreign Office saying a country is too dangerous for UK citizens to visit, but the Home Office seems to think the same country is safe for refused asylum seekers. Who knows why? Last week Iraq was put back on the White List. Can you believe that? The good news is that Kenya is complicated. Its White List status only applies to men. The Home Office still admits that the dangers facing women are severe enough to not send women and girls back there. Now, they change their minds *a lot*. They're bloody impossible to predict, but I think you've got a strong chance of a favourable decision.

This is good news, smiles Daniel.

Phil raises his shoulders to his ears. I don't want to get your hopes up, but here's the most important thing to remember: during their Substantive Interview the biggest mistake people make is to tell, in great detail, all the terrible tragedies they've been through and then expect that to be enough for them to stay in the UK. It isn't. Let me make something very clear: Leave to Remain is *not* a reward for the injustices you've suffered. Leave to Remain is *protection*. It's a protection from the dangers you'd be in if you were sent back. You understand?

Dalila nods.

So when you tell your story, obviously, you have to give them all the reasons why you fled Kenya. Don't leave anything out. But, and here's the smart thing to do, don't focus on the past, focus on the future. You've got to understand that your job is to prove what harm will come to you the moment you return to Kenya, and if they decide to send you back, then *they* will be responsible for putting you in harm's way.

Daniel nods slowly. Yes, he says.

Spurred on by Daniel's nodding, Phil continues, You'll need evidence. Documents, articles, signed letters, anything to support your story. And you'll need to prove who is after you and how they're likely to find you, even if you're sent back to a different region in Kenya. Have you got friends you can contact in Kenya?

Yes, on Facebook, says Dalila.

Perfect. Ask them what's going on back home. Get them to write letters and gather signatures. Find anything to support your story.

This one is a journalist, interrupts Daniel, with a hint of pride in his voice. With computers, she can find things.

Great, Phil says to Dalila, because what you have to do now is build a solid story for yourself. You've got to spend the next few days focusing on this. You can even write a report and hand it to your case owner as an opening statement for your interview.

I can do this, says Dalila.

Now, there'll be a small panel of interviewers and they'll ask all kinds of questions, trying to find a gap in your story, a flaw, but with a strong story, that's properly evidenced, I think you'll have a chance.

The three of them nod, happy with the plan that's been formed.

How do you know this? Dalila asks Phil.

Oh, you know, that's a whole story in itself, says Phil.

Dalila feels a sudden stab of guilt. She can't believe she just put him on the spot after he was delicate enough not to ask her any awkward questions. Lowering her head, she's about to turn to leave, when Phil says, I mean, it's no big secret, but I used to work at the Home Office.

Really? says Daniel. You?

It's not something I advertise, but, yes, I used to work down in England. I was a case owner.

Hmm. Yes, and now you do this, says Daniel.

Phil glances around the crowded room and shrugs. And now I do this.

Why did you change?

Lots of reasons really, but the toy monkey was the final straw.

Dalila glances at Daniel.

I started at the Home Office straight after uni. It was a solid job, my parents were proud, I rented a nice flat, the whole thing, and, you know, I took it seriously. I researched each case that crossed my desk, studied the law and tried to make the best, most informed decisions I could. But after 9/11 it got . . . more political. We were given quotas and encouraged to reject as many cases as we could. So, one day our supervisor announces to the whole office that we're going to play a game. At the end of each week, the case owner who's granted the most asylum seekers Leave to Remain would be shamed with a stuffed monkey placed on their desk.

Phil wipes his hand across his forehead. Believe me, the symbolism of a monkey wasn't lost on us. In fact, most people in the office thought it was bloody hilarious. Anyways, by the end of the month, I had won that monkey three weeks in a row. And so, now I'm here.

It's clear now what she has to do. Dalila goes straight to the library and books a computer for two hours. With pen and notepaper ready, she starts.

First, she logs onto Facebook and sends Muthoni a private message.

> Xaxa Noni! I need a BIG favour. Can you find out what my uncle is doing now? How is his business? Etc.
> I have an important interview here with the UK government in 4 days. They want proof and statements of the danger I face if I go back home. Maybe you can start by asking BB and Anne and those guys. But be smart girl. Ask quietly, and only people you can really trust. No Mungikiz!
> Be safe! Asante.

She googles her uncle's name, *Kennedy Kimotho Mwathi*. An old newspaper article pops up. It's from the days when her uncle and her father first expanded their matatu business together. There is another article covering her family's funeral, which she hurriedly reads twice.

As she scrolls through the results she discovers another man with the same name as her uncle who opened a training camp for long-distance runners. There are many articles for this man, including links to his website, Facebook and LinkedIn account.

She clicks on *Images*. Only two pictures of her uncle appear, pictures connected to the two newspaper articles. The other images are of the runner Kennedy Kimotho Mwathi.

Dalila pauses for a moment, her fingers stroking the keyboard, thinking. For her interviewers to understand a man like her uncle and the reach he has, to understand the danger she faces, they would need to know about Mungiki.

She googles *mungiki sect Kenya*.

She googles *mungiki sect politics*.

There are three excellent articles, from which she takes notes, detailing how the Mungiki sect came from the Kikuyu, her own tribe. Starting as a religious sect, they have recently become more politicised, even shaving off their signifying dreadlocks to integrate into mainstream political and civil positions of power. The article highlights how they control the vast slums like Kibera and many other neighbourhoods of Nairobi, often providing electricity and security in return for mandatory payments from the families living there. How they operate out of the matatu terminals, giving their influence an instant network that extends right across the city and indeed the country.

Just as her time is about to run out, she goes to the library desk and asks to print out the articles she has been studying.

She is told she cannot.

Dalila quickly jots down the web links for each article, before pulling on her coat and leaving.

She marches three blocks back to the Solidarity Centre. Only Abbi and one other person sit on the sofa. Phil is sipping from a mug; he looks up and smiles at her.

Excuse me, Mr Phil, she asks.

Phil. Just call me Phil.

Phil, she says. I found articles to help my interview, but at the library they don't let me print. Could I . . . ?

Yeah, sure, you can do it now if you like, he says, getting up from behind his desk and offering her his chair.

Dalila sits down at his desk and says, It is only a few pages.

Absolutely, no problem at all. Did you, uh, did you get hold of a solicitor yet?

No. Me, I didn't phone.

Well, you could use this phone while the pages are printing, he says.

She stands up but Phil slides the phone towards her. No, no, it's okay, he says. You just sit there and make your calls.

She calls Mr Rafa, but there is no answer. When she phones the Dundee office, they keep her on hold and then ask for her mobile phone number and promise to call back.

At home, lying on her stomach across her bed, she starts scribbling notes, composing her statement to her case owner. She can't remember the last time she worked like this. Part of her mind is writing and part of her is watching herself. It's calming to be writing longhand, like doing homework, she thinks.

She works late into the evening. Her head nods once, twice, before she lays her cheek down onto her application form and a deep sleep wraps around her. She dreams of walking to college with Noni. They discover they both have the exact same mobile phone, which Noni finds hilarious. We're so alike, Noni laughs. We're like twins. But Dalila begins to feel uneasy without knowing why. There's a sense of being late, or perhaps she should be somewhere else. She holds both phones, one in each hand. They are the same. In fact, they are exactly one and the same phone.

The morning wind is strong as Dalila short-cuts her way across the flat mud and concrete remains of where a factory once stood. It occurs to her to drop into the Solidarity Centre and warm her fingers around a hot mug of tea. Perhaps have a quick chat with Phil? But no. She should get to the library early, stay focused on her application. She crosses the street, passing the corner shop as the Polish owner nods hello and rolls open the shutters for business.

Her bag feels heavier than normal with all the paperwork she's carrying. It sits uncomfortably, the strap digging into her neck. She shifts the weight, hooking the strap over her other shoulder when, between the traffic, in the periphery of her vision, a shape moves. Her body recognises the shape before she does, her muscles primed by their own volition, poised to sprint, to fight. She casts the shape a quick look and immediately drops her head, tilting her shoulders away.

It's him.

The rolled shoulders, the solid neck, the way his head dips forward making him peer at the world through his heavy brow.

Markus. No mistaking him.

Her body locks. Her will and power sapped into the vacuum of fear.

He's strutting away from her, looking down at his phone, but it's certainly him. Here in Glasgow.

She has to move. She knows she has to. With one big stride she hides herself behind a pair of phone boxes, blocking his view of her should he happen to glance back. Her heart is thrashing in her chest. She sees herself lying on that sofa in that flat in

London. Markus standing over her. The sensation of his hand over her mouth, the way her forced her knees apart.

Droplets of sweat start forming on her face. Her forehead itches under her woollen beanie. She tugs the hat off her head, trying to cool down, trying to think. Is that really him? Why would he be here? But she can't play dumb with herself. It's him. She'll never forget his bulk. He's here for her. She did this to herself. She was safe, hidden. But now trouble is back, sniffing the air to find her.

As Markus turns the corner, Dalila scoots off in the other direction, trying to walk quickly at first before finally giving in and sprinting as fast as her legs will run.

Dalila bursts through her front door and bolts it closed behind her. She runs to the bathroom and finds Ma'aza in there, scrubbing the toilet.

It was Markus, gasps Dalila, trying to control her breathing. He was there. He was . . . near the library, he was there. Me, I saw him. I know that one. I saw him there.

Who? asks Ma'aza, dropping the brush into the toilet bowl. Who did you see?

Dalila exhales, knowing she is going too fast. She unzips her coat and flings it towards the coat hook at the front door, watching it fall to the floor. In London, she explains as slowly as she can, there was this man, and also a woman. But the man, Markus, he . . . I was sleeping and he came to me, and he tried to . . . They were supposed to help me. Those ones met me at the airport.

Dalila feels her mind's urge to tumble down into that memory, to dwell in it. She sets her feet as if to steady her balance and says, He attacked me but I ran away.

And you saw this same man today? asks Ma'aza, as she peels off her pink rubber gloves.

Yes.

You are sure?

She can't believe Ma'aza would even say that. Does she think she's bragging, trying to impress her? What she saw today could endanger them both. Is Ma'aza even on her side? The words can't come fast enough for Dalila so she throws Ma'aza a look expressing all her thoughts at once.

Don't be like that, my sister, says Ma'aza. I can see you are frightened. Okay. But in our fear we can see fearful things. That is why I am asking, are you sure it was this man from London?

It was him, snaps Dalila, her anger rising. He was there. I saw him. It was Markus.

Ma'aza sets her hips and places her hands on them. Did he see you?

No, I don't think so.

Are you sure?

Yes. Yes, I'm sure, yells Dalila. He turned and I ran away. He didn't see me and I just ran.

Ma'aza looks at Dalila, her eyes scrutinise and analyse but don't yet blame. Maybe this man is here for somebody else, Ma'aza says.

He is here for me. For me, shouts Dalila, thumping her own chest. Because of stupid Facebook. Because I told my stupid friends that I am here in this stupid city. Because I am stupid, stupid, stupid.

Okay, I believe you, says Ma'aza, reaching her arms around Dalila. I believe you. He doesn't know where you live. He didn't see you. For now, we are safe.

Dalila wriggles out of Ma'aza's embrace, struggling between the hope of being safe and the guilt of dragging Ma'aza into danger.

Ma'aza retreats and grabs the toilet brush. She holds it up and declares, After today, you and me, we go all places together. Okay? It's safer like this.

The following morning Dalila and Ma'aza both march across the empty site where the factory once stood. Ma'aza strides out in front, head up, blotting out the rest of the world, focusing only on her destination. Dalila walks quickly behind her. She can't shake the horrible sense that Markus is stalking up behind her. She'd rather be in bed but yesterday she lost the whole day worrying about Markus and she has to get back to the library to complete her application. She scans the windows of a passing bus, studies the shapes of people across the street, peeks through shop doors but she doesn't see him.

Back inside the library, it feels a little safer. She and Ma'aza book computers next to each other. Dalila sits down and rubs her sweating palms across the tops of her thighs. As she logs on to the internet her head is alive with questions. Hoping the focus will calm her, she leans into her thoughts. What does her case owner need to know? How much context should she write into her statement? What is her uncle likely to do to her if he finds her? Is there a way of linking him to other violence to prove what he is capable of? And, if she was sent home, who could she trust? Who might meet her at the airport? How would they even get past the airport matatu and taxi rank without her uncle's employees spotting them? Where could she possibly go to hide? To Naivasha? To Lamu? If anyone informed her uncle where she was, there would only be one possible outcome for her. But before the end, before that quick passing over, he would want his revenge and that is what she fears the most. She knows how angry he can get and he would want to make it bad for her, worse than he had done before, worse than she could possibly face.

Her fingers tremble on the keyboard. She bites down on the inside of her lip and then opens her mouth, easing out the tension building up around her jaw.

Things might change, she tries to convince herself. Her uncle might die. It could happen. He has many enemies. When he dies, she can go home. The thought excites her. Just as fate put her here so, too, fate may erase her problems. But for now she has to wait. If it takes a lifetime, she will wait.

Ma'aza stretches her arms above her head and yawns. Ish, she sighs, everything in the news is people coming to Europe. More and more people on boats, dying in the water. Even more are walking. somebody is making money from this, believe me.

Dalila looks at the blinking cursor on her screen. She can't think about Syrians right now, she has to focus on herself, focus on her own safety.

She googles *matatu gangsters*.

She googles *police corruption Kenya*.

She googles *matatu gangs police corruption Nairobi*.

She writes out quotes and notes the source and date of every article. After an hour of reading, she sits up straight and stretches her back, pointing her elbows towards the ceiling. What she's gathered so far is good. It supports her story, showing precisely how the Mungiki members are known to operate across Nairobi via the matatu networks. They pay off the police, or the police simply tolerate the Mungiki running the slums. Since her uncle is a Mungiki member and runs a matatu business, he has incredible reach. He will definitely find her if she goes back. And if she goes directly to the police they are likely to inform him that she is in their custody.

What else would her interviewers need to know? What was Phil's advice? Asylum isn't a reward. She's got to show the danger she faces, but she hasn't established that yet.

Closing her eyes to think, her fingers slip under the neckline of her blouse and find the twisted, hardened skin of her scar. She remembers the screaming, her screaming. She remembers the belt buckle whipping down. The blood. She remembers him dropping his trousers. She remembers her face being pressed down hard against the carpet. His smell comes to her. Heat rises on her neck and it feels as if her uncle is standing right behind her, right here in the library. She opens her eyes and stares at the door to the toilets, hoping she doesn't throw up.

With jittery fingers she googles *victims of Mungiki.*

She googles *police brutality Nairobi.*

She googles *Nairobi rape statistics.*

She googles *Mungiki retribution, murder.*

At noon Ma'aza says, I have to go, I am too hungry.

Dalila looks up from the screen. Okay, she says. One minute.

Only one minute, says Ma'aza. She hangs her head to one side, stretching her long neck.

As Dalila logs off and gathers her notes she asks, Can you walk with me to the Solidarity Centre? It's just there. I will be safe with them and you can go.

Ma'aza nods, before tilting her head to the other side.

At the centre, Dalila again asks to print off a few web pages. She calls the Dundee solicitors' office but the results are the same as yesterday: after putting her on hold they take her number and promise to call back.

When she phones Mr Rafa, he answers on the first ring. He listens to her situation for a few minutes before interrupting her. I am unable to take on any more clients, he says. With this recent shift in political mood, my workload has doubled. I'll be honest with you, Miss Mwathi, stress levels are high. I'm in court hearings all day and I've filed so many appeals I can hardly keep up. So, attending a Substantive Interview is not a priority.

But, she says, would you . . . ? Maybe, if you have time you could—

You should be able to present your case clearly at the interview, he interrupts again. Your command of English is obviously excellent, which is an advantage, believe me. If you need any more advice, you can always try the Scottish Refugee Council. Of course, if you have any issues further down the line with your case, then feel free to call me. In the meantime, why don't you try this new solicitors' office in Dundee, I believe the Solidarity Centre has their details. Apparently they are taking on asylum cases.

Dalila drops the receiver and thumps her forehead down on the desk.

Is everything okay, Dalila? asks Phil.

Yes. Okay. Everything is fine.

What is it?

I don't know. I don't understand, says Dalila. Everything is confusing me.

She stands up and grabs her papers from the printer. Everything is too complicated and, me, I read it but . . . Why are there so many papers? She waves them at Phil and then throws them on the desk. It's too much. I don't understand anything. And every day on the news it's Syria, Syria, Syria. All those people coming here. What about Kenya? We have danger too, but the news is silent. No one cares about us. If you come from Kenya it is just papers and more papers. Every day I'm trying to make sense, and to fill these papers, and report to Festival Court, but they don't care. Better if I walked from Syria, with my face in the news. Then people will believe me.

Abbi and a few others in the centre are staring at her. Dalila lowers her head and starts gathering her application notes.

I know it can be overwhelming, says Phil, his voice calm and contained. I appreciate that. How can I help? What exactly don't you understand?

Phil's face is open and she's sure she'll cry if she keeps looking at him.

This, says Dalila, flipping through her notes. This, I don't understand. She points to a section on her Statement of Evidence Form. For these parts, I don't know what I must put, she says. I must put one for the basis of my claim. Look here, section C2 is for race or nationality, and C3 is for religion and C4 is my politics and for C5 it says *any other reason including membership of a particular social group.*

Phil is already nodding as if he knows what she is about to ask.

You know about my . . . the reasons I had to run away from Kenya, says Dalila, but my reasons don't fit with this form.

Yeah, I see this a lot, says Phil. It's a common problem for women claiming asylum.

Why only for women? Her voice pitches higher than she expected. She leans closer to Phil and almost whispers, They don't want women in the UK?

No, no, it's not like that. It's a historical issue, says Phil. You see, the key legal document that defines who qualifies as refugee was put together in Geneva in 1951 just after World War Two. At that time, they were focusing on the problems in Europe, so refugee status was granted to those who had been oppressed because of their race, nationality, religion or their political affiliation. Those were the main legal definitions. That's why it's listed like that on your form. It's the law.

Dalila looks down at her form, still unsure how to fill it in.

The problem is, Phil continues, back then they weren't actually thinking about the rest of the world. It simply didn't cross their minds to consider issues like forced marriages, FGM, famine, child soldiers, rape or domestic violence. That's why women often fall through the net, because what they are fleeing isn't covered by the law. To be fair, the laws have widened in scope a bit since 1951, which is why you have section C5 on the form. See there, where it says, *any other reason including membership of a particular social group*. That's for people in your position. You understand?

Dalila nods. So what must I put there?

Well, just put that you're a woman, says Phil. The violence you're fleeing and the persecution you fear is specific to being female. Now they might argue with you, okay? You're going to have to be prepared for that. My guess is the Home Office will say that what happened to you was just a tragic set of domestic events, that it's hardly a nationwide policy targeting women. They'll argue that it's not like all women in Kenya suffered the way you did. So they might try to send you back to a different part of Kenya.

No, I cannot, says Dalila. My uncle can find me anywhere. Even here, in this city, I have fear for myself.

I understand, Phil quickly replies. Let me just ask . . . would you mind if I asked you a personal question?

Dalila studies Phil's eyes, trying to guess at what he might ask. Has he heard about Markus?

Is your uncle or any of your family part of the Mungiki sect?

Yes, my uncle, he is Mungiki. How do you know about this?

I'd say almost all the Kenyan women who come through here have had problems with the Mungikis, says Phil. The Home Office knows all about those bastards. When presenting your case, I'd recommend you try to show how *politically* connected your uncle is. Show that if you went back to Kenya you'd be silenced as a political dissident, simply by being there, even if you don't speak out against him.

It's a clever point and Dalila likes the force behind it. Yes, she says, this is good. I can say this.

It'll definitely strengthen your claim, Phil assures her, because you'll be claiming as part of a particular social group under section C5 and for your political opinions under section C4.

The rain comes down hard and Phil offers to give Dalila and the few others in the centre a lift home. The van stops outside her building and Dalila waves goodbye to Phil as she jogs inside. She steps into the lift and presses number 17. Her toes are numb and damp inside her basketball shoes. She removes her hat and shakes out the silver droplets of rain trapped between the fibres.

As the lift doors open, a little girl bounces towards Dalila. Clamped between the girl's ankles is a ball wedged into a disc, like a plastic Saturn, on which she pogos, squealing with delight. She rides her planet into space for only a second, arms flapping outwards, skirt billowing, her dark tangles of hair reaching, weightless, before gravity reclaims her and all goes limp. Up and down, up and down.

A taller girl skips after her saying, My turn. My turn.

They appear to be sisters, with the same thick wavy hair. Their open front door is right next to Dalila's. As she approaches her door, key in hand, the older sister says, Do you live here now?

Before Dalila can answer, Mrs Gilroy opens her door across the landing and her little dog wriggles between her feet and escapes.

Both girls squeal with delight, falling to their knees to greet the little dog. Toby! Hi, Toby. Come here, boy. Ears back, tail wiggling, Toby darts from hand to hand, licking their fingers.

Standing in her slippers and dressing gown, Mrs Gilroy shakes her head and says, Right, you girls, I know it's raining but yous have got to keep it down if you're gonna play on the landing. I can hardly hear the telly for all this commotion.

Toby is licking my fingers, laughs the littlest girl, her Scottish accent almost as strong as Mrs Gilroy's.

Aye, he's known to do that. Now, did you hear what I said, Rosa? Irene here's just moved in and yous are making a God-awful racket.

The little one, Rosa, looks up at Dalila. When did you come here?

Me, I moved here one week ago.

Oh, says Rosa. Then she says, Do you know what? We did sports at school today and, you know what, we did running and I'm the fastest girl in my class but Ashley Worsdale is faster than me.

Really? says Dalila, squatting to the child's height. Even me, I used to run in my school, ten thousand metres around the soccer field.

The older sister watches Dalila through the tangles of her fringe. Her eyes are wary. Dalila smiles at the elder girl and stands up.

Can Toby come and play in our house again, Mrs Gilroy? asks the little one, as she rubs the dog's ears back with both hands.

Perhaps another time, love, says Mrs Gilroy. She shuffles towards them. Toby's had a long day already.

Mrs Gilroy picks up her dog and lightly touches each girl's head before she goes inside. Dalila, too, unlocks her door and goes in. She hangs up her coat and unlaces her shoes, placing them neatly together against the wall.

A knock at the door startles her.

She attaches the chain and opens the door two inches. The sisters stand side by side, staring up at her. The elder one speaks. My mother said we have to ask you something.

Yes?

Do you want to come and eat with us today?

Oh, uh, yes. Thank you, says Dalila. When?

The older girl leans and yells to her mother in the next-door flat. An exchange happens in a language Dalila doesn't understand and then the girl tells Dalila, My mother says in twenty minutes. Just come to our house.

That's my house there, says little Rosa, pointing at the door next to Dalila's. A fit of giggles suddenly grips the girls and they run into their flat.

Dalila changes into her floral dress. She rubs moisturiser into her cheeks and along her forearms. In the kitchen she opens cupboards hoping to find a gift to take next door. There is a large bag of nachos, unopened. She grabs it.

When she knocks on their front door, a voice calls out from inside, Who is there?

It is me, from next door.

The older sister opens the door and says hello as little Rosa grabs Dalila's hand and drags her into the flat, calling to her mother, She's here! The lady is here.

Dalila kicks off her open-toed shoes as she is led down the hall, stepping over toys scattered along the hallway floor. She gets a glimpse of the bedroom. It is a nest of toys and clothes and school bags, Disney and pop star posters, magazines and teddy bears. A bunk bed lines one wall with a chest of drawers and a desk pushed up against the other wall, leaving just enough room to move down the middle.

That's my room, boasts Rosa, and this is the living room.

Dalila is met by a stout, tired-looking woman with the same dark, wilful hair as her girls. She introduces herself as Olcay.

Sit. Sit. Please, says Olcay, motioning to the table and chairs in the kitchenette.

Thank you for inviting me, says Dalila. I brought this for you.

With a dip of the head, Olcay takes the bag of nachos, saying, Thank you. You . . . very . . . kind. She tries to say something else but gives up and starts talking to her elder daughter in another language. The daughter sits down at the kitchen table and translates. My mum says she's happy to meet you and you're welcome in our house any time.

Thank you, Dalila smiles.

Olcay pours tea from a pot into a pink Barbie mug and places it in front of Dalila.

You . . . are . . . welcome, replies Olcay, clearly delighted and then self-conscious about her English skills. She opens the packet of nachos and pours the contents into a plastic mixing bowl and places it on the table. The elder daughter takes only one crisp. But the youngest puts her whole hand into the bowl and then the other. She stands looking up at Dalila, nibbling fistfuls of nachos.

Dalila can't hold back the giggles. She hasn't been around children for such a long time and feels herself falling in love with little Rosa.

Rosa whispers into her big sister's ear. They giggle and scramble out of the door calling, We're coming back in a minute.

Dalila holds the Barbie mug, enjoying the heat seeping into her cold fingertips, as Olcay attends to the food on the stove. On their balcony is a clothes horse and two children's bicycles. A toy kitchen set stands in the corner, the colours faded by weather. Only a sheet of metal panelling separates this family's balcony from the balcony in Dalila's apartment.

The television is on, quietly chatting to itself, holding back any awkward silences. Their living room is neat yet packed with furniture. A sofa, a bookcase, a wardrobe, framed family pictures, DVDs stacked under the glass coffee table. A double mattress is tucked against the wall behind the sofa. Its faint blue colour almost complements the wallpaper. Almost. She stares at it, as if this mattress is, somehow, important.

This flat, Dalila realises, is a mirror image of her own. The girls' room is backed up against her own room and it is, she realises, their voices that she has heard coming through the wall. Their kitchenette and living room sit back-to-back against Ma'aza's room and kitchenette. Their flat is exactly the same size as hers, with the same dimensions. She glances up at the mattress again. It dawns on her that while the girls sleep on bunk beds in the bedroom, the parents must sleep through here, laying the mattress out each night and tucking it away again in the morning.

The girls come bursting into the kitchen and the little one announces, Me and Parla are gonna do a play and you have to watch.

Of course, grins Dalila.

Rosa takes Dalila's index finger and pulls, leading Dalila to the sofa. You have to sit here, she says.

As soon as Dalila sits the play begins. Parla perches on the sofa's arm, raises a recorder to her lips and starts a tune. She's awkward and self-conscious while Rosa picks up a toy guitar and wildly strums open chords, skipping from one end of the living room to the other. Their mother smiles and half-heartedly tries to shush them, but this only makes their little performance even more dynamic.

The girls suddenly stop and look towards the front door, their ears attuned to a sound that Dalila had not heard. Delight bursts across their faces as they scramble towards the door calling out, Baba. Baba's home.

Dalila stands, Barbie mug in hand, unsure where to be. She moves into the kitchen and places her mug on the table. She smiles at Olcay, who is wiping her hands on a dishcloth.

Baba, Baba, this is our friend, says Rosa, leading her father by the finger. She lives next door and she is called Irene and she also did athletics in her school.

Oh, says her father, that is very nice. His accent is thick but his command of English is much better than his wife's. He places his hand lightly on his chest and bows ever so slightly as he addresses Dalila.

Welcome. Welcome to our home, he says, I am Mr Erdem. He offers his hand and Dalila shakes it.

I am Irene, says Dalila.

It is a pleasure to meet you and always a pleasure to have guests for dinner, he says, glancing at his wife and the food she is preparing. He touches Olcay on the shoulder and whispers something in their language. He is heavyset, dressed in a brown suit with a grey tie and black polished shoes. Close-shaved, with greased grey hair slicked neatly to the side. He moves deliberately, almost slowly, around his family and when he smiles, Dalila notices that his mouth appears more pleased than his eyes.

Olcay gives her daughters tasks and soon all the women, including Dalila, are setting the table, laying out knives and forks. Parla fills a Tupperware jug with water. Rosa folds square sheets of kitchen roll into triangles. Dalila puts a glass at each place setting, while keeping one eye on their father.

Mr Erdem sits on the sofa and unties his shoes and carries them down the hall. He returns still wearing his suit and tie but his feet are clad in slippers. There is a weariness to his movements, and it is not lost on Dalila that the girls have become less animated since his arrival. He sits back down on the sofa and switches the TV to some foreign news channel.

Little Rosa comes waddling through, struggling to carry the chair from her bedroom desk, and places it at the table.

You have to sit next to me, she tells Dalila, and Parla can sit there and my mama there and Baba there.

Olcay lays out a plate of warm flatbreads wrapped in a tea towel. She places a bowl of rice and a dish from the stove on the table too, before calling through to her husband.

Everyone sits.

Olcay stands again and leans over the table and hands some bread to Dalila. Please . . . eat, she says.

That glass is for you, Baba, says Rosa, and this one is for me.

Thank you, my child, says Mr Erdem, touching the back of his daughter's head. He takes a deep breath and looks at each member of his family in turn. He nods gently to himself before scooping some rice onto his plate.

He offers rice to Dalila and tells her in a rather formal tone, It is a blessing to have you join us today. You are always welcome at our table.

Thank you very much, replies Dalila as a swell of gratitude grows up around her. It has been so long since she sat with her own family like this and she wants to explain how good, and sad, it feels just to sit here, pretending to be part of their family. Just to be included feels like waking up with sunlight on her face, after a long, restful sleep. And before she starts crying she knows she should say something, so she says, Me, I am . . . I feel blessed to be here.

With only one day left before her interview, Dalila hurries back to the library to prepare her case. An email from Muthoni lies in her inbox.

Xaxa Dali,
I have news! Your uncle has been busy these past months. He is always out, smiling and shaking hands. People say he is generous, always buying tea and presents. It is also rumoured that he has made large donations to the Narc political party.
These days he is always in a suit. Many believe he will run for a city council seat.
When I spoke to BB, he said last month two bodies were found, bodies of matatu drivers who used to work for your uncle. These two were not Mungiki. There is speculation that those ones who can harm your uncle's reputation are disposed of. But, of course, I can't get proof of this. But I can say that in Nairobi many respect him and many fear him.
I have attached two links to articles in the Standard newspaper. One speculating about his move into politics, and the other suggesting that the death of the two matatu drivers was not accidental.
I am also putting together a letter for you, supporting your stay in the UK and gathering signatures from trustworthy friends and colleagues here at the college.
Your friend,
Noni

PS I feel like a real reporter gathering all this information. I have my first real story before I even graduated!!

Dalila reads the letter twice and then carefully picks over the
articles. She spends the rest of her morning typing up her statement, detailing exactly how she believes she will be captured
if she returns to Nairobi and what her uncle is likely to do to
her. She references all her concerns, linking them to similar cases
in Nairobi, showing that her specific case and her particular fears
regarding her uncle fit with the general climate of corruption
and violence towards women in Nairobi and those whom the
Mungiki dislike.

In conclusion, she states that, more than anything, she wants
to go home. Her only wish is to complete her studies, to visit her
family's graves, to rebuild her life. To live where she belongs. But
she cannot do any of this while her uncle is still alive. She needs
a safe place until the day comes when she can return.

Dalila sits back, satisfied. She emails the document to herself.

Feeling confident, she decides to walk towards Govan. Autumn
leaves lie pulped in a heap along the pavement. The surface of a
puddle is crusted with ice. She touches her toe to it and it splits,
fragile as eggshells.

A bell tinkles as she opens the door to a charity shop. The assistant
comes through from the back, a stout woman with a dark fringe
touching the frames of her glasses. They nod to each other and
Dalila browses through blouses.

Is there anything you're looking for? asks the assistant.

Me, I want a jacket, answers Dalila.

Like a coat?

No, maybe like this one. Dalila holds up a beige two-piece suit.
The skirt is knee-length and the jacket wide with heavy shoulder
pads. But, for me, I only need the jacket, says Dalila. I have an
interview tomorrow.

Ah, right you are. Well, we might have your size over here.

She follows the assistant to the end of the rail.

The woman lifts her chin and appraises Dalila's size through the bottom of her glasses. She turns to the clothes and picks out an item.

How about this? says the assistant, holding up a pale green suit. Or perhaps . . . this? She holds up a navy blue jacket.

Dalila points to the jacket.

She tries it on and stands in front of the mirror. The sleeves are a good fit but the shoulder pads are broader than she imagined. It's a bit loose for her narrow frame. But the effect is strong. She fastens the single button at her stomach and it suits her even more.

You're such a slip of a thing, smiles the assistant, but I think that one's alright on you. Now, you'll need to finish it off with something like . . . Let's see now. The woman fingers through the hangers and selects an ivory-coloured scoop-necked blouse. Here. What do you think of this? Why not try them both on together?

When Dalila steps out of the changing room, the assistant lifts her chin again, to see through the bottom half of her lenses. Very nice, she says, very smart. You're bound to get the job wearing that.

Dalila turns to the mirror. The scooped neckline is an improvement and the jacket collar covers the scar on her shoulder, just. But it works. She looks like a serious person, a professional. She looks like a newsreader.

In her dream, that night, she is back in Nakuru, in the village where she grew up, in the primary school she attended. She is an adult sitting on the little bench surrounded by unfamiliar children who stare and giggle behind their hands. The desk is so low she has to sit with her knees to one side. Being here is ridiculous. She can't believe she's here but they said that something on her record was incomplete. They insisted that she goes back and does it again. They were very firm about this. She simply can't go on until she takes this class again. She is livid, her anger sits high up in her throat but she doesn't want to lose her temper and frighten these little children. She blinks her eyes, trying to focus on the chalk scribblings on the blackboard, but none of the words make any sense.

On the morning of her Substantive Interview, Dalila showers and puts on her new blouse and jacket with her black trousers. The dark blue of the jacket doesn't match her black trousers, but it's all she has.

She goes to the bathroom and says to Ma'aza, Are these trousers okay? I don't know.

Ma'aza continues brushing her teeth as she gives the outfit a side-on glance. With her mouth full of toothpaste, she lifts her thumb in approval.

And for shoes? says Dalila. My basketball shoes are warmer but maybe not good for the interview. She says this hoping Ma'aza might pick up on the hint.

Ma'aza spits and rinses. Without a word, she walks past Dalila and goes to her room, returning seconds later with a pair on black slip-ons.

These are better, says Ma'aza.

Are you sure?

The shoes won't help your case, but they are better for interview.

Thank you, says Dalila.

Ma'aza and Dalila take one more trip to the library to see if there is an email reply from Muthoni. There is.

Dali, my friend,
I put together this letter and got as many people as possible to sign it, but some are too scared to sign.
I hope it helps. Good luck! Xxxx

In the attachment is a scanned copy of a letter.

To the Government of United Kingdom, regarding the case of Irene Dalila Mwathi in the application for safety and refugee status,
We, the people signing this letter, are worried about the safety of our sister, friend and fellow student.
Irene Mwathi's family were tragically killed during the political riots following the Kenyan General Elections.

Many people believe the killings were random acts of violence, others suspect that they were maliciously lynched for business gain. There is an ongoing police investigation into this matter but the judicial system here cannot be trusted since there is a lot of corruption. Irene Mwathi's uncle, Mr Kennedy Kimotho Mwathi, has been questioned by the Nairobi police with regard to this case but has not been arrested. No one else has been charged.

Mr Kennedy Mwathi is a powerful businessman in Nairobi and all over Kenya. Recently, Mr Kennedy Mwathi has announced his interest to run as a councillor in Nairobi. Some of his opponents who have spoken out against him have later been found dead. Others have been badly beaten. When questioned by the police, the wounded claim to have been in accidents or the victims of robbers. There is a culture of fear surrounding Mr Kennedy Mwathi and presently he is implicated in five separate police investigations involving murder, extortion, tax evasion and drunken driving.

We believe that if Ms Irene Mwathi is returned to Kenya, she will be killed just like the people who have spoken up against her uncle, Mr Kennedy Mwathi.

She is an honest and very hard-working student leading her class in the School of Journalism and Mass Communication at the University of Nairobi. She also had many friends and would never hurt anyone. We would all dearly love to see her again. However, we would ask that you allow her to temporarily stay in the United Kingdom where she is guaranteed to be safe until the police investigations against her uncle have been concluded.

We ask this in good faith for our kind and hard-working sister, Irene Dalila Mwathi.

The letter is signed by nineteen of her former classmates and friends at college, and by three lecturers, including the head of the Media and Communications Department.

Her eyes tear up. She wraps both hands across her nose and mouth in case a tide of emotions bursts out of her. As she rereads the list of names who signed the letter, the face of each friend blooms in her memory. Their friendship and courage are astonishing and a deep homesickness shifts in her stomach. Tears roll down her face as she wishes she could hug each one of these beautiful people, her true friends, her true family.

Outside, the fresh wind is bracing and helps to settle Dalila's emotions as she walks with Ma'aza to the Solidarity Centre.

Be lucky today, my sister, says Ma'aza, as she gives Dalila a brief hug. I will see you tonight?

Thank you, says Dalila. Yes. Tonight. Maybe I take a lift home with Phil. I can text you.

Inside, Dalila signs the registry book and prints out the scanned letter from her friends. While she waits, she accepts a mug of tea from Abbi.

You look good, sister, he says, noticing her blouse and jacket. And no gold shoes? What happened?

Dalila looks at Ma'aza's slip-ons on her feet. Me, I have my interview today, she explains.

Ah, you look good. You look like a lawyer, from the TV, says Abbi. They give you Leave to Remain for sure.

Dalila shakes her head but smiles warmly at him.

And if you smile at them like that, for sure, you even get their phone number.

She laughs, a little embarrassed, and gently slaps Abbi on the shoulder.

As her documents are printing, Phil leans over his desk and types on his keyboard. He prints another document, signs it and hands it to Dalila. Here, you should put this with your file. It can only help.

He gives her a cardboard folder for all her papers and then reads over what she has.

This is good, Dalila. It's good. It's going to help, Phil says. He gives her a letter. It's on headed notepaper with the Solidarity

Centre's logo and address. The letter states that Irene Dalila Mwathi is a valued member of the centre and has integrated and contributed to the local community. Glasgow should be proud to have her and if she should be granted Leave to Remain in the UK, her academic and interpersonal skills would be an asset to the city.

Thank you, she says. Thank you so much, you are very kind to me. She feels the tears rising again, but Phil cuts in before she can display any more emotions.

Right, so, you have everything? Are you all set? You look ready. How do you feel?

Dalila holds the folder up to her chest. With her statement and supporting articles, her letters of support from Kenya and from the Solidarity Centre, and in this outfit, it is the best she can do.

I am ready, she says.

Dalila exits Festival Court. Ears burning, her heart wedged high into her throat, as she strides out of the gate under the bored stare of the security guard. She breaks into a run, pointing her hot face into the cold wind. Her head is crawling with cicada beetles, buzzing, shrilling, filling the space inside and around her.

As if from afar, yet whispered, the questions of her inquisitors return to her.

Miss Mwathi, you suggest that the tragedy which befell your family was somehow masterminded by your uncle, a Mr Kennedy Mwathi. Do you have any proof of this theory? Something to link him to those murders? Is there anyone who can support your claim?

The handsome face of Ms Colgan reappears before her. She remembers shaking hands, and the smile on her case owner's lips. She can still feel the silence in the room while the three questioners read her statement, the supporting documents and letters of support. Then that telling moment when Ms Colgan put down the papers, lifted her eyes and something in her face closed over.

Miss Mwathi, if you suspected that your uncle had a hand in your family's murder, why did you go with him to his house? Why not go directly to the police?

Dalila slows to a brisk walk. The tower of the Science Centre points up towards the darkened clouds. She heads towards it. She remembers entering the interview room. The three of them waiting for her. The hard plastic chair. The coarse brown carpet tiles.

Miss Mwathi, in your statement you claim you were physically and sexually assaulted by your uncle. Yet, in your initial interview in Croydon, you failed to mention this? Why have you changed your story?

She sees him, her questioner. One eyebrow raised, his pen tap, tap, tapping on the desk. That is when she knew and that knowing feeling remains, lingering on her skin, in her bones.

Miss Mwathi, you came directly to the UK to seek safety from your uncle, yes? However, when you arrived at Heathrow you failed to claim asylum immediately. In fact, you said you were here for a holiday, to visit your aunt for twenty days. This was lie, was it not?

She walks, stooped towards the oncoming wind. At the top of the road she turns left into more oncoming wind. As she crosses the park the buzzing in her head becomes the swirling, rushing of wind through the trees. She passes behind the BBC building and stands on the bridge. Cold river wind from the Clyde. Cold in her knees, cold toes.

Something is not the same. A shift has happened. She delivered her report. She told her story, all of it, left nothing out, gave them every shame-filled detail. But underneath all the talking, under the questions and answers and assurances and polite tone, something had become apparent and then become something else.

Miss Mwathi, you claim you were assisted in entering the UK. Is that correct? Could you provide us with the names and contact details of the people who assisted you in getting all the documents necessary for entering the country?

Miss Mwathi, it would be helpful if you provide us with the names of the people with whom you stayed in London and the address of that flat.

Why do you keep asking me about that? I don't know anything about those people, she finds herself saying out loud.

The wind whips the water. She crosses the concrete space between the BBC and the Science Centre, alone, head bent against the wind. Now the rain comes, thick and wind-thrown, darkening the concrete with bloated full stops. Too far from home to run, she resigns to the wet, accepts the cold. All around her, rain weeps across the city.

Miss Mwathi, you claim not to know the address of the flat nor the names of the people you stayed with in London. Are you asking us to believe that, having arrived in a foreign country, you willingly went to stay with people you had never met? Indeed, you didn't even know their names?

She walks on, the rain slanting against her. Her woollen hat saturates. The wet gathers at her coat collar, slips down her back. Her sodden trousers cling to her shins. The wet seeps through her flimsy shoes and settles around her toes.

Under a tree, still rain.

All of it cold. All of it very cold.

Miss Mwathi, you have described your uncle as a volatile and violent man who kept you as a prisoner in his large Nairobi home. You claim he is an active member of the Mungiki sect. And yet you say that one of his devoted followers took pity on you and provided you with money and documents. This man helped you escape and took you to the airport. Could you perhaps describe for us, again, how all this is possible?

I don't know how it's possible, she says aloud.

Dead, damp leaves against the fence, shivering. Wet wheelie bins guarding wet houses. At the kerb she hops across a puddle.

Her building looms, the top disappearing into the grey. She clenches her house key in one pocket and her phone in the other. The phone vibrates.

Hello? Dalila?

Yes?

This is Phil, from the centre. Just checking in to see if everything is okay, because you didn't sign out this evening. Is everything okay?

I don't know.

Are you still in Festival Court? Did they detain you?

No. No, I am okay. But I think it was bad.

Your interview?

Yes. They asked me many strange questions. I think they were angry, but I don't know why. Even, I told them everything but they . . . I don't think they listened.

But you're safe, yes?

Yes. I am nearly home.

These interviews are tough for everyone. It's horrible, I know, but don't let it get to you.

She has nothing to say.

Have you got someone you can visit? Maybe chat things over with a friend or something? That might be a good thing to do.

I have a friend in my house. Ma'aza.

Good. Good. It's better than sitting in the flat by yourself all night.

She doesn't know what else to say and her silence grows across their connection.

Okay, so I'll see you tomorrow at the centre, will I?

Yes. Maybe, I will come tomorrow.

Alright. Glad to hear you're safe.

She ends the call.

Squinting against the rain, she looks up at the tower.

In the middle of the night she wakes. Did she hear Ma'aza come home? She listens for footsteps. For a long time, listening, but there is nothing. Ma'aza isn't here.

She pulls back the covers and stumbles down the dark hall to the kitchen. She pours herself a glass of water and as she drinks she becomes aware. They are here with her. All three of them. Her brother and father stand together on the balcony, staring out across the city lights and the auburn under-lit clouds hovering over the world.

Her mother is here too, sitting by the table, looking down at her hands.

In the silence, Dalila sits and stares at the shape of her own hands.

Back in her bedroom, Dalila removes her three photographs from her handbag. She squats down till her armpits rest on her kneecaps, and holds the photographs out in front of her. The first one is of her by the cook fire with her mother. In the photo, her younger self stirs the food and in her left hand she has a torn piece of cardboard for fanning the flames. The kale and onions whisper their scent to her. She remembers the day this was taken. Her father was beginning to make a little money and he had just bought a small pocket camera. He was snapping everything. Her mother thought it was a wasteful extravagance and she flapped her hand at him, telling him to point that camera elsewhere. But then she would exchange a secret glance with Dalila and try not to smile.

Dalila brings the photograph closer to study her mother's expression. There is love in her eyes, maybe a touch of playfulness too, but her arms look thin. She looks exhausted. For many years her mother worked in the flower factory, walking the long rows of flower beds inside the polytunnels, weeding, prepping the soil, cutting roses, lilies and carnations and wrapping them to be flown to Europe. That's how her parents met. She had been told the story many times. Her father drove a delivery truck and saw her mother at the gates of the compound. He had rolled down the window and asked, How could a flower be tending all these weeds? That's always been her favourite part of the story. After they got married they lived together on the compound where her brother was born. But with all the chemicals sprayed in the polytunnels her mother had developed breathing problems. There had been complications with the pregnancy and her mother was told she could never have children again. She, Dalila, was born small and fragile, with her eyes wide open. So the story goes.

That's how she got her name. Dalila – the delicate one.

These stories had been told and retold. They were facts she could easily recite. Yet, looking at the frail woman in this photograph, Dalila wonders how well she really knew her mother.

There was always a cool air about her mother whenever she met other women and children. She had a meek, straight-lipped acceptance that she had been given so few children. But hidden in this mood there lived an unspeakable longing. The silence of this longing unsettled Dalila, even as a little girl. She remembers working extra hard in school and studying every afternoon. Every year she was always in the top group of her class. She cooked and did the laundry and fed the chickens without being told to, as if to compensate for her mother's lack of daughters, as if by working extra hard, by doing the work of two daughters, she might prove herself to be twice as worthwhile.

Dalila lays the photograph on the floor and studies the next one. It's her father, as a young man, hoisting up her brother.

Did her mother take this photo? Perhaps her uncle took it. There is something so uninhibited about her father's expression. Most photos of him are too staged. He is often well dressed and serious, posing, putting forward his business self, his persona as a provider. But this photo shows a truer self, the father Dalila knew in private. He was a gentle man, good in a way that makes her proud. His arms are strong and he is clearly delighted by his son. Her brother, still just a toddler, has his arms up and his head back, completely secure in the embrace.

She remembers being held like that.

She touches her finger to her father's smile, to the gap in his front teeth. It's so genuine Dalila smiles too. She can almost hear her father's laughter. As she hears it, the giggles take over and she can't stop. Giggling breaks out of her. It's so funny and wonderful and heart-wrenching. Through the tears she sees her brother's baby face and he seems to be laughing too, frozen in his laughter, and her father is holding up his only son and they are both so beautiful, so tremendously beautiful that she can hardly breathe.

Her sadness is sudden and powerful, rising from deep in her chest, from even deeper down, choking the air out of her. She sobs and sobs. Deep, unrestrained, howling sobs, till she is emptied out but weeping keeps washing over her, eroding all parts of herself till nothing is left upright.

She wakes up and finds herself lying on the carpet. She shields her eyes from the glare of the bare light bulb. Raw misery sits so heavy in her she doesn't have the strength to switch the light off. She drags the duvet from the bed and covers her head.

In the blackness, she drifts.

She sees her brother. He is walking the path towards the bus station. When the troubles started he went straight home, but she stayed. She stayed because she had exams, because her brother was the eldest and it was his job to take care of their parents' worries.

But in this darkness all those meticulously painted lies hold no colour. There is only the truth, cold and hard as stone. And the truth is she stayed because being the best in her class was more important than being with her loved ones. She stayed because she's a vain and self-centred girl with grand dreams. She stayed because she is truly a worthless daughter. A disgrace. The pollution in her family's story.

She cries for her mother, for her dignified father and for her brave brother. More than anything she wants to go back to Kenya, to feel the sun on her shoulders, to stand at the graves of her family and apologise.

From within the folds of sleep, Dalila hears keys in the lock. The front door closes and the security chain is slid into place. Ma'aza is in the flat, Dalila thinks, and her thoughts are so stark she wonders if she spoke them aloud.

The faint voice of the TV whispers down the hallway. Dalila tries to move but her body drags with heaviness, as though each limb is bound to her but belongs to someone else. She remembers Ma'aza coming into her room and looking down at her, yet distrusts this memory. It feels more like a wish. But when she pulls the duvet from her face she notices her light has been turned off. She heaves herself onto her bed and hides under the duvet. Curling her body around the pillow, she begins sinking down, down.

In her dream she stands in a house, staring out of the window. The sun shines orange as it sets. A great leafless tree is silhouetted on the plain. In the tree sits a dog. Its ears pointed straight up, watching the house. Higher up in the tree a hyena, stooped and powerful, stalks up behind the dog. The dog sees the hyena and leaps from one branch to another as the hyena gives chase. To the other people in her house, to her family, she says, Look. I think that dog is going to fall.

And the dog falls, yelping as it hits branches on the way down. The hyena, too, loses its footing. Both animals land badly in the dust. The hyena's jaw snaps, only just missing as the dog scrambles to its feet. Limping and desperate, the dog runs towards the house for shelter with the hyena giving chase.

She stands at the window, watching them come.

Close the doors, she screams to her mother. Close the doors. They are coming.

But no sounds leave her throat.

There is a voice. She can't make sense of the words. Dalila senses a person nearby.

Ma'aza tugs back the duvet covering her face. She opens the curtains, allowing a sharp light into the room.

Come, says Ma'aza. Wake up.

Dalila covers her eyes with her elbow.

For two days, you cry and sleep, says Ma'aza. This is good. Everyone makes like this when they come to the UK. Now, crying is finished.

Dalila rolls away from Ma'aza.

I will put water in the bath, says Ma'aza as she leaves the room.

A strong wind howls outside. It buffets against the window.

Water starts pouring into the bath. Dalila covers her face with her hands. The great gnawing sadness is still with her but no more tears will come.

Ma'aza returns. She sits down on the bed and says, Come, Dalila.

I want to sleep.

I know this feeling, says Ma'aza, to sleep and sleep and wish to sleep for ever. And when you wake you sit the whole day waiting for something, you don't know what. This is a life for a plant, not a person.

Ma'aza takes Dalila's wrist and peels her hand away from her face. Later, you can sleep. Now you must come.

Too tired to resist, Dalila allows herself to be pulled to her feet and guided towards the bathroom.

The bathroom is thick with steam. Water gushes from the hot tap while the cold tap only lets out dribbles. Ma'aza tugs the cord on the extractor fan and it drones to life, then she turns up the cold tap.

When the water is ready, get in, she says, closing the bathroom door.

Dalila stares at the steam rising off the water. She feels weak, teary. A lump in her chest is making her nauseous. She can feel it with her hand, right there, above her stomach and below her ribs, right in the centre of herself, a knot or a ball that she can't massage away.

Her mother is in this room. She can feel her. Her father is here too, sitting upright on the toilet lid, waiting. They want to talk and she knows they want to ask, Why were you not at the funeral? You never said goodbye. Why didn't you say goodbye? They are waiting for her to say something. Tears well up again as she pictures her brother. The time when they were little, how they spread picture cards face down on the back step, turning them over two at a time to see if they were the same or different. He always won at that game, because he was older, but she remembers hating him for it and now she only has herself to hate.

She breathes in, deeply, trying to inflate her chest, to expand that collapsed sensation around her ribcage. She wipes the condensation off the mirror and knows she should try to calm down, perhaps go for a walk later. But she remembers Markus just standing by the sofa, staring down at her. Markus. He could be here right now, waiting outside her building. He could be right outside the front door. If she goes out Markus could grab her at any time. She won't let him take her. She will not let that happen again. She will not be taken, not by Markus or her Uncle Kennedy or the Home Office. Except there was that look on Ms Colgan's face. She can't get it out of her mind. For the whole interview that woman's eyes carried the same look. A look that says, You lied. You're a liar. You lied to us and you're lying to yourself if you think you can stay. You got yourself into this. Whatever happened to you is your own fault. You've only got yourself to blame.

The more she thinks about Ms Colgan's face, the tighter that knot above her stomach gets. It's as if each of her organs, each of her bones, is attached to a string and every string meets in this knot in her chest. When the knot turns, every part of her gets pulled in on itself.

It's your fault, she whispers to herself.

Why did her uncle stop her from going to the funeral? He didn't even tell her about it. Why? What is the point of that? Why did he even kill them? That was his family. His only family. And to do what he did to her. For what?

It's not fair, she says. Why? I didn't . . .

The anger in her is so hot, so ferocious, she wants to howl. To scream right in each one of their faces. Ms Colgan. Markus. And if she ever sees her uncle again she's going to grip his ears and scream right into his fat, disgusting face till her throat burns, till it bleeds.

She presses her palms over her eyes, squeezing her head as hard as she can. The ball in her gut turns, pulling her tighter and closer in on herself. In that dense darkness there is only space for loathing. She hates herself for being taken. For being weak. She's such a stupid idiot. And now look what's happened, she's been used up and broken. Just a useless, disgusting, horrible piece of rubbish. That's all that's left of her. Someone should throw her out, get rid of her.

She sees her mother looking at her, her father and brother too. Dispassionate faces, unblinking. Ms Colgan raises her eyebrows and looks at her. Markus staring down at her and then the face of her Uncle Kennedy right up close. His mouth open, his eyes black and depthless.

Dalila opens her eyes to make the faces disappear but all those eyes are still on her. Everything winds in tighter, strained to its very limits.

The bath is almost full. Through tears and the steam she reaches to turn off the hot tap and touches the spout, burning herself. All those faces shake their heads. Useless, pathetic. You get what you deserve. Her body reels against itself, snarled and tighter than she has ever felt, just ugly knotted slops of what she used to be.

She suddenly forces the inside of her wrist against the tap's scalding metal, pressing down on it with her other hand. Pain flashes through her but she keeps pressing down, till the faces disappear, till everyone in her head is wiped out, till all the anxiety and rage is seared into one tiny point of outrageous pain. The knot in her chest spins loose and she is released, limp and exhausted.

The pink mark on her wrist instantly starts to swell into a blister, but she can breathe again.

Ma'aza knocks on the door. Dali, you are okay? she calls. Dali?

I'm . . . Yes, I'm fine, says Dalila, trying her best to sound fine.

She undresses, lets the cold tap run for a while and steps into the bath. The water is almost too hot. She stands with both feet in the tub, her toes prickling as they adjust to the temperature.

Slowly, she sits down, keeping her burnt wrist out of the hot water, her hand still quivering in shock. She sinks her torso lower till the water touches her chin.

The waters calm. The surface becomes flat as glass, reflecting the light bulb above her, hiding her body beneath. She closes her eyes and dissolves.

Without her moving, the water tilts and runs back on itself. There's another unsettling shudder as the wind shunts against the tower and the bathwater leans and rolls against her chin.

When she has washed and dressed, she sits on her bed and pulls the duvet around her shoulders. Ma'aza knocks on her door and enters.

You feel better? Ma'aza asks.

Dalila lowers her head.

Ma'aza lays a plate on the bed. On it are two pieces of toast with slices of avocado. She holds out a mug of tea for Dalila to take.

No, thank you.

For two days you don't eat or drink anything.

Me, I'm not hungry.

Ma'aza sits down on the bed next to Dalila. I know this sadness, she says. I also cried for many days. I became too, too thin. But you cannot give so much time to mourning. Will it bring back the dead? Will it change your problems? Now is the time to be strong again. This tea is warm and sweet, my sad little sugar sister. Take it.

Dalila smiles weakly and takes the tea.

I know your interview was bad, says Ma'aza.

Who told you?

Ma'aza shakes her head and smiles sadly. Everyone has a bad interview, she says. That's how they do.

They will send me back?

Probably, they will. Too many get sent back. Who can say what will happen? But now you must wait.

For how long?

Who can know? says Ma'aza. Some wait for months, some wait for years. Nobody knows how long they must wait, but the waiting is the hardest part. The waiting can kill you before the Home Office sends you back.

Maybe . . . I deserve to go back, whispers Dalila.

Ma'aza shifts closer. Shh, don't speak like this.

Dalila's bottom lip begins to tremble. You don't know . . . what I did, whispers Dalila. How stupid and . . . and selfish.

You are wrong, Dalila.

Dalila swallows hard, trying to compose herself. My mother, she whispers. My mother said God can see everything. Even, He can see in your heart. After I was born I was very small and my mother was angry in her heart. After that she believed God gave her no more children. She always said to me everything happens for a reason.

My mother believed this too. She even cut her beliefs into all her children, says Ma'aza, running her finger down the centre of her forehead across her tiny crucifix scar. She says we are given to God, protected by Him, and we cannot be out of His love, but it is not true.

Dalila lowers her mug and wipes a finger across both eyes. Ma'aza moves the plate of toast onto the bedside cabinet and sits cross-legged on the bed.

In Ethiopia, I was in a camp for five months, Ma'aza says, like a refugee camp. People were hungry. Everyone knew great sadness. One NGO ran the camp. Sometimes volunteers would come to help. Some of these people, the white ones, they always say to us, Don't worry, everything happens for a reason. God will help you. Everything is God's great plan.

One day, goat herders bring a Somali girl in the medical tent. They find her lying in the road. Some women in the camp spoke

Somali. They speak softly to the girl and find out how she came to be here.

A militia came into this girl's village. The men raided the village for supplies, they took water. They grab her father's goat and throw it into their jeep. When her father protested they shoot him. The girl, she screamed and ran to the body of her father. The soldiers lifted her up and took her with them. They kept her for three weeks, always moving, driving here and there. When they stop they tie her to a tree or to the truck. They rape her every day and night. They broke her teeth with the butt of a rifle and used her mouth. They tortured her for sport. Sometimes they traded her to other soldiers for a night in return for a spare tyre.

I don't want to hear stories like this today, Dalila whispers.

The soldiers don't give her food, Ma'aza continues. They leave her in the road believing she was dead. She was not. In the camp they give her medical treatment but her wounds were too severe. She was double incontinent, she couldn't walk. This girl was fourteen years old.

The wind billows against the building. The room wavers. Ma'aza takes a deep breath and continues.

Every night I sit with this girl. She don't speak Amharic, I don't speak Somali, but some days you need people close without talking. She would not eat. She don't like if I touch her. So, I only sit with her in the dark. In that tent was so much sadness. I thought, What bad things have this girl done to bring her this horror? But I couldn't even invent reasons. Other nights, I think, Maybe God let this happen. Some priests say from small evils we learn small truths and when God allows great evil we can learn the deepest truths. So I thought, Maybe this girl is part of God's great plan. Everyone who knows her story will understand a deep truth.

Ma'aza shifts round on the bed till she is facing Dalila, and says, About that time, I become very angry. Because what great lesson is equal to the suffering of this child? If God says to me, You can know My wisdom but only through the suffering of one girl. You know what? I will choose safety for the girl. Every time, I would choose this. God can keep His big boss plan for Himself.

Ma'aza gets to her feet, unable to sit any longer. She says, Anyway, the next day the girl died. Most people in the camp never hear her story. Nobody learn anything. She was tortured and died for nothing. That day I knew for myself, God is a false trader. He asks for us to believe. He wants us to think He has a big plan for everything, but there is no plan. No reasons. God has nothing.

She picks up the plate with the toast and avocado, and says, Everything happens without reasons, Dalila.

She places the food in front of Dalila. Now, you must eat.

Dalila moves the plate away. I cannot.

Ma'aza reaches over and gently pulls Dalila's hand closer, staring at the raw, burst blister on her wrist. The tiny crucifix scar on Ma'aza's forehead draws Dalila in. It folds slightly as concern pulls Ma'aza's eyebrows together. When she looks up, Dalila looks away.

Avocado is good for you, my sister, Ma'aza whispers. You should eat.

Why?

To become stronger.

Why?

So you can keep going.

I go out this morning, says Ma'aza as she comes out of the bathroom. Her hair is pulled back into a tight bun and Dalila notices she is wearing her old jeans and hiking boots.

Where are you going?

Out, says Ma'aza. And you also must go out.

Me, I will stay, says Dalila. It's too cold out there.

No, says Ma'aza, you will fight. Remember, I told you, they want for you to stay inside and be alone. You must fight them, not with stones but with your life. You go out because they want you to stay inside. Walk, because they want you to be weak. Talk to people, because they want you to be alone. If you want to survive this place, you must move.

Ma'aza pulls a leaflet from her back pocket and gives it to Dalila. When I come to Glasgow, I went to this place. It's good. Many people go there and they give free lunch.

Dalila reads the leaflet and looks up at Ma'aza. English classes? For me?

It is conversation class, not only for learning, says Ma'aza. The people are nice there.

Dalila pushes the paper away. I don't need this.

You cannot wait here, you will get sick, believe me, says Ma'aza. You must go out. Use your days.

Ma'aza pushes the leaflet back towards Dalila. Come. Get dressed. The class starts in one hour. Come, come.

Dalila presses the buzzer on the door frame of the YWCA building. She peers through the door's frosted glass and sees a wide-hipped woman shuffling towards the door.

Oh. Hiya, says the woman. Can I help you?

I have come for the . . . the English conversation class.

In you come. Ma name's Gemma.

Irene, says Dalila as she shakes the woman's hand.

The building has a stuffy warmth. It smells of dusty carpets and baby food. Blue-and-white-striped wallpaper reaches up past an old chandelier. Gemma moves behind the small reception desk at the bottom of a curling staircase. Posters cover the walls, most featuring pictures of women. Happy groups of women, bruised women, women in shadow. The words on the posters rush at Dalila. *Women's Aid. Mother and Toddler Group. Women's Asylum News. Introduction to Yoga. Domestic Abuse is a Crime. Fair Trade.*

She looks back at the door and imagines herself simply walking out. Leaving. She doesn't need an English class.

Gemma slides a ledger towards Dalila and asks her to sign in. Now, remember to sign out again when you leave. The class is upstairs, says Gemma, first on your left. You'll see the others waiting outside the door.

The wooden staircase creaks under Dalila's steps. The banister has been rubbed smooth by the grip and slide of a million fingers. At the top of the stairs stand five women. Dalila stands with them. In silence, they wait. One woman, dressed all in black with a black headscarf, holds a baby boy in her arms. He is absorbed with a pink Post-it note which is stuck to his fingers.

Leaflets, children's drawings, taxi numbers and handwritten notices decorate a large cork noticeboard. To avoid looking at the women waiting with her, Dalila reads the posters pinned to the wall. *Rape Crisis. Thursday Cooking Class. Girls on the Move Leadership Courses. Positive Body Image Campaign.* The flat eyes of the models on the posters stare straight into the camera, straight at her.

The door opens. Twenty or more women pour out, talking excitedly, stretching their arms into coat sleeves, carrying handbags, grocery bags and umbrellas. The push of people forces Dalila against the wall as they brush past her without acknowledgement.

When the class has emptied, the women waiting in the corridor file in. Dalila follows. It's cooler inside the class. Large sash
windows let the heat from radiators escape. Four tables have been
pushed together in the centre of the room, surrounded by black
plastic chairs. Two towers of chairs stand stacked in the corner.
She notices a flipchart leaning against the wall, a fire extinguisher,
paint flaking from the corner of the ceiling.

The other women sit down around the tables. No one takes
off their coat. The woman in black sits with her son on her lap
and starts pulling paper and crayons out of her handbag. The
child grabs at the crayons and immediately tries shoving them
into his mouth. Next to this woman sit two giggling girls in
multicoloured headscarves. The three of them appear to be sitting together. Their unconscious comfort with each other gives
Dalila the feeling that the woman in black is, somehow, the girls'
chaperone. At the top of the table sits an older woman with
meticulously styled bronze hair. A Chinese-looking woman flips
open a palm-sized electronic dictionary and begins prodding
the keys with her index finger. Perhaps this woman is Japanese?
She can't be sure, having only ever met two people from the
Far East.

Dalila chooses a seat close to the door, sits and tugs her
sleeve down over the bandage on her wrist. The only sounds
are the child scrunching paper, the tapping of buttons on the
dictionary's keypad and the hush of traffic outside. She lowers
her head, sure she's made a mistake coming here. Better to be
in bed, than this.

Sorry I'm late, says a woman as she hurries into the room,
weighed down with a handbag, a bottle of water and an armful
of folders. She goes to the far end of the table and props up the
flipchart. Is this the teacher? Dalila wonders. Teachers usually
dress up, don't they?

An African woman comes in.

Hello, Constance, says the teacher. Could you please close the
door?

Constance shuts the door and sits next to Dalila.

Well, says the teacher, unbuttoning her coat, it's lovely to see you all again. And it looks like we have a new face joining us today. What is your name?

Irene.

Well, Irene, it's lovely to have you here. I'm sure you'll be made to feel welcome. We're all very friendly here.

The entire class stares at Dalila. The bronze-haired woman gives her a nod.

Have you been to an English class before? asks the teacher.

No. But I learned to speak in my country.

Where are you from?

Kenya.

And, so, where did you learn English?

In school. From my grandparents. Everyone speaks English in Kenya.

Really? I mean, right, of course. The teacher blushes. So, why have you decided to join us today?

Dalila hesitates. The honest answer is shamefully exposing. She knows why she is here. It's the same reason Ma'aza dragged her out of the flat this morning. It's why she stalked the neighbourhood repeatedly looking over her shoulder in case Markus was around while staring at the pages of the *Glasgow A–Z* hunting for the YWCA. It's why she can't sleep and then sleeps too much and then struggles to get out of bed and why she never feels hungry and why the tears come. She has lived with it, but never forced herself to say it.

I came . . . for conversation.

Okay. Lovely. Excellent. That's why we're all here, says the teacher, rubbing her hands together. She nervously tucks her fringe behind her ear. Well, why don't we start with a wee warm-up? Turn to the person next to you and for five minutes let's use *who what why where when* questions to get to know each other.

The three Muslim women huddle together and begin to debate who should go first. The Asian woman shuffles her chair closer to the bronze-haired lady. Instead of turning her chair Constance slumps across the table and props her head up with her hand. She sighs and says, What is your name?

Irene.

Where do you live?

Flat seventeen two Iona Court, Ibrox, Glasgow.

What is your favourite colour?

Um, blue?

What is your date of birth?

The twentieth of December, nineteen ninety-four.

Where is you come from?

Dalila's throat tightens. It's always the same list of questions. Housing staff, the Home Office, hostel owners, everyone demands the same list of facts. The more she answers these questions, the more she feels the truth peeling away from her replies. Where does she live? She sleeps at the same address, but does she *live* there? What is her true name? Why is her date of birth so important?

Where is you come from? Constance repeats.

Where *do* you come from? says Dalila.

No. Me, I'm asking first.

Okay, but you must say, where *do* you come from?

Constance sits up. I said like dis, where *do* you come from?

Dalila folds her arms. Debating the issue is too depressing. Me, I come from Kenya, she says.

How many children you have?

None.

You are married?

Dalila stares out of the window at the last leaves on the branch fighting the stiff breeze. She lowers her eyes at Constance. No, I am not married.

The teacher claps her hands. Okay, everyone. Once the first person has asked the questions, remember to switch around and let the other person do the asking, that way everyone gets to practise.

Okay, ask me, says Constance.

I thought this was a conversation class?

If you ask, we have conversation.

Fine, says Dalila, giving up. Are you married?

Yes.

Does your husband live with you?

No, he stay in Congo.

Do you have children?

Yes. Four. Three boys and one daughter.

Where are they?

Through her heavy Congelese accent, Constance explains. The bigger boys is with they father in Congo. The other one, he is four and half years and my baby girl, she is two. They are downstairs in crèche.

Fifty questions sprout in Dalila's mind all bidding to be asked.

Constance continues, My husband say he is coming soon. Money is a problem. Maybe next year, he come.

The teacher claps her hands again. Okay, everyone, can I have your attention? Well, that was a nice little warm-up. Now, if you can all face the flipchart we can move on by reviewing some grammar. Does anyone remember what we were doing last week?

The bronze-haired lady raises her hand, while glancing at her notes. The present continuous tense, she says.

Very well done, says the teacher. That's right. For the past few weeks we have been studying the present continuous tense. We've learned how to make positive and negative statements and how to form questions.

Who can give me a positive sentence using the present continuous tense?

One of the Muslim girls puts up her hand.

Yes, Aiesha? says the teacher.

The baby is eating the paper, replies Aiesha. The two girls burst into giggles. Everyone smiles at her choice of sentence. Dalila finds herself smiling too.

Perfect, laughs the teacher. She writes it on the flipchart and turns to the class once more. What is the verb in that sentence, Aiesha?

Eating.

Good. And the auxiliary verb?

Um . . . is?

Very good. We know that to make a present continuous sentence you must use an auxiliary verb, and add –ing to the action verb.

Now today we are going to learn *when* to use this tense, says the teacher. She draws a diagram on the flipchart.

PAST -------------| NOW |------------- FUTURE

The teacher points at the diagram and explains. We use the present continuous when referring to what is happening now, this very second. For example, we might say, *I am breathing*. Or another sentence could be, *I am sitting*. We can also use this tense to describe temporary states. For example, we could say, *I am reading a book*. Now, you might not actually be reading at exactly the same time as you say this sentence, but it still refers to a short time in the past when you started reading the book and assumes you will finish reading it in the near future. Do you understand?

Dalila suspects the teacher is speaking too quickly and too technically for the level of English she is teaching, but everyone nods their heads, eager to show that they are keeping up with her.

The teacher continues. So, it is a temporal state. The present continuous refers to positive or negative actions that are unfinished.

Dalila stares at the word NOW, hemmed in by parallel lines. Cut off from the past and the future. Shut in on itself.

So, who can give me another example of a present continuous sentence? asks the teacher. Anyone?

Sentences of temporary, unfinished states flash through Dalila's mind.

Dalila is living in Glasgow.
Dalila is waiting for the Home Office to decide.
Dalila is spending her day alone.

How about you? says the teacher to the bronze-haired woman. Can you think of a sentence?

The bronze-haired woman thinks and replies, I am enjoying this class.

Very good. Well done. Anyone else? How about a negative sentence?

Dalila isn't eating properly.
Dalila isn't sleeping.

The woman in black answers, I am not standing up.

Excellent, says the teacher. How about some more examples?

Dalila is trying not to give up.

Dalila isn't crying today.

Me, I'm speaking every day English, says Constance.

Well, you have the right idea, smiles the teacher. But just say, *I am speaking English.*

I said like this, I . . . am . . . speaking . . . English.

Good, says the teacher. Any more examples?

Dalila is sinking.

Okay, why don't we form two groups and discuss what we plan to do for the rest of the day. This is a perfect way to use the present continuous tense. Especially for short-term future arrangements. For example, I have theatre tickets for this evening so I can say, I *am meeting* my friends at 5 p.m. We *are having* a few drinks because we *are celebrating* my sister's birthday. Then we *are watching* the show. See how this works? Why don't you try?

As the other students arrange themselves into two groups, Dalila raises her hand. Excuse me, she says to the teacher, where is the bathroom?

Downstairs and on your left, says the teacher.

Dalila stands up, loops her bag over her shoulder and leaves.

At home, Dalila goes straight to bed and sleeps for the rest of the afternoon. She wakes, groggy and stiff, and waddles to the bathroom. Sitting down to pee, she blows her nose at the same time, wondering if perhaps she is catching another cold. When she stands up, there is blood on the toilet paper. She blinks and stares into the toilet, then checks her crotch. It's here. She hasn't been regular for over a year, not since her uncle took her. When was the last time? Three months ago? Four? But here it is again, it's back.

She glances at the missing bathroom tiles before staring back down into the bowl.

Lifting onto her toes and splaying her fingers, she quickly presses the latch on the toilet and watches everything get flushed away. All that's left is clean, white porcelain.

She washes her hands and face when something rushes over her, a feeling of being drawn down, of her whole self being flushed clean. She sits down on the edge of the bath and bursts into tears, sobbing out a horrible weight she forgot she had been carrying. Right after the relief comes delight. Sheer, sparkling delight at being free. Her giggles gurgle out amongst her tears as she wipes the back of her wrists across her eyes.

No baby, she whispers to herself.

No matter what he did to her, there will be no baby.

When Ma'aza arrives home she dumps her backpack on the kitchen table and pulls out two frozen pizzas, a bottle of Pepsi, crisps, salsa and a large tub of Asda's own-brand vanilla ice cream.

Where did you get all of this? asks Dalila.

Ma'aza undoes the bun at the back of her head. She rakes her fingers across her scalp and shakes out her hair till her loose curls spring out in all directions. Tonight, my little sugar sister, we get fat, fat, fat, she says, snapping her fingers and throwing her hips.

Try this one, she says, passing Dalila a Tunnock's teacake.

What is it?

Ma'aza raises her shoulders. It's like a . . . a sweet. It's very good. Try.

Dalila unwraps the foil and holds up a half-dome of chocolate the size of a small pomegranate. How can I eat this?

You just . . . Ma'aza gestures for Dalila to shove the whole thing in her mouth.

As Dalila bites into it, the chocolate shell collapses, sending sweet white marshmallow paste over her chin and fingers.

Ma'aza bursts out laughing. Is good, huh? Ha ha, you have some on your nose.

Dalila grins with her mouth full and wipes the back of her hand across her nose.

Tonight, we eat and laugh, says Ma'aza as she turns the oven on and peels the wrapping off the pizzas. I got this DVD in the market. We can watch tonight. It's about these two American women, they are police, and the fat one is funny.

Okay, says Dalila, picking up the DVD and trying to read the badly printed sleeve notes. I can make some tea?

No, no, says Ma'aza, wagging her finger. You Kenyans always want tea. But no, tonight we make coffee and popcorn, Ethiopian style. You sit on the sofa. Go. Turn the TV on and take these nachos.

Halfway through the film, the two of them are slumped side by side on the sofa. Ma'aza's feet are up on the coffee table. Now and again her hand dips into the bowl of popcorn on Dalila's lap.

So the class was good? Ma'aza asks.

What?

The English class. Did you go?

I went there, says Dalila, keeping her eyes on the TV screen.

And the people are nice?

Dalila shrugs and pops some popcorn into her mouth.

Ma'aza watches the movie for a few minutes and then says, Dali, did you stay till the end of the class?

There is no answer. Ma'aza sits up and opens her eyes wide in mock shock. She says, You didn't even stay, I know it.

Dalila tries to fight the smile coming to her face but she can't. It was too boring, she laughs. I couldn't stay. I tried but I couldn't.

Ma'aza sighs theatrically but her smile betrays her real mood. She grabs a handful of popcorn and tosses it into Dalila's face.

Dalila approaches Daniel's tower. The bonnet of a car is open like a basking crocodile. Daniel is bent forward, leaning into the mouth.

Men bent over cars – same.

He looks up, gives her a quick wave.

I will come back tomorrow, she says. You are busy.

No, please, says Daniel in Kiswahili. I am almost finished. I would be honoured if you kept me company. But don't get too close, everything here is dirty.

My father loved cars, says Dalila. He was always fixing them.

I think I would have liked him, says Daniel, sitting down on the ground. He reaches his arms into the machine, feeling for something.

How are you, my sister? he asks.

Okay. Dalila sighs. Some days are better.

I haven't seen you. What have you been doing?

Nothing, says Dalila, just walking.

Only walking? Oh, but you should see people, too. Did you try an English class?

I tried one, but . . . Dalila leaves the rest unsaid, not knowing how to explain it.

Some weeks are difficult for me, too, says Daniel. He stands up and wipes his hands on a rag. There have been many days when I did nothing, he says. In those times, I become unfamiliar to myself, an old man who gazes at the TV and waits for the rain clouds to pass.

Dalila suspects he is saying this just to identify with her, to make her feel better. She can't picture Daniel slumped indoors.

Every time she meets him he is busy, motivated, facing the world unafraid.

But today is not one of those days, he says. Look at us. We are out. There is peace. And the sun is . . . Daniel squints up at the sky. Well, the sun is probably shining in Africa.

Dalila smiles. Yes, Africa has stolen all the sun from this place. We are guilty of that.

My sister, have you eaten? asks Daniel.

I will eat at home, she replies.

Well, I am going to my favourite food van. It is full of Scottish food. Would you like to join me? You can add the experience to your *different* list.

I have no money for this.

I have a little money. I will treat you and you can repay me by keeping this old man company.

Daniel bends over a bucket and scrubs his hands with a nail brush. He throws the water out across the lawn and dries his hands off on his trousers. He locks up the car, puts on his hat and they set off.

Dalila strolls, making sure Daniel can keep up. A light drizzle starts and she keeps her hands warm in her coat pockets.

So you have had your interview? asks Daniel.

Yes.

And so now you wait, he says.

Yes, now I wait.

How do you feel about this?

She wants to say that she is fine and she knows everything will be okay. Instead, she lets his question rest with her.

I feel . . . I don't know, she says. I see myself alone in a great desert. I can see for many kilometres in all directions and everything is flat. I don't know which way to go. All directions are the same, they all go nowhere. So sometimes I think, Why continue? Why not just stay here?

Hmm. Yes, says Daniel. I believe you see the world correctly. It doesn't matter which path we choose. In the end, we are all going to the same place. The emptiness you feel will always be there. I feel it too. It is there for everyone. If you pretend it isn't there, it is there still. Better to make friends with it, stay in it. It is simply a feeling like joy or anger or boredom. If you become familiar with it, you can watch its approach, unafraid, and accept its embrace with grace.

Dalila looks over at this old man, surprised by him.

But I believe your questions are confused, says Daniel, more as if he is talking to himself than to Dalila. When you ask, *Why go on?* It cannot be answered. There are no clear directions. So we are left with how to proceed. How to go on? says Daniel, jabbing his middle finger against the open palm of his hand. Now that . . . that is the interesting question. Maybe if we know *how* to continue, we glimpse *why* we should continue.

Her father always had a plan, that was always evident. He was always preparing for the future and counselling her and her brother to choose their paths and stick to them. But Daniel? This old man is different and less like her father than she first thought.

We should stop here, says Daniel, leading Dalila by the elbow across the street towards a van.

One entire side of the van is flipped open and propped on poles to create a stiff awning. She notices that the inside of the van has been converted into a little kitchen with a hob, deep-fat fryer and fridges. There's a small glass counter housing chocolate bars, drinks and pink-glazed doughnuts. Beside the counter a small printed menu has been taped to the panelling.

So this must be their version of street food, Dalila thinks. No wonder she hadn't seen any until now. She had been looking for open charcoal fires and hawkers selling roasted corn on the cob and goat sausage or some sugar cane to nibble.

Street food – different.

They huddle under the awning as the rain picks up. Faint aromas of hot cooking oil and burnt sugar comes from inside the van. Inside, a large, bald man turns to look at them. Afternoon, Daniel, he says, wiping his hands on his apron.

Big Chris, my friend, says Daniel, shaking the bald man's hand. How is that Toyota? Is she behaving herself?

Aye, good, says Big Chris. Been running it to Paisley and back every day. Never had any bother.

I told you. Those ones are the most reliable cars, chuckles Daniel. One day your son will be driving it.

Well, mibbe. We'll have to see about that.

Last year I sold a car to this gentleman, Daniel explains to Dalila. He turns back to the man in the van and says, This is my good friend Dalila. She has recently moved to this neighbourhood.

Big Chris reaches over and shakes Dalila's hand. Good tae meet you, luv.

He places his elbow on the counter and leans heavily on it to relieve some of the weight from his legs. Some weather this, aye?

Yes, Daniel replies, but me, I like rain.

Well then, you're in for a treat. Forecast says it'll be like this till the end of the week.

Rain is good, says Daniel. Scotland is too lucky.

Lucky? Big Chris smirks. We've been called many things, but I'm no sure about lucky. Big Chris places both hands on the counter and raises himself up. So what can I get yous?

Daniel turns to Dalila and asks her in Kiswahili, Have you ever had a bacon roll?

What is this? Dalila asks.

It is a Scottish delicacy and this particular establishment prepares the best bacon rolls in the entire country. You must try one. It is my treat. But I wouldn't try the tea. It's like Kibera sewer water.

Okay, says Dalila, trying not to smile, no tea.

Daniel orders two bacon rolls.

Right you are, says Big Chris. You wanting yer rolls soft or crispy?

Soft, please, says Daniel.

They wait, watching gutter water flow down the side of the street. The smell of frying bacon drifts out of the kitchen van behind them. It's a deep and marvellous smell. Dalila swallows the saliva gathering under her tongue.

Daniel cleans his glasses with a paper napkin and looks out at the rain.

So, asks Dalila, trying to adopt the tone of their previous conversation, how do you know . . . how to . . . ?

Daniel nods, appearing to understand what she is trying to ask. It is only a simple thing, he says, but an easy thing to forget. Ubuntu reminds us *how* to live. You know about Ubuntu?

It's a word from her childhood. A word often said, but rarely emphasised. Yes, I know this word, says Dalila. I think it means sharing, or kindness.

It is about sharing, of course, Daniel nods, but the true meaning is higher. Ubuntu says, I can only be okay if you are okay. I am, because of who we all are. Do you understand?

Dalila nods, unsure.

My sister, Ubuntu is simply a way of being. If your efforts are used to give value to others, it will bring purpose and dignity to yourself. Be like this, and you will possess the hours you live.

You wanting sauce, Daniel? asks Big Chris.

Yes, please.

Red or brown?

Brown for each one.

The man squirts brown sauce on each roll, wraps them in paper and hands them over. He returns to leaning forward on his elbows. Daniel places enough coins on the counter.

That's perfect. Cheers, says Big Chris.

The rain comes on heavier. Daniel and Dalila eat under the canopy to keep dry. As she chews she studies the bacon in disbelief.

I told you it was good, smiles Daniel.

It's really good, she says, taking another bite. This is not like the bacon in Kenya. She wipes the sauce from the corner of her mouth and sucks it off her thumb. I like it. What kind of sauce is this?

Daniel shrugs. It is brown sauce.

But what is it made of?

A mischief plays across Daniel's face. It's made of brown things.

She takes another bite and peers out into the rain. A car drives slowly by and comes to a stop. The reverse lights flick on and the car comes back towards them, stopping across the street. With the bacon roll poised in front of her mouth, she watches the rain water dribble down the car's metalwork, the windscreen wipers sweep and pause, sweep and pause.

The door opens and Markus gets out. His eyes are fixed on her, but he makes no effort to approach. He just stands in the street, arms dangling at his sides, rain soaking his T-shirt, and glares at her.

She drops her roll and steps behind Daniel, ready to run, sure she can outpace him if she bolts now. A twist of nausea tightens in her. Unable to swallow, she spits out the mouthful of half-chewed sandwich.

What is it? asks Daniel.

That man, she says in Kiswahili. Daniel, we are in danger, big danger. We must go. Right now.

She pulls at his sleeve and, for a moment, thinks of leaving him, just running off by herself, ducking and weaving between the flats and warehouses of the neighbourhood. But she finds herself holding on to Daniel's coat, unable to abandon him.

Who is that? says Daniel.

He has come for me, whispers Dalila. He is Mungiki.

They both stare at Markus. Markus holds their gaze, unaffected. Behind him the car is still running. The driver's-side door is wide open, causing an alarm to ping pleadingly for its driver to return.

Markus takes two steps forward to the middle of the road. He pulls out his phone and holds it up towards Dalila. She sees the flash as he takes her photograph, and then another flash.

Mr Big Chris, says Daniel. Please, call the police. Now.

Leaving his umbrella, Daniel limps straight out into the street, stopping a few feet in front of Markus. Daniel lifts his own phone and takes Markus's picture.

Markus's only reaction is to lean his head to the side, keeping his gazed fixed on Dalila.

Dalila strides out into the rain behind Daniel, surprising herself, aware of how fearless she must appear. But what looks like courage is in fact worry. She can't help herself, she has to protect Daniel. She shoves her hands into her pockets to hide how much they're shaking. As she arrives behind Daniel she hears him say to Markus, You have no power here, young man. You should go home.

Ho, you, shouts Big Chris as he marches towards Markus. Is that your car, aye? It's parked in a loading zone, mate. I've had to call the polis. You better get a move on, afore the cops get here.

Markus glances back at his car and then up and down the empty street. He leers at Big Chris, measures up his size. Big Chris doesn't break his stride, forcing Markus to take a step back and then another. Aye, and I see you've parked in front of a fire hydrant an awe. That makes you a fucking fire hazard. You parking that car there's put ma business in danger, mate. And I fucking hate being in danger, you get my meaning? So better get yer arse in that motor and fuck off.

And he does. Dalila watches him get in the car and slowly drive off.

Are yous a'right? asks Big Chris.

Dalila and Daniel look at each other. Dalila is shaken but since Daniel seems quite calm she tries to act calm too.

'Mon then, says Big Chris, I'll drive yous home.

The only sound from the outside world is muffled shouting from neighbours in the flat below. The mute grey TV screen waits in front of her. Time is rough and gritty this morning. Every second scours across her. How long has she sat like this? Three days?

Her senses momentarily sharpen and the details in the room become hyperreal. The groove she has nervously rubbed down the centre of her thumbnail, the nacho crumbs resting in the fibres of the carpet, the dust between the buttons on the remote control, the synthetic lemon scent on her hand from the washing-up liquid.

A brooding gulps down through her stomach. How unexpected, how unforeseen her life has become. Everything is off. This trapped freedom. This safe danger. This full emptiness. Are any days supposed to unfold like this? It's like living with her uncle. Only, in this town, she is her own captive.

Maybe Ma'aza is right? She has to get out. So what if Markus is out there? Moving is living. The time is now. It is time. Time to take the bus.

Rain spatters across the bus-shelter roof. Dalila stands in the corner, up against a poster of a white family on a sunny beach. With a blue marker pen, someone has drawn a moustache on the father and a pair of drooping breasts over the mother's yellow bikini. A cartoon joint hangs from the little son's mouth. No matter how deep into the corner she presses her shoulders the wind finds a way of flinging raindrops at her.

Four other people wait with her. An Asian woman, an old woman with a walking stick and two teenage boys, both with their hoods up.

The four of them stare at the crest of the hill.

The Asian woman and the teenage boys were waiting when Dalila got here, while the old woman arrived only a minute later. This means, according to British etiquette, Dalila is fourth in line. Even though the old lady is her elder by at least forty years, Dalila reminds herself that, in this land, queuing is more important than age.

The bus arrives. Its sides are covered in a wet grey-brown silt splashed up from the city traffic.

Dalila lowers her head against her upbringing and steps in front of the old woman. The driver is patient and helps her find the exact fare from the change in her hand. She moves down the humid aisle scanning the bus for a safe seat. Most people sit alone on a seat for two, staring at their phones or out of the window. No one acknowledges her as she walks up the aisle. No one offers her a place to sit. She claims the only empty seat opposite the two teenage boys, sits down and wipes the condensation off the inside of the window with her sleeve.

The engine revs and the bus lurches forward. Outside, a woman runs towards the bus, holding down her hat, handbag swaying at her elbow. She flaps her free hand at the wrist. The woman's eyebrows are highly arched and her overly red lips make a neat circle as she shouts, Stop. Whether the driver sees the woman or not, Dalila isn't sure, but the bus doesn't slow. The woman's thin eyebrows sink downwards and her red mouth flattens.

Near the front of the bus, a young woman holds a child. A man raises a newspaper, opens the back page and lowers it to read.

It is good to be out, to be going somewhere. Dalila wonders if Muthoni is riding the bus right now too. She pictures her in a matatu somewhere in the Nairobi gridlock and then she wonders about Markus. Is he driving around the city? Is it just him or are others looking for her? Should she even be going out today? This is madness.

The teenage boys on the seat next to her snigger and snort as they watch something on a phone. The closest boy has no lips. His mouth is neat as a slit in a papaya. Yet his nose is wide as a finger, built like a wall down the centre of his face, and flush with his forehead. His eyes sit deep in his skull under a canopy of eyebrows. He must be able to see the bridge of that nose at all times, Dalila thinks. What must it feel like to hide inside his face? Turning her head to the window, she crosses her eyes trying to see her own nose, but the space in the centre of her face is almost flat. She stares down at the out-of-focus orbs of her nostrils.

The boys snicker and tap the small screen to upload another clip. The one closest to the window is skinnier than the other. His nose curves down and ends sharply with two upward-facing slots for nostrils. It's an elegant, delicate feature but Dalila worries about his breathing. Perhaps he has to draw hard, as if he has a permanent cold? That's probably why he is so thin. Not being able to breathe easily would mean he struggled to run and play with the other children, preventing him from growing strong.

The boy nudges his friend and whispers. Dalila realises she's been staring at them and turns her head towards the window.

Ho. You, says the bigger boy. What you gawking at?

A movement catches the corner of her eye. Instinctively, she looks. The boy places his fist on the seat next to him and uncurls his middle finger.

She turns away, her heart thumping against her chest. She rings the bell and scrambles down the narrow aisle.

Paki bitch, says the boy. They both snigger as she hurries to the front of the bus.

The bus stops. Dalila gets off, praying the boys don't follow her. They don't.

The bus pulls away and through the mucky windows she sees the boys preoccupied with the phone as if she had never been on the bus at all. Her heart beats fast as she looks back up the road from where she has come. Though the drizzle has stopped, the sky seems thick with gathering rain, a sign that has always warned her to seek shelter. Yet all around people go about their day, content to live as usual in this foreboding and deepening dark. She wants to be like them. To live, unaffected.

She turns her face into the wind, towards the city. The air is brisk and clean against her skin. She chose to come out, to feel the life and rhythm of the city around her, to be part of it. But to stay out, she'll need to continue making that choice moment by moment. She takes a deep breath and steadies herself on the exhale.

They were only boys, she whispers to herself, just boys.

Putting one foot in front of the other, she lowers her head and strides into the wind.

She walks, moving her limbs to the cadence of her heart. Moving for the rhythm of it, enjoying the simple mechanics of one leg swinging past the other, each golden shoe planted and uprooted in turn. The pavement rolls beneath her, while shop windows, fences and graffiti pass beside her. One moment unfolding into the next.

She crosses a river and, checking her map, confirms it is the same river that flows by the BBC building. Soon she finds the city's heart, a shopping district with imposing old buildings and very modern shopfronts full of brands she recognises. There are shopping plazas and fast-food outlets, buses and cars and thousands of people moving about the streets. She wants to explore it all and email each exciting finding to Muthoni. But for now it's enough to know it's here. Instead, she follows the broad brown river named Clyde.

She walks and she walks. A calmness comes to her along with thoughts of her brother. The faces of her mother and father appear. They are close for a while but they float off, finding their own way. Then she sees her uncle, standing in the room she had to live in. She remembers his hand on the back of her neck forcing her face down across the table. She picks up her pace a little, striding out, worried that if the dark thoughts come, they might rise up and crush her. Yet somehow the walking focuses her more completely into herself. These memories are as potent as before, but as long as she keeps walking, they seem less cohesive, they slip off her, unable to find their usual purchase.

She keeps placing one foot in front of the other, in front of the other.

By the time she gets home, she knows she has found something. Something she can cling to. A thing that is herself.

A text arrives from Ma'aza.

> **Dali. U have money? Buy milk eggs green onions. Tonight we make omelette.**

Dalila pulls on her jeans, her golden boots, her black puffer coat, her black woollen hat and gloves. Grabs her purse and keys and locks the front door behind her. After shopping she could go for a walk by the river. This will be her day, shopping and a walk.

The landing smells of disinfectant. A new, violent scrawl of graffiti decorates the lift's metallic doors. She presses the down button and waits for the lift. The lift arrives with a ping. She steps in and presses G.

As the double doors begin to close a hand wedges in and pulls them apart. A man and a woman join her in the lift. Her neighbours. She has seen them go into the flat next door to Mrs Gilroy, but she has never spoken to them. They both wear white tracksuits. Blue Kappa stripes run down his sleeves while hers has a yellow V shape across the chest. They stink of alcohol and speak to each other in loud slow voices as if they are deaf.

Dalila slips to the back of the lift, avoiding eye contact.

The doors close. The man goes to press the G button but it is already glowing green. He sways very slightly and stares at Dalila with his head tilted to the side. The woman licks a tiny piece of paper and sets to building a joint with her fingertips. He mumbles something to his girlfriend. Dalila looks at the floor.

You fae Africa? says the man.

The woman taps the back of her hand against his chest. Leave her alone, Mick, she says.

It's a'right. I'm no doing anything, just talking. He turns to Dalila. Where're you from? From Africa? You from Nigeria?

Dalila stares at her gold shoes, her breath beginning to rise in her chest, her leg muscles tightening.

Here, I'm no meaning anything, by the way, says Mick. I'm no meaning . . . See me, I don't care where you come from. I'm just making conversation here.

Just leave her be, Mick, c'mon, says his girlfriend.

I'm *just* talking to her.

Dalila's hands start trembling. She clenches her fists and forces them down in her coat pockets.

The man leans in a little closer. His face is red with drink and he seems older than his clothing suggests. Mid-thirties.

I'm Mick, that's Alison. What's your name? Go on, tell us.

Irene.

Irene? he says, glancing at his girlfriend to see if she heard what he did.

Yes, says Dalila.

No way, man. That's ma mum's name, he laughs. Ally, d'you hear that? She's got ma mum's name.

Aye, I heard it, Mick.

Put it there, love, says Mick, offering his hand.

Dalila flinches and stiffens against the wall. They are only at the tenth floor. The surface of this man's face seems friendly but it's difficult to read the deeper parts of him. She looks at the woman, who is absorbed with building her smoke. Dalila takes the man's hand. It is sticky and cold. He clasps her hand in both of his and shakes them up and down.

Right then, Irene. Nice to meet you, by the way. Here, you're no a Rangers fan, by any chance? He grins at her.

I . . . I don't like football.

Aye, well, if you did, you'd be Gers fan. A True Blue. Best team in the world. Definitely. D'you get Rangers on the telly in Africa?

I don't know.

Where are you from again?

Kenya.

Kenya. Kenya. Right, aye. See that Obama, he's fae Kenya, is he no?

He is half Kenyan, says Dalila.

Mick keeps his grip on her hand. Listen here, Irene, says Mick. Want to know something? I'm fae Africa too.

What you on about? says Alison. Bloody Africa. What are you like? She leans in and whispers to Dalila, Don't listen to him, hen. He's a bit pished.

No, really, says Mick. See, I know things. See if you go right back to the cavemen, afore them even, right, right into history, to the first people. The very first were from Africa. It's true. I seen it on the telly. We came from Africa. You. Me. Everyone. 'Cept for Alison, she's fae East Kilbride. He laughs sweet, beery breath into Dalila's and Alison's faces, expecting them to join in.

Alison rolls her eyes and says, Mick, you're a fuckin bawbag. She licks the end of her joint and tucks it behind her ear.

The lift stops at the third floor. The doors roll back and Alison tries to step out, but Mick holds her back with one arm.

This isn't us, he says.

As he pulls Alison back into the lift he nonchalantly switches his grip on Dalila, holding her by the wrist.

We're going all the way down, he says. Right to the bottom.

The doors close. Dalila imagines herself running, jumping out between the doors and racing up to her flat. But Mick's grip is firm, his mood volatile.

Right to the very bottom, Mick mumbles to himself. Here, Irene, you got a job? he asks.

No.

Aye, me neither, he says. See what I mean? Both fae Africa, both got nae jobs. We're the same, you an me. You got a telly, Irene?

Yes.

Aye, me too. A big telly. What about a toaster?

Yes.

Really? Is it new?

I don't know.

You don't know? Mick broods on her answer for a moment, then says, Right well, answer me this. Have y'got a washing machine?

Yes.

Bet that's new. Am I right?

Maybe it is a new one. Me, I don't know, says Dalila.

Bet you've got a microwave an aw, don't ye?

Dalila lowers her head. She glances at her arm in his possession.

Aye, yous've got aw that stuff, he says. Fuckin right you do.

The lift stops and the doors open. Dalila is first out, tugging at her arm but he won't let go. His grip tightens, hurting her.

C'mon, Mick, leave her alone, says Alison, pulling at Mick's tracksuit. C'mon, let's just go. Let's go.

Get off us! Mick shoves Alison back while keeping his grip of Dalila.

Don't fuckin push me, ye fuckin prick, shrieks Alison, as she stumbles drunkenly against the wall. She steadies herself and lurches at Mick again.

Get off, Alison, or I'll fuckin do ye. I mean it.

Just leave her alone and let's go, she says.

I'm just *talkin* to her, he roars.

Please, says Dalila, her trembling now visible.

Please what?

Please. The tears break loose and roll down her cheeks. I don't want trouble.

C'mon, Mick, let's go, Alison screams at him.

Shut the fuck up, Ally. Mick wipes the heel of his hand across his mouth and focuses through the alcohol at Dalila. He lets go of her wrist and spreads his arms wide so she can't get by. We're just talking, right? Just a proper conversation, okay? Then I'll let you go.

Dalila backs up against the wall and wipes her cheeks.

Right, so, says Mick. Answer me this, he steps towards Dalila but doesn't touch her, see your spankin new washing machine and your wee toaster. Who gave you that?

Dalila whispers, Nobody.

Don't fuckin lie to me, Irene. You've no job, so you didn't *buy* that stuff, did ye?

No.

No, you didn't. He puts his face right up to hers. So who did?

Dalila swallows hard and makes herself answer. When they put me in the flat everything was there.

Aye, that's right, says Mick, grinning. *They. They* gave you it. *And* a bed *and* new carpets *and* a toaster *and* flowery fuckin curtains. *They* gave you that too. Am I right?

Dalila nods, her tears flowing easily now.

So yous come here wi nothing and yous get a sofa and a nice wee bed. But me? Me and Ally have lived here wer whole lives and we get nothing. Fuck all. Now I'm asking you, Irene. Is that fair?

I don't know about these things, she says very softly.

Aye, you do know. It's an easy question. Is. That. Fair?

No.

No, he says, backing off. No, it's fuckin not. You think about that, by the way.

Alison grabs his sleeve and pulls him towards the main exit.

See you later, Irene, calls Mick, as the two of them stumble out into the wind.

Dalila covers her mouth with both hands. She tries not to make a sound, tries to hold it in. She jabs the up button and waits for the lift to arrive. When it opens a family spills out towards her. She turns, pushes through the fire-escape doors and starts running up the stairs, she keeps going for seventeen floors, right to the top.

At her front door she fights with her keys, breathing hard, barely able to stand. She looks over her shoulder, feeling they are right there. That they might rush up behind her at any moment. The key fits, the door opens and she slams it shut behind her, bolts it, flicks the bolt on the Yale lock, clips on the chain and peers through the spy hole. The landing is empty. Her legs tremble with adrenalin till they can't hold her, and she slumps to the floor.

A knock at the door startles her. Dalila holds her breath, certain the drunk man, Mick, is banging on her door. She hasn't seen him since yesterday and never wants to see him again. Is he drunk, trying to get in? Another knock. It's softer, almost hesitant. Maybe it's Mrs Gilroy? Or Paul from the Housing Association, but Paul never knocks.

Dalila approaches, placing one bare foot carefully in front of the other. She listens. Someone is out there. She hears movement. A whispering.

The knock comes again, more deliberate this time. Dalila freezes in the hallway. She knows she should just go back to her room and ignore whoever is outside. If the knocking continues she'll look for the number to call the police.

Dali, shouts Ma'aza, from the bathroom. Who is at the door? If Paul is there, say he must go away. He must fix the heater in here or leave us alone.

Dalila moves closer and peeps through the spy hole. Olcay's face bulges in the lens.

Hello? calls Dalila.

Hello? comes Olcay's voice. Hello . . . is . . . Olcay.

Dalila opens the door a few inches.

Hiya, says Parla, the oldest daughter. My mum wants to know if it's alright if we stay with you for a bit 'cause she's got to report and my dad is at computer class and hasn't come back yet.

Dalila looks at the two girls and then at the mother.

My mum thinks it's safer if we stay with you while she signs. We've got homework to do and stuff. We won't bother you.

Little Rosa grins up at Dalila and says, I've got colouring to do. Two whole pages.

Dalila unclips the chain and opens the door. Come in, please, she says.

Olcay talks to Parla and Parla quickly translates for Dalila, saying, My mum says she'll only be away for an hour. She's gonna text my dad and tell him we're here. He might be back before she is. She says thanks for looking after us.

Thank you. Thank you, says Olcay, taking Dalila's hand.

It's okay. It's no problem, says Dalila, feeling quite enthusiastic about having the girls in the flat with her. Please, you are welcome.

The girls run into the flat as Olcay pushes the lift button. Dalila glances around the landing before closing and locking the door.

When Dalila comes into the kitchen she finds the girls standing side by side staring at the room.

Who is that? says Rosa, pointing at the photographs Ma'aza has taped to the wall by her bed.

Those are not mine, says Dalila. There is another lady who lives here too. Those pictures are her family, I think.

Where is the lady?

She is in the bathroom.

Oh.

What happened to your arm? asks Rosa.

Dalila glances at the bandage around her wrist. It's nothing. It just got burned . . . an accident.

The girls stare at her.

Her mind rummages for a diversion. What would her mother do? Who wants to have snacks with homework? she asks.

Me, shouts the little one, hopping on one leg. Me, me, me.

Okay, if you start your homework, I'll make us all snacks.

Rosa crumples to the floor, opens her schoolbag and spills pencils and crayons across the green carpet. She is soon kneeling and colouring with focused effort while her sister sits at the kitchen table and opens her books. Dalila looks through the cupboards while the girls work. There's a couple of apples and a single Mars bar. She slices them up and arranges alternate slices of chocolate and apple around a plate.

Ma'aza enters wrapped in a towel with another around her head. Dalila and the two girls are sitting on the carpet in the middle of her room. Dalila is reading aloud from a story book while the girls squish chocolate slices between their fingers.

Ma'aza's hands go to her hips. She dishes Dalila a flat, ice-cold stare.

They are the children from next door, says Dalila.

I know who they are.

Are you the lady what lives with Irene? asks Rosa.

Yes, I am. I am Ma'aza.

Irene is reading us a story.

I can see, Ma'aza replies.

I think Ma'aza is a bit tired, says Dalila to the girls. Who wants to finish the story in my room?

Me, me, says Rosa.

Dalila gets up and says, Before that, we must tidy up all these pencils and put them in your bag. Okay?

While the girls repack their school bags, Dalila drags Ma'aza into the hallway. I'm sorry, she whispers, but the mother just brought the girls. She said her reporting time was changed. What could I do?

Ma'aza sighs through her nose. How long will they stay?

Dalila glances back towards the kitchenette. I think one hour, maybe. The father might come for them. I'm sorry, Ma'aza, I didn't mean . . .

Is okay, says Ma'aza, flicking away the apology with the back of her hand. They like you. I can see. Better for them to stay here and not be alone next door.

Dalila nods. Yes, I will keep them away from your room.

Is okay. Really, is okay, says Ma'aza. I am not angry, only tired. And the children are good for you. Is okay.

In her bedroom, Dalila sits on her bed with her back against the wall. The girls sit either side. As she is about to continue the story, Rosa asks, Why have you got no hair?

I have hair. But it is just very short.

Do you cut it all off?

Yes.

Can I touch it?

Okay.

Rosa climbs up onto Dalila's lap and her fingers reach out and explore Dalila's scalp.

I like it, she says. I want hair like yours.

Dalila laughs and says, And I wish to have hair like yours.

Maybe we can swap? says Rosa, grabbing handfuls of her own hair and leaning towards Dalila's face.

I know, says Parla, you stand behind her and put your hair over her head.

At this, all three of them get giggly. Rosa jumps up and stands on the bed behind Dalila, placing her cheek on top of Dalila's head, allowing her thick wild curls to flop down across Dalila's face.

Parla lets out a snort of laughter and reaches for her phone.

Take a picture. Take a picture, squeals Rosa.

Dalila is almost limp with laughing as she arranges the hair down one side of her face, and for a moment she can feel the laughter's pull threatening to tilt over into tears. But it doesn't. The shutter sound clicks on Parla's phone as she takes one photo after another, while Dalila's emotions settle.

Let's see. I wanna see. Show me, says Rosa, leaping off the bed and grabbing for the phone. She hoots and flops to the ground, rolls onto her back in fits of laughter. Show Irene, she insists, show her.

Dalila takes the phone and looks at the screen. A smiley woman with black hair all across her face stares back. A thin, uncertain woman she hardly recognises.

When Olcay returns, her face is flushed. She rubs warmth back into her knuckles as her eyes dart around Dalila's flat looking for her daughters.

I will make tea, says Dalila.

Rosa gets off the bed as soon as she sees her mother and hugs her thighs. But Parla waits in the doorway, studying her mother.

Dalila offers tea again, looking to Parla to translate.

After exchanging a few words with her mother, Parla turns to Dalila and says, We have to go. But my mum says you're welcome to come and visit with us.

Yes, okay, says Dalila.

The four of them move next door as mother and daughters negotiate over something until it feels to Dalila like a plan for the evening has been formulated and each of them knows their tasks.

Dalila sits at their kitchen table as Olcay sets the kettle to boil. She watches Olcay move around her kitchen, placing chicken thighs to roast in the oven, chopping vegetables and rinsing utensils. She works with fervour, as if to distract herself, or perhaps to assert herself so solidly into this kitchen that everything outside becomes distant.

From the bathroom comes the sound of water running into the bath and the girls talking busily to each other. Soon, Parla comes through into the kitchen carrying an armful of dirty laundry. In English she says, Rosa is having her bath. Is there any juice left?

She shoves the laundry into the washing machine. Then she opens the fridge door, gazes at the shelves and closes the door again.

For the first time this evening Olcay slows down. She wipes her hands on a dishcloth and leans her hip against the counter. She chats with Parla, but soon her mood becomes more intent and her voice lowers so the little one in the bath can't hear.

Dalila watches, wondering if she should even be here, but the feeling of being included in a circle of women who are discussing important things is a feeling she can't walk away from.

Is everything okay? she finds herself asking Parla.

Parla twists her mouth in a manner which indicates things are difficult and there are problems with no easy answers.

We've been refused, she says.

Dalila looks from daughter to mother, not exactly sure what they mean.

Last week they refused our claim, says Parla. They said we have to go back to Turkey. Yesterday they changed the reporting times for my parents and they stopped giving us money. Everybody is upset because we cannot go back. My sister was even born here.

Olcay sits down at the table. It's clear she understands more English than she speaks. She says something to her daughter in Turkish. Parla looks at Dalila and says in English, My mum wants to thank you for looking after us this afternoon.

It's no problem, says Dalila. You have lovely children.

Olcay nods her thanks. She says something else to her daughter and Parla translates, My mum thinks that when they change reporting times, it's a sign. It means they want to get us out of the country.

Parla listens to her mother again and then says, That's what they do. It's like a trap. They change the reporting times to after school hours, so the mums have to show up with their kids and then they take everyone together. They'll put us in a van and take us to the detention centre. After that, it's a plane to Turkey. It's happened like this before to other families. My friend at school, Jamilah, they did this to her family and now they are back in Somalia.

The mother talks and the daughter listens and then says to Dalila, Mum wants us to stay with you when she signs, if that's

215

okay. It's safer. They won't deport the parents and leave their children behind.

Dalila nods. You are welcome any time. Please, any time.

For a moment the three of them sit and look at each other. All three smile as they listen to little Rosa talking to herself in the bath. It surprises Dalila that she has been trusted with so much so quickly. What will you do? she asks.

Olcay understands the question without it having to be translated. She explains through her daughter that, apparently, nothing can be done. Their solicitor has appealed but she holds little hope for a positive outcome. They refuse almost everyone and recently there are stories of dawn raids happening again.

What is this? says Dalila.

Here Parla answers directly without waiting for her mother to speak. It's when the Immigration people come into your house, she says. They come early in the morning, and break the door and take everyone away. My other friend, they also took her. I phoned her in the detention centre and she told me everything. She said they came early, lots of them, and they all looked like police or the army. They woke everyone up and made them get dressed and put them in the van. They drove far, to England somewhere, and put her whole family in detention. She said they put handcuffs on her father and after a while his hands swelled up and he couldn't move his fingers.

Olcay explains something to Parla and points for her daughter to translate. My mum says the Immigration always come in winter, says Parla. They come early, early in the morning because they know the whole family will be at home. Now some people are even sleeping on the stairs. You know the stairs next to the lift?

The fire escape? asks Dalila.

Yes. They stay there all night, listening for the footsteps. It's very cold and sometimes we bring them tea.

What happens if they take you back? asks Dalila.

Parla shrugs and says, We can't go back. Also, I have exams soon so I have to stay for that.

Olcay looks directly at Dalila and starts telling her story. Parla translates every word. My dad is a good man, she tells Dalila. Every day of his life he gets up early, washes and shaves, and gets dressed for work. Even in this country he gets up and puts on his suit and goes out. My mum says he is dignified. He gave a home to his wife and education to his daughters. He worked at the airport in Turkey, checking deliveries from all the different planes. He was a customs officer. One day some co-workers in the airport told him to sign for crates that were not on the list. They asked him because my family are Christians. These men said they knew his address and they knew he had a daughter, so it was best if he signed.

Parla tells the story with dispassion, suggesting she has told it many times before. My father refused, she goes on to say, because of his honour. He went to his manager and filed a complaint and he informed airport security about these bad people.

The next morning, Parla translates without glancing at her mother, when we woke up my father's car was on fire. He called the police but they could do nothing. When he went to work they threatened him. His boss told him he should just sign the papers and don't worry about nothing. But my father wouldn't sign.

Olcay's hands tremble as she speaks and Dalila feels the force of this woman's story moving into her own heart.

Two days later, we found a cat and a kitten in front of our house, both females, their bellies split open.

Dalila glances at Parla as she translates these details. The girl shows no reaction, concentrating only on the sentences flowing through her.

My father took our money from the bank and bought a new car and my mum packed clothes and photographs into our suitcases. In the night, we drove away. We drove all across Europe, because it was not safe to fly from Turkey. My uncle lives here, in Glasgow, so we came to stay with him. When we arrived here there was not much room to stay in his flat. He said we must claim asylum, because they will help us. So now we are here.

Dalila nods, not sure what to say next. Where is your father now? she asks.

I think he is at computer class, says Parla. He always goes out, to English class, to the library to use the internet, or to sit with the other men at the cafe.

Olcay talks, as if to herself. Parla translates anyway. My dad is sad. He says it's his fault that we are here, and because of him we all suffer. He wants to make everything okay. But he can't do nothing because it's not safe to go back and he can't work. It is very bad for him here.

Rosa calls from the bathroom and her mother calls back. Giggling, Rosa comes running into the kitchen with a towel around her shoulders, her hair is wet and flat against the sides of her face. Olcay stands and starts complaining in Turkish and Rosa whines and darts out of the kitchen, leaving little wet footprints on the linoleum. As Olcay goes to check on the little one, Parla turns to Dalila.

We are worried for my father, she whispers. He is a good man . . . but he is so sad. Mama believes he might go back to Turkey alone, to make it safe for us. But if he goes . . .

Parla glances towards the noise in the bathroom and turns back to Dalila. I am scared for my father.

Dalila counts thirteen days of rain. Thirteen days without sunshine. Some days, spits of moisture hang stationary in the air. Other days, rain drenches the city.

Every day she walks. Hands stuffed deep into her pockets, hat pulled down to her eyebrows. She squints this way and that, watching out for Markus or a shape that might be him. But every day she walks.

She sometimes takes Ma'aza's umbrella, sheltering under its hood, and there are days when, believing the pale sky holds no rain, she ventures out into the wind clad in her puffer coat and woollen cap, but returns damp nonetheless.

Nothing changes. Sameness is the way of things. One day resembles the next with yawning openness.

She walks to Festival Court twice a week and sits in the waiting room for hours with others of her kind before swiping her ARC card. She walks to the Post Office in the semi-deserted mall and collects her money.

For a while, Muthoni is her sunlight. Every morning there is a new Facebook message waiting for Dalila. They type furiously, telling all there is to tell until her time runs out and she has to leave the library. But after many afternoons of typing, Dalila finds that all the telling is told and the replies from Muthoni get shorter. Some days Dalila finds herself sitting alone at the computer flicking through Facebook photos. Each picture is a window to a life she used to love and wants to have again, but also a reminder of how removed she has become.

In the park, she tramples on rusted autumn leaves sprinkled across the tarmac pathways and she moves across the green grass between old trees, running her gloved finger across their bark, and on good days she senses their ancient calm wash down on her.

The overpass above the motorway is her favourite place to stop. Leaning on the handrail she stares down at the cars. Three lanes of white headlights coming towards her, while across the central reservation red brake lights glide off in the opposite direction. All in perfect rows. All neat and obedient and so unlike the chaos of Nairobi city driving.

In the supermarket, she touches the unusually small fruits and vegetables, trying to decipher their readiness. She buys milk and tea and bread and crisps and apples. Apples were a rare treat back home but here there are boxloads of many varieties, and they are always good. On her way home she passes the crumbling tower block with its internal wallpapers exposed to the elements. The crane scrapes and nibbles at the masonry and she marks its daily disassembling.

She walks to the city, where the friendliness of the people is apparent. They smoke and talk outside the pub entrances. They call to each other across the street. Friends sit side by side in coffee-shop windows and show each other things on their phones.

In the city square, she sits on a bench like a tourist, or an elderly person, watching the people with purpose move from one necessity to the next. The square is paved with red tarmac. Statues and ornate buildings stand in silent decoration. Not a single tree or bush or flower bed is to be seen. Only the pigeons, pecking at the concrete, remind her of the natural world.

In the noise of it all, she is silent.

The people are foreign to her and their histories and struggles are hidden. What she knows of them may be different from what is there. Sitting in this square, her home feels remote and dream-like and among these pale faces she struggles to recall the face of her own mother, her father.

She doesn't sit for too long, always feeling the need to keep walking.

From the city centre, she takes the path along the river named Clyde. The water never noticeably flows in any direction, boats rarely cut across its wind-chopped surface, but the river has presence, a brown-grey stillness built on curling currents of profound power. The proximity of water changes people. Cyclists give a quick nod as they pedal on against the wind, and some pedestrians, the older ones, even say a brief hello. The air carries a mulchy scent of seaweed and engine oil and rainwater rests in the straight furrows between the paving slabs.

She walks on and on till she loses herself or feels she has got to know herself, and on longer walks she wonders if losing and finding might be the same thing.

Dalila opens her eyes, fully aware of herself, her senses poised. The dark blue predawn enters between the curtains. The threads of a dream linger, waiting just behind the door of her thoughts. She tongues her lips and turns onto her side, wrapping the blankets tighter across her shoulders, rearranging the pillow under the curve of her neck.

Outside, in the hallway, the lift door opens with a *ping*. The fire-escape door on the landing also creaks open. Footsteps climb the stairs, but the placement of each foot is too deliberate, too careful.

Dalila raises her head.

Shuffling, perhaps whispering, comes from outside the front door.

She holds her breath to sharpen her hearing.

An open hand slaps the door three times.

Immigration! shouts a male voice. Open the door. Open the door!

In a burst of panic, she scrambles, wrestling with the bed-covers, knocking her glass of water on the floor. She trips, her chest slamming to the ground. Winded, she rolls backwards under the bed till she's pinned against the wall. She tucks her knees up to her chest, the muscles in her neck pull rigid. The bed springs suspended just above her face.

Immigration! We know you're in there, right, so open up. Open the door!

A scream comes through the wall, the sudden noise having frightened little Rosa. The officers hear this too and the door-slapping becomes prolonged and vigorous.

You *have to* open the door. This is Her Majesty's Office of Home Affairs. We need to talk to you. Open the door.

Dalila's heart hammers against her chest, blood pumps up her neck, through her ears, dampening the sound of the door being bashed. She twists the blankets around her fists, clenches her teeth.

We are not going to hurt you. But if you don't open the door we have the authority to force our way in. Open the door. Now!

She doesn't answer, she can't. The water glass lies broken on its side, the carpet around it dark and wet. Maybe, if she keeps silent, they will give up and go away. Will they believe she isn't home? If she stays silent, they might move on to the next case, and perhaps, in time, forget about her altogether.

She shakes her head, angry at herself for daydreaming. They are coming, Dali, she says to herself. What will you do?

The urge to run is powerful, to move quickly, with purpose, fully in charge of her own body, her own direction. But the front door is blocked and the back door leads to a small balcony seventeen floors up. Perhaps she could climb, or jump, across to a neighbour's balcony? She imagines the freezing morning air rushing through her nightdress as her bare feet balance on the railings. If she could make it down the stairs and out, her feet carrying her across early-morning streets and football fields and through the woods, she would just keep going, settling into long strides. She would run for miles.

A fist pounds the door. Then the voice, Open this door!

She wants to try the balcony. Her breath comes in short gasps, her arms won't stop quivering.

The door to her bedroom opens. Dalila squeals, kicks, pushing herself deeper into the corner under her bed.

Dalila, my sister, don't be afraid. It's me, Ma'aza, she whispers.

The bare feet approach her bed.

Dalila? Where are you?

Ma'aza touches the mattress. She kneels down and looks under the bed.

It's okay. Don't be afraid.

Dalila exhales, short and sharp. What's happening? she asks. Will they take us? As she speaks the tears rise in her throat.

Ma'aza places her finger to her lips. Shh. They only take one family at a time. Today, we are safe. We are safe.

Dalila looks at her, but doesn't move.

Ma'aza points to her ear, then to the wall. Together they listen. They hear crying, children wailing, words called in Turkish.

They come to take the Erdem family, says Ma'aza.

The officers bang the door three more times and stop. This time the sound is easier for Dalila to discern, it's not her front door being hammered, but the one right next door. The Erdems' front door. Screaming, pitched with fear, comes through the walls. A child's screaming. To Dalila's ears it sounds like little Rosa. There is more banging on the door. Then a voice from inside the neighbours' flat calls out.

Okay. I . . . open . . . door. Just wait.

It's Olcay's voice. Hoping to hear more clearly, Dalila turns onto her back, staring straight up through the darkness at the faint criss-cross of bed springs.

We . . . get . . . dress, she hears Olcay say.

No. You open the door *right now*! We aren't going to harm you or your family but it's important that you open the door immediately.

Shuffling and movement come from inside their flat. A frantic, hushed energy seeps through the walls as Dalila's mind races to make sense of the sounds. Is that bare feet running down the corridor? A cupboard door being slammed? Whispering? Something heavy being moved? Sobbing? She thinks she can hear Rosa crying.

This is your last warning. If you don't open right now we are—

Okay. Okay, says Olcay. We . . . no . . . make trouble.

For a second, a breathless silence exists, everyone is listening. The sound of the Yale lock and then the chain being taken off the latch.

A stampede of boots rushes into the small flat, forcing their way down the corridor from the front door. Many voices are talking at once. Shouting. Barking orders at the family. The voices of male and female officers carry over the sobs and cries from Rosa and her mother. It's impossible for Dalila to work out how many people are moving around in that cramped living space. She imagines the officers stepping on toys, opening cupboards, looking through the bathroom cabinets, checking the contents of the fridge, opening curtains.

Ma'aza reaches under the bed and touches her on the shoulder. It is okay, she whispers. It is safe. Come out. She motions for Dalila to crawl to her, out from under the bed. Come, she says.

Slowly, Dalila drags herself free from the tangle of bedding and pulls herself out from under her bed. As soon as she is out, Ma'aza embraces her. They stand together in the darkness. Dalila's toes grip the thin, coarse carpet. She allows her arms to ease themselves straight. She spreads her fingers, sensing the room, feeling her way to the next move.

We are safe today, Ma'aza says. You understand? They only take one family at a time. We are safe. So be strong, my sister.

Dalila tries to control her trembling and nods. Maybe we should leave?

No, says Ma'aza, we stay. We don't go out. We can hear everything better from this room.

They sit down on the bed with their heads near the wall. Through the chaos of sounds and movement, certain phrases punch out with clarity.

. . . We are representatives of Her Majesty's Office of Home Affairs and we have orders for your immediate removal . . .

. . . Get dressed . . .

. . . note, there *are* children on the premises . . .

. . . Where's your father? . . .

. . . I've got a minor through here . . .

. . . Calm down! . . .

. . . No! No phone calls . . .

I want . . . phone . . . my solicitor, Dalila hears Olcay demand.

We are holding your mobile phones for the meantime but they will be returned to you. Besides, it's Sunday. You understand

Sunday? Yes? Your solicitor won't be at work today. Now come, put some clothes on.

. . . Where's your father? Where's Mr Erdem? . . .

. . . No, don't pack anything. You can't take your bags, just get dressed and come . . .

There is more banging, scuffling, closer this time.

Parla, the oldest daughter, suddenly shrieks, Get away from me! Don't touch me!

Her voice is clear, close, inches away. Only cream-coloured paint, stippled wallpaper and cold concrete separate them. Parla's voice is angrier, more assertive than her mother's.

Leave me alone! she screams. We didn't do anything. Why are you doing this to us? We didn't *do* anything. You can't do this to us.

A Scottish woman's voice shouts back, Miss, if you keep kicking we'll be *forced* to restrain you. Now, *stop* crying and try to calm down. You're going to be fine. We're taking you back to your *real* home.

I can't leave now. I have exams at school and everything.

Just get dressed and come quietly.

Take your hands off me! screams Parla. I want to go to my mother.

No, first get dressed. It's cold outside.

I want my mother. Mama! Mama!

Be quiet, shouts the Scottish woman officer. If you don't calm down you'll be the first one out the door, right? And you'll sit in the van by yourself till your family's ready. Do you understand?

Silence.

I said, do you understand? The voice is angrier now.

Yes.

Right, well, take off those pyjamas and put on some proper clothes.

Okay, close the door, says Parla.

No. The door stays open. Officer Mackenzie and I have to stay with you while you put your clothes on. Quickly now!

I hate you! shrieks Parla. You are all dogs. Less than dogs!

This is your last warning, miss. Keep your voice down. Here, put these on. And you better wear this too, it's bitter out there and you've a long journey ahead of you.

Other voices start shouting now, with renewed intensity from deeper in the house.

Ma'aza grabs Dalila by the hand and leads her to the front door. The voices are louder here. Ma'aza places her splayed fingers against the wall by the door. She rises onto her tiptoes, arching the pale undersides of her feet, and moves her eye very close to the spy hole. No part of her touches the door. She balances and watches.

The sound of officers' voices and boots squeaking on the tiles come through the door. Then Dalila hears Olcay's voice on the outside landing. She hears the lift *ping* open.

Ma'aza turns around and says, They take the mother and the little one. Look.

Dalila edges towards the front door. She places a hand on the wall and peeks through the spy hole. For a moment the fish-eye lens distorts the landing and the people right outside her door but her vision quickly adjusts. Olcay and Rosa aren't there. Five male and two female immigration officers are discussing something. They look like police, with their black uniforms, bulletproof vests and handcuffs glinting on their belts. One woman is holding a clipboard. Their body language is nervous. A plump officer is pointing at the clipboard and telling the others what to do.

The door across the landing opens and Mrs Gilroy steps out, dressed in a pale blue dressing gown and slippers, her white hair wild and uncombed. She has Toby in one arm, who starts barking incessantly.

Yous should be ashamed o yersells! she says, pointing her finger at the group of officers. The lot o you! It's a disgrace what you're doing to that family. An absolute bloody disgrace! These are decent folk you're messing with. It's no right what yous are doing.

A female officer turns to her and says, Ma'am, we understand you might be upset, but this doesn't concern you. Please return to your home.

Toby barks and barks.

It bloody well does concern me! These are my neighbours. They're good people. You cannae just burst in here and do this to them.

Calm down, ma'am, says the female officer, raising both hands as if to push Mrs Gilroy back into her flat. If you wish to lodge a complaint you are free to send a letter to our Brand Street offices. But you need to lodge your protest peacefully. You will be charged if you interfere with our operation. The officer keeps moving closer and closer to Mrs Gilroy as she speaks, forcing the old woman back into her flat.

Oh, you'll be hearing my protest right enough, shouts Mrs Gilroy, as she backs into her flat. It's no right what's going on here. This is a free country!

Two officers exit the flat, trying to manoeuvre Parla into the lift. She lurches towards her flat, clawing at the door frame, screaming, Baba! No, Baba! Baba, please!

The officers prise her fingers loose and hoist her up by the armpits, dragging her out. Kicking and thrashing, she breaks free and scrambles back into the flat, howling, Baba, Baba, no!

What is happening? asks Ma'aza.

Dalila moves away from the spy hole. I don't know. They are trying to take Parla, she says.

Let me see, Ma'aza demands. She places her face against the spy hole, not afraid this time to touch the door. She watches for a few seconds.

Sounds of shouting and crying and shuffling push through the wooden door. Dalila places her hands on her face and listens. She picks out Parla's voice but loses it among the other deeper voices.

The shouting escalates and then, oddly, there is a change of tone. The barked orders become a heated discussion. It is difficult to pick out phrases but Dalila senses something isn't right. Their energy has shifted from aggressive to anxious.

Ma'aza quickly turns to her and says, Come.

They run through their dark flat to Ma'aza's room. Mr Erdem is shouting, his voice getting clearer as they approach the kitchenette, and then the balcony. Dalila can make out the threat in his voice. Ma'aza peels back the curtain on the balcony door and tries to see what is going on. The officers' voices are more distinct.

. . . come with us, sir . . .

. . . Mr Erdem, there's no need to get upset . . .

. . . quick, somebody grab him, for God's sake . . .

Ma'aza opens the door and frosty air rushes into their flat.

What are you doing? whispers Dalila, grabbing Ma'aza's arm. Don't go out there!

Ma'aza looks at her and calmly says, Is okay. She steps out onto the balcony, her flannel pyjamas rippling in the wind.

The voices from next door are very clear now.

. . . you better get the bloody fire service on the phone. Call an ambulance too, just in case . . .

. . . he's taken a freaky . . .

. . . Mr Erdem, we need you to calm down. No one is going to hurt you or your family. . . .

Ma'aza places both hands on the railing and leans over slightly, trying to see what is happening next door. The sky is lighter now but the sun has yet to rise. The tower block across the street is a violet silhouette. Black birds move across the navy sky.

. . . Sir, I am asking you to please step inside . . .

Mr Erdem is talking wildly in Turkish, switching now and again to English. Stay away! I do nothing wrong.

Ma'aza is peering more intently over to their neighbours' flat and Dalila finds herself stepping out onto the cold concrete balcony floor. She places her hand on the railing and sees the ground swim seventeen floors below. Leaning out, she peeks around the panel dividing the balconies. Mr Erdem is straddling the railing, his bare left foot planted firmly on the balcony, his right dangling free. Many of the people in their tower block have woken up. Heads appear from the windows and balconies above and below.

More shouting comes from inside the neighbours' flat. Parla is sobbing and crying for her father. Baba! Baba, please!

Somebody get her out of here! shouts an officer.

Leave my child! shouts Mr Erdem. He moves to go to his daughter and at the same time the arms of officers reach out to grab him and pull him in. Everyone is shouting. Mr Erdem fights the officers off and struggles free. He swings his other leg over the rail and everyone backs off.

. . . whoa, calm down. Just relax, sir . . .

Only his bare toes balance on the balcony, his fingers clutch the railing.

Go away! Go away! Leave my family! he shouts.

. . . Okay, Okay. Sir, just calm down . . .

A siren sounds in the distance.

. . . That's the Emergency Services on the scene . . .

. . . Thank Christ. Right, everybody just back off . . .

The blue lights of a fire engine flicker in the distance as it races along the road. When Dalila turns back to look at Mr Erdem he has moved. He is facing out, balancing on his heels, his arms stretched out behind him holding the railing.

. . . Mr Erdem, just remain calm. This will all be over in a minute . . .

I don't go back to Turkey! shouts Mr Erdem. They will hurt my family, my girls. We do nothing bad.

On the ground below sit the two white vans waiting to take away the family. Officers on the ground stare up. A few residents in their dressing gowns stand on the lawn, looking and pointing up. The officers move them back and start creating a perimeter. The wail of the fire engine siren calls across the morning. Mr Erdem looks out at the horizon towards the place where the sun will soon rise.

Ma'aza turns to Dalila. This is bad, she whispers. Very bad.

The fire engine approaches their tower block, another one is coming along the road followed by two police cars.

Mr Erdem doesn't look down. He lets go with his right hand. He touches his mouth, his forehead, and lets his hand drift up to the fading stars. Then his left hand lets go.

He falls.

He makes no sound.

The wind rushes through his clothes.

No one, not a single person, can breathe.

Wind.

A hard wind.

The squawk of seagulls.

Sirens and screaming.

Hysterical screaming.

And the squawk of seagulls on the wind.

Each sound distinct. Each with its own weight, drawing closer. The wind, the screaming, the sirens, the squawks, converging and growing louder and higher, into horrific harmonies rattling in Dalila's skull. She feels dizzy from the screaming, the awful, hysterical screaming. The world blurs.

You okay? says Ma'aza. Hey. Sister. You okay?

Dalila throws herself towards the kitchen counter and vomits in the sink.

Ish! Ma'aza jumps back, checking to see if any got splashed on her pyjamas.

Dalila heaves again, but nothing comes and she slumps to the floor. When the room returns to focus, she finds herself on a chair. Ma'aza turns on the tap and rinses the sink and then offers Dalila a glass of water.

Drink, says Ma'aza. Breathe and drink.

Ma'aza returns to the balcony and leans over the railing. She glances left and then right, looking far off towards the horizon. She twists, leaning over backwards, peering up at their own building.

Dalila has to look. She rinses her mouth, spits in the sink and then rinses again. Still holding the glass of water, she steps back out onto the balcony. An icy wind gusts up against the side of the building and her toes splay and rise off the freezing-cold concrete. She reaches for the railing and looks down.

The body lies face down on the lawn near the car park.

Like a sleeping man.

No blood.

No mangled limbs.

People in uniform edge towards the body, taking little steps, as if not to disturb him. Finally, a man kneels down close to Mr Erdem's face and places two fingers against his jugular.

Residents, out in their dressing gowns and slippers, gather closer. Everyone looks. People in the crowd cover their mouths, some put their hands on their heads. In turn, each face gazes up, open-mouthed, at where this body came from.

The body just lies there.

Dalila waits for him to twitch, half expecting Mr Erdem to get up, dust off his clothes and apologise to the police. But he continues to lie there, face down.

This is bad, says Ma'aza. Believe me, is bad.

But Dalila can't believe. She can't believe he is gone. That is Mr Erdem lying on the grass. It is his body, not a dead body. That is still him. He is right there.

Ma'aza sucks air through her teeth. Bad, bad, bad, she says. We must move. Now.

She grips Dalila's arm and pulls her back into the kitchenette. Come. Get dressed, she says. We have to get . . . Hey, Dalila. Look at me. We *have* to get ready.

For what?

I don't know. Anything. The police, maybe they come here to ask their questions. Maybe they can evacuate this floor, say we must all leave. We must get ready now.

Running to her bed, Ma'aza scoops a pair of jeans off the floor. She steps out of her pyjamas and, hopping for balance, steps into the jeans.

Go, she shouts at Dalila. Get dress. Now.

Dalila rushes to her bedroom and throws on her warmest clothes. She takes two ten-pound notes from her purse and slips one into her bra and the other into her sock. The rest of the change she leaves in her purse. Her family photos, Home Office papers and extra underwear all get stuffed into her handbag. She runs into the bathroom and grabs her toothbrush, a bar of soap, moisturiser. Ma'aza moves along the hall and the front door opens and closes.

Dalila steps into the hallway. Ma'aza? she calls.

Nothing.

Ma'aza, are you here?

She goes to the front door and peeks through the spy hole. Officers. Police.

She checks Ma'aza's room. Nothing.

She steps out onto the balcony and sees that someone has pulled a sheet over Mr Erdem. The fire engine's red light sweeps across the shocked faces of the onlookers. Police are sectioning off a large perimeter with tape and there are more white vans now, and police vans with wire mesh across the windscreens. Over to the side, she spots Ma'aza walking towards the scene with her long, determined strides. Ma'aza pushes her way to the front, right up to the tape. She looks at the body for a moment and then lifts her face up. Dalila can feel Ma'aza looking at her. Knowing Ma'aza would have picked her out among all the other residents huddled and watching from their balconies.

She waits for a wave but Ma'aza lowers her head, shoulders her way through the crowd and marches off towards the city centre. Dalila runs to her room, slings her bag over her shoulder, snatches her keys and runs back to the balcony to get one last look at the direction Ma'aza is heading. But she can't see her. She traces the empty streets but Ma'aza has disappeared.

Where will she go? Dalila thinks. Who would she go to? She thinks hard about all the people Ma'aza knows. Tries to predict the most likely places Ma'aza would visit, but she has no idea. And in failing to come up with answers a deeper answer gradually opens inside her. She has no idea where Ma'aza goes or who she knows or what she does while she's away. She doesn't know Ma'aza at all. There has only ever been the sense, the assumption, that Ma'aza is busy doing something.

From somewhere comes a muffled ringing. She checks her phone but it's not that. The ringing continues, coming from elsewhere. She checks Ma'aza's bed, lifts the duvet, the pillow, looking for a phone, but finds none. She checks the coats hanging by the front door, the pockets. It sounds like it's coming from her bedroom. A long urgent trill, then a pause, before another a long, questioning trill. The sound comes from near her bed. Dalila stares at her bedroom wall. The ringing is coming from there. It's the Erdems' phone from next door, ringing and ringing, refusing to go unanswered. The officers talk in lowered voices and still the phone calls out.

She stands in her bedroom staring at the wall, wondering what to do next. The ringing stops and, for a moment, the only sound is her own blood pulsing and pulsing.

The phone starts up again, shrill and insistent.

Dalila splashes water on her face and rinses her mouth. The bitter taste of vomit still lingers. She brushes her teeth with shaking hands, working the bristles hard against her gums and never daring to look at herself in the mirror. She spits, rinses. Her stomach turns and she quickly sits on the toilet as her bowels void themselves.

What should I do? What must I do? She takes out her mobile phone and calls Ma'aza. No answer. Daniel. Will he be up yet? Will he even have heard what's happened?

Someone raps the letterbox on her front door. There is more knocking. Dalila approaches, her hand covering her mouth. Through the spy hole she recognises the face of Mrs Gilroy. The knocking comes again and she opens.

Oh, will you look at yourself, says Mrs Gilroy. Poor thing. You've the fear of God on your face. C'mon, let me in.

Dalila glances at the policemen crammed onto the landing. She unclips the chain and opens the door. Mrs Gilroy, still in her slippers and holding her dog to her chest, enters and Dalila locks the door again. They stand facing each other, waiting for the other to speak. Dalila opens her mouth, her throat braces up and the tears trickle down her face.

Och, love, you've had an awful fright, haven't you? Mrs Gilroy reaches out and gives Dalila's hand a little squeeze. There now. It's alright. You're alright, love. Why don't we make some tea, heh? Have you got tea?

Dalila nods. She sniffs.

Right then. Old women like me need wer tea first thing in the morning.

They move to the kitchenette, where Dalila sets a pan of milk to heat on the stove.

Mrs Gilroy puts Toby down and he starts exploring the floor, nose down, tail wagging. Dalila edges away from the dog.

Mrs Gilroy opens the back door and steps out onto the balcony. She places both hands on the railing and looks down. Jesus, God Almighty. That's him, isn't it? She shakes her head and pulls her dressing gown around herself. I cannae believe it. It's a sin what happened here.

A noise distracts her, and Mrs Gilroy looks across at the neighbouring balcony where the immigration and police officers are standing.

It's a sin what yous have done here, she hisses at them. A sin, you hear me? Yous should be ashamed. Think what you've done to this family, to they kids! Ashamed!

Ma'am, please step inside, responds a policeman, and allow the officers to conduct their investigation.

I will not. For shame! The lot o yous.

Toby starts barking.

Dalila steps out as the officer says, Ma'am, if you don't step inside—

You've no right to come here and tell me what's what. You're a bunch o arrogant . . . no-good—

Dalila places her hand on the old woman's shoulder.

Oh, yous make me so angry. Acting like the bloody Gestapo. I'll be writing a letter to your superintendent, to the council, to the First Minister, the lot o them. Then you'll see. You cannae just do this to folk.

Ma'am, you're welcome to write down your grievances, but for now I'd ask you to please step inside.

The tea is ready, Dalila whispers to Mrs Gilroy. Come. Come inside.

Come here, Toby, says Mrs Gilroy, lifting up her little dog. Let's get away from these . . . these good-for-nothings.

They re-enter the kitchenette and Dalila pulls the door against the wind and locks it.

Oh, it makes me so angry. All these bloody thugs coming in here and scaring folk. Mrs Gilroy pauses, her lips flatten out to a hard line. Just think of those poor lassies, she says. Oh God. She puts her hand to her face. I hope they didn't see him fall. Were they in the flat, when he . . . you know?

I don't think so.

Oh, it doesnae bear thinking about.

Dalila removes the tea bags from the pan and fills two mugs. She places the mugs on the table. Mrs Gilroy puts Toby down. She cups the mug with both hands and drinks.

This is good, she says, taking another sip. D'you put ginger in this, aye?

Yes, for my cold, says Dalila, and cinnamon also.

They both sip. Mrs Gilroy looks into her mug. I used to like living here, she says. When Sam and I first moved in, this block was very smart. Posh, even. You felt safe living so high up. My Sam would say he felt modern, part of the modern world. We all knew each other and summers we'd all sit doon there on the grass, whole families thegether. But no the now, she says. No the now.

Mrs Gilroy stares deeply into her tea.

Used to be the drugs. The families moved out and this block was full o junkies. One day they took a laddie up the top. Those days the top was open and anyone could just go up there and look out. I'd even dry my washing up there, if the wind was fair. Well, some poor laddie owed money, so they took him up there, knifed him, threw him aff. The scream he gave out, God, I'll never forget. It chilled me, so it did. I'd hear that scream for days after. After that, the council started moving the junkies and troublemakers out and filling the empties with asylum seekers. Only took fourteen months afore the first one jumped. He was a sad boy. They said he wasnae right in the head. One night he just stepped aff. A month later another one fell from the flats just across the way. Some say he was in a fight, others say he fell of his own will. Hard to know. But here's the thing, when asylum seekers fall, there's no scream. They just drop through the air without a sound. It's enough to give you the shivers.

The image of Mr Erdem comes to Dalila. The hairs on the back of his hand, his fingers opening, letting go of the railing.

They did this before? The Home Office? asks Dalila.

Oh aye, plenty o times. All over the place. Cardonald. Easterhouse. Sighthill. Castlemilk. They come in like bloody gang-busters, shouting and the like, all dressed in black. And always early in the morning, mind, when they know the families will be in their beds. Folk would run out to block and slap the sides of the immigration vans, trying to get them to stop. Caused a right upset. Made the news. And there was plenty o hot air from they gasbags in Holyrood. For a while the families felt safe, but soon the raids started again, quiet and sneaky-like. They'd pull folk from their homes and hide them away in detention centres, somewheres out in the country. Or they'd shove them straight on a plane and send them away. Some folk you'd never hear of again. No one knew what happened to them, they'd just be gone. I mean, God sake! What's happening to us? My Sam fought the fascists in the war. He was a trade unionist his whole life. He'd be horrified to see what's going on, to see what's happening on his own street!

The telephone next door starts ringing again. Calling and calling, hoping for an answer.

Mind if we turn on the telly, love? asks Mrs Gilroy. There'll probably be stuff on the news about what's happened.

They sit side by side on the sofa, Toby on Mrs Gilroy's lap. The first station has a breaking news item involving a man falling from a multistorey building in the Ibrox area. Dalila flicks to another channel which seems to be a cooking show. A guest has splashed flour on themselves and the host is slapping his thighs and laughing into the camera.

On a different channel, a reporter in a neat charcoal overcoat and blue scarf announces that he has just arrived at the scene. He stands in front of the police cordon and in the background Dalila recognises her building. Behind him is a tent covering the spot where Mr Erdem landed. A forensics team in white overalls and white gloves enters the tent as the reporter delivers his story. His relaxed and professional style doesn't escape

Dalila. He stares straight at the camera, never once glancing at the locals gathered around him. He talks of a tragedy involving a man whose name and country of origin cannot be confirmed at this moment. But what we do know is that he recently had his claim for asylum in the UK rejected and there appear to be details coming in suggesting that he was on medication for a mental health condition but as yet that has not been confirmed. Then it cuts to the studio.

Christ, I cannae watch this any more, says Mrs Gilroy. Time to take Toby out anyway.

The old lady gets to her feet. Thank you for the lovely tea, Irene. You be sure and pop by if you need anything. I'm just across the hall.

Thank you for coming, says Dalila, as she follows Mrs Gilroy down the hall.

She opens the door and the landing is full of police and forensics people and UK border agents. Toby starts barking and a policeman turns to Mrs Gilroy and says, Ma'am, we'd ask you to stay in your home for the time being.

Och, shoosh! That's my flat there, she snaps, pointing across the landing. She pushes through the crowd, Toby barking all the while.

Dalila shuts and locks the door. She gathers the mugs and washes the dishes, dries them and puts them in the cupboard. She wipes the counters, the table, the top of the fridge. Squatting down, she sweeps the linoleum floor with a dustpan and brush.

When the kitchen is completely clean she stands looking at it. Her mind replays the moment Mr Erdem let go. The hairs on his hands. His fingers splaying to release. She hears the girls crying. Little Rosa crying. The boots. The shouting. Ma'aza pulling her arm and Mr Erdem's fingers letting go, and letting go, and letting go.

She inhales and finds herself standing in the kitchen, her kneecaps quivering.

She calls Ma'aza again. No answer. She texts,

Where RU? Did I make U angry? I'm sorry.

There's the sound of a door slamming in the hallway. Even standing in the kitchen, she can hear the voices of the police right outside her door. She can't leave, so she runs the vacuum cleaner over the green carpets and then gathers all the clothes from her room and Ma'aza's room and puts them in the washing machine and turns it on. She scrubs the toilet and sink and loose tiles around the bath. She makes her bed and tidies her room and after a while finds herself standing in the kitchen, picturing Mr Erdem's fingers uncurling from the railing, his thumb straightening, his hand letting go.

By the evening, only one police van and one TV crew remain. The tent and body have been removed and the police tape taken down.

The residents of Iona Court Towers keep nervously distant from the area where the body lay only a few hours ago. Huddled in coats and hats, hoods up, they shuffle their feet to keep warm. The forensics team have removed some turf as evidence where the head and hands had been, leaving a misshapen depression on the lawn. Dalila tries not to look at this patch of grass, but her eyes betray her. Every time she glances that way, her mind invents horrific malformations of Mr Erdem's limbs.

People place candles in jam jars, and lay them out in a wide semicircle around Mr Erdem's final resting place. Some residents have brought flowers, which they lay out between the candles. Three football jerseys have been laid out, too. Children, holding their mothers' hands, place teddy bears on the ground. Some people open flasks and pour the steaming-hot contents into cups, others sip from bottles and pass them to their neighbours. Most stand in silence, gazing at the flickering candles.

The evening darkens and the orange glow of the street lights shines down on the gathering. Standing among the crowd, Dalila picks out faces from Africa and the Middle East, some from the Far East, but under this false light each face lacks colour. There is only shadow and contrast. Those who are new to this neighbourhood are marked out by their confused expressions. These people who have given up their lives to flee from death, who have travelled halfway across the planet to escape men in uniforms only to find everything they fear in the safest place they could imagine. She sees the disappointment in their faces as sharply as she feels it in her own heart.

Fear – same.

Sadness – same.

Death – same.

Next to the foreign faces are the others, the people born to this. The old locals with watery eyes gazing at the scene where another person has died. They do not hide their weariness. They stand, hands in pockets, stooped by deposits of disaffection. Whereas the younger locals seem hardened by something more elusive. Fierce-eyed and angry, glaring at the candle flames as if they have just glimpsed their inheritance and feel betrayed by it.

Daniel arrives on the other side of the vigil. He nods and makes his way towards her.

Habari, Dali, he says, and they shake gloved hands.

Daniel, says Dalila, switching to English, this is my neighbour Mrs Gilroy.

Daniel removes his glove and shakes her hand.

It's lovely to meet you, Daniel, says Mrs Gilroy.

A pleasure to meet you also.

The three of them go silent.

Daniel removes his hat and clasps his hands behind his back, staring across the candles and the uplit faces. He lifts a tall candle from a jar, cupping the flame, and uses it to relight a smaller candle. He stands again, pulls his woollen hat over his ears.

Erdem. I knew this man, says Daniel, in English. He was good. He only cared for his family.

Aye, he was a good one, says Mrs Gilroy. Always well dressed, he was.

He was my neighbour, says Dalila.

Daniel looks at Dalila, searching her face.

I looked after his daughters, she says. I ate with him and his family.

It is a difficult day, my sister, Daniel says. Did you eat something today?

Dalila takes a tissue and blows her nose.

Aye, it's been rough, says Mrs Gilroy. What they've done to this family, it's no worth thinking about.

A TV news crew sets up close to the vigil. The reporter wears a tweed coat. She crouches near the candles while the cameraman sets up the shot.

I've been thinking about my Sam all day, says Mrs Gilroy. I cannae help it. I keep wondering what he'd make of all this.

It is right to think of our loved ones now, says Daniel.

Dalila listens to the murmurs in the crowd. She studies one face and then another, as if expecting to see someone. She stares into the flickering candles and it begins to feel as if her mother and brother are here, standing with her. Her father seems to be in the crowd, too, somewhere among these faces.

Daniel clears his throat. While staring at the candle flames, he says, When I was a young man I went to one funeral in Uganda. We stayed there three days. At this funeral there was an old man, a healer. They said this old man was a priest before, and then became a common witch doctor. But people believed in his gift. On the first day, the brother of the man who passed spoke to the healer. He asked what he knew of the next world. But the healer man, he didn't say anything.

Daniel stares out, as if looking between the crowd, at the darkening evening beyond the towers. Will he continue his story? Dalila wonders. Perhaps she should say something. But Daniel draws back into himself and starts talking again. On the third day, Daniel says, all the men, we sit together. The healer said to us, he said this, As we live our days, every person must make their own narrative or it is made for you. That is the great struggle. From this struggle all stories are told and by their story each one is known, each one is remembered. When you pass over, only the story stays behind.

Aye, that's one way o looking at things, says Mrs Gilroy.

Daniel continues. This old healer, he said to us, Your story remains in this world, but even more, it passes with you to the other place. Your story is all you have. In the next place it is all anyone has. There, our ancestors sit by the Great Fire and tell about their lives. Some tell stories of long journeys, others explain concepts. There are tragic stories and mysteries and tales of great adventures. Vast family sagas are coupled with romantic meetings which are met with braggings. When one speaks the others listen, paying close attention to what is told and closer attention to what is left untold. Every detail is collected. The weight of each word is tested, remembered. The more our ancestors listen, the more evident it becomes that every story is connected. Parables are linked to tragedies linked to jokes linked to legends. Together, all our stories become the Great Story. To all the men gathered at that funeral, the healer said this, It takes a lifetime to create your story, the rest of time to see how it fits in the Great Story. This is the only true work there is.

See, I like that, says Mrs Gilroy. That makes sense to me. It's easier to believe than all that bloody claptrap you hear from the pulpit. I'm sure ma Sam is up there the now, just gabbing away.

Daniel chuckles. My daughter, Dembe is her name, she is there also. Ish, that one can talk. She never stops. Right now she is telling a very big, big story, believe me.

She'll be doing well to get a word in edgeways with ma Sam, so she will, chuckles Mrs Gilroy.

Dalila watches the two of them smiling at each other. She never knew Daniel had a daughter and can't believe she hasn't asked him more about his family.

A silence descends and their eyes return to the candle lights.

What do you think the Great Story is about? Dalila asks.

For a moment no one answers and then Mrs Gilroy says, I couldnae say exactly what it is, but I'll say this, ma whole life I've always thought we're building something, something good. And no just for our weans but for werselves. I dunno. In ma old age, I wonder if we've actually built anything at all. But if there is a Great Big Story, I'm sure it will show we're all in this thegether. Like it or not.

Yes, Daniel says, I believe this. It is like a long drama and everything is so, so important. Sometimes, when I am quiet, I think I can feel the shape of the Great Story. From its shape, I sense how it is moving.

How does this story end? Dalila asks.

Too many things will happen. In the end, everything will happen. But I believe after all is done, and after all is told about what was done, after every deed and word is consumed in the Great Fire and all is gone, there, in the deep for ever, a silent beauty will remain. I believe, in the end, beauty wins.

As the vigil starts to break up, Dalila says goodnight to Daniel and Mrs Gilroy and goes back to her flat. In the lift, on the way up, she checks her phone for messages.

None.

Ma'aza is sure to be back tonight. She left without even taking a bag. She must come back soon. Dalila decides to wait up and watch the news, it'll be better than trying to sleep alone in the flat. A hot bath will also be good. To soak in it till she is drowsy and her bones feel warm again. Then she will wait on the sofa, maybe watch a film until Ma'aza returns.

The lift doors open and Mick is standing right in front of her, staring down at his phone. He doesn't look up. Dalila stumbles back and touches the button to close the doors, but Mick reaches out and stops them.

A'right, he mumbles.

She imagines running past him, but finds herself unable to move.

You coming out, Irene?

His eyes are bloodshot as if he's been crying or drinking, or both. There's a weary pull to his movements, a slowness. He steps back, keeping his hand across the door closing. He spreads his other arm wide, signalling her free passage.

C'mon. You can come out. I'm no gonna touch you.

Dalila glances past him at the two police officers guarding the Erdems' flat. She walks straight to her front door without even glancing at Mick. The key goes in the lock and as she opens the door and steps in, Mick says, Here. D'you see what happened this morning?

Dalila turns her head halfway towards him and nods.

The lift doors starts to close and Mick lets them shut. He glances at the police officers, who are watching him without looking directly at him, and takes two careful steps towards Dalila. He whispers, You seen what happened, aye?

Yes, she says softly.

Looked like there were about thirty polis or something.

Dalila nods.

Mick takes a step closer and throws the policemen a sideways look. He whispers very quietly, So, they just burst in and threw him off, is that it?

Dalila lifts her eyes. But Mick struggles to look at her. He glances again at the officers. He turns his head and spits.

They did not throw him, Dalila whispers.

He jumped?

No. Mr Erdem, he . . . he stepped off.

He stepped aff?

Yes.

Fuckinhellman, says Mick under his breath. He sniffs and wipes a hand across his mouth. Were the weans in the flat when he . . . ? I mean, did they see their da . . . step aff?

I think the officers, they took the girls out before, whispers Dalila. But if they saw, I don't know.

I seen him, whispers Mick. I seen him just lying there, like he was drunk or something. No movin or nothin. Just lying there.

Mick swallows hard. His bloodshot eyes become redder as if he is about to scream or cry.

I cannae get that picture oot ma head. Aw day I just seen him lying there. Mick swallows again. Know what I mean?

I know, whispers Dalila. And then she says, One day, it will get easier.

She steps inside and as she shuts the door Mick says, Here, Irene.

She leaves it open an inch, waiting.

See last time, whispers Mick, I didnae mean . . . I know I was a wee bit . . . I'd been on the bevvy and, and I know I went on a bit about fuckin toasters and the government and that, but

I didnae mean it. I was just a wee bit . . . Mick points a finger at his temple and twirls it.

The sign for crazy – same.

Dalila nods and closes her front door. She lies down on her bed and listens to her heart pulsing. She takes a slow breath. In and out.

Where is Ma'aza? Where could she have gone? And where are Parla and Rosa? Where would they have been taken? They must be with their mother. Do they even know what happened to their father? And the police? How long will they be here? Will they come for more people?

She gets up, goes to the bathroom and blows her nose. She washes her face with hot water and massages her sinuses and then blows her nose again.

She drags her duvet through to the sofa in Ma'aza's room, turns on the TV and lies down. The news is still reporting on this morning's events. There's a clip with the body lying on the lawn covered in a sheet. She thinks about Mick, about his bloodshot eyes.

There is a sensation in her stomach and she can't tell if it is hunger, so she stands up and goes to the kitchen and opens the fridge. Nothing in the fridge looks appetising. She doesn't want tea.

Her mind goes back to Mick, about the look he gave her as she closed the door. It was a look she understood, yet could not explain.

She unplugs the toaster, shakes all the crumbs into the bin and wraps the cable around it.

As she opens her front door the policemen outside the Erdems' flat halt their conversation. She crosses the landing and places the toaster right in front of Mick's front door.

One of the policemen raises his eyebrows. Before he can speak, Dalila says, This one is for him.

Something grabs her foot and Dalila wakes, startled.

Wake up, says Ma'aza, yanking off the duvet and dumping it on the floor. This is not your room. You cannot sleep on this sofa.

The TV is still on, adverts mutely flashing across the screen. The window is dark.

Dalila stands too quickly and stumbles onto the neutral linoleum flooring of the kitchenette. She runs water across her fingers and rubs her face with her wet hand.

Where did you go? Dalila asks.

Out.

Ma'aza switches on the overhead light and clicks off the TV.

What time is it? asks Dalila.

It is late. No, it is early, says Ma'aza. She pulls her rucksack out from under her bed, unzips it and throws it on the bed. She pulls a pair of jeans from the drawer, inspects them and rolls them down the length of her torso into a tight scroll and shoves them into the rucksack. A T-shirt and pullover get the same treatment. A pair of shoes and a scarf are also stuffed into the bag. Kneeling on her bed, Ma'aza starts taking down the photographs of her family taped to the wall.

What are you doing?

Moving.

But where are you going?

I'm going. Finished.

Ma'aza, please, you must stay at this place, this address. What about reporting? They will refuse you if you don't report. You are scared, even me, I am scared, but you must stay.

I will go.

Where? Where can you go? They can find you anywhere. They will take you and send you back.

Ma'aza gets off her bed and struts right up to Dalila, her scarred eyebrows raised. You have seen revolution? she asks, jabbing her index finger towards the ceiling.

Dalila hesitates and says, I have seen election troubles.

You have seen famine?

No, she concedes.

I have seen both. Both times, the ones who stay are the ones who die. Believe me. Moving is living, I told this to you before, she says, with another jab of her finger.

But, yesterday, with the police, this was not a revolution.

I see people like this before, says Ma'aza, her voice a little softer. They will come again. They will take you and you will be gone. In detention, back to Kenya, it doesn't matter. You will be gone. I see this before, believe me. You have to go, Dalila.

But where? There is nowhere to go.

Ma'aza moves closer. You are right, she says, if we go frontways or back or left or right, they find us. Only a rich man can go up. If you have money and there is trouble, you go up to those places where they don't come looking for you, or you pay them not to find you. You can hide up there. But for you and me, we don't have money, so we go down. No papers, no phone, no address. If we go down, they don't find us.

Dalila blinks, not sure how to reply.

Ma'aza takes hold of her hand. I know some people. We can work in their shop. We sleep there. In the spring, we pick fruit. We make money. With money, we go to Canada. Canada is better. Come with me, sister, please.

Dalila looks away.

Where do you want to go?

I want to go home, to Kenya. As she says it, the homesickness descends. The longing to be back home again.

Ma'aza gives her a flat look. And your uncle?

Dalila has no answer to this.

When he dies, you go home. Maybe next week, maybe in twenty years. But where will you wait until you go back?

Here?

Why?

In her mind the answer is poised, ready. What better place to be than in the UK? It is the Father of the World. But she catches these words before they leave her mouth, the authority of them having somehow shifted. Instead, she looks at Ma'aza and says, It is safer to stay here.

Ma'aza shakes her head. Was it safe for them? she says, pointing through the wall.

At the first hint of dawn, Ma'aza is packed and ready to leave. Dalila watches her zip up her coat and tie her bootlaces.

You won't tell me where you are going? asks Dalila.

Ma'aza shakes her head.

Can I phone you?

I won't be able to answer, but if you text I can reply, says Ma'aza. She stands up and places her hands on Dalila's cheeks. Don't be sad, little sugar sister. I will be okay. One day I will phone and you will say, who is this? And I will say, Ish, you don't know your sugar sister?

Dalila can't help but smile.

And I will say, Come and visit me in my house in Canada.

Your *big* house, adds Dalila.

Yes, my very big house. Come and visit me in my so, so big house. I have a very big TV and you can stay and we watch movies every day.

Dalila starts giggling. She wipes away the tears and says, We will watch comedies with coffee and popcorn.

Yes. Of course. Lots of popcorn and ice cream and cookies and Coke and lots of BBQ, only BBQ all the time. You and me, we watch movies every night and we get fat. So, so fat.

The two of them are giggling and Dalila says, I would like that.

Ma'aza nods. She opens the door and checks. There is no policeman on the landing. She turns and says, Dalila, if there is trouble, you go, okay?

Dalila looks at the floor.

Promise me, girl. You just go and keep going and then you call me, okay?

Okay.

Ma'aza hoists her bag onto her shoulder and disappears down the fire escape.

Two hours later, there is a tapping at the door and Dalila jumps up from the couch, thinking it might be Ma'aza returning, having changed her mind or perhaps she forgot something. She opens the door and Alison, Mick's girlfriend, is standing there holding the toaster.

Is this you, aye?

Dalila glances around, unsure how to answer that question.

The fuck is this? Alison holds out the toaster. D'you do this?

Yesterday, I—

Is this your toaster, aye?

Yes.

So what's it doing in ma flat?

I thought . . . Mick said . . .

You thought what?

Dalila takes a breath. This one is a gift, for you and for Mick. We are neighbours. If we don't have, we share.

You've got some fucking cheek, hisses Alison. You think we want your toaster? You think you're better than us? Is that it?

No, I don't think this way.

Here, Alison shoves the toaster at Dalila, keep yer shite to yersel. I don't need yer charity, ya fucking cheeky fuck.

Alison marches across the landing to her front door, but then turns and marches back towards Dalila. And see here, she says, if I ever see you talking to ma man again, I swear to God, I'll fuckin do you.

Dalila shuffles from room to room, hoping for a distraction. The dishes are washed, her clothes are clean, floors vacuumed. A walk would help but she's not going out, not today. Not after what's been happening.

Trying not to think about Alison, her mind jumps to an image of Ma'aza walking towards the front door. Then she's wondering where Parla and little Rosa might be. How must they be feeling? Do they even know what's happened? The sound of Mr Erdem falling comes to her exactly as it was yesterday. That moment of in-breath. His trouser legs flapping as he dropped through the air. She wraps both arms across her midriff as her stomach cramps. Bending over, breathing through it, she has to do something before these feelings overwhelm her again.

In the bathroom, she turns on both taps and watches the water pour into the bath. Steam begins to fill the room. She checks her phone, again. She has sent nine messages to Ma'aza, all of them unanswered. She sends another one anyway.

Thinking about U. Pls text me. Let me know U R safe. D. xx

When the bath is full, she climbs in and sits down, fanning her fingers through the hot water, trying to be herself again. Her jaw aches from clenching down so tightly and she opens her mouth as wide as she can, easing her chin from side to side.

Ma'aza will come back, Dalila says out loud, but she knows Ma'aza is gone. She will have slipped downwards like she said she would. Gone underground, where you don't need papers. And the Erdems are gone. Those girls won't be back.

Cupping her hands together she lifts a little pool out of the bath. The water dribbles out between her knuckles. She tries again, squeezing her fingers, trying to create a watertight basin in her hands but still the water drains away.

After her bath, she drags her duvet to the sofa in Ma'aza's room and turns on the news. A protest is taking place about the treatment of refugees. Once again, the words MIGRANT CRISIS scroll across the bottom of the screen. Video footage shows people walking along a motorway. It cuts to images of men climbing into the back of a lorry. Currently, three thousand migrants are camped in Calais, says the news anchor's voice, as they try to cross through the Channel Tunnel from France into England. Calais has increasingly become the focus of attention because the numbers of migrants has swelled quite considerably over the last few months. The report cuts to footage of men standing outside tents. The conditions are squalid. Rubbish on the ground. Mud splattered up the side of the tents.

Dalila's anger rises. Why are they showing this? It's always about Calais or boats in the Mediterranean. Always Syrians, Syrians, Syrians. What about the rest of us? Why aren't they talking about Mr Erdem? Is he not important enough?

She switches to STV, where another protest is taking place. People are angry. They jeer and shout at the camera, some wave banners calling for justice. Dalila recognises her tower block in the background. There are very few clips of asylum seekers, some even hide their faces as the camera pans towards them. The segment cuts to a local man being interviewed while still behind the wheel of his van. Well, if you ask me, the man says, leaning out the driver's-side window, this never would have happened if they hadn't been allowed into Scotland in the first place, would it?

The news item cuts to the studio, where two people speculate about Mr Erdem, claiming he had been on medication and suffering from depression.

Ish! He was not crazy, Dalila shouts, flapping her arm at the TV.

The news anchor interviews a different expert, asking, Was the UK Border Patrol consistent in their orchestration of this particular forced removal, compared to the similar operations that have taken place, uneventfully, across the city in recent weeks?

Why are they asking this? she shouts, jumping to her feet, pacing the living room. They dragged those children from their beds. This is so . . .

For five minutes these questions get pushed around the studio, and then pushed aside. The programme cuts to a reporter standing near the spot where Mr Erdem died. She is surrounded by locals who listen in on her report. I have with me Ms Carol Kerr, a spokeswoman for various asylum charities across the city, begins the reporter. She claims many asylum seekers are frightened of sharing their opinions or of demonstrating because they believe their actions may harm their case and lead to their being removed.

Yes, that is why we're protesting, replies the spokeswoman, looking directly at the reporter instead of the camera. We have to give a voice to the voiceless. To show our solidarity with those vulnerable people who are too scared to speak out for themselves. You've got to remember, these people are not statistics in faraway lands. Their children play with our children. They're our neighbours and friends. They share our places of worship. Just like you and me, these people are the essential ingredient that makes a house into a home, that makes a street into a neighbourhood. And that's why we will not stand by and watch these abuses take place. These dawn raids, carried out by the UK Border Agency, are an attack on our neighbourhoods and our communities. They're an affront to the people of Glasgow. So we're collecting signatures from right across the city and tomorrow we'd like to invite all citizens of Glasgow to march with us. There'll be a gathering outside Iona Court at 10 a.m., after which we'll be marching right to the City Chambers to deliver our concerns directly to the Lord Provost and other members of the City Council.

*

The next day, Dalila watches from her balcony. A crowd gathers in the mist below. Banners are unfurled and held up. More people arrive and the police stand by, observing. She had considered joining the protest, but the thought of the news cameras made her wonder about who could be watching. If her face was included in a shot that got broadcast across the UK, Markus or Mama Anne might recognise her. She won't take that risk.

A woman holds up a megaphone and gives a muffled, tinny speech. The crowd claps. Then a man takes the megaphone. He leads a call-and-repeat chant. It takes a few attempts to gain momentum but soon the crowd is chanting as one. There is cheering and clapping. A troop of drummers, it looks like women from up here, starts banging its drums. They're pretty good, and the drumming draws more of a crowd. She estimates between about five and seven hundred people are now standing in the car park below. She spots several mothers with pushchairs and even a man in a wheelchair.

Protests – same.

Protestors not dancing – different.

Protest marches led by the bagpipes – different.

Length of protest speeches – different.

Protestors drumming – same.

After about forty-five minutes the woman with the megaphone stands in front of the largest banner and leads the march down the street. The crowd is escorted front and back by police on motorbikes. Yellow-coated officers walk alongside the crowd to keep it contained. They head off towards the river and the BBC offices.

Dalila watches them disappear into the mist. The bright yellow police jackets hold out a little longer against the elements. Soon they are all gone. Only the drumming and the whine of bagpipes linger.

It takes her most of the following day to build up the courage to walk out of the front door. She takes the fire escape to avoid the possibility of sharing the lift with Mick or Alison or policemen or reporters who may still be in the neighbourhood. Descending the stairs, she passes two separate groups of asylum seekers who are camping out on the landing in case another dawn raid happens. The people say hello but Dalila only nods and steps across their sleeping bags.

At the footbridge over the motorway, she leans on the railing, looking out across the heavy traffic. A darkness is growing across the horizon. It is only 4:35 p.m., yet the day appears to be ending. Below her, cars rush by in something similar to silence. It's better up here, peaceful. Hundreds of cars speeding along in six perfect lanes, following the gentle curve of the motorway, each car knowing exactly where it is going and precisely how it should behave. Their lights are pretty. One river of red brake lights and an oncoming stream of twinkling headlights. It reminds her of the rows of flowers where her mother used to work.

These endless overcast days are gnawing at her, shaping her. A change has happened, is happening. And it's not to do with her uncle . . . not only. On her strong days she can push those memories away and they don't trouble her too much. It's not him, it's something else.

From within is a deep and foreign urge to be quiet, to spend all day alone. This can't be who she is. There has to be something more. She has to find something more. She has lost everyone and now, like water through her fingers, she is losing herself.

Dalila – same.

Dalila – different.

She has not seen Daniel for almost a week. She texts him, suggesting they go for a short walk. After an hour, Daniel has still not replied. She sends him another text asking if he is okay. This time she gets a reply.

Just tired.

She decides to go for a walk anyway. Perhaps up through the park. Lacing up her boot she stops, takes out her phone and rereads Daniel's reply.

She phones him. No answer.

Five minutes later she is knocking on Daniel's door. She waits, knocks again. Could he be sleeping? Perhaps he isn't feeling well and the best thing would be to just let him rest, alone. Yet she stands closer to his front door, listening. There is an unsettling sensation in her stomach. She phones him again and this time she can hear his phone ringing inside his flat. She knocks on the door again and calls out, Daniel? Baba Dan, it's me, Dalila. Please come to the door.

She lifts the guard on the letterbox and peers into the darkened flat. Something stirs inside.

I know you are there, Daniel. Please come to me.

She dials his number again and this time the ringing inside the flat grows louder. She bends forward and looks through the letterbox to see Daniel approaching.

He opens the door and steps back. He is unshaven and is not wearing his glasses. In his hand, his mobile phone is still ringing.

Are you sick, Daniel? I was worried.

He looks past her and glances back into his flat.

Dalila lifts her own phone and ends the call. In the sudden silence, Daniel sighs and says, I am just too tired.

His eyes still refuse to meet hers.

Can I come in?

Daniel steps back from the door.

Dalila enters and unties her laces, as Daniel disappears down the hall. The flat is dark and musty with that particular smell of old people. It is a smaller flat than the one she shares with Ma'aza. The bathroom is off the main hallway, and beyond that, an L-shaped room with a kitchenette. That's the whole flat. Old fish-and-chip wrappers litter the floor. Socks and underwear are thrown in the corner, trousers are draped over the arm of a sofa. The kitchen sink is full of dirty dishes. The fridge door stands slightly open, dripping water onto the dirty linoleum.

She finds Daniel sitting on his bed. A weak afternoon light pushes through the brown curtains.

Are you sick, Daniel? You don't look well.

I'm okay. He lifts his head but his eyes struggle to rest on any specific thing. I'm just . . . tired. I'm sorry you have seen me like this.

Dalila squats down in front of him. I also get tired, she says. Why don't you rest some more? When you are ready I will make tea for us.

She helps Daniel to lie back on his bed.

She takes off her coat and hangs it up on the hook by the front door. The bathroom is filthy. Dried urine stains on the toilet bowl and floor. Hair gathering in the corner behind the door. A rim of brown scum in the bath. Mould on the tiles. An empty toothpaste tube on the sink next to a thin sliver of soap. Tucked behind the toilet are some cleaning products.

She starts scrubbing. First the bath and tile surrounds before moving on to the sink and then the toilet. Using a little scouring brush, she kneels down and scrubs the floor.

When all is clean, Dalila runs a bath and goes through to check on Daniel. She finds him sitting on his bed. He reaches for his glasses as soon as she enters.

You are still here? he says.

Yes. Is that okay with you?

Daniel puts on his glasses and places his hands on his knees. I don't mind, he says.

I am running a bath for you. It helps me when I am . . . tired. Maybe you would like to try it?

I don't know.

Try.

Okay.

Maybe later, when you have finished washing, we can have some tea together. I will make it Kenyan style, says Dalila, smiling.

Yes, says Daniel, gently rubbing his knees, this is the best way for tea.

Come. The bath is almost ready. Do you have a clean towel?

Without looking up, Daniel points. In the cupboard, he says.

She takes a towel to the bathroom, turns off the taps, hangs up the towel and switches on the extractor fan. She pauses and looks at the hot tap. When she touches the metal, it's still quite hot. She runs the cold tap and splashes handfuls of cold water across the hot tap to cool it.

As Daniel comes in she exits, closing the door behind her.

She throws open the curtains and the window in his room. In the new light, she notices he has the same green carpet as she has in her flat, it's the same carpet as in the Erdems' flat too. But Daniel's is covered in bits of rubbish and crumbs and grey fluff. A little path amidst the dirt has formed where he walks from his bed to the kitchenette.

She strips the bed, gathers the dirty clothes off the floor and pushes the whole bundle into the washing machine. In the cupboard under the sink, she finds detergent.

She opens the kitchen window and allows the brisk air to gust through the flat. She scrunches up the fish-and-chip wrappers into tight bundles and drops them in the bin. She folds two pizza boxes in half and shoves them in the bin too. Nachos packets, biscuit boxes, three beer cans and a pile of old newspapers all go in. In the fridge, the milk has curdled. Two old tomatoes and half a packet of greying sliced ham, all gets thrown out. She wipes away the stagnant orange water in the bottom of the fridge and cleans the shelves, then gathers up the cups, plates and cutlery lying around the room and washes the dishes, leaving them to drain on the plastic rack.

The only food in the kitchen cabinets is four tins of oxtail soup and half a packet of sliced white bread that is speckled with mould.

Dalila throws out the bread and looks around for something else to do. She hears his weight shift in the bath. On top of the fridge are Daniel's keys. She grabs them and leaves.

Back in her own flat, Dalila fills her left coat pocket with tea bags and the right with a quarter bag of sugar and a stem of ginger. She takes the vacuum cleaner from the cupboard and wrestles it into the lift.

The vacuum cleaner rattles along the pavement as she drags it towards the corner shop. There is enough money in her purse for a pint of milk and a loaf of sliced white bread but there isn't enough for a packet of biscuits. As she pays, the Polish woman behind the counter doesn't even glance at the vacuum cleaner.

When she gets back to Daniel's flat she finds him clean-shaven, wearing a blue-and-white checked shirt tucked into his green corduroy trousers. He is barefoot and fiddling with the kettle.

You look better, she says.

He sits down on a stool as soon as he sees her and says, I feel a bit better.

I bought milk and bread.

Good. Yes. Daniel stands up and scratches his scalp. I think I have . . . He goes to the cupboard and opens it, but it is empty. He opens the next one. You know, I'm sure I have some . . . Yes, here it is, some oxtail soup. I find this is the best thing to revive the senses whenever I get really tired. Would you like to stay for dinner, Dali?

I would be honoured to join you, says Dalila. We can warm it in the pan while I quickly clean the floors.

No, no. You've done enough. Besides, this old man is better with machines than he ever was in the kitchen. Daniel takes the vacuum cleaner, plugs it in and begins running the head across the carpet. He cleans the sofa arms and vacuums down the hallway while Dalila stirs the warming soup. She sets two bowls on the table and arranges the sliced bread on a plate.

They eat together in silence. Dalila watches his mannerisms for signs of sickness and wonders what he's going through.

Daniel focuses on his food.

They finish and she takes their empty bowls and places them in the sink. She warms milk and ginger for tea and when it is ready she brings a mug to Daniel.

Thank you, he says.

You're welcome, Baba.

For the first time that day Daniel looks directly at her. Thank you, my sister, he repeats and his eyes suddenly fill with tears.

It's okay.

I am an old fool, he says. I'm fine . . . and then sometimes, I can't . . .

I understand.

. . . sometimes, I can't make it past the front door.

Dalila puts her mug down. If it happens again, where you feel . . . where you can't get past the door. Just call me.

I don't know how it happens, says Daniel, peering down into his mug. I just get . . .

Dalila reaches out and takes his hand. Remember when you bought me the bacon roll and you told me about Ubuntu. You said, I can only be okay if you're okay.

He looks up at her and nods.

So the next time you feel this way, you phone me, okay?

Okay.

Dalila's phone vibrates. It's a text from Daniel.

You report today? We go together? Meet at my house 10 am.

The morning is bitterly cold and Daniel insists on taking his new car. He gently revs the engine two or three times, tilting his head to one side to better hear the song under the bonnet. Dalila fastens her seatbelt. Daniel keeps well under the speed limit, stooping forward over the steering wheel as he drives. He turns his head all the way left and then right as he navigates the first roundabout. They pass the Asda supermarket and the tower block being eaten by the crane, now only a few storeys tall. At the traffic lights, Daniel turns to Dalila and grins. This car, she is a good one. Maybe I will keep her and sell the other.

He sounds so like her father. Dalila tucks her cold fingers under her thighs and enjoys the feeling of being driven through the city.

They park near the Solidarity Centre. Eight men are standing outside the entrance. Dalila recognises Abbi, with his hood up, smoking. As they approach he takes one last drag and flicks the stub away.

How are things, my friend? says Daniel, shaking Abbi's hand and nodding to the other men.

Ah, you know how they do, says Abbi. They been taking here and there. Times is bad.

A few of the men nod in agreement.

They have six raids now, says Abbi.

Six? says Daniel.

Believe me, six. Two even this morning. Families every time.

Daniel shakes his head. Ish, I did not know it was so bad.

That's how they do. It's like this. All attention is at your block, so they take their vans and pass by other places, waking up families and taking them. Dungavel is filling up, man. No joke.

Abbi nods at the other men. They step back a little and let him speak. Yesterday, they go very early and take this family. They from Syria. They put everyone in the van but the girl, the daughter, she says she has to go to the toilet. Them officers said no. They said is too late, you can't go out. So she had to, you know, to make water in the back of the van. And the officers, they don't care. They just drive.

Dalila and the other men wait for Abbi to tell more of what he knows but he has nothing left to say. They stand, each one, and stare at their feet. Daniel puts his hand on Abbi's shoulder. He gives Dalila a nod and they enter the centre.

Inside, it's full of women, the men having elected to stand outside while the women stay in the warmth with the children. Women sit three to the sofa and one on each armrest. Others stand and wait while they read over documents. A large lady in tight jeans stands with her back to the gas heater, warming her hands and the back of her thighs.

Dalila and Daniel nod hellos to the others and shuffle to the desk at the far end of the room to sign the registry book.

No, says Phil into the phone, as he untangles the cord from his arm and scrawls something on the notepad in front of him. No. Look. No, that's not . . . If you're going to be that way, then I'm sorry but they're going to be out there all night.

Phil waves for attention from one of the other volunteers and points at a folder on top of the photocopier. The volunteer puts down the two mugs of tea he is carrying, passes the folder to Phil.

Look, says Phil, into the receiver, it's not like we had a committee meeting and, you know, petitioned the board of directors to give us permission to have a protest. They went out there on their own, of their own accord, as it were. They chose to lock themselves to those gates. It has nothing to do with me.

Phil listens. Then he says, You're not hearing me. I do *not* have the keys. Or any idea where the keys are, they are acting alone. I'm not part of it. No . . . No . . . Hey, don't start threatening . . . Well, if you hadn't, Phil raises his voice, if you hadn't, sir, if you hadn't pulled those families from their homes at six in the bloody morning then these protestors wouldn't have chained themselves to the gates of your facility, now, would they?

Behind Phil, another volunteer cleans the whiteboard while she talks into her mobile phone. The sides of her head are shaved clean. A mandala tattoo decorates the back of her neck. When the board is clean she writes a name, a country and yesterday's date along the top in small neat handwriting. Next to the name, in red marker pen, she writes DETAINED: DUNGAVEL. She listens to instructions on the mobile phone and writes the next name.

Phil slams the phone down. He stands up and places his hands on his head.

As Daniel happens to be standing right in front of his desk, he extends his hand. Phil takes it. They shake and Daniel nods his support and encouragement to Phil.

You are fighting a noble battle, my friend, says Daniel.

I'm losing, you mean, Phil replies with a tired smile.

We must report today, says Daniel. It is safe, you think?

Phil fills his cheeks with air and rubs his temples. It's all a bit nuts at the moment, as you can see. There's been a bunch of raids but I think you'll be alright reporting.

Dalila glances up at the whiteboard. Half of it is now covered in neatly written names. Beside each name is their fate.

DETAINED: YARL'S WOOD
DETAINED: DUNGAVEL
DETAINED: DUNGAVEL
REMOVED
DETAINED: COLNBROOK
REMOVED
DETAINED: DUNGAVEL

The phone starts ringing again and Phil picks it up. He turns his back and grabs a folder as he says, Yes, just give me a minute, let me write those addresses down. As he sits down at his desk, Daniel nudges Dalila and says, I am going to enjoy the fresh air and smokers outside. Do you want to join me?

I will stay, says Dalila. It is warmer here.

Very wise, says Daniel. He looks at his watch. We go to report in forty minutes, okay?

Yes, okay.

Dalila sits on the edge of the sofa and warms her hands in front of the gas heater.

Next to her, a Scottish woman is trying to discuss something with an African woman. The conversation starts and collapses and begins again as the African woman battles with her English words. But Dalila thinks she recognises something in her accent.

A Pakistani-looking woman comes into the centre, with her child in a pushchair. She quickly signs the ledger and says to the Scottish woman, I have to report. I leave my baby, okay?

Aye, of course, replies the Scottish woman, who Dalila assumes must be a volunteer at the centre.

Thank you, says the Pakistani woman, thank you. I come back soon.

It's no bother. I'll be here when you get back. She stands up and lifts the child out of the pushchair and bounces the toddler on her hip.

Dalila smiles at the African woman left on the sofa. She takes a chance and, in Kiswahili, asks if the woman has been here long.

Ah, my sister, you speak Kiswahili? Thank God, replies the woman. Thank God. I have been trying to give them my information but they don't understand.

Maybe I can help you? says Dalila.

Oh yes, please. No one here understands me and my English is terrible. I come from Tanzania.

I'm from Kenya, says Dalila. My name is Irene.

I am Beatrice.

The baby starts gurning and the volunteer rummages under the pushchair for something to distract the child.

Excuse me, says Dalila. Excuse me, madam? May I help my friend with her form?

The volunteer looks up. You two speak the same language? she says. If you could help her that would be great. We weren't getting very far. Once you've written down her details just check things over with Phil.

For half an hour the two of them chat like old friends while Phil argues on the phone and people constantly come in and out of the centre. They talk about Africa and the strangeness of Scotland. They talk about food and their troubles and their confusion with the Home Office. Beatrice explains how her father became too ill to work and her family eventually lost their home. A lorry driver offered to marry her. She didn't want to get married. However, her mother encouraged her to accept the offer, for the sake of her family. Soon after the wedding her husband moved her family into a newer home, he provided food and even found a job washing cars for her younger brother. But one night he became angry and shoved Beatrice's head against the wall. She ran back to her family. At that time her husband was away, driving his truck for two weeks, but when he came back her mother forced her to return to her husband. Again, he beat her. It went on like this for many months. Beatrice suspected he was unfaithful and she worried constantly about AIDS. When she discovered she was pregnant, she had to act. She would suffer beatings for her family but she could never expose a child to what she had to endure. So she fled. First to Mombasa and then to France and then the UK. Her son is now four years old. He is healthy and goes to crèche, but the Home Office have just rejected her case and cut her support. Now on Section 4, she has no home and is sleeping on a friend's sofa.

Dalila listens, fascinated at how, in many respects, their stories are one. The emotions are the same, though the details are different. She translates Beatrice's story and writes it up neatly on the Solidarity Centre's registration form, double-checking each detail.

I see you have found your work, says Daniel as he limps into the centre.

Dalila glances up at him, unsure what he is trying to say. I am nearly finished, she replies. I just need two minutes. Dalila stands up and hands the registration form to Phil, who quickly reads it.

Did you, umm, fill this in for that woman? Phil asks Dalila.

Yes. Dalila stands aside and introduces them. Phil, this is Beatrice. She is new here.

They shake hands and Phil says, It's lovely to meet you, Beatrice.

We speak the same language, Dalila tells Phil. Me, I helped her. I checked with her, all the information is there. It is correct.

This is good work, says Phil.

Oh, Dalila is very good, Daniel chips in. She is a journalist, this one. Her English is excellent. You should ask her to be a volunteer for you.

Dalila looks at Daniel, trying to read his motives.

Well, you know, we could use your help, says Phil. You'll need a bit of training, and uh . . . But yeah, we'd love to have you. You can come back tomorrow if you like?

Dalila lowers her head as gratitude and embarrassment flood into her. She tugs at the zip on her coat, trying to hide how she feels. Yes, tomorrow, she says. Me, I will come tomorrow.

The protestors outside Festival Court chant as one.

Together! United! We'll never be defeated!

Large home-made banners are held up over the heads of the protestors.

STOP DAWN RAIDS. STOP DETAINING CHILDREN.

On either side of the crowd a police car blocks the road, redirecting traffic away from the protest. The people are wrapped in scarves and heavy coats. Mothers with prams, Sikhs, two white boys with blond dreadlocks, women in headscarves, local men with their pale bald heads. A faint steam rises off the crowd as they chant and jeer. As Dalila and Daniel move closer, she even recognises faces from her tower. Policemen stand to one side, hands tucked under their body armour for warmth. One policeman smiles and chats to two Home Office security guards.

The main gates of Festival Court have been bound together with bicycle locks and three protestors have chained themselves to the gates and handcuffed themselves to each other. Roped to the gates and along the fence are more signs.

SOLIDARITY!!! ASYLUM SEEKERS AREN'T CRIMINALS. DOWN WITH DAWN RAIDS.

Daniel points out Abbi, who is in the crowd, jumping from one foot to the other and punching the air. When he sees Daniel he grins and sings, Together. United. We'll never be defeated!

The two men grip hands.

Brother, says Daniel, raising his voice, today we must report. Can we go in?

Yes. Yes. No problem for you, is a problem for them. They cannot get out. Them gates are locked.

Yes, I see.

But you can pass by that side. Abbi points to a side gate manned by two security guards.

Thank you, my friend, says Daniel, as Abbi resumes his jumping and fist-pumping.

Inside, the reporting centre is crowded. Security is tighter than usual and people fidget in line before going through the methodical checks. Dalila puts her phone, belt and hat into her handbag. She takes off her coat and hands everything over. She takes off her gold basketball boots and gives them over, it's easier than taking the laces out and having to rethread them later. She and Daniel join the line behind the metal detector. Once through, they each get patted down.

The waiting room is a mixture of bad breath, sweat and damp clothes. It's a hushed mood. Children cuddle close to their mothers or sleep on the floor. Dalila walks across the waiting room in her socks and, near the front, she and Daniel find two seats together.

Daniel leans towards Dalila and quietly says in Kiswahili, I just heard they are not removing the Erdem family.

How do you know? says Dalila, turning more fully in her seat to face him.

I passed by the centre yesterday and Phil told me.

Why didn't you tell me?

I'm telling you now, says Daniel. Phil told me the family were initially taken to Colnbrook Detention Centre in England. But charities and campaigners across the country were outraged. They sent thousands of texts and emails complaining about holding those children. How can the Home Office detain children? How can they send little Rosa to a country she has never seen? And all this after they lost their father in an incident provoked by the Home Office itself. The news agencies also kept enquiring about the family. What will become of the Erdems? they kept asking. In this way, the family's story grew. The pressure began to grow. It became very difficult for the Home Office. Blame was being passed up to ministers in London. So the family were quietly released. The Home Office claims their case won an appeal due to new evidence. Phil says they are in Liverpool for the moment, because the Home Office knows it would be a disaster to bring them back to Glasgow.

This is wonderful news, says Dalila, immediately lifting her hand to her mouth, feeling horrible for saying it. I mean it is good they are staying, but they must be suffering.

Those girls will have a safer life here, Daniel says.

The next number bleeps onto the board. Across the waiting room, all faces lift to see if it is their number that has been called. Daniel lowers his gaze and speaks. I only met Mr Erdem three or four times. Here, and outside your building. He gave me the impression of a sad man, a guilty man.

How do you know he was guilty? says Dalila, shocked at Daniel's opinion. What did he do?

I only mean that he appeared to carry a heavy guilt, as if he accused himself of things he would never forgive.

Dalila folds her ticket around her ARC card. She unfolds it, straightens it out. Did you know his wife, Olcay? she asks Daniel.

I saw her, but I don't believe we met.

She told me her husband worked at the airport in Turkey. He refused to help some men smuggle goods. To keep his family safe, they fled. She believed he blamed himself for taking his family out of their home and bringing them to this place.

I imagine him up there with the officers shouting at his back, says Daniel. Even before those men came bursting in, he must have known his case was not strong enough. It was a sad man who stepped off that balcony, but also a brave man. His act, maybe we should call it his *gesture*, transformed their sad, quiet story into one so mighty it could not be denied. Stepping off the way he did was a selfless act . . . maybe even a wise act.

Do you really think he thought about all this up on that balcony? asks Dalila.

I believe he thought about these questions all the time.

I can't stop thinking about his girls, says Dalila. That little one, Rosa. It makes me so . . . I just . . .

Daniel nods. I hold a great sadness for those girls.

He looks at her. In the silence that draws out between them Dalila feels he is seeing parts of her she prefers to hide. She rubs one socked foot over the other to keep her toes warm and then speaks to cover the silence.

When I came to London, I thought I had lost everything, she tells him. My father. My family. My future. But I am still losing, more and more, all the time. I can feel myself . . . I don't know. It's like I am becoming very small.

In my first weeks, says Daniel, I would lie on the bed for hours, not eating or sleeping. I felt driven from my life. He lowers his head and places his palms together. As you have seen, I can still get this way, he says.

Dalila takes his hand, wanting to reassure him. She says, Ma'aza told me that we asylum seekers only have to survive. That is what we must do.

Daniel nods and squeezes her hand. Ma'aza is right, he says, we must survive. But the man whose hands and feet are cut off, but still breathes, he survives, doesn't he? Survival is simply your heart receiving and expelling blood. It's essential, but I wonder if it's enough.

He coughs once onto the back of his hand. He shifts a little in his seat to face her. Did you know I was in prison? he says.

No, says Dalila. She leans closer to try to meet his eyes, but Daniel adjusts his glasses to evade her.

I was there for seventeen months. In Uganda. I was there because of my politics. In a way, I was lucky, he says, because I knew why I was there. I knew what they wanted from me. Other men had been locked between those walls for many years without ever knowing why, or how long they might remain.

The prison was overfull, he continues, and they kept us locked together in small cells, sometimes ten men to a cell. At any time, the guards would drag one of us away. They would take you to a room, sit you down, tie your ankles to the chair legs and then push the chair over backwards. As you lay there, they beat the soles of your feet with a cane. The pain was extraordinary. No man could hold back his screams.

Daniel rubs both hands down his calf muscle. My foot has never healed from those beatings, he says. Sometimes the guards would ask you questions, sometimes not. I remember that room, where the beatings took place. It smelled of urine and even today that scent brings a panic into my heart.

Dalila watches the side of his head. Daniel, I am so sorry, she whispers.

Fights would break out in the cells, Daniel goes on. Some prisoners were worse than the guards. It was as if they took the beatings put onto them and put it onto others. That's how they survived. Everyone avoided these inmates.

He breathes in deeply. He leans back in his chair and crosses his legs. For many months I shared a cell with this older man. His name was Absolom. When the guards dragged him back into the cell after questioning his feet were bleeding and his trousers were wet, just like every other man. Sometimes he was punched by other inmates or his food was stolen, but mostly he was left alone. I began to watch him. Absolom didn't smile very often yet he spoke with this look in his eyes as if he was about to smile. It was more than humour. There was a quality about this man that made everything outside of him incidental. I wanted to be close to him.

One day a fight broke out in a cell next to ours. A man was stabbed. Later that night the man died of his injuries. I sat next to Absolom and asked him what he thought of the night's activities. He said they were just men scrambling to stay alive and in their efforts they kill each other. They hadn't yet learned to lose, that is what he told me.

To lose? asks Dalila, unsure if she had heard him properly.

Yes, says Daniel. Absolom explained it to me like this, he told me, It is the fate of every being to lose. It will all gradually slip away. You might fight and struggle. You may even see great signs to prove the world has a different plan for you. You may assure yourself that you are the first ever to face such problems and you, alone, will be the first to conquer them . . . and then you will lose. You will lose track of your plans and you will lose hope. Your health will leave you, your family members will pass and, finally, you will also be gone. Everyone loses. It is the single truth of our lives.

Absolom then said, Those who are strangers to this truth refuse to accept that their fate is identical to those pathetic creatures who have lost so much. We might think they hate people, but in truth they fear the suffering they see in others. And their fear diminishes them, it makes them aggressive. It turns them into monsters.

Daniel turns to her with a stoic expression. Every day I think about Absolom, he says. His idea was very powerful. I remember when I first came to the UK. I worried about the change that was happening. Somehow, from somewhere, I was being fashioned into a new person. He gestures to all the people in the waiting room, and says, For people like ourselves, while we wait for our papers, something else is happening. The way we are treated is not for nothing. Believe me, I have seen this. The enforced idleness, the stress we must live under, all of it is an effort to reduce our lives, to hide us away, to keep us out of their offices or universities or hospitals. Most of all they want to remove us, to send us away. Why? Because our suffering frightens them. Because they see what we have lost. Because they refuse to accept that they are just like us.

Another number bleeps across the screen. All faces gaze up. A mother and daughter stand up and go to the nearest booth to report.

I sometimes even wonder if Ubuntu is really about loss, says Daniel. If we understand that we're all losing, then we can sit with each other in our loss. We may find one another through what we share. This is the greatest gift of Ubuntu.

When I think of Mr Erdem, I remember how he walked, continues Daniel. He carried himself with dignity. Always composed and courageous. Even in his loss, he chose how to be, moment to moment. This is what truly shaped him. His wife, his daughters, his friends, he will be carried in their memories. He will become part of their stories and help them choose the manner in which to face their own loss. In this way, our stories inform the stories of others, on and on till we form the Great Story. Do you see, Dalila? This is not how we survive. This is how we prevail.

Dalila's first job at the Solidarity Centre is to make hot drinks for everyone. She wants to make proper sweet tea, with hot milk and cinnamon and maybe ginger. But they don't have a pan for the milk. All they have is an old kettle, tea bags, instant coffee, sugar and stained mugs. She sets about washing each mug properly in the tiny sink while the kettle boils. She takes a drinks order from everyone in the room and then opens the front door and asks the huddle of men sharing a smoke if they would like a drink too.

With a teaspoon, she presses the tea bag against the wall of the mug, making the tea as strong as possible, and then she pours in a dash of cold milk. It's the best she can do under the circumstances. She hands out the drinks and goes back to the sink to wash some cutlery while secretly watching people sip their tea and clutch their mugs to keep warm.

Later in the morning she helps the volunteer with the mandala tattoo, Tracey, to sort through a new donation.

This is all going to the Easterhouse flats, explains Tracey. But we need to sort it a bit first. Go through all these bags here and make three piles, women's clothes, kids' clothes and men's clothes. Check there's no mould on anything 'cause sometimes people just give us shite.

When the clothes are sorted, Dalila helps Tracey and Abbi load the bags into a van. They also load up four boxes of tinned food, blankets, children's toys and three bags of shoes.

Let's go, says Tracey, sliding the van door shut. She pulls the keys from her back pocket and gets into the driver's seat. Abbi jumps in the passenger side and Dalila is about to ask if she can go with them when Phil comes outside and says, Dalila, sorry, are you busy just now?

No.

You see, thing is, we've got this gentleman who's come in for the first time. He needs to fill in his registration form but his writing skills aren't the best. We're run off our feet and he's been waiting an hour. I was wondering if you'd, you know, well, if you wouldn't mind helping him fill it out?

Ah yes, of course. Yes, I can do this.

Great. You'd really be helping us out. Now, you'll make sure you ask him all the questions listed here and then jot down his story. Make sure it's all there.

Okay. Yes, says Dalila, taking the clipboard and registration form. She follows Phil inside and he introduces her to the man.

Dalila, this is Abit.

They shake hands. Dalila sits down on the sofa beside Abit and rests the clipboard across her knees. She starts the interview with the basic questions and soon Abit is relaxed and talking freely, telling his story as she writes it down.

Abit explains that nine years ago government soldiers attacked his village. The soldiers killed his family, burned everything. But he ran away. He was thirteen years old. The following day a small anti-government militia arrived at his village. They gave the survivors, who were sitting among the ashes, a choice. Either join the SPLA and fight against the corrupt forces of the Sudanese government or face execution.

This was how he joined the war.

Abit didn't even have a weapon. He simply followed the militia, camped with them, and collected food from nearby villages as part of the war effort. They lived like this for a year and a half.

When the fighting started, he huddled down and passed ammunition to anyone who had a gun. But their small band of rebels was soon overwhelmed and they were captured by government soldiers. Abit's hands were tied behind his back. He was marched, with the few other survivors of his militia, to the nearest town. The town had no jail, nowhere to keep prisoners. In the houses, the windows had no bars, no glass.

Abit pauses in the telling of his story and grins at Dalila. Me, he says, patting his chest, I am too, too clever for them. They don't keep me. I run away. Abit chuckles and flings his arm out to show how far away he ran.

By dawn the soldiers had caught Abit again. This time they didn't put him with the rest of the boys. Instead, he was taken to a room furnished only with a wooden table.

Those men, they put my arm like this, says Abit, and they take a nail gun. You know what is a nail gun?

I know, says Dalila, cringing, but trying to keep her face straight.

They take a nail gun and put it like this, he says, shaping one hand like a gun and pointing it at the wrist of his other hand. They shoot two times, *bah bah*, through this part of me, he says, as he leans forward to show Dalila the scars on the side of his wrist where the nails penetrated both bones, pinning him to the table.

He tells Dalila he vomited immediately. The soldiers left him there with one arm nailed down. The nails were too deep into the wood for him to pull them out with his right hand and because his bones were pierced, he could not rip though his flesh to free himself. He tried sitting down but there were no chairs and the table was too tall for him to sit on the ground and too heavy to push out of the room. The nails were side by side through his wrist, he couldn't even swivel round to the other side of the table. So he stood, half slumped across the table.

He stood like that for three days.

His legs swelled up and his feet became painful to stand on. He watched the vomit dry out and become specks of half-chewed corn. Delirium set in. He spoke to his dead mother, who shouted at him and told him to Go out, leave, tend your goats. She couldn't understand why he wouldn't leave.

When the soldiers came back they lifted his arm and hacksawed through the nails. He was too weak to walk and his fingers were going green, so they dumped him near a refugee camp.

When I was better, smiles Abit, I run away from that place. After many months, I get a boat and arrive to Cyprus. Then I run away to Italy. After Italy, I run away to UK.

The Home Office rejected his claim, stating that he should return to Cyprus and claim asylum there, since that was his point of entry into the EU. He was placed on Section 4 support and forced out of his hostel. That support has now stopped too because he refuses to report to Festival Court every day.

They want to catch me, Abit says. Put me in those blue vans and send me away. But, me, I'm too clever. I move here, I move there, I sleep in the park.

He smiles at Dalila, and for the first time she wonders if he is flirting with her. She writes the word DESTITUTE under the form heading Current Address.

Abit winks and says, They not catch me. I run away.

That evening, Dalila turns off the TV and sits replaying moments from her day in the silence of her flat. She sets a few potatoes on the stove and while she waits for them to boil she gazes across the city lights and the sparse stars above. One of the first assignments she had at college was to interview someone and write a report. She chose Muthoni's aunt, an elderly widow who had sold fruit in the markets, raised five children, buried a husband, travelled to Uganda, worked in an orphanage and built a house, among many other jobs and adventures. As she pictures sitting under the trees with this old woman, the heat of the dappled morning sunshine comes back to her. She remembers Muthoni being impatient, wanting only to gather a few stories, write them up and pass the assignment. But Dalila had been really challenged by the instructions of her tutor. Listening is giving, their tutor had said. Give people time to invite you into their stories. And so she sat with pen and paper on her lap, spellbound by the stories of Muthoni's aunt. It was a privilege to be there, to be invited into those private memories, to hear about her sufferings, her yearnings. It was one of the most intimate things Dalila had experienced. Days after she had handed in her assignment, she still carried those stories around inside her, feeling more connected to the old woman than Muthoni seemed to be.

Dalila turns off the stove, drains the hot water and soaks the boiled potatoes in cool water. She brings salt and lemon to the table. Her mind replays Abit's story from earlier in the day. She imagines him nailed to that table and sees again that odd smile on his face at the end of the interview.

With a pinch, she dips some warm potato into the salt and lemon, and sits chewing, licking her fingers in the dimly lit kitchen. She liked Abit. Sitting next to him on that sofa, listening and writing, she could feel his story pass through her, yet at the same time it tethered itself to her, and her to him. It was a sense of being perfectly placed in the world.

Her minds drifts to Abbi and then to Phil, as she eats some more potatoes. Phil has been so helpful to her, she thinks. Tomorrow she'll go back to the centre, meet more people, listen to their tragic stories. This might be the way, she thinks. If she is ever to have a hand in this world, this might be it.

Dalila returns to the Solidarity Centre most days. Sorting through clothes and making tea becomes her routine. Now and again she bounces a baby on her knee while the mother reports. She interviews newcomers and shows them how to sign into and out of the logbook. Phil teaches her how to type up the interviews into the database. She listens to the many complaints about housing. Broken windows, mould through the wallpaper, damaged plumbing, stinking carpets, broken heating, water dripping from the ceiling; the complaints come every day. She writes each one down, taking note of the name and address, and then emails the complaint directly to the responsible Housing Association. But still the complaints come. One woman, Nawal, comes to the centre for three days running. She enters the centre looking exhausted. Her oldest child immediately sits down on the carpet, opens a book and begins quietly colouring in while the baby in the pushchair cries and cries.

Everything is still broken, says Nawal. Yesterday they didn't come. It's the same, the water is coming through the roof. The heat is broken. I cannot keep my children there. You must tell them again. Tell them to come today. Now.

I emailed them yesterday, says Dalila, but I will tell them again.

Have they still not fixed the leak? interrupts Phil.

No. Nothing, says Nawal. It's cold for three days, my children are getting sick.

Godsake, says Phil. He phones the Housing Association and argues with them for twenty minutes. When he slams the phone down he tells Nawal, Okay, so they are coming this afternoon. Can you be at home from two to six?

Yes, says Nawal, I will go home now. Thank you, Mr Phil. Thank you.

As the evening draws in, Dalila pulls on her black puffer and beanie. She waves a goodbye to Phil as he chats on the phone and gives Abbi a shoulder-bump hug. Ducking under the half-closed shutter, she steps out into the still, cold air. Someone grabs her elbow, pulling her, and in the quarter of a second it takes for her to turn she assumes it's Abbi or one of the volunteers, catching her before she leaves. Has she forgotten something? But as she looks back, the face of Markus appears behind her.

Come, he says, we go. Back to work.

What does he mean? she finds herself thinking, as she stands stunned and blinking, before the weight of recognition, of dread, lands on her. She pulls her arm in, but he doesn't let go. She tries to yank her arm free, sets her feet and tugs again, harder, and then, as if of its own volition, her open palm push-punches Markus on the mouth. She rips free of the grip he has on her puffer jacket. But he's quick. He snatches her wrist, pulls her in and locks his hand around her neck, shoving her against the wall, lifting her to her tiptoes. Her free hand fluster-flails about his face and she kicks, aiming for the groin but her basketball boot connects with his knee. He grunts as his balance falters but his fingertips dig deeper into her throat and she kicks again, knee-ing him right in the chest. They break. Markus stumbles back. Dalila collapses against the front door of the centre, gulping air back into her lungs. She should be on her feet. She knows she has to get to her feet.

Mr Kennedy will have you back at work, says Markus. I must bring you.

My uncle? spits Dalila, scrambling to her knees. I don't work for that pig.

Now you do. You have debts.

Markus rushes at her and Dalila screams, trying to get up and run, clambering right into Abbi.

You okay, sister? says Abbi, glancing from her to Markus.

Help, she shouts, her voice rasped and desperate. This man is—

Markus lunges again, grabbing at Dalila's jacket, but Abbi wedges between them. Hey! Hey, you don't do that, shouts Abbi. He gets up into Markus's face and the two of them edge into the street, glaring at each other.

If you are smart, you will step off, says Markus.

Ayeee! Ha, ha, laughs Abbi, smoothing his hand down across his beard. What you will do, fat boy? You will rob me? You want to punch my face? Is already broken! Ha! Come. Do it, says Abbi, splaying his arms as he dances and taunts Markus further into the street. Maybe you want to kill my dead family? Too late, fat boy. So what you gonna do?

Markus retreats further back, pulls out his phone and takes Abbi's picture. He snaps photos of the centre and Dalila and Phil and two centre members who have come out to see what's going on. Dalila instinctively turns her face from the violating little eye on his phone.

People will come for her, Markus says, pointing at Dalila. And now they come for you, too.

At this Abbi gets even more animated, stomping and war-dancing in front of Markus. I know fire and hunger and death, he shouts. But you? You only know chicken nuggets, baby boy. So, bring to me the Devil! It will be nice to see him again.

Leave him alone, Abbi, says Phil, walking into the street. I've called the cops, they're only blocks away. No need for you to get into trouble.

As Abbi dances he flashes his splayed fingers in front of Markus's face, making him flinch. In that instant, Abbi snatches the phone out of his hand and hurls it against the wall. Dalila ducks as bits of glass and plastic casing shatter against the wall above her. The phone splits, scattering onto the pavement by her feet.

Abbi, that's enough! shouts Phil. Just step back.

Abbi and Phil stand in the street as Markus paces back and forth, each man waiting for the next move. Dalila's urge is to run. Shifting round, crouched, so only her fingers and toes are on the wet pavement, she is ready to sprint but held by the thought that she might be safer with her friends.

You better go, says Phil.

Tomorrow I will come again, sneers Markus.

I will never go with you, spits Dalila, pouncing to her feet, ready to fight. Me, I did nothing to you. Nothing! What do you want from me?

Mr Kennedy wants you back, says Markus.

My uncle can go to hell! And you, screams Dalila, pointing a bony finger at Markus, if you ever touch me again, I will have your eyes! Do you hear me?

Phil puts his arm out to keep Dalila back. You better go, he tells Markus.

In the distance come the first howling echoes of a police siren.

Markus takes a backwards step, and then another. He glares over his shoulder as he makes his way to the car, with two revs of the engine, he speeds off. Abbi skips after the car, jeering. He scoops up a bottle and hurls it. Surprisingly, it doesn't shatter on impact but careens, rattling and clattering across the potholed tarmac.

The group look at each other in silence. Phil and Abbi and Dalila in the street, the shocked faces of the two women standing in the centre's doorway.

Phil calls out, You better get going, too, Abbi.

Why? I'm not afraid of police.

I know, mate, but I think it's best you go. Your blood's up, says Phil. You did well, but there's no need for you to get sucked deeper into this. Honestly, mate, you shouldn't be here when the police arrive.

Abbi's shoulders droop. He jogs over to Dalila. You are okay, my sister? he asks, looking at the scratches on her neck.

I . . . I am fine. I'm okay, says Dalila, feeling shaken, furious, but stable.

The police sirens wail closer now and Abbi looks at Dalila and then at Phil. Okay, I go now, he says. Without another word, he gives Dalila a wide grin before jogging off towards the library. The two women in the centre, wanting no interaction with any police, quickly say goodbye and hurry off into the darkening evening.

Dalila rubs her neck, peering down at the bits of circuit board that once were Markus's phone. She squats down to examine a piece and from it she slides out the perfectly intact SIM card. She clasps it in her fist. All those photos, those moments taken from her, are now back in her possession.

When the police arrive, she and Phil sit on the sofa in the centre and give their statements. Her hands are shaking but Dalila manages to detail the incident clearly and tell all she knows about Markus. You must take this also, she tells the police officer, handing him Markus's SIM card. Me, I took it from his phone, after it was . . . when he dropped it. It fell to the ground when he grabbed me. I think there is information in there. It will help you to find him.

The police officer holds up the SIM card, examining it. Yes, he says, we'll take a look at this.

An hour later, Phil drives her home in the van, but instead of going into her building Dalila stops by Daniel's flat. He answers the door holding up his filthy hands. Welcome, Dali. Please come in. I've been changing brake pads all afternoon, so you must excuse me while I wash my hands.

His flat is quite messy and Dalila distracts herself by gathering up mugs and dishes and placing them in the sink while Daniel scrubs his hands in the bathroom. Before he comes out, she sneaks through his bedsit gathering up dirty clothes and puts them into the washing machine. She sets a pan of milk to warm on the stove and quickly sweeps the linoleum floor with a dustpan and brush.

When Daniel comes in he sees his clothes turning in the washing machine and the dishes in the sink. Oh, I was just about to do that. You don't need to trouble yourself.

I don't mind, she says.

I can take care of myself, you know.

I know, she says, scrunching up fish-and-chip wrappers and placing them in the bin. She gathers up stray bits of cutlery and places them in the sink and begins to wash the dishes.

Why don't you come and sit down?

Let me just finish these, she replies. And I'm making tea. Would you like some?

Dalila puts the final dish on the drying rack, wipes her hands and goes to the pan of milk. She adds tea bags and sugar.

Daniel places his hand on her shoulder. Come, child, sit.

She pours out two mugs of tea and sits.

Daniel takes a small green banana from the shelf and sits down opposite her. He pushes the banana towards her.

I'm not hungry.

Eat.

Yes, she replies.

The banana peels easily. The taste is sweet at first and then absolutely radiant. It fills her with homesickness, and yet calms her.

How do you like it?

Dalila nods, her cheeks full.

I bought those ones at the Afro-Caribbean shop. They are so much better than the bananas they have in this country. Those long yellow things? I don't know, they have a powdery texture on my tongue that I don't like.

Banana colours – different.

Banana tastes – different.

I have another if you want? says Daniel.

No, that one was good. She lowers her eyes, trying to steady her emotions, and says, Thank you, Baba.

Daniel smiles and says, Drink your tea, Dali, and tell me what you did today.

She sips her tea, relieved to be in this cramped flat with Daniel. She sips again, hoping for the right words to come.

Today was . . . difficult, she begins. I saw Markus again.

On Friday morning it's raining hard. Daniel drives Dalila to the Solidarity Centre. Before she gets out Dalila takes a deep breath to compose herself. She wants to be here, she reminds herself. She is needed and she'll be safe here.

You will be okay today, says Daniel.

I know, says Dalila. Thank you, Baba. Will I see you this evening?

Of course, I'll be here at five to collect you.

The centre is packed. Only two other volunteers are in. Abbi is helping Phil refill the gas canister on the heater, while people stand in their coats gripping mugs of tea. Tracey puts Dalila straight to work. Dalila, this is Divine, she's from Congo and she'd like to join the centre, explains Tracey. Would you mind seeing that she fills out the registration correctly?

Of course, says Dalila, giving Divine a welcoming smile.

The two of them stand to one side and look at the form together.

Maybe you speak French? asks Divine.

No. Me, I only speak English and Kiswahili.

No one in these parts speak French, says Divine. French is very easy, but nobody speaks. Yesterday, I take my lawyer to visit my Scottish MP, even this one he doesn't speak French.

I'm sorry, says Dalila.

Unsure what to say next, Dalila asks, Do you want to join our centre?

Yes, I want. I join everything. Scottish Refugee Council, Positive Action in Housing, Glasgow Asylum Network, Royston Road Project, everybody. Everybody must help because the Home Office refuse me. They say I must take my children and go back.

Dalila shoots a glance over at the desk to see if Tracey is free to talk to this woman, but she appears to be arguing on the phone. Dalila scans her notes and asks, So you already have a lawyer?

Yes, yes. My lawyer we meet with the Scottish MP and explain everything. He shows all the papers from the Home Office. I tell him everything about Congo, about prison and the beatings I suffer, about many, many terrible things. But you know what that MP say to me? He say, You must get used to the idea to go back. That's what he . . .

Divine coughs a few times and then she unzips her coat.

. . . that's what he say. He just look at the papers and say, The war is finish now. You have to go back. Divine takes off her coat and dumps it on a pile of plastic bags in the corner.

You are writing this? she asks Dalila.

Yes, it is here. Look.

Good, says Divine, so I say to him, to this man I say, I will never go back. In Congo, what they can do to me, to my children, is worse than death. No, I cannot go. I love my children, believe me, I love them too much. But if you force me to go back, I will take a knife and cut the throats of each child before I put the knife in my own heart. Before God, I will do this.

Dalila stares at Divine. The woman is wide-eyed and already talking faster and faster about her lawyer. She's scared and it's a fear Dalila recognises in her own heart. If this woman wasn't talking so much, Dalila knows she would reach out and hug her.

I went outside and my lawyer she will drive me home, continues Divine, but the MP, he runs outside and comes to the car. He says he was sorry. He says he promises to help me and he give to me his card. So now I come here. I am fighting for my children. I want anyone to help. That's why I come to this place.

Okay, says Dalila, touching Divine on the arm. We can try to help. We will fight for you.

That afternoon, Dalila goes to Festival Court to report. She leaves her coat and shoes at reception and goes through security. When her number is called, she sits at the allotted booth and slips her ARC card under the glass to the officer on the other side. It is an officer she has never seen before. He is young, plump, with sloping shoulders, as if he has spent his entire life at a desk. Reading the computer screen, he fiddles with a pencil with a Santa Claus rubber propped on the end of it. Place your thumb on the scanner, he says.

She does.

He studies the screen for a few moments and then re-examines her ARC card. An officer appears at the booth behind her.

Irene Delilah Mathy?

She turns in her seat. Yes?

Please, he says. Come with me.

She stares at the young officer on the other side of the glass. He lifts the pencil and taps Santa's head against his lips, but his eyes never rise to meet hers. She looks back towards the waiting room, beyond the body scanner and towards the afternoon light coming through the glass front doors. A hand rests on her shoulder, it slides down her arm and pulls at her elbow till she stands up. She is taken to a room and told to sit.

There is a problem? she says.

Just wait here, please.

The muscles in her jaw want to bite down hard. She inhales, expanding her lungs, and, with control, lets the air release through her mouth.

There have been no letters from the Home Office. Maybe there is a problem with my ARC card? she wonders. Or Ma'aza? Maybe they want to ask about her? Her mind drifts to the centre. She has work to do this afternoon. She promised Divine she would help her make phone calls.

After twenty minutes, an officer arrives and asks Dalila to follow her. The officer is a woman, older, skinny, with red-tinted hair going grey at the roots. They enter a room that looks like the Post Office, with a chest-high counter and bulletproof glass. Behind the glass is a male officer and Dalila's case owner, Ms Colgan. She comes out from behind the glass carrying papers and Dalila's ARC card.

Irene, it is my duty to inform you that your application for asylum in the United Kingdom has been denied, says Ms Colgan.

What? says Dalila. But I didn't . . . Why? I didn't get any letter.

I've just issued your letter of refusal. There is a matter of negative credibility regarding your claims, but all the reasons are stated here quite clearly. She hands Dalila the letter as she says, I need you to be calm and to listen to me very carefully.

Dalila stares at the Home Office insignia at the top of the letter. The words are there in front of her but it's as if she has just woken up and can't quite make sense of where she is, who these people are.

Irene, could you look at me when I'm talking to you? Irene?

Dalila looks at her, this strange, rigid woman with a prim expression on her face. It's an expression full of accusation.

Ms Colgan raises her thumb. Your case has been refused, she repeats, that's the first thing. Secondly, she says, holding up thumb and forefinger, we have removal directions to put you on a flight to Kenya in five days' time, leaving from Heathrow airport. And thirdly—

Me, I cannot go to Kenya, Dalila says, searching the face of her case owner and then the red-headed officer.

And thirdly, repeats Ms Colgan, raising her thumb, fore- and middle fingers, we are required to detain you until you are placed on the flight.

But . . . I told you, whispers Dalila, I cannot go back. Please.

Well, it's out of my hands now. Officer Mitchell here will see to you now.

Could you please empty your pockets? says Officer Mitchell.

Ms Colgan turns and walks towards the door.

Please, Dalila calls out. If I go back, he will find me. Please.

The skinny Officer Mitchell steps between Dalila and Ms Colgan. Miss Mathy, if you don't cooperate, I'll be forced to restrain you. Do you understand? Officer Mitchell unclips the handcuffs from her belt. There is a hard edge to this woman that Dalila doesn't want to provoke.

Ms Colgan swipes her pass across the door lock and leaves.

Please don't send me back, Dalila whispers to the red-headed officer.

Do *not* touch me, barks the officer. That's your final warning. You understand?

Okay, says Dalila, backing off. Okay, but please listen. You cannot send me back.

That's not for me to decide. Now, I need you to empty your pockets, please. Just place everything here on the counter.

Dalila places some cash, her library card, lip balm and her favourite photograph of her father and brother on the counter.

The officer fingers through the items and without looking up she says, Could you please remove your clothes.

My clothes?

It's procedure. We need to check for items that may pose a threat to yourself or others. You can keep your underwear on.

Dalila glances up at the male guard behind the glass. He is yawning as he stares at his phone. She steps out of her jeans and places them on the counter. She pulls her T-shirt over her head and crosses her shaking arms over her chest. Officer Mitchell dips her hand into each pocket, she feels along the seams of the clothing.

Can I phone, please? Dalila asks. I want to phone someone to tell them what is happening.

Do you have a phone?

It is with my bag at reception.

Does it have a camera?

A camera? No.

Then it'll be returned to you once you arrive at the detention centre. You can call from there.

But I need to phone now. Don't I have the chance to make one call?

You're being detained under the Immigration Act, Miss Mathy. You're not being arrested and you're not being taken to jail, so you don't get a phone call. Now, if you'll get dressed and follow me, please.

Dalila is escorted, by the elbow, down the corridor. Her feet, in socks, make no sound as she moves. She can't really feel her feet. Only a weightless feeling. She blinks hard with both eyes and deliberately looks down at her arm in an effort to keep her mind in her body, to keep herself here, with what is happening now.

A door opens to the outside. A blue van, the size of a regular matatu, has been backed right up against the doorway. In the back is a cage containing six chairs. She is put in the cage and told to sit. Between the cage and the driver's cabin is an uncaged section where an immigration officer sits, facing her.

Another woman is brought to the van. Her hands are cuffed behind her back and she is sobbing. The officer escorting this woman dumps her on a seat beside Dalila. The cage is shut, locked. The officer flops down into the seat next to his colleague and slides his door closed. The van moves forward, passing through the gates, along the road and past the library and then out towards the motorway.

A light rain starts. Droplets trickle sideways across the tinted windows.

Why? sobs the woman next to her. Why? The woman cries and cries, with her head resting on the seat in front.

The van picks up speed as they leave the city. Rows of pine trees and fields of mud move past the window. The heads of the officers sway in unison with the van's movement.

Dalila keeps looking out of the window to avoid making eye contact with the male officers. She tries to think about Phil. If she can call Phil, he will know what to do. He can get her out.

The crying woman sits upright and groans, Why? I do nothing. Why? I'm pregnant. Her sobbing grows louder, more intense.

Hey, calm down, says one of the officers.

Stop, please, says the crying woman. Stop. I'm pregnant, she moans, crying with renewed strength. I am sick. Stop.

The officers look at each other. You think she could be pregnant? says one.

God knows, says the other. They'll say anything.

Aye, well, perhaps we should take the cuffs off, all the same.

If you want to take the cuffs off, says his colleague, on you go. But, I'm telling you, half an hour ago she was hysterical. Scratching and throwing things. She's fine now. She's just screamed herself out, she'll be alright. He leans forward and taps the cage. We'll be there soon enough, he says to the crying woman. Just calm down.

The crying goes on and on. Suddenly the woman sits up and says, Stop. I am sick.

We're almost there, says the officer. Just try to relax, you're making things harder for yourself.

The crying woman leans to the side and vomits all over the floor of the van.

Oh, for the love of Christ, yells the officer. He opens the latch and tells the driver, You better pull over. We've got a puker.

There in ten minutes, says the driver.

The crying woman retches and vomits again.

Just pull over, shouts the other officer. It fucking reeks in here.

Dalila tucks the neckline of her T-shirt up over her nose, but it hardly helps, she gags and almost throws up herself.

Smell of vomit – same.

The crying woman slumps towards Dalila, moaning and talking in a language Dalila does not understand. Keeping one hand over her nose and mouth, Dalila reaches over and brushes the damp hair away from the woman's face. She gently runs her palm across the woman's forehead, trying to soothe her.

The van pulls over and stops. The first officer slides open the side door and steps away from the smell. Godsakes, that's rank.

The driver steps out. Where is it?

It's all over the fucking floor. Have you got anything to wipe it up?

Dunno. Think I've got a wee towel in the glove box, says the driver.

Well, you better get it.

The van is stopped near a pine forest. It's quiet. Steam rises off the wet tarmac. Through the tinted glass Dalila sees a wind farm on the nearby horizon. The white blades slowly rotate. She had assumed they would be synchronised and finds herself hoping that they might align and turn together, even just for a second, but each mill silently spins to an individual rhythm. One of the officers catches Dalila looking out and, curiously, she finds herself saying, I think you must take off the handcuffs. She is not well.

To her surprise, one of the guards unlocks the gate, climbs in and takes off the handcuffs. The woman doesn't move. She just lies across the seat groaning.

The driver comes back with the hand towel and gives it over.

Me? says the officer. Why me?

She's your catch, so she's your responsibility, says the driver.

He's right, says the other officer, grinning.

Holding his nose, the officer kneels down on the floor of the cage. With the bunched-up towel, he pushes the soupy puddle towards the back doors and flicks it out onto the sodden brown pine needles by the roadside.

Honestly, man, fuck this job, says the officer, as he flicks more vomit out the back door. I'm serious. I've already done fifty hours this week and I'm on right across the weekend. And for what?

Dalila raises her feet onto her seat as the officer cleans the floor in front of her.

Fifty hours, the officer repeats. I may as well be working in Tesco. The money'd be about the same but you only have to put up with half the shite you do in this job.

Here, give it a skoosh with this, says the driver, holding up a bottle of Evian.

The officer sloshes water along the floor and wipes it towards the back, gagging and dry-heaving as he works.

Feeling a bit bokey there, are you? sniggers the other officer. The driver starts chuckling too.

Fuck off. I don't see you doing any work.

The driver and officer burst out laughing. Careful not to get any on your boots, laughs the driver.

Honestly, fuck the both of yous. Why don't you come back here and do this? He climbs out and tosses the towel into the bushes. He wipes his hand on his trousers, while the other two giggle.

Right, let's go.

After a few miles the van turns off the main road past a sign announcing,

Dungavel Detention Centre.

The building they approach is one of the most beautiful Dalila has ever seen. She isn't sure what she was expecting, but not this. It's a white castle on a mound, as if from a children's story book. On the right is a turret four storeys high, capped with a cone-shaped roof and an ornate weathervane. To the left, a tall square keep and a parapet with long stately windows. Twin stone staircases lead down from the front entrance onto the neatly mowed lawn. In the centre of the grounds is a flagpole flying a soaked Union Jack. Surrounding this castle are ten-foot-high fences capped with coiled razor wire. Spotlights shine onto the grounds. CCTV cameras stare down from their perches, patient as marabous.

The van passes through one checkpoint, and then a second. It stops in a small courtyard behind the building. The crying woman is helped out and assisted by both officers into the building. A guard, dressed in a different uniform to the border control officers, comes out of the building to escort Dalila. As she steps onto the coarse, wet tarmac her socks soak up the bitterly cold water. Inside, the crying woman collapses to the floor, wailing and howling. Two more guards jog up the corridor to assist the officers. Dalila is led away, down a long corridor with beige walls and blue flooring, clean except for her wet footprints. She is taken into a holding room and left on her own.

Two female guards enter.

Welcome to Dungavel Detention Centre, says the older guard. Her hair is very short and dyed copper. The other guard has a softer face with brown hair twisted into a bun on the back of her head. Both are wearing stab-proof vests and heavy boots. Handcuffs and mace are clipped to their belts.

You're going to be here for a while, says the older one. We'll need to quickly process your details and then take you to your room. Is that okay with you?

Dalila bunches her toes, shivering with the cold.

It's getting on a bit. Have you had anything to eat? asks the other guard. We've got sandwiches. Or perhaps a Coke? Would you like a drink?

There are no windows. Instead of a door, there is a locked metal gate. She is locked in here with these guards.

It'll be easier for everyone if you answer us, says the copper one.

No.

No, what?

No. Thank you. No Coke.

Good, then we can get straight to business. You'll need to remove your clothes.

Again? says Dalila, checking both guards' faces to see if they both agree. The impression she gets from the older guard is one of stone, something closed off. Whereas the younger woman is nervous but trying to act distant, almost bored.

It's only procedure, says the older one. We are required to search your clothes.

Dalila peels off her wet socks. She almost stumbles over as she steps out of her jeans and then she removes her top and places everything on the table. It's impossible to control her shivering.

Her clothes are searched and returned to her and when she is dressed they take her to a different room. They take a photograph of her face, scan her fingerprints, type her details into the computer. She is allocated the number DG3331. Her outgoing flight number is logged along with the departure time. Destination Nairobi. She is also given a bail application form as the younger guard quickly explains how and under what conditions she is allowed to seek bail but most of the information swims right by Dalila. Echoes creep along the corridor. Her mind skips to little Rosa. To Ma'aza. She wants to phone Phil. Daniel. What will Daniel do if she can't get out?

A male guard appears on the other side of the gate. Yous almost done here, aye? he asks.

Just a couple of minutes.

The male guard moves on.

Dalila's phone and handbag are returned to her.

Do you have my shoes, also my coat? asks Dalila.

The older guard says, No. That's everything we got. Must have left your shoes in Brand Street. Not to worry, we'll look into it.

A different male guard enters, a short fat man. He collects papers from the desk and reads them. So you're Irene Delilah Mwatty DG3331?

Dalila steps back towards the wall.

Come on, follow me.

Clutching her wet socks in one fist, her arm wrapped around her bag, she follows. The male guard wheezes as he moves. He walks with a toe-splayed waddle, his boots squeaking on the rubber floor. Dalila moves barefoot and silent beside him.

He leads her to a wing named Loudoun House. They enter a room with several bunk beds. All talking in the room stops and the faces of four different women turn towards them.

Evening, ladies, says the guard. You've got a new roommate tonight. I expect you all to get along nicely.

A small boy in his school uniform moves out from behind one of the bunks and stands by the side of a woman, presumably his mother. He gazes up at Dalila, blinking. Dalila looks at the guard and back at the little boy. She can't believe a child is in here, in this prison, before realising that she must be scowling at him because the child ducks behind his mother.

You can take any bunk you like, says the guard. Now, there's no lock on the door but you've been assigned this locker where you can keep any valuables. You'll need to sign here for the key.

The guard hands Dalila his clipboard and as she signs he says, Through there is the laundry room should you need to wash your clothes. There's showers along that way. Tomorrow you'll get to meet the nurse and someone will talk you through the procedures and all that.

Dalila hands back the clipboard and the guard gives her a locker key.

Right then, says the guard, just relax and get comfortable. The night staff will be coming round shortly to check on you.

The guard leaves. All the women in the dormitory remain silent, listening to his footsteps squeak down the corridor. The women quietly resume their conversations. None of them makes any effort to acknowledge Dalila.

The mother sits her son down on the bottom bunk and removes his shoes, getting him ready for bed.

Dalila checks her phone. It's half charged and low on credit. She is about to dial Phil's number but remembers that the centre will be shut by now. She tries to clear her head, to think. Her hands are shaking so violently, it takes her three attempts to dial Daniel's number.

Yes? His deep voice comes to her ear.

Baba. It is me.

Dali?

She hurries to the corner of the dormitory for privacy. They took me, she says in Kiswahili. You have to help. They have taken me. They have a flight ready to take me to Kenya, but I can't go back and I'm trapped here. It's like a prison.

Dali? Dalila. You are talking too fast. I don't understand.

They took me.

Where are you?

I went to report but they put me in a van and brought me here. You need to tell Phil.

Dali, be calm, my sister. Phil has already contacted me. You didn't sign out of the logbook this afternoon, so he has already started looking for you. Tell me where you are.

I'm in detention. In Dungavel Detention Centre.

Okay, okay. I will call Phil. He is the one to help you.

I'm scared, Baba. They said my case was refused. There is a plane waiting for me in five days to take me directly to Nairobi. I'm so scared, Baba, what can I do?

Dali, listen to me. Are you listening?

Yes, I can hear you.

You need to be calm. Try to calm yourself. You are a smart woman. If you are calm, you can think better. Okay?

Okay.

Breathe slow, says Daniel. Always good to breathe slow.

Okay. Okay, says Dalila. She inhales and exhales.

I will phone Phil immediately, tonight, says Daniel. Maybe we will get a solicitor. Phil will know what to do. Maybe appeal the decision. But we will help you, I promise.

Yes. Yes, do this.

But now be strong and calm. Many people, they are taken but then they are released. We know this. You have spoken to people like this at the Solidarity Centre, haven't you?

Yes.

And we know they try to scare you to go back. So don't sign anything, don't agree to anything until you speak to the solicitor, okay?

Okay . . . yes.

There is still hope, Dali.

Is there?

Of course. Phil can find a lawyer who will argue your case. They will get you out of there. In time, you will be granted status and then you will be safe and live in the UK. Things will be okay. You will find friends and work and happiness. That is how it can be. Trust in how it can be. Focus on that.

I will try, Baba.

Good. Good. Now, do you need anything?

She tries to think. Uh, I don't know. Phone credit, I need this. And a charger. A Nokia charger.

I can bring this.

And shoes, she says. They took me without my shoes.

Her phone goes dead. Out of credit. She taps the screen, hoping to somehow thump money into the SIM card. Her whole body is trembling. She wants to scream, to throw herself against the wall and shriek till her throat burns. She shoves the phone in her pocket and lies on one of the bunks and stares at the corner of the ceiling, breathing in and letting it out. Daniel will come. She breathes again. He will come. He knows how to get help. She rubs her eyes and presses hard against the sides of her head.

The mother crosses the dorm, puts some clothes in her locker and turns off the lights. She gets into bed next to her son and holds him, whispering to him as he falls asleep. Another woman lies down and pulls the blanket over her head. While the other two sit on the floor in the light of the bathroom doorway and talk quietly.

Dalila listens to the whining extractor fan in the bathroom and the rattle of the guard's keys as he patrols the corridor. The dorm is stuffy, airless. The skylight is a square of purple against the dark ceiling. She exhales slowly, deliberately. She splays her fingers as wide as she can to try to stop them quivering.

Daniel will come. He will come.

For hours she lies in the darkness feeling her heart hammer against her ribcage.

Darkness — same.

It was the same in her home, in college, in her uncle's home. The same in her flat and the same here. Thick, frightening darkness. Empty, uncertain darkness. Familiar, deep darkness.

In the quiet, she pictures her mother. The face doesn't come easily but her hands do, she can feel her mother's dry, nimble fingers. She goes back to a time in history when she knew those hands. From there she reimagines what happened. The riots came, and she imagines it was her uncle who was killed. And now, instead, she lives in Nairobi and graduation is just around the corner. Her mother and father have inherited her uncle's large home and they visit her regularly. Her mother has picked out a dress for her graduation but it's too long and she is adjusting the hem herself. Her brother wants his own car but her father thinks he should concentrate on his studies. On Sundays they meet for a big lunch of ugali and stewed goat and she brings her friend Muthoni because she fancies her brother.

The woman in the next bed starts to murmur in her sleep and Dalila is newly aware of the room and how dark it is.

The skylight above her gradually turns from purple to blue to grey. She hasn't slept at all.

One of the women takes a shower while the others use the bathroom and make their beds. The little boy, wearing only his underpants, runs by Dalila's bed and opens his locker with the key. His mother follows him. She helps him get dressed and kneels down to tie his shoelaces. He is perhaps eight years old and he's wearing his school uniform. Dalila wonders who is going to take him to school. The guards? Will they really take him all the way back to Glasgow?

The boy waits for his mother as she ties her long black hair into a bun and then wraps a hijab around her head and tucks it under her chin. As she watches, Dalila suddenly understands. This boy isn't going to school. Like herself, he is wearing all he owns. He was taken in his school uniform and he will wear it until he is released.

As Dalila makes her own bed, the mother comes up to her and asks, Do you speak English?

Dalila stands upright. Yes, I do.

It is time to eat, says the mother. Come, I will show you.

They leave their dormitory and they are joined in the hallway by other women from the room opposite. The mess hall is a clatter of cutlery, crockery, languages and chair legs being scraped across the floor. Each noise bounces off the walls and ceiling, making all sounds come from everywhere. A milky smell mixes with a steamed pulpy scent of scrambled eggs. Sharper still are the conjoined odours of plastic and instant coffee. The mother and son join the back of the long food queue, and Dalila stands beside her, conforming to the order of the room. Beside the vending machines is a stack of wet trays. One guard watches the food line and another watches detainees having their food dished up. At every exit is another guard, watching.

Men and women mingle freely in the hall. There are a lot more men than women. Strong, wiry-looking men. Asian men. Agitated men. Bearded Muslim men and frightened, swaggering men.

Dalila looks back down the corridor she just came from and is relieved to see a sign declaring Loudoun House as a women and family wing only. She quickly works out that the women and children must be kept separate from the men.

With no intention of eating, Dalila slips out of the queue and sits at a table being used by other women. Among the faces, she spots another child. A girl of about fourteen with her head lowered, eating eggs. Two large women sit either side of her, as if to hide her.

When breakfast is over, people move out of the hall. Unsure where to go or what to do, Dalila finds the mother and follows her again. The corridors are full of people leaning against the wall, chatting, walking one way or the other. Most of the languages brush by her but it is the eyes that are the most difficult to ignore. Confused eyes, pleading eyes. Every pair seems to reach out and grasp her. Angry, pain-filled eyes.

She comes to a small library. One guard sits at a desk next to a white woman, possibly a UK border official. Another guard stands near the window. A queue is already forming to use one of the six computers and people are also lining up to speak to the white woman at the desk.

Her thoughts return to Daniel. She takes out her phone to double-check her credit. There is none. She could use a computer but the queue is already long. What is she supposed to do all day? And why are people waiting to talk to this white woman? She lifts a *National Geographic* off the shelf and sits down, hoping to camouflage herself as she flips the pages.

In here most people talk in lowered voices. Some sigh in front of the computer screens, tapping away at the keys. She overhears bits of conversations in English, people trading phone credit, toiletries, cash. There are lots of discussions about shoes and she notices many people walking around in socks and flip-flops. Two women gossip about a third woman who was recently taken to the medical wing.

The boy in school uniform enters the library with his mother. They sit at the table opposite Dalila. The mother opens a book and encourages her son to read to her in whispers. Dalila keeps her eyes down, flicking through pages of camera advertisements.

By midday Dalila's feet are cold. Her socks are still a bit damp from the night before. She goes back to her room and lies on her bed, keeping her feet warm under the blanket. She wonders what Daniel is doing. Her mind moves to Ma'aza. What would Ma'aza do in this place? She always said moving is living and Dalila pictures her walking with those fast, determined strides. I should have gone with Ma'aza, she thinks. Just taken what I had and left. Kept moving. Instead, I froze like a scared little girl. I should face it, I'm a coward full of stupid little dreams. They were never going to let me stay in the UK. Ma'aza told me, she told me. She said they were coming to take us.

In the canteen at dinner time, her mood is low. Dalila sits with a bowl of soup in front of her. She tries a mouthful. Nausea churns and tugs at the back of her throat. She pushes the bowl away. Across the hall, the boy in school uniform is also not eating. He sits on his hands, head down. His mother nudges the tray of food towards him, but the boy simply turns his head.

Dalila lifts the bread roll and forces herself to take a bite.

By 7 p.m. she is waiting outside the visitors' lounge with a group of men. Some push forward to ask the guard if their name is on the list, if they have a visitor, their solicitor perhaps.

Dalila stands back from the group, against the wall.

The guard reads the list of names and numbers of those who have visitors.

DG3331 Irene Matty? calls the guard. Her heart leaps and Dalila forces her way to the front of the group. A female guard asks her to raise her hands. She does. The guard pats her down.

Daniel stands as soon as he sees her and it takes a strong and steady willpower not to cry and run towards him.

They shake hands. Hello, Dali, says Daniel. He clasps both his hands around hers.

Thank you, Baba.

How are you?

Thank you. It's bad here, Baba. Thank you for coming.

It is not a problem. I will come again tomorrow, if you like. But sit, please. I have lots to tell you.

They sit. The room is similar to an airport lounge. Lounge-style benches with low coffee tables. Dalila looks at Daniel. She has so much she wants to tell him, to explain, but looking at him, here, she can't find the words.

Daniel adjusts his glasses and looks around the room. In Kiswahili, he whispers, You know, I believe this to be the ugliest hotel I have ever seen.

Dalila almost smiles. She reaches out and touches his arm, so thankful that he is real and here with her.

I have good news, Dali, he says. The solicitors from Dundee think you have a case. Phil spoke to them this morning. He emailed everything to them. They are going to put together an appeal and they'll probably call you tomorrow.

She thinks she understands but her mind is struggling to focus. What? is all she can say.

Daniel leans forward. The Dundee solicitors are filing an appeal against the decision to deny you Leave to Remain. They will make an appeal. The Home Office cannot put you on a plane if there is an appeal. So you are safe, for now. You won't be taken to Kenya in four days.

She hears that last sentence but does not believe it.

They appealed my case?

Yes. They will call you tomorrow to explain everything. I gave them your number.

So they will let me out?

I don't know. Phil told me that you're likely to have the hearing soon, at that time you will be given their decision. He thinks you have a good case. You are a woman. Kenya has a bad reputation with women. And your uncle is becoming political, this new information will strengthen your claim. It is good for you.

At the back of the visitors' lounge a couple sit close together, caressing each other. He is clearly the detainee in his sweat pants and flip-flops. She wears a long green shawl and her black hair flares out from a hair tie on the back of her head. She lifts her legs onto his lap and nudges his cheek with her nose.

Have you eaten anything today? asks Daniel.

She watches the couple. The boy adjusts her legs on his knees and starts fiddling with the buckle on her shoe.

I believe, says Daniel, that those vending machines only sell food with absolutely no nutrition. It will be like not eating at all. He stands up, goes to the machines and brings back two hot chocolates in paper cups, a packet of Maltesers and two bags of crisps. He opens out the crisp packets till they are flat silver sheets on the coffee table.

A picnic, says Daniel, holding his arms out wide.

Dalila smiles and runs her hands along her thighs. She looks up at him. The lenses of his glasses are smudged, he hasn't shaved in a few days but his face is beautiful. Seeing him here, in this place, is such blessed relief. Beautiful, beautiful Daniel, with his little jokes and easy manner. She watches him sip from the paper cup. He leans forward on his seat and fiddles with the visitor's tag on his wristband. Gratitude overwhelms her. She wants to thank him, and hold him and kiss his hands for every smile and reassuring word he has ever given her, to tell him that he is the only true family she has now. Her tears are rising, building, threatening to gush over into full-blown weeping.

Thank you, Baba, is all she can manage to say, taking a Malteser and popping it into her mouth.

You like the food? he asks.

Dalila nods as she chews. Her tears spilling down her smiling face.

I brought shoes for you, he says, looking at the socks on her feet. I also have phone credit and ten pounds in cash and I brought a jumper in case you get cold. What else? Oh, yes, a toothbrush.

You brought me a toothbrush? she asks, as salty tears slip into the corner of her mouth.

Yes, says Daniel. He moves to sit next to her and places his hand on her knee. She puts both of her hands on top of his, squeezing his knuckles to thank him again, her throat too tight to say the words.

I had to leave everything at the desk when I went through security, says Daniel. I'm not allowed to bring anything in here, but the guards will make sure you get your package.

They sit close together and eat their picnic but every time Dalila feels herself starting to unwind she is tempered by the sense that their visit is passing far too quickly. At the end of the hour a guard announces that they have five minutes before visiting hour is over. Daniel leans closer and says, Dali, I will come again soon. I think tomorrow. But listen to me carefully now. He takes her hand and looks right into her.

I know what it is like to be in these places, he says. You cannot change all this, instead, you must guard a secret place inside you. Keep that place good and full of beauty. Some people, like your uncle, are hyenas. They will hunt you and kill you, even eat your bones. But the ones here, he says, directing his chin to the guards, these ones are termites. They take small bites, always eating at you. In the end, the hyena and the termite are the same. They devour everything. You must protect what they cannot eat. Keep your heart secret. Find a purpose for your days, a reason bigger than this place. It will keep you going. When I was in prison, the men who found this, even if they did not survive, they prevailed. You must prevail, Dali. Do you understand me?

Before breakfast, Dalila pulls on the slipper-like shoes Daniel brought for her. They are a little too big, but warm. The fleece jumper he brought is thicker than a blanket and she feels less shivery as she goes to the canteen. Determined to eat something this morning, she manages half a banana and a bowl of cornflakes. She buys herself a hot chocolate from the vending machine and sits at the table watching the other detainees. The mood in the canteen is quieter than yesterday. People talk in huddles and shoot worried, wide-eyed looks at the guards.

The mother sits down opposite Dalila, and helps her son into his seat.

Hello, says Dalila. I am Irene.

Zainab, says the mother, placing a hand on her chest. This is my son, Mohammed.

The boy looks down at his cornflakes and pushes the plate away.

Zainab speaks quietly to her son in a language Dalila doesn't know, then she turns to Dalila and says in English, He is not feeling well today. I think he has pain in his stomach. Every day he says he feels sick. But I think today everyone is sick.

Dalila is surprised at Zainab's neat English accent. She leans in closer and asks, What is going on? I notice that everyone is quiet today.

Last night they brought in women from Yarl's Wood, whispers Zainab. Do you know Yarl's Wood?

It is a detention centre like this, says Dalila.

Not like this. Zainab shakes her head. This place is alright. It's relaxed here and they don't treat you bad. But Yarl's Wood is different. It is a place only for women. Pray they never take you there. The stories from that place are horrific.

Zainab places a hand on her son's back and encourages him to eat.

She turns back to Dalila and says, Last night, they brought in six women from Yarl's Wood. Four of them were put in the dorm opposite ours. They said the other two are in the medical unit. They are hunger strikers. When there is trouble, like a hunger strike, they'll do this. They'll move the hunger strikers and troublemakers to other detention centres so they don't have power together.

Those women will bring trouble here? asks Dalila.

I don't know, but I don't fear them. I am worried about the vans. When the van comes here with new people, they don't leave empty. Some of us will be taken today or tomorrow.

Lying on her bed, Dalila clutches her phone. It vibrates. A text from Daniel.

Solicitors coming today. 3:30. They have your number. Be strong.

Moments later, she gets a text from the Dundee solicitors' office confirming the appointment.

At 3:30 p.m., Dalila is searched before being allowed into the visitors' lounge. A man in a silver-grey suit stands and puts out his hand towards her. Hello, you're Irene, I take it?

Yes, she replies, shaking the man's hand.

I'm Duncan Finley and this is my associate Helen Foster.

He stands aside, allowing Dalila to shake his associate's hand. This woman, Helen, appears to be only a little older than Dalila. Her hand is damp and cold. Her heavy eyeliner gives her a slightly startled appearance.

We're having a coffee. D'you want one? says Duncan, pointing at the vending machine.

No. Thank you.

You sure?

Maybe hot chocolate, says Dalila.

While Duncan buys the drink, Dalila sits down and watches Helen's eyes dart around the room. Helen leans back in her chair and then seems to notice Dalila. She slides forward on her seat and says, So you're from Kenya?

Yes.

That must be nice, smiles Helen. All that sun.

Yes, Dalila replies. In an effort to keep the conversation going she adds, Sun is good.

Helen looks at the guards and then up at the CCTV camera. She picks up her notes and studies them.

Duncan returns with the drink, and says, Looks like you two are getting to know each other. That's great. Helen here is one of our bright young stars at the firm. Very competent. She'll be representing you during the hearing. I'm just a glorified taxi driver, me. He laughs out loud and Helen manages a weak smile.

You are solicitors? Dalila asks. From Dundee?

That's us, says Duncan. Now, we've been sent most of your documents from, let's see here, from Phil at the Solidarity Centre. We've filled out the appeal form and got that in. But there's a few things we need to discuss in preparation for the hearing. Mibbe we can start with you telling us why you left Kenya?

As they discuss the case, Dalila struggles with their thick accents and often has to ask them to repeat themselves. Duncan does most of the talking while Helen takes notes. She seldom glances up at Dalila, preferring the familiarity of her notes. Her nails are perfect and her eyebrows tightly shaped. The suit she wears is newer and smarter than the one worn by Duncan, who looks like he's been living in his suit for years.

Well, this has been great, Irene. A lot of interesting things have been flagged up. So, here's what we're gonna do, says Duncan. Looks like you've got a strong case for an appeal, given that sending you back would contravene the Human Rights Act because you'd be in immediate danger. So we're – well, actually Helen is – gonna push for Discretionary Leave to Remain, aren't you, Helen?

The young solicitor looks up from her papers when she hears her name and says, Yes, that's right.

Duncan waits for her to continue, but she goes back to her notes. He smiles at Dalila.

The, uh, the other thing that's interesting is the political dimension, says Duncan. With your uncle entering politics we could argue you'd face political oppression back in Kenya.

Dalila nods.

I'm optimistic. I mean, the truth is, over eighty per cent of asylum cases are rejected straight off, but it's in the appeals that a case gets to be heard by a proper judge. I don't think your case was properly thought through by your case worker. Looks like you've got a good chance.

Will I go with you to the court? Dalila asks, hoping to get out of detention, even for a day.

No, no. It's all done by video link now. You'll be able to hear and see everything that's happening on the screen. You'll see Helen, she'll be there. And if the judge needs to ask you a question, he'll speak to you directly. It's exactly like being there. The whole thing will take about forty-five minutes.

The judge will ask me to speak, to tell my story again?

No, you shouldn't need to go over it all again. It's just that you might be asked a question. But not to worry. Helen will deal with everything. She's very competent. One of our bright young stars.

Crying and movement in the dormitory wake Dalila in the middle of the night. Mohammed writhes in his bed, inconsolable. As Zainab tries to soothe him, his crying gets louder until he is openly wailing. By now, all the women in the room are awake. Some turn over and try to ignore the commotion. One woman hisses, Shh.

Zainab gets up and calls one of the night-duty guards. The guard comes in and switches on the light to groans from the other women. When Mohammed sees his mother with the guard his crying intensifies.

He is not well, Zainab tells the guard. He says his stomach hurts and I think his temperature is high.

The guard looks down at the boy and he looks around the room at the rest of the women sitting up in their beds.

Right, uh, well, says the guard, I guess we better get him down to the medical unit. Can you carry him? he asks Zainab.

Yes, I can take him.

Zainab wraps her son in a blanket and lifts him up onto her hip. The guard leads her out of the room and shuts the door. After a moment one of the women lets out an annoyed sigh. She hops down from the top bunk, switches off the light and returns to bed.

After breakfast, Dalila asks for directions to the medical unit. When she finds it, the guard at the door stops her.

My friend, she is in there. She came last night with her son, Dalila explains.

But the guard tells her, There's no visiting just now.

When can I visit?

Depends on who it is.

My friend Zainab, says Dalila. Her boy is Mohammed. Last night the boy was not well.

Yeah, I know who you're talking about, says the guard.

Can I see them? I brought apple juice.

You'll have to come back later, says the guard. The doc's in there just now doing her rounds.

Dalila returns after lunch and this time they let her in. The medical ward is a room sectioned off by curtains. Mohammed is asleep. He looks pale. Zainab is sitting next to him, holding his hand.

Hello, Zainab whispers.

How is he? whispers Dalila.

He had a fever during the night, but I think he is doing better now. He is very worried and says he wants to go to school. Can you believe that? Zainab smiles. He never wants to go to school.

I brought this for him, Dalila says, placing the carton of apple juice next to the bed. When I am feeling bad, sometimes apples help.

You are very kind, says Zainab.

Her son murmurs and shifts in his sleep. Zainab stands up and places her palm across his forehead.

Dalila waits, hoping Zainab might create an opening for conversation but she is too focused on her child.

Also, I want to thank you, says Dalila. When I came here, it was only you who spoke to me. Thank you for that.

It was nothing, says Zainab.

A nurse comes in, pulls back a curtain and checks the chart of a man with a swollen face and his arm in a cast. After seeing to the man, the nurse sweeps back another curtain, revealing two beds, with a woman in each.

She signals to the guard at the door. These are our two hunger strikers, she says. They're still refusing to eat so I've been ordered to separate them. Could you bring some help?

The guard steps out and returns with three other guards to assist the nurse. Two guards begin rolling the first bed out of the ward. Dalila stands well out of the way. On the second bed is a thin woman with loose curly hair spread across the pillow. As the guards wheel the bed out, Dalila gets a proper look at the patient. The recognition makes her step back.

Ma'aza? Ma'aza, is it you? Excuse me, I know this woman, says Dalila, approaching the bedside.

Stay back, barks the guard.

She is my friend, explains Dalila. I know her. Is she okay? Ma'aza, are you okay? What happened?

Right, you, says the guard. Back. Now.

Mohammed wakes up with all the shouting and starts crying.

Where are you taking her? says Dalila. Is she sick?

I said, get back.

But me, I know this one, Dalila shouts. We lived together. I just want to—

The guard puts his arm up and pushes Dalila back, away from the bedside. She moves his arm out of the way, saying, I only want to speak with her. I know this woman. Ma'aza? Hello? Ma'aza?

More hands are on her, spinning her around, and she loses balance, stumbling, grabbing at the guard as he grabs her. She lands on her knees and from behind a force knocks her onto her stomach.

Stay down, shouts a guard.

It's okay, she says.

Her arms are pulled behind her back and her wrists cuffed. She can hear Mohammed shrieking and crying over the shouts and orders being barked in the room.

Dragged like luggage, the handcuffs biting into her wrists, she gets dumped in an isolated room. The guards leave without removing the handcuffs. She lies there, alone in the room, with her face to the side and all she can think about is Ma'aza. She must have been one of the women brought in last night. They said Yarl's Wood. She was brought in from there. Is she on hunger strike? How did she get caught and taken there?

She rolls onto her back, wriggles her hands down, and by pulling her knees right up she is able to squeeze her forearms around her hips. She unhooks one leg at a time till her cuffed hands are in front of her. Digging into her pocket, she retrieves her phone and calls Daniel.

I found Ma'aza, she says into the receiver. They brought her here. I saw her in the medical unit, because now she is a hunger striker.

What? says Daniel. Ma'aza is there, with you?

Yes, I saw her. But they won't allow me to talk with her. She looks sick, Baba.

She is a fighter, that one.

I know, says Dalila, but I am worried for her. She will fight and fight but it will change nothing. She will die for nothing.

Okay, Dali, be calm, says Daniel. It is best if you can speak to her.

I tried but they won't let me near. They put handcuffs on me and locked me in here.

I see. Well, first you must think and be calm. When you are ready, when there is a good time, you must try to see Ma'aza again, says Daniel. She will need you, Dali.

Okay. Okay. I will call Phil and tell him everything.

I will tell Phil all of this, I am going to the centre now. You must keep your credit, in case we need to get in touch or if something else happens.

Thank you, Baba. We have to help her.

What can I bring for you tonight? asks Daniel.

Even me, I don't know. If you can bring some more money, because no one here has cash, she says. And phone credit top-up cards.

Okay, anything else?

Dalila thinks, as she wriggles in the handcuffs and puts the phone to her other ear. When you see Phil, could you look in the clothing bank for boys' clothes? I need clothes for small boy. Eight years old.

Dalila is taken to an office she has never seen before. She stands in front of a desk while a guard waits at the door behind her. At the desk sits a woman who is dressed in the same uniform as the other guards but introduces herself as the Residential Units Manager.

Miss Mwathi, says the manager, I believe you speak English?

Yes, I'm from Kenya.

Quite. The manager lifts a sheet of paper from her desk. I'm also aware that you have completed this complaint form regarding the incident that took place in the medical unit earlier today.

Me, I only want to know where is my friend, says Dalila. She looked very ill and I was worried. Is she still here?

We'll get to that, says the manager, placing the form on her desk and interlacing her fingers. But first I need to make a few things clear. You are here at the taxpayer's expense and as such your behaviour should reflect the appropriate gratitude. It has been explained to you that in this centre we run an Incentives and Earned Privileges scheme. At the moment you are on the Enhanced Level but if we should see fit to downgrade your status to Standard Level we could remove your phone and internet privileges. And if you ever again lift a finger against one of the employees in this facility we will place you in temporary confinement for as long as I see fit. Have I made myself clear?

Yes, says Dalila.

Now, to the matter of your friend. How do you know this woman?

When I was moved to Glasgow, they put me in a flat together with her. Me, I known Ma'aza. We are friends.

Glasgow, you say? Yet Ma'aza was arrested for working illegally in Luton and detained in Yarl's Wood Detention Centre.

Ma'aza ran away. Me, I know nothing about her work, says Dalila. There was a raid, a dawn raid in the flat next to ours. She became frightened and ran away.

I see, says the manager. You mentioned in the complaint form that you were, quote . . . *only trying to help. If I could see Ma'aza, I could help. She will talk to me. She won't fight with me and maybe she will eat.* Do you still believe this to be the case?

Yes. We are friends and I know her. I want to help her.

Okay. Thank you, Miss Mwathi. You can go now. The guard will escort you to your room.

That night her visitation privileges are withheld. She texts Daniel.

Sorry Baba, they won't let me C U. THX for coming. I know it is a long drive. If they let me have visitors again I will SMS U.

His reply comes a few minutes later.

I like the drive. I left a package for you. Did you see Ma'aza? Will email you tomorrow. Be strong.

Before breakfast the next morning, Mohammed and his mother Zainab enter the dormitory. The boy has more colour to his face though he looks a little sullen. Zainab takes her son to the shower and makes sure he is properly washed and dried. As they come out of the bathroom, Mohammed is wrapped in a towel. Dalila approaches and says, Hello. How are you, Mohammed?

The boy doesn't answer but his mother says, He's doing much better. We are going to try and have some breakfast.

Good, says Dalila. Breakfast is good. Also, I have something for you, Mohammed. Do you want to see what it is?

The boy lowers his head.

I have it here, says Dalila. She goes to her locker and brings out some folded clothes. This is for you.

The boy looks at Dalila's swollen, bruised wrists. He glances around the room at what else might be out of place this morning.

Please. Dalila holds the clothes closer. It's okay. It is a gift. I have a friend who comes to visit me, she explains to Zainab. He brought these.

From the expression on her face, Dalila knows she consents to the gift.

Zainab crouches down next to her son. What do you say to the nice lady?

The boy looks at the clothes and points to the T-shirt. Are they Ninja Turtles? he says.

Dalila looks down. Uh, yes, I think they are. Do you like the Teenage Mutant Ninja Turtles?

I only like Batman, says the boy.

Well, you know more than me about this, says Dalila, but I like the colour. What do you think?

The boy shrugs.

Zainab runs her hand over the back of her son's head. If you put these on, then when we get home I promise to buy you a Batman T-shirt. Does that sound fair?

The boy nods as he takes the clothes.

Thank you, Irene, says Zainab as her son gets dressed. Please, you must sit with us for breakfast.

Dalila spends the afternoon in the library, hoping to use one of the computers. As she sits at the table, reading the newspaper from two days ago, a man approaches the table. She looks down and shifts away.

Sister, don't be afraid, says the man. My name is John. From Sudan. Can I ask you a question?

She waits, knowing the guards are nearby, planning to scream if he tries anything.

I know you give clothes to the boy. You are very kind. Please, I ask, where do you get such clothes?

Dalila looks up at the man. My friend brought them from Glasgow. Did you buy these things?

No, there is a charity. They have a clothing bank. Sometimes they can get things.

I understand, says John. He glances around to see who is watching. I have problem, he says. I can show you? His sweatshirt is tied around his waist. He lifts the flap covering his buttocks. Underneath, his jeans have a large L-shaped rip, exposing his underwear.

Dalila swallows.

He shifts the sweatshirt to cover himself again. When they remove me from Colnbrook, he says, this happened. I have no other trousers and I don't know anybody in Scotland. Is cold here, but I can't wear this jumper in the day because my trousers is teared.

Dalila nods. I will ask my friend.

Thank you, says John. My size is 34–32. Thank you.

*

Within four days, word has got around that Dalila can get things. Detainees ask her for clothes. Socks, shoes, headscarves, jumpers and underwear are the most requested items. But people also need credit for their phones, cash and printouts of documents. She keeps a precise list with each person's name and request and a check to see that they receive what they have asked for. Everything is relayed to Daniel or Phil via text. Daniel visits every evening and sometimes brings Tracey, the volunteer from the centre, to help him. They meet other detainees and offer advice about their cases, promising to contact solicitors or friends and family members in other parts of the UK.

I'm sorry for always asking you to do this, Daniel, she tells him one evening.

It's no problem, Dali, he says. This is all Ubuntu. Our pain is shared, as well as our purpose. I get up and do this now. It's a life larger than my own. And my flat is much cleaner, because I am never in it.

Dalila laughs out loud. That's a good thing, she says. An unbelievable thing.

One evening, after visiting hour is over, Dalila distributes the clothes and phone cards Daniel has brought. She checks off each item against her list and writes out the new requests for the following day.

As she is about to go to bed, two guards come to her room, with them is the Residential Units Manager.

DG3331. Irene Dalila Mwathi? the manager reads from her clipboard.

Yes?

Pack your things. We are moving you.

Dalila gathers her few possessions and is taken down a corridor sealed off from the general population. The last time she came this way, she was in handcuffs. She is shown to a room where she recognises Ma'aza lying on one of two beds.

This is an isolation room, says the manager. Ma'aza will be kept here until she eats. You said you can make her eat?

Yes, I think so, says Dalila.

Good. Stay with her. Make her eat. There'll be a guard posted outside should you need anything.

Thank you, says Dalila.

The door closes and she kneels by the bed.

Ma'aza is gaunt and drowsy. Her eyes roll towards Dalila, she swallows slowly and says, You look terrible, my little sugar sister.

Dalila laughs and puts her hands on Ma'aza's cheeks and says, And you are absolutely beautiful. She kisses Ma'aza's forehead.

Why did you run? says Dalila, stroking her friend's hair. Ma'aza's eyelids close and open again.

Dalila sits on the floor next to the bed. I thought we made big plans, remember? You and me, we are supposed to get a house in Canada, and watch movies on a very big TV.

Ma'aza's eyes close and her mouth stretches into a smile.

You promised we would eat junk food and BBQ every day and grow very big and fat, remember?

I remember, Ma'aza says weakly. And you? You promised the manager you will make me eat, didn't you?

Why are you doing this to yourself?

I do it because . . . I choose it. They don't control me. You do not control me.

But you will die, Ma'aza.

Maybe it is better. Ma'aza turns her face away. After a few moments she says, I'm sorry I left you.

If you are sorry, then eat something. Do it for me, so we can be strong and get out of here.

They will never let me out, says Ma'aza.

Maybe, after time, they will. Please eat, just one small bite.

I was working . . .

What? says Dalila. I can't hear you. She sits on Ma'aza's bed and leans closer.

I went to Luton, whispers Ma'aza. I was working there, in a kitchen, like a factory. She licks her lips and says, The police, they arrest many of us. After four days in the cell they take me and some others to Yarl's Wood. The Home Office says I am a criminal because I work in the kitchen. They reject my case and want to send me back to Ethiopia.

Shh, says Dalila, reaching over for the water bottle. Here, take this. Drink.

Ma'aza drinks a little before pushing the bottle away. They try to make me fly back but Ethiopia doesn't accept me, she says. They say I am Eritrean. So I don't fly.

But that's good news, says Dalila. You can stay.

Ma'aza opens her heavy eyelids and says, You don't understand. You never understand. The Home Office do not release criminals and my country won't accept me. Like this, I am trapped. They will keep me in Yarl's Wood for years. To stay in that place? It is better to die.

Ma'aza closes her eyes and says, I have lost everything.

Okay, whispers Dalila. I understand, I do. But I am going to stay here till you go. I am your friend. I will lose with you.

She lies down on the bed, takes hold of her hand and turns off the light.

Fifteen minutes before her appeal is about to begin, a guard escorts Dalila to a small room near the main reception. On the table in this room is a flat-screen TV. Above it, a webcam pointed at the single chair. Dalila is told to sit on the chair.

The guard switches on the screen and fiddles with the cables leading under the desk towards a computer terminal. He closes the curtains and adjusts the camera to point at Dalila. An image flickers onto the screen of a man's face.

Hello, can you hear me? he asks. Testing. Testing.

Dalila nods and the guard says, Aye, we can hear you. How's things at your end?

All looks good here, says the man on the screen. Can see you fine. Sounds alright. He moves away from the camera to a desk in a courtroom of plain pine furniture. The judge's desk is higher than the large table in the centre of the room. There are floor-to-ceiling windows behind the judge's seat and through them, in the distance, Dalila recognises the white and black spires of the churches near the YWCA where she went to her one and only English class. The man comes back to the screen and says, Good morning. I am the court bailiff and this is the Asylum and Immigration Tribunal Court in the Eagle Building in Glasgow. Are you Irene Dalila Mwathi?

Yes, she says to the camera.

Good. You'll soon see the judge come in. He'll sit up there straight ahead of you. Your solicitor will sit here to your left and the Home Office presenting officer will be seated over there to your right. If at any time you cannot see or hear what's going on, you just let us know, okay?

Yes, okay.

Don't need to talk so loudly, says the bailiff, we can hear you fine.

He goes back to his desk, as Helen Foster enters the courtroom. Wearing an expensive suit, with her make-up perfectly done, she looks just like a professional lawyer, a TV lawyer. She comes up to the camera and says, Hello, Irene. How are you today?

I'm okay.

Good. That's nice, says Helen. Right then.

The judge enters. The court bailiff and the two other people in the courtroom rise.

Dalila stands, awkward and alone in the small room, not sure if she should participate in these formalities. When the people on the screen take their seats, Dalila sits, too.

The judge begins proceedings by asking Helen Foster a few questions about Dalila's statement and the articles and letters of support submitted during her Substantive Interview. The judge has a clipped grey beard and his manner is direct, yet he is soft-spoken with his questions. Dalila watches her solicitor, who leans forward to the microphone on her desk to answer each question, otherwise keeping her head down over her notes. The judge then looks at the Home Office presenting officer and asks, Would the Respondent like to begin cross-examination?

Thank you, my Lord. I only have a few questions for the Appellant. He stands and addresses the camera.

Miss Mwathi, could you describe for us how you came to the UK?

She thinks back and says, My friend, he helped me, his name is Charles Okema. He took pity on me when I was in my uncle's house. He said, if he had money, he can get papers for me and help me to get away. So I, I stole money from my uncle and gave it to him. After two weeks Charles took me from the house and brought me to the airport. There I caught the plane to the UK.

And where did this Charles Okema get these documents? asks the presenting officer.

He told me he received them from a man called Eddie.

Do you know Eddie's second name? His address?

No, says Dalila. I never met him. I don't know him.

So, he gave you false papers and put you on the plane, is that correct?

No, the papers were not false, she says. The passport and ID card are mine. They are real ones. The tourist visa is also real, but he had to buy it. And also pay for the flight ticket. That is why Charles needed the money.

The solicitor rubs his forehead and thinks for a second before saying, But he did tell you what to say at Border Control when you arrived in the UK, did he not?

Yes.

You were instructed to pose as a tourist, all the while knowing you were going to claim asylum once inside the UK. Am I right?

Yes.

The presenting officer lifts a photograph from his desk, walks up to the camera and holds it up for Dalila to see. Miss Mwathi, do you know this woman?

Yes, says Dalila, this is Mama Anne.

Her full name, please.

Dalila thinks back to the name written on her instructions when she first arrived in the UK. Her name is Anne Nafula Abasi.

And this person? Do you recognise him? The solicitor holds up another photograph.

This one is Markus, says Dalila.

That's not their real names, is it?

I only know these names, says Dalila.

When you arrived in Heathrow you lied to the Border Control and told them that these people were your aunt and cousin, respectively, didn't you?

Yes, says Dalila, lowering her head.

Speak into the microphone, please, interrupts the judge.

Yes. Me, I said this.

According to your statement, you went directly from the airport to their house and spent the night with them, did you not?

Yes.

Could you provide the court with the address at which you stayed?

I don't know the address, says Dalila. I only followed them. I told the Home Office many times, I don't know the address. It was dark. I ran away from there because Markus, he . . . attacked me, so I don't know where the flat is.

I see. So you maintain that you don't know the real names of these people or where they live, yet you were happy to arrive in a foreign country and stay with them. Why is that, Miss Mwathi?

I don't know, says Dalila. Me, I didn't know anyone at that time. I only wanted to be away from my uncle. I went with them because it was arranged for me. They promised to help me.

Very well, I have one more question. You claim your uncle abused you and kept you prisoner in his home, is that correct?

Yes.

Did your uncle tie you up or restrain you?

No.

Did he lock you in a room somewhere?

The man on the screen in front of Dalila is like a character in a strange film. She has to concentrate to answer him sincerely and not to simply watch him perform.

The doors of the house were locked, she says, and the gates of the compound were always locked.

Were all the doors of the house locked?

The back door to the kitchen, it was open so I could cook and wash in the courtyard there.

Thank you, Miss Mwathi, says the presenting officer and he sits down.

Any final questions for the Appellant? asks the judge.

Helen leans towards the microphone and says, Yes, My Lord. She checks the notes before asking, Miss Mwathi, the man who helped you escape from your uncle's compound and who provided you with the documents you needed, this Mr Charles Okema, are you still in touch with him?

No, says Dalila.

Why not?

Because he has died. I saw on the internet they found his body. He was murdered.

Thank you. With the court's permission, may I refer My Lord to the submitted evidence article C3, the one referring to Mr Okema's murder. While no one has been convicted of that crime as yet, there appears to be strong evidence that it was carried out by members of the Mungiki sect, which is consistent with Miss Mwathi's version of events.

Still seated, Helen turns her face towards the camera and says, Your uncle, Kennedy Mwathi, is a member of the Mungiki sect, is that correct?

Yes, he is.

Miss Mwathi, could you remind the court of the treatment you received from Mr Kennedy Mwathi?

Yes. Dalila clears her throat. He kept me in his house. Me, I was like a prisoner there. He beat me with his hand and he hit me here with a belt, cutting the skin. She peels back the collar of her T-shirt to reveal the scar on her shoulder. He also, he raped me and threatened me with a knife.

Thank you, Miss Mwathi, says Helen, cross-checking her notes.

During your initial interview in Croydon, you omitted to mention that you were sexually assaulted. Why is that?

Dalila takes a deep breath. I don't know. I was scared. Because I was very nervous to be in a room with these two men.

Which two men?

The officers who were interviewing me.

Did you ask for a female officer to be present during the interview?

Yes.

But only men interviewed you, is that correct?

Yes.

Thank you, Miss Mwathi. That is all, My Lord.

Thank you, Miss Foster, says the judge. We are now ready to proceed to the closing arguments.

The presenting officer immediately stands up. He shifts out from behind his chair and puts his hands on his hips. My Lord, he starts, the position of the Home Office is the same as when it first refused the Appellant's case for asylum. Very little new evidence has been presented here today, but what we *are* witnessing is a story with facts that have changed and changed again. The Appellant claims to have been abused and imprisoned by her uncle. While the Home Office does not condone this treatment and sympathises with victims of abuse, it is not enough for this court to function on hearsay. Clear evidence needs to be provided, and in this instance, regarding these claims, it has not. Indeed, after claiming to be imprisoned for almost a year, when the time came to flee the house, Miss Mwathi seems to have had little to deter her. Furthermore, she appears to have had the money and contacts to arrange for her safe passage to the UK. Upon arrival, she did not immediately claim asylum but elected to perpetuate a lie that she was visiting family for a holiday. Later, when she did claim asylum, she withheld vital information regarding her case and regarding the names and whereabouts of the criminals who helped her.

Dalila watches the solicitor on the screen go to his desk and lift up the photographs of Markus and Mama Anne.

These people, who the Appellant claims not to know, are one Mark Kayode and Mariam Olushola, both wanted by the police in connection for human trafficking, falsifying documents, fraud and working illegally within the UK. Having paid these people for their services and stayed in their house, Miss Mwathi has consistently denied knowing their names or whereabouts. Miss Mwathi obviously has strong connections to an international criminal network and this government does not harbour people who consort with criminals. If released, I believe Miss Mwathi would quickly go underground in an effort to stay here illegally.

The solicitor adjusts his suit jacket and steps away from the camera and back towards the judge. With regards to the risks she faces if sent back, he continues, the Appellant has argued that Mr Kennedy Mwathi is a politician, a member of the Mungiki sect and a ruthless businessman with a vast empire who abuses and destroys those who oppose him. However, with a quick bit of research, we know that he is not *yet* a politician and his new interest in politics is speculative and opportunistic at best. The man owns a taxi business, that is all. To claim political asylum would be to stretch the definition. Indeed, Kenya is classified by the Home Office to be a safe and politically stable country. It is an economic powerhouse on the African continent and a holiday destination to thousands. There is no reason to believe that when Miss Mwathi is returned to her country of origin she would be unable to find a safe place to live outside of Nairobi. Upon removal, we propose that she be placed in the custody of the Red Cross, who would provide for her, and that the initial decision by the Home Office to deny her Leave to Remain should stand.

He buttons his suit and sits down.

Dalila stares at the screen in confusion. She cannot get over the feeling that this is all happening far away and might even be unreal, yet right now, here in this tiny room with a TV and camera something is happening to her life. It is being decided and she has no power to affect it.

Helen Foster remains seated and leans towards the microphone as she reads from her notes for her closing argument. My Lord, she starts, I would like to begin with the issue raised by the presenting officer regarding the discrepancies in my client's presentation of events. During my client's initial interview, we have just heard testimony that she requested a female officer to be present but the request was not granted. The Home Office has a responsibility to accommodate vulnerable female asylum seekers, which, in this instance, it failed to do. I would further point out that my client has since provided us with all the necessary information regarding her case and this information has remained consistent. There was a large amount of fear and confusion on the part of my client during the initial interview, she did not fully understand the asylum system in the UK and I would request that this is taken into consideration.

Helen removes the top sheet of paper and starts reading from the next page.

My client's uncle, Mr Kennedy Mwathi, has been campaigning for a seat on the Nairobi city council and elections are due to take place next month. This political dimension to his reputation is real. With regards to my client's case, the politics are real too. You do not have to be an elected official to politically oppress people. Mr Mwathi is a known member of the Mungiki sect, who are very politically active. As she made clear in her initial interview, my client is an eyewitness to Mr Kennedy Mwathi committing murder. She watched him brutally kick a boy to death. Also, the man who helped my client escape, Mr Charles Okema, has since been murdered. Furthermore, if My Lord would refer to the statement provided by my client's colleagues and college professors, it claims that Mr Kennedy Mwathi has been questioned by the local police in connection with two other murders and, at present, is implicated in numerous police investigations regarding extortion, tax evasion, and driving under the influence of alcohol. In light of Mr Kennedy Mwathi's alleged murderous activities, I believe the safety of my client could not be guaranteed. Indeed, by returning her to Nairobi, I believe Her Majesty's Government would be placing my client directly in harm's way. Also, considering Mr Mwathi's new career path, I believe there is now an undeniable political dimension to my client's asylum claim, and to deny this would be to ignore a fundamental tenet of the Geneva Convention Relating to the Status of Refugees 1951.

Dalila watches the judge sit back. He taps a pen against his notepad, but Helen does not look up. She presses on.

With regards to the allegations that my client consorts with an international criminal gang, I will reiterate that these claims are preposterous. The truth is Miss Mwathi has been hounded and attacked by this gang. They even attempted to kidnap her. This gang has links to Mr Kennedy, who, as we know, is linked to the Mungiki sect. My client's attempted kidnap is clearly detailed in the police report, of which you have a copy, and she provided the police with the SIM card from the phone of the man Miss Mwathi knew as Mr Markus. It is clear that she is working against this gang in an effort to bring them to justice. Miss Mwathi is not working with them.

Finally, I would like to remind the court that although Kenya is a holiday destination for many, the Home Office has it blacklisted for its many human rights abuses directed against women. My client would face a real and serious risk of harm and even death if she was returned. For the UK government to place my client at such risk would contravene the European Convention on Human Rights. I therefore believe that the initial decision to reject Irene Mwathi's claim for asylum was wrong. And I would recommend that she is released from detention in Dungavel Detention Centre immediately and given Discretionary Leave to Remain in the UK until such time as it is safe for her to return to her country of origin.

The solicitor stops and looks up at the judge. That is all, My Lord.

The judge gathers up his papers and stands as the bailiff calls, All rise.

The camera feed dies and Dalila is left staring at a screensaver ball bouncing around the television.

Dalila is escorted from the video-link room back to her room. Walking down the corridor, it's difficult to process what just happened. If only her solicitor had been more charismatic, more vigorous in her delivery. But when Dalila thinks about the arguments her solicitor made they all seem solid. Everything was backed up by documents. Still, there is an uneasiness she can't escape.

Her phone buzzes. There is a text from Daniel asking how her appeal went. She replies,

Don't know. Maybe good.

For days Dalila stays with Ma'aza in the isolation room. She moves her bed closer to Ma'aza's and at night she listens to the murmurs of her delirious sleep. She washes her friend with a damp cloth. While she braids Ma'aza's hair, she tells her all about Daniel and providing clothes and phone cards for the other detainees.

Yet Ma'aza never eats, and Dalila never asks her to.

Dalila keeps her lists. Every morning in the canteen after breakfast she meets with detainees and writes down their requests, and then emails the details to Phil. She gets some more clothes for Mohammed and a scarf and blouse for Zainab. She keeps a strict list for phone top-up cards and hands them out on a first-come-first-served basis.

One evening, as Dalila enters the visitors' lounge, Daniel approaches carrying two cups of hot chocolate. He hands one to her and says, Heri ya Krismasi.

Is it Christmas already? she asks.

Not for a few weeks yet, shrugs Daniel, but look around you.

Tinsel adorns the picture frames and on each coffee table is a small origami Christmas tree.

How do you think they celebrate in here? asks Daniel. Maybe they will roast a goat for dinner?

I wish, sighs Dalila, slumping onto the couch.

Don't worry, says Daniel, I believe you could be out before Christmas.

Really? Why do you say that?

Daniel sits down next to her. There is now a big campaign for your release, he says. Phil has put together separate posters, one for you and one for Ma'aza. They list the basic details of your cases and they call for your immediate release from detention. He has posted these all across different forums on the internet. Mrs Gilroy has got involved, too. She has been on the phone to the council, to different Scottish MPs, the Housing Associations, charities, women's groups and even her husband's old trade union to gather whatever support she can.

This is unbelievable, says Dalila.

Oh yes, says Daniel. Even Abbi is helping. He has been handing out flyers around the neighbourhood. People care for you, Dali. There is hope.

I'm trying to believe that, she says, sipping the sweet hot chocolate.

Just before lights out, Dalila dashes to the library and grabs a large red book in the children's section called *One Thousand and One Jokes*. She convinces the guards to let her take it into her room.

Look what I found, she says to Ma'aza, holding up the book. I know you like comedy but we have no TV so I will read for you.

She switches off the light and gets into bed next to Ma'aza. Using the torchlight on her mobile phone, Dalila opens the book at random and reads.

What do cats eat for breakfast? she whispers to Ma'aza.

There is no response from Ma'aza, so she reads the punchline.

Mice crispies.

She tilts her head towards Ma'aza. Nothing.

Even me, I don't understand this, says Dalila. It's not funny.

Flicking through the pages, she reads out another joke. What did the envelope say to the stamp? After a pause, she reads, Stick with me and we'll go places. I think this one is good, says Dalila. Ma'aza rolls her head towards her and raises a scarred eyebrow.

Dalila turns the page and tries another one. How do you make God laugh? she reads. Tell Him your plans.

Ma'aza smiles. Raising her finger, she whispers, That one is funny.

The morning light is different, paler and more diffused. Without waking Ma'aza, Dalila rises and goes to the window. The world is white. Snow lies untouched on every surface. Large flakes twirl as they drop, landing in the white with silence. She puts on all her clothes and heads out to the recreation yard. It's freezing, bitterly cold, and exhilarating. The snow is cat-like in its disregard for rules, resting on top of the CCTV cameras, clinging to the razor wire, adorning the tops of cars and trees.

She dances around the yard, grinning at the other detainees. It's as if the world is reborn, pure and breathless. They lift their faces to the sky and hold out their tongues, lapping at the falling flakes, chasing tiny, fragile portions of this beauty to take into themselves.

A letter arrives at the detention centre for Dalila. It is titled, **A Determination**. As she reads it, she understands that her appeal has not been successful.

She texts her solicitor and the solicitor calls back right away. There is a long discussion about a Judicial Review, about the possibility of bail, about even appealing directly to the European Court of Human Rights, but Dalila can tell by the tone of Helen's voice that the news is bad.

Instead of having lunch, Dalila returns to her room. She lies down on her bed and rests her elbow over her eyes.

In a frail voice Ma'aza says, What?

They rejected my appeal.

Ma'aza struggles up to a seated position. What will you do now? she asks. More appeals?

No. It is over, says Dalila. Every time, you told me they will send me back. Now I understand. There is no escape.

You cannot talk like this, says Ma'aza. I also told you, many times, to survive, to be strong.

Dalila gets up and paces to the door and back. I can't believe what I am hearing, she spits. You lie there like a bony, dehydrated cat and lecture me about survival. Why are you allowed to give up? You think you have all the answers, but you are trapped in here with the rest of us. She levels her eyelids and throws Ma'aza a hard, flat look.

Ma'aza sighs long and slow, trapped by her own logic.

I can only be okay if you are okay, says Dalila.

Ma'aza raises her hand in defeat and lowers it across her eyes. Fine, she says. If I eat, you must believe, okay? Together we survive.

Dalila crosses her arms, unsure if she can really trust Ma'aza.

After a moment Ma'aza says, When you stand like that, you look like my mother. Come, bring me food.

Dalila goes over to the stash of food she received from the manager. She picks up an orange, forces her thumb into the crown and tears away the peel. Sitting down on the bed, she hands over a segment. Ma'aza's thin hand takes the fruit and puts it in her mouth.

Chew, says Dalila.

Ma'aza rolls her eyes. She chews and swallows.

More, says Dalila, giving her another segment.

As Ma'aza eats, Dalila folds up her Determination letter and tosses it onto her bed. I am so tired of surviving, she says.

What else can you do? says Ma'aza.

Dalila nibbles the rough edges around her thumbnail. She pictures herself sitting on a plane, circling down and down into Nairobi, but quickly shunts that image from her mind.

In those last weeks with my uncle, she tells Ma'aza, I would lie on the floor for hours. Only lie there, surviving, with my face against the tiles. Almost nothing was left. He had taken everything. I was empty, so empty. I didn't care any more.

Ma'aza opens her mouth as if to speak, but stays silent.

Me, I cannot be like that again, says Dalila. I have to mean something. My life has to mean something real. I cannot only run and survive, always going from place to place. I want to help others, you know? I want to give and be like . . .

Dalila fights back her emotions and in the process loses track of what she is trying to say. She looks at Ma'aza and clasps her hand, allowing the turmoil to settle for a moment. Every day I am trying, my sister, she whispers to Ma'aza, I am trying so hard to prevail.

For the next week, Dalila fights. She fills in another application for bail and, with the help of her solicitor, she applies for a Judicial Review of her case. When Phil visits the detention centre, Dalila tells him all about Ma'aza's case. They draft a letter to include in the ongoing internet and letter-writing campaign calling for the immediate release for Ma'aza on health grounds and Phil assures her that he can secure many high-profile signatures before the letter is submitted to the press, the Home Office and key members of the Scottish Parliament.

One morning, Dalila is standing in line for breakfast, checking over her list of requests from detainees.

A guard approaches and says, Irene Mwathi? DG3331?

Yes? says Dalila, looking up at the man.

Come with me please.

She is escorted by the guard to the office where the Residential Units Manager is waiting for her. The manager waits for the guard to enter and close the door behind him. She begins by saying, Miss Mwathi, we have two matters to discuss. First, I would like to congratulate you on the progress you have made with your friend Ma'aza. She appears to be eating regularly and the nurse informs me that her health has improved dramatically.

Yes. Now she is eating soup, replies Dalila. I bring it from the canteen.

And I believe Ma'aza is now able to walk around a little, even to use the bathroom by herself?

Yes. Every day she is a little stronger.

I don't know how you convinced her to abandon her course of action, but I am impressed with your efforts. You kept your word, and for that, I thank you.

Thank you, says Dalila. She is my friend. It makes my heart glad to see her become strong again.

The manager nods. She slides a paper across her desk and says, This bring us to our second matter for discussion. I understand that you have received a Determination letter informing you that your recent appeal was not successful.

Yes, but my solicitor has applied for bail and we will try for a Judicial Review.

Well, I have to inform you that since your appeal was not successful, I have received new orders for your immediate removal. These are your new removal directions. As you can see by the details listed here, your outward flight from London to Nairobi is in four days' time. Today you will be transferred to Yarl's Wood Detention Centre, where you will be housed until your flight. Your personal belongings have been collected for your convenience. Officer Malcom here will escort you to the vehicle.

Dalila sits, caged in the back of the van, for nine hours. By the time they drive through the security checkpoints of Yarl's Wood Detention Centre, she is exhausted.

The building feels like a hospital. Long white corridors with hard rubber floors. Every door she passes through has to be unlocked first and then locked behind her. On some doors there is even a small sign reminding the guards to *Lock it! Prove it!*

At the small reception area, she once again has her photograph and fingerprints taken. They ask for her name, nationality, date of birth and double-check everything against her file. Her belongings are examined and she is told to strip to have her clothes checked.

Dalila undresses and waits for the female guard to go through her things.

We'll need to check your bra too, says the guard.

Dalila unhooks her bra and wriggles out of the shoulder loops. She wraps one arm across her breasts and drops the bra onto the table.

The guard steps towards her and says, I'll need to check these. She puts two fingers under the waistband of Dalila's underwear and feels all the way around for hidden items. Dalila raises her face to the ceiling, her body tight and shivering. She feels herself wanting to rise up and hover near the corner of the ceiling.

Her bra has no underwire, so it is returned to her.

Get dressed, says the guard, opening the door and standing in the hallway.

Dalila pulls the T-shirt over her head and then puts her arms into the jumper Daniel brought for her and zips it up. She shoves her bra into the pocket of her jumper and as she is stepping into her jeans a male guard comes into the room.

Let's go, he says.

She follows him down a long white corridor. An argument is going on somewhere and Dalila can hear crying and shouting. A door is slammed shut, and then another door.

The guard brings her to a gate in the middle of the corridor. He leads her in, shuts and locks the gate behind them. Two metres ahead is a similar gate. The two of them are caged in the corridor. Dalila flattens herself against the wall, as the guard brushes past. His keys are attached to an extendable cord which is fixed to his belt. He yanks the cord out in front of him, fiddles with his keys and unlocks the next gate.

They come to a door. The guard opens it and flicks on the light. It is a small room with two single beds, a toilet and shower. One bed is empty and neatly made. On the other lies a woman in the foetal position with the pillow over her head. She stirs and squints against the light, pulling her long black hair away from her face.

Irene Delilah Mwathy, says the guard, this will be your room. It's lights out now. Breakfast at 7:30 a.m. Goodnight.

She steps into the room and the guard locks the door behind her. The woman on the other bed lies back down and pulls the pillow over her face.

Dalila lies down and her fear presses her to the bed like a physical force. She struggles to breathe under the weight of it. She sends a text to Helen, her solicitor, telling her where she is and asking for help. She texts Phil and Daniel, listing her flight details and location and the word **Help**, and then she holds the phone to her chest and waits.

She listens to boots marching down the corridor, the rattle of keys and a slamming gate. She hears crying. Someone nearby is crying and soon they are wailing. It becomes a desperate, frustrated howling as some woman, somewhere down the hall, pounds her hand against the door again and again and again.

*

At 7:30 a.m. the gate at the end of the corridor slams open. Keys jangle and the stamp of approaching boots is unmistakable. A door is thrown open. Two in One, barks a guard.

Dalila sits up in her bed.

The boots march closer and the next door is thrown open. Two in Two, the guard calls.

The door to her room is flung open. A male officer tramps in and switches on the light. In the corridor is another guard with a clipboard. Two in Three, shouts the guard to his colleague standing just outside the door. The guard leaves. The footsteps and roll call continue down the corridor. The woman on the other bed gets up and shuts the door. She shuffles over and uses the toilet. She showers and comes out dressed and towelling her long hair.

I am Shada, the woman says. From Iraq.

She appears to be in her forties. Her eyes are slightly swollen and she looks exhausted and withdrawn.

I am Irene. From Kenya.

Wash, says Shada, pointing at the shower and sink. Then breakfast.

Dalila rises and uses the toilet while Shada wraps a scarf around her head. Since she has no toiletries of her own, Dalila washes her hands and face at the sink and stands ready in the clothes she slept in. When she comes out of the bathroom, Shada has placed her towel on the ground and is saying her prayers.

When Shada is finished, she says, We go.

The canteen is similar to the one in Dungavel, except here there are no loose chairs, only wooden booths. Dalila buys a hot chocolate from the vending machine and sits down with Shada. Shada nods, takes out her phone and texts. Within a few minutes another woman sits down at their booth next to Dalila.

This my friend, says Shada, introducing the other woman. Her English better.

Farida, says the friend. Can we borrow money?

Dalila sits straighter.

We will pay you back, tomorrow. Only four pounds.

Me, I don't have, says Dalila.

You buy from the machine, says Farida, so you have.

Why do you want money? For what?

For toiletries.

But you have in your room, Dalila says to Shada, even me, I saw them.

Farida leans in closer. They don't give us what we need. We must buy toothpaste, Tampax, shampoo. If we have these things it is easier for us, but they only give us seventy pence per day.

Dalila looks at one face and then the other. She doesn't trust these women but doesn't want to make enemies of them either. So we need toiletries?

Yes, we all need, says Farida. You also need this. If you give us money, we can show you where to buy these things.

My cousin is visiting tonight, says Farida. He will bring money for you, but now we need to buy.

Okay, says Dalila. She takes a one-pound coin and two 50p pieces from her pocket and slides it over.

Shukran, says Shada.

The three of them leave the canteen and go to the small kiosk. Taped to the wall is a price list and beside it a poster of a cartoon snowman in a red hat and scarf, wishing everyone a Merry Christmas. Dalila buys toothpaste, a toothbrush and a bar of soap. For now, that is all she needs. She has a little more money stuffed in her sock but she is cautious about exposing it.

Farida and Shada each buy two small bottles of shampoo and nothing else.

An announcement on the loudspeaker asks all detainees to make their way to their units for roll call. The people waiting in line at the shop glance at each other. They look at the guards, who immediately start herding everyone out of the hall. In the corridor people are moaning and shaking their heads and Dalila gets the feeling that what is happening is not part of the regular routine.

In the crowds, Dalila gets separated from Shada. She gets to her room and wonders what she is expected to do next. Shada bursts into the room a minute later and the two of them stand side by side listening to the count starting at the bottom of the corridor. Two in One. Two in Two. The guards walk up to their door, lean in and scan the room. Two in Three. The keys and boots and voices move to the next room. Two in Four.

Shada closes the door and lifts both hands up against her mouth.

Something bad is happening? asks Dalila.

I hear they find a woman, says Shada, she cut her arms.

They are kept in their rooms all morning. Shada lies down on her bed with her knees tucked, while Dalila takes a shower. She quickly gets dressed and as she brushes her teeth the guards do another roll call. She tries to think. There are only three days left till her flight. She has to do something.

She sits on her bed and looks at her phone. She has her charger with her but she is low on credit. Perhaps they sell top-up cards at the kiosk? She could use the little money she has left to buy more credit. As soon as she is allowed out of her room she will do this. The phone rings in her hand and she almost drops it.

Hello? Dalila?

Yes, it is me.

Hi, it's Phil. Listen, I am—

Phil, they put me in Yarl's Wood, she blurts out. Please help me, I am scared. They want to put me on a plane in three days.

I know, I know. Look, I am doing what I can. I have contacted the airline and complained. A volunteer will call them every two hours to complain. This can be effective, because the flight captain has final say about who is allowed on his plane. If he decides you are too disruptive or whatever, he can refuse to have you on board and they will have to delay your removal.

Good. Thank you. You have to do this, she says. I can't go back, but it is very bad here.

I know, Dalila. You've got to be strong, okay? Now, I've also contacted some friends in London. They have your flight details and they are going to try to go to the airport on the day of your flight and protest against your removal. So, we'll just have to see if this has any effect, but usually, if people can, you know, cause

344

a ruckus, then the Home Office often backtracks. They like to do things quietly.

Thank you, Phil.

Don't thank me yet. I have to go, but I want you to know we are doing what we can, okay? Be strong, Dalila.

I will try.

Phil hangs up.

Dalila grips her phone tightly in her fist. Phil's plan sounds good. It could work, but she won't know until she gets to the airport. The silence after his phone call is awful and she desperately wants to talk to someone. She texts Daniel again.

Baba. Phil called me. He has a plan. Can U pls contact my solicitor? If U visit tonight, ask to see Ma'aza. She is stronger now, but make her eat. Make her laugh, like U helped me. She will need you.

By mid-afternoon, they are finally let out of their rooms. Dalila goes straight to the kiosk and buys more credit for her phone. She walks around till she finds a common room where many women are watching TV. She sits down and wonders what to do next. She can feel the minutes slip away, pulling her ever closer to the moment of her departure. There must be some action to take. Perhaps a form to fill out or advice from a local charity. She wonders if they have similar visiting hours like she had with Daniel up in Dungavel. But then she remembers that guests have to specifically request a visit with a detainee. She texts Phil.

Maybe you have friends in London who can visit me tonight?

After a few minutes her phone rings. It is her solicitor, Helen, who explains that she is unable to represent Dalila any more because Yarl's Wood is in England. Scotland and England have different judicial systems and she isn't qualified to work in England. This is a well-known trick of the Home Office, to move detainees from one part of the UK to another where they will have to seek new legal help. But Helen assures her not to worry. She will try to contact a few solicitors that she knows in England. Perhaps one of them could come and meet with Dalila.

The phone call leaves Dalila feeling unsettled and she walks the corridors trying to compose herself. Breathing steadily, reminding herself that Phil has a plan. People are trying to help. It will all be okay.

That evening before lights out, Dalila sits on her bed listening to Shada talk to herself quietly as she showers. A gate is unlocked and boots march up the corridor. The door to their room is thrown open, and five male guards enter. One guard opens the door to the bathroom and Shada screams as the man looks at her.

Get out, screams Shada. Get out. Pigs.

Dalila scoots back against the wall with the covers pulled up to her neck.

The guard in the bathroom reads out Shada's name and number and says, Get dressed. Get your things. You have five minutes.

Where you take me?

Just dry yourself and get dressed. You've got five minutes. The guard shuts the door.

After a few minutes Shada comes out with only a towel wrapped around her. Her eyes move from guard to guard. I get my things, she says.

C'mon. Let's go, says the guard. We haven't got all night.

Shada grabs her clothes and toiletry bag and walks back to the bathroom, slamming the door behind her.

Quickly, says the guard.

Two guards sit down on her bed. Another starts gathering Shada's possessions and putting them into a plastic grocery bag.

One of them looks at Dalila. Just stay where you are, alright? This will be over soon, he says.

After a few minutes a guard knocks on the bathroom door. Shada? Let's go.

Okay, I come.

Minutes pass.

The guards look at each other. We should go in, says one of them. He pushes the door but it's jammed. The others help him and Dalila squeezes back into the corner, making herself as small as possible.

Shit, says a guard, you'd better get a medic. Call the medic.

One of the guards rushes out while the others drag Shada from the bathroom. She is naked and delirious, white foam drains from her mouth.

What the fuck happened? shouts a guard. Is she having a fit?

Could be, says one guard.

No. She's not epileptic, says another. It's not on her file.

It's this, says another guard, coming out of the shower cubicle with shampoo bottles in his hand.

She's drank the bloody shampoo. How the fuck did she get four bottles of shampoo?

It's another long night of crying and the sound of doors being shut and locked. In her sleeplessness, Dalila pictures Shada's naked body, the glazed eyes, the soap oozing from her lips. It was stupid to give her money. Why didn't she suspect something? Why couldn't she tell Shada was so desperate?

Death is close tonight. Dalila senses it stalking the hallways. She holds up the photograph of her father and brother and tries to imagine the men who came into her home. Did her father know immediately that the men were there to kill him? She imagines her brother would have shouted and fought. But her father? Her mother? How did they choose to act? How did they choose to lose? They are not in the room with her, she can't feel them, but she wonders if they are watching to see how she holds her head. How will their daughter define her own story? Will it be any different from their own?

By the next afternoon, there is still no message from Daniel or from Phil. While she waits for a reply she manages to log on to Facebook and sends Muthoni a message.

Xaxa Noni, I need help. Things are bad. I think they will send me back. I have a flight tomorrow morning. I arrive in Nairobi at 8:10pm. Flight KA 1078. I don't know what they will do with me. I am so so worried some person will see me there. There are too many matatu drivers at the airport. If one of those Mungiki sees me he will tell my uncle.

Please Noni, can you meet me there? Maybe I can stay with you? Please.

Her time runs out on the computer, but in the evening after dinner she is able to get another half-hour slot to check her mail. There is a reply from Muthoni.

Dali, don't worry. I will come. My friend has a car, he will bring me. He has family in Lamu and maybe you can stay there with them. If he can drive to Mombasa, from there you can go to Lamu. It is so far from Nairobi. You will be safe there.

Excited to see you tomorrow, my sister.

Dalila runs her hands across her face in relief. She reads the message three times. She types a short reply and then logs out. She can't imagine going back. She will not go back because Phil has a plan to stop her getting on the flight, so everything is going to be okay.

But if she does go back, if something goes terribly wrong and at the airport they somehow get her on the plane, then at least Muthoni will be there when she lands. She could wrap something over her head, disguise herself, quickly get in the car and slip away without being recognised. It could work.

In the evening she gets a phone call. It's Daniel.

Dali, where have you been? I have been trying to call you for two days.

I have been here, says Dalila. But the phone didn't ring. Maybe reception is bad?

Well, it doesn't matter. Are you okay?

I'm scared, Baba. They will take me tomorrow.

I know. I spoke to Phil. He believes he can stop you getting on the flight. You might have to stay in Yarl's Wood for a while, but you will be safe.

Dalila quickly answers, saying, I emailed my friend Muthoni. She might be able to meet me at the airport. Then I will go to Lamu. She says she has a friend there. Lamu is far away. Safe.

Yes, Lamu is good, says Daniel. You will like it. The ocean is very, very beautiful.

But why is she even thinking like this? It's not the warm ocean she wants to see. I'm scared, Baba, says Dalila. I'm so scared.

I know, Dali. It's okay to be scared, says Daniel, switching to Kiswahili. But listen to me, my sister, listen. You are my friend. Always. I am with you. I am there with you. We suffer together. Our stories are one. You have a great indestructible dignity, always hold to it. Do you hear me?

Yes, Baba. I will. She takes a deep breath. I will.

I have Ma'aza here.

She is there? Where are you? In the visiting lounge? In Dungavel?

Yes, we are here. She is drinking coffee. She wants to speak with you.

Hey, sugar sister, comes Ma'aza's weak voice. You need to be strong, okay? For me.

I will, if you promise to eat.

I'm serious. I know what you did for people, for me. People never listen to me, but you did. You listen to people, you hear them. It is a great gift you give to them. Now listen to me.

I'm listening, says Dalila.

When you get to Kenya, you run, okay?

Okay.

You run immediately, my sister. Just go. Don't be a nice girl. Don't do what they tell you. You run and be safe.

I will.

You must promise.

Dalila wipes her tears away and says, I promise.

And then, my sugar sister, when I go to Canada, I will call you. You can live in my house and we can get old and fat.

Yes, whispers Dalila. She clamps her hand over her nose and mouth so Ma'aza can't hear her sob.

Hello? Dalila?

I am here, she says. I am still here.

The day of her flight arrives. Before the dawn, Dalila lies awake in the dark. Her mother is in the room. Across from her waits her father, looking out of the window at the moon. Her brother stands near the door.

When the boots march up the corridor, she knows they are coming for her. She lies on her bed, so scared she finds herself hovering near the ceiling, terrified, away from herself, in a place the guards would never see.

Okay. You're okay, Dalila whispers to herself.

She exhales long and slow, sinking down with every breath till she is fully inside herself again. She imagines Ma'aza standing in this room, chin up, hands on hips, ready to defy the guards. She pictures Daniel, leaning on his good leg, adjusting his glasses, with a quiet smile to his face. She imagines Phil here, arguing and resisting them as they come in. She imagines Mr Erdem standing in the corner with his arms around Olcay and his two girls. And Mrs Gilroy, if she was here, they would all be safe. She pictures Abbi and Abit and the face of each and every person she met at the centre till the room feels full of people, all waiting beside her, waiting for that door to open.

When the guards enter, Dalila stands up. She raises her head with a fierce dignity and meets the eyes of every man, looking right into them, unafraid of what she sees or what she allows them to see.

As one approaches with handcuffs Dalila calmly says, Why do you think you'll need those? She walks out, down the corridor to whatever awaits her.

Epilogue

As is his habit, Daniel visits the library. He removes his gloves and flirts with the receptionist before he books an hour's session on the computer. His ankle joint is stiff from the cold and he favours his good leg as he climbs the stairs to the mezzanine.

He googles *NTV Kenya* and scans the news headlines. A story, three items down, catches his attention and he clicks on the attached video. The clip begins with villagers and locals peering and pointing towards the bushes. The voice of a female reporter delivers the story.

Local residents from the village of Ruiru are still in shock at the discovery of a woman's body in the early hours of yesterday morning. The body was discovered in a locality by the side of the road between the village of Ruiru and the Jomo Kenyatta University of Agriculture and Technology.

The segment cuts to an interview with a strong young man in a green T-shirt.

When I passed by to there, he says, *I was astonished to see a . . . a body, down behind those trees, and what made me to know that it was a human being's body? I saw the . . . the foot.*

The piece cuts back to shots of a police truck. People gathered at the site. A woman's worried face. The reporter continues.

There were four knife wounds on the victim's body and indications that she had been raped. Early police investigations were centred around discovering the victim's identity, believing that she might have been a student at the Jomo Kenyatta University. But it has recently been confirmed that the victim is in fact twenty-one-year-old Irene Dalila Mwathi, a former student of the Kenya Institute of Media and Technology and niece of the businessman and Narc political candidate Kennedy Mwathi.

A photograph of Dalila appears on the screen. She is in a crowd, glancing over her shoulder, about to smile.

Neither the killer nor the motive for the killing has been established and investigations into this matter continue. It is understood that the victim moved in with her uncle shortly after the murder of her family members during the political riots in Naivasha last year.

In a statement this morning, Mr Kennedy Mwathi described his niece as a good student who suffered from depression after the loss of her family. He had recently sent her on a holiday to the UK in an effort to help her overcome her emotional difficulties but he fears she may have become involved with narcotics. He also added that the criminal who did this should face the maximum force of the law and that he would support the police investigators in any way possible until her killer is found.

Watiri Mutono, NTV, near the town of Ruiru.

The screen goes black.

Daniel blinks, unsure of what he has just seen.

He watches the news segment again, waiting for her face to appear and when it does he pauses the clip.

It is her. She is there, on the news. The expression in her eyes is extraordinary, as though she is a holder of a remarkable secret. It's a look of grace.

Daniel logs off. His fingers fumble and he struggles to button his coat. He hobbles down the stairs looking for air, fresh air.

The librarian waves as he passes. Cheerio, Daniel. See you tomorrow.

He nods, but finds he cannot reply.

Outside, the pavement is slick. Brown slush gathers around the base of the lamp-post and is cast in the gutter of the road. He takes short, deliberate steps, but soon stops. He cannot face being alone in his flat. He squints up through his glasses, wondering where he might go. The road is dark and wet. The blackening clouds announce the day's early end and the city emits the constant sound of traffic, like wind, like the hushed prayers of a million souls. He sets his feet, lost and listening for the reassuring silence of the world's heartbeat.